PRAISES FOR

REFRACTION and JAN DYNES

"It delivers..."

"THIS BOOK OPENS WITH A BANG AND NEVER STOPS PROPELLING YOU TO THE AMAZING CLIMAX."

—Beaufort Review

"EXPERTLY EXECUTED ENTERTAINMENT.......WITH EVER INCREASING MOMENTUM, ROMANCE, SUSPENSE AND A HEART-BEAT...... THIS IS A GREAT HOT-SUMMERS DAY READ, YOU WON'T BE ABLE TO PUT DOWN."

—MIdwest Readers League

"ADVENTURE'S THAT TAKE YOU TO EXOTIC PLACES AROUND THE WORLD, WHILE AFRAID TO TURN OUT YOUR LIGHTS AND GO TO SLEEP FOR FEAR YOU WILL MISS A TWIST OR TURN IN THE PLOT; A REAL PAGE-TURNER."

—Ninilchik Book Club

"A SINISTER REVENGE PLOT THREATENS THE LIVES OF A WONDERFUL CAST OF UNIQUE CHARACTERS; THAT WILL HAVE YOU FALLING IN LOVE, WITH GREAT STORY-TELLING. IT HURTLES YOU PAGE AFTER PAGE."

—Readers Unite

"A BIG-BONED THRILLER, THIS WOULD MAKE A TERRIFIC MOVIE. READING IT IS ALMOST LIKE WATCHING IT ANY WAY, THE SCENES COME SO VIVIDLY TO LIFE, AS YOU READ THIS FINELY HONED AND SPIRITED ADVENTURE."

—Anchorage Readers Guild

"WHEN A FIRST NOVEL STARTS OFF WITH SUCH MOMENTUM AND CREATES SUCH WONDERFUL CHARACTERS; YOU CAN LITERALLY CHEER FOR THEM, YOU SIMPLY CAN'T WAIT TO SEE WHAT'S NEXT. THIS IS AN AUTHOR WHO HAS EARNED A FAN-CLUB. I WILL BE ANXIOUSLY AWAITING THE MOVIE AND HER NEXT LITERARY OFFERING."

—Portsmouth Book Review

Visit the author on her website for information on events and new releases: *www.jandynes.com*

Watch for Raw Justice which will be released just before Christmas of 2008.

Ask your local bookseller for her books and her upcoming events in their stores.

Her books can also be found on:

www.amazon.com
www.amazon.co.uk
www.jandynes.com
www.abebooks.com
www.alibris.com
www.biblio.com
www.booksurge.com

Books in Print with R.R. Bowker
Baker and Taylor
Nielsen Book Data (UK distribution)

ISBN: 1-4196-8517-1
ISBN-13: 978-1419685170

#1 Book

Publishers
www.1bookpublishers.com
sales@1bookpublishers.com

DEDICATION

This book is dedicated to my sister Diane. I grew up coveting her name, along with her beauty and her character. She is my big sister; and I've always been proud of her. So when I wrote my book, I used her name for my main character, simply because I loved it, as I do her. I never intended my novel to be prophetic. This book was written and completed and she had a copy of the manuscript before September 19th.

After Diane's and her husband Bill's very real accident on that day, and now throughout her continued hospitalization and constant rehabilitation; as I became aware my book was to be published so soon, I considered changing my heroine's name, as life had in a very small way imitated fiction. My sister Diane and her husband had been in a terrible accident and Diane would be in for a long and difficult journey on the road back; just like my fictional character had endured.

I decided that the original version should stand as it was written and I'd let the coincidence of having used her name honor my sister, instead of my changing it at the eleventh hour. It was already laid out in print, when I added this dedication for her. There was 'no way' I could have foreseen what was to come, when I was writing my book at the beginning. Diane was the vibrant, energetic center of her loving family and had the world by the tail at its inception.

Diane is my real life heroine as are her husband and sons who must share this recovery with her. They tell us it will be a long, slow process, but our hope is boundless. We all join in our determined belief; one day she will recover completely. We and so many friends believe in her, she is much too loved and needed, not to go home soon to the people who love her.

I respectfully request your prayers for my sister Diane Flett, as you begin the adventure Refraction, which is the story of Diane Lindsey who is a purely fictional character along with her entire adventure.

Now please enjoy my book, a suspenseful fiction, intended to be simply entertaining.

Thank you so much for reading my novel.

Sincerely grateful,

Jan Dynes

Re`fract´ion

1. Bent backward angularly, (as if half-broken); as a; refracted stem or leaf looks bent when seen partly submerged in water. As, a shard of glass refracts light to bend an image or perception at an opposite angle from where it entered the refracting agent.

2. Turned from a direct course by refraction; as, refracted rays of light change appearances of objects, as they emerge past the change in substance. Refracted materials appear bent visually and the product of the Refraction appears changed. An illusion that matter changes form, when traveling through, light, water, glass or sound.

Thank you to my husband Ken for all of your support
and patience through out the writing of this book.

I love you with all my heart.
Your encouragement means the world to me.

Refraction

e
f
r
a
c
t
i
o
n

a novel by Jan Dynes

www.jandynes.com

PREFACE

Killing was a rush. It was great to be paid to do what he loved.

He slowly closed the gap on the road between the vehicle he drove, a sturdy Dodge Ram pick-up truck and the one ahead of him, a flashy silver Mercedes Benz.

The car held a man and a woman in the front seat and he had seen them strap a child into a safety seat in the back.

He'd been following them, since they'd left their home in Cherry Creek. Now that they had all reached this totally deserted spot on the Continental Divide, away from the overly populated I-70; his whole plan fell into place. Ad-libbing was his strong suit.

They couldn't have made it any easier for him. The driver had unknowingly colluded in making his assignment easier, simply by choosing this route; they hadn't passed or seen another car for over a half an hour. He could not have picked a better place himself, for what he needed to do.

Loveland Pass was hardly ever used, except in the summer and early autumn. It was a treacherous road as soon as the weather became undependable. No one used it in the winter even when the road was clear and the sky was blue like today.

The man in the luxury sedan was distracted as he drove, apparently in an animated discussion with his wife. She was reaching over the back-seat, probably consoling the kid. Neither of them even glanced at the truck gaining on them. This would be too easy. He began to gradually increase his speed to pass them. At his right thigh, warm in his palm was his gun.

He pulled even with the car and for a split second, the driver glanced over and they made direct eye contact; and in that one instant, before the trigger was expertly squeezed, he had known what this was about and had foreseen with horror, what was about to happen to him.

The dead-on bullet entered his right eye socket and exited his skull, taking most of his brain matter with it.

With a simple easing up on the gas pedal and a considered bump of the assassin's right front bumper; he launched the victim's car over the ledge.

He slowed, backed up a little and parked on the edge of the road, directly above where the other vehicle had landed forty feet below. It had bounced and rolled several times, turning it into a twisted mangled chunk of silver metal, which no longer resembled its sleek predecessor.

Placing a second perfectly placed bullet into the gas tank, he guaranteed the vehicles explosion. He enjoyed his handy work far below him. His aim had been exact. He stood and appreciated the beauty erupting below. Flames licked upward with orange and blue tipped crackles and red-fired spits of disdain. The scrub-brush and ground covers burst spontaneously into yellow and white balls of combustion. Dry and dead in the winter, all the vegetation surrounding the car conspired to obliterate any trace of the inhabitants.

This hadn't been as hands on, as he might have preferred, but it had been effective.

He'd met the criteria of the assignment perfectly.

Twenty-Three Months Later

Having amnesia certainly seemed like a tired old cliché. Yet that's what Diane was up against. It seemed more like a plot line for a bad television movie, yet this was her truth and her circumstance.

Only thirty-one on her last birthday, she'd been forced to relearn the basics it took just to exist normally, simple things like how to walk and talk. All the things that most people took for granted. With an absolute single minded resolve, she had achieved normalcy, but her mind was still devoid of a history or memories.

Now she needed to figure out who she was.

Although the authorities had supplied her with the details of the murder and accident that had hospitalized her and killed her family, she still felt totally detached from all of it. None of the events which had contributed to who she was, and who she'd become, were familiar. She needed those memories back now, even if they were going to be painful.

Diane remained unable to incorporate the facts given her, into any kind of reality prior to her awakening in the hospital, nearly two years ago.

She only knew what she'd been told and that seemed surreal; since the facts felt alien to her and lacked being anything more then graphic and horrible details.

It may have been crucial at the beginning, to direct her absolute focus on healing and she had understood that then. But now, she needed more.

This hospital had been her only world; where she lived in a mint green microcosm and every bit of her energy had been devoted to a physical recovery. Most of the first three months had involved surgeries and the setting of bones and just waiting for the swelling and the bleeding in her brain to stop and return to a healthier state. Diane really didn't remember much of that drug filled time period.

It had taken almost twenty more months after that in physical, occupational and speech therapy until she had relearned everything. Those months she remembered, as often being hard and frustrating. She was glad they were behind her and she had come all the way back. Grateful of everything now, she took nothing for granted.

Doctors admitted that they knew very little about the forensics of amnesia. It differed so completely from case to case, and was rare enough, that none of her doctors had ever dealt with it. She would have preferred not to have been such a rarity.

Opinions and textbook findings varied, sometimes people just 'spontaneously got their memory back', sometimes 'bits and pieces' returned, however there were also cases where it 'never did'; and she found that thought intolerable and unacceptable.

The staff psychiatrists had made it very clear; there was absolutely nothing they or she could do, to force the memories. In fact; 'to try too hard', might have exactly the opposite effect.

So as frustrating as it was, Diane was forced to be patient. And while Diane might not know much about her past; the one thing of which she felt certain, was patience was not one of her virtues, and trying not to push it was damned impossible.

Diane determined to take stock of what she did know, and go from there. There was no other choice.

She knew that she had been married for five and a half years, to Rand Lindsey. He'd been an International commodities broker. They had conceived one child, a daughter, Alexandra, who had just turned three, a week before her death in the car crash.

Although she'd spent hours and hours looking at the pictures given to her by the police detective who came in nearly every day, and was handling her case; neither her husband, nor the beautiful little girl evoked any response.

It was disorienting and heart-breaking to have no memory of her family and not to be capable of answering the myriad questions asked her, about the day of the accident.

Diane hated herself for the cowardice inside her own psyche that held the memories at bay. For a long time she'd refused to acknowledge that Rand had been murdered, and always thought in terms of a car crash. The actual facts were sad and brutal, but it was time that she faced them. They might not seem real to her; but they were her history. Rand Lindsey had died instantly from a gunshot to the head and the car had gone off the road. Alexandra's immediate death on impact had been referred to, as a blessing, since the car had been consumed by flames. Both bodies had been burnt beyond recognition. Her doctors speculated it was that image; too horrible for Diane to even begin to grasp, that had simply blanked out all possible recollection of those events. The mind is evidently very protective and complicated at times, yet simple too, in it's ability to throw up a shield to spare itself what it can't handle.

Diane had been spared the furnace, which the car had become upon impact. She had been catapulted, clear of the car, through the smashed windshield, which indicated she had not been wearing her seatbelt.

The light refracting through the broken windshield glass had caught the attention of a passing pilot in a small plane; otherwise she would have died in the elements very quickly with all of her injuries. Only just barely surviving the accident, Diane had arrived at the hospital unconscious, given only a very slim chance to live. Her neck and back had been broken, her pelvis was shattered, and there had been countless other less dramatic breaks and lacerations to her extremities. The brain trauma had been the most critical problem and although the speech center damage and her motor control issues had been addressed successfully in the last year, the brain injury could still account for her inability to remember anything before it.

A team of four surgeons had worked on her for seventeen straight hours just to stabilize her vitals that first night. Internal organ damage and her bleeding and swollen brain were the biggest concerns at first. Later they worried about bones and breaks and tears. An indomitable spirit had been on her side. Now she wanted more then just total recovery and walking out of the hospital; she wanted a life back.

It was New Year's Eve and she would leave the next day, on a brand new year.

There had been no visitors for over a year, except the police detective and hospital personnel. Ultimately, all her visitors had dwindled due to her total unfamiliarity to them. Even the most well-meaning visitors got discouraged when not recognized. It had become awkward, for them and for her too.

There had been theories to answer the mystery of what had happened that night, but nobody really knew. There were no witnesses except Diane.

The general consensus dictated it was a professional hit based on the accuracy and precision of the shot. That was certainly a sobering thought. A drive-by shooting might have been senseless, but at least it wouldn't have insinuated a bigger conspiracy.

There had been a police guard placed outside her door for many months. That had been daunting when she was aware enough to understand it. But as nothing was attempted and the case grew cold, the steady guard was stopped and only regular visits from Detective Matthews had continued. But she had no answers to give him, and he'd run into brick walls and very little information to solve the case.

The shooter had disappeared without a trace. All they had was a tire track at the edge of the road that could have been made anytime and matched hundreds of vehicles. Rand Lindsey's past, had proved too minimal in content to provide a motive.

The detective had his own suspicions, but he'd also had other cases, and been pushed by the department to move on regarding this one. It was cold. Still he stuck his head in to say hello nearly every day. This was an amazing woman who'd endured so much, and he worried about her. If her husband had been professionally murdered and this had been a hit, than she was a witness.

Diane knew from the police detective who'd questioned her so many times over the last twenty three months, that she had no other family, she'd been an only child and her parents were dead, yet another sobering thought and dead end.

Tomorrow she would be sent home, to a place she didn't remember; to a house likely to be full of memories, with ghosts of her family, living within its confines, all the tokens of her life, before the murder and the accident, and all a mystery to her.

CHAPTER 1
HOME AGAIN

Checking out of the hospital on New Years Day went smoothly, even though it was full of emotional good-byes. Diane had made so many friends among the hospital staff.

Now she had been taken to the home of her past, and with the key she'd been handed, opened the front door and walked over the threshold alone and prayed for it to all be familiar.

The neighborhood and house hadn't been, not from the curb, or from the front, and then she found herself wandering over to a side entrance, which just felt more like where she normally would go. It wasn't a memory, but rather an automatic reflex. The key worked and she entered and realized it made sense to enter there, it was the kitchen entrance. After all don't most women use the kitchen door directly when bringing home groceries and coming home with small children who desire snacks after playtime? It just seemed right to her to use this door instead of the grand front entry.

The house was gargantuan, much larger than she believed a couple with only one child would ever possibly need. Unfortunately, so far it wasn't even vaguely familiar, as she glanced around the kitchen. Yet oddly enough, she automatically reached into the correct cabinet in the kitchen, to get a glass to pour some water, on reflection wondering, if it was actually a rote response.

Thinking it through; she believed, that most likely, in any place she lived, she would have kept her glasses in the cupboard above and just right of the sink. So in point of fact, all that Diane had learned at this juncture was more about her self, then about having any real familiarity to this kitchen. She mentally moved on in her thought process.

The kitchen, "wait a minute, *my* kitchen", she mentally corrected her disassociation, was so much more utilitarian and cold than she imagined her taste to be. She vaguely wondered, if she'd liked this before, because she hated it now. Decorated in an abundance of startling white marble and relieved by only even more antiseptic stainless steel, the ambiance certainly wasn't very inviting to her now. She idly wondered, if this had ever have been her taste? Surely people don't change this much. A loss of memory shouldn't change who a person is in the fiber of their being, should it? Could it?

She walked slowly out through the butler's pantry, into the dining room, glancing around at everything with the detached feeling of prowling through a builder's model home or that of a stranger.

The dining room was much more to her taste; it was very warm and inviting with lovely old tapestries. A fresco graced one entire wall, featuring a pastoral English country scene. The tapestries, portrayed unicorns prancing through a forest, the colors were all rich and mellowed by the ages. These were obviously antiques, truly outstanding ones, chosen with a love and knowledge of such things. The furniture was rosewood, delicately carved, and obviously expensive. There was a huge oval table in the rich, dark wood and around it twelve lovely Queen Anne side chairs and two brocade upholstered arm chairs that dominated the room.

It crossed her mind, that the furnishings were eighteenth century. Then she felt pleased with herself, realizing intuitively, she knew it with some certainty. Diane thought abstractly, in a somewhat disassociated thought; we must have entertained a lot, to have a dining room that seated fourteen so easily. Had we been people who enjoyed entertaining? Idle questions ebbed and flowed through her mind.

What Diane felt instinctively was that she had lovingly selected the furnishings of this room. It was warm and inviting, and it made her feel at home in it. The room also included an antique china hutch and sideboard, a teacart and a filigree wine rack that were eclectic to all the rest of the furnishings. The filigree was a whimsical touch, but beautifully introduced and full of lovely vintage wines. At least the bottles were lovely. Diane didn't know if she liked wine, she wondered vaguely if she was knowledgeable on the subject. Walking over for a closer look, reading the labels; she had to admit to herself, that if she had ever been a wine connoisseur, she wasn't any longer. The labels meant nothing to her. Maybe Rand had been the wine aficionado.

Where the kitchen had been vividly uninviting, the dining room was its antithesis. Diane knew in her heart that she had enjoyed planning this room. It was comfortable and gracious and she could feel a kinship with the choices.

As a second and abstract thought she realized she and Rand must have had an obscene amount of money, to warrant a house of this incredible magnitude. It was in the old-moneyed and posh part of Denver, 'Cherry Creek' was 'the neighborhood' so to speak, and somehow she knew that. Diane couldn't help but wonder, what her financial status was now, and realized that she had absolutely no idea.

It was startling to realize just how many questions arose, simply walking through her home, and how just looking at these furnishings, seemed to be revealing more questions.

Diane felt both daunted at what she still couldn't remember and a certain peace, that some things in her home felt comfortable and at least vaguely familiar.

On further inspection, wandering room to room, their home exhibited huge contrasts of warmth and starkness. Vaguely she wondered if she had done this all herself; or if perhaps Rand or a decorator had influenced alternate rooms? For it was uncanny how almost every other room felt right to her, while the others felt distinctly alien.

A warm living-room in deep forest green and burgundy with lovely carved European antiques and multiple equestrian bronzes, spilled onto floors inlaid with rich multi-color slate, and then covered with Oriental and Persian rugs, while walls were graced with rich oils and soft watercolors which contrasted pleasingly giving a feeling of gracious welcome.

The living area segued uncomfortably into a stark, mahogany paneled library, a room that featured an ultra-modern, glass desk and library tables, the total opposite of user-friendly. This room completely devoid of any ornamentation or human touches, dismally empty, the books perfectly matched leather bound classics all appeared to have never been touched, much less read.

Diane loved to read, but would never have been inclined to do it here. It was a room abysmally lacking any inducement to enter it. Diane felt sad just looking in from the doorway, and even somewhat repelled by the ambiance in the room. Was this room her deceased husband's legacy?

She had a gut feeling that came without preamble; that this room personified him, cold and devoid of outward expression. She didn't know how she knew it, but she did. More than a memory, it was an intuition.

So many questions were raised as she walked deeper into the house.

Questions that only left her wondering, who to ask?

It was a shame that there were no close family members on either side. The police had told her, they'd found very little information about Rand's past. It had been another total blank wall when searching for answers. The people who had visited her at the beginning had seemed more neighbors and acquaintances then close friends. Probably the reason no one persisted in staying in touch. Diane felt a really good friend would have stuck it out, to help her.

She did have a game plan forming in her mind though, as she thought about her need for answers. She would begin tomorrow by calling everyone in her address book and then in Rand's too. Her plan was simple. She would call everyone that she and Rand and Alexandra had ever known and interview them all now that her head was clear. Asking them about everything they could possibly tell her, no matter how trivial, about her husband, her child and her own life before the accident, had to yield something that would promote memories. With determination and persistence she would find herself. She would figure out everything that had happened up to and on that day, and why? Even if it meant that with success she would be forced to accept a very catastrophic grief, and some difficult truths.

As things stood now, she only felt the loss of her family in a detached way. She empathized with the story, but nothing felt personal. She needed her own life back, no matter how painful it might be. She was ready to make it personal.

The emotional pain of remembering everything had to be experienced, to go on with any kind of a future. Diane knew and accepted that it would probably be her most painful hurdle to face what had happened in all its horrific detail and remember it as happening to her.

It appeared the police had reached a dead end in trying to locate or identify Rand Lindsey's murderer or a motive. But she had a much more vested interest in the truth, and it wasn't possible to put it behind her, not without first pursuing the answers with a vengeance. There was still the possibility that she might be a target, although the police had told her that they doubted it because her amnesia, which had been documented in the news, kept her from being a threat as an eye witness.

Nevertheless for the time being there was a police car parked out in front of her house, and an officer was on guard duty, and the kind Detective had escorted her home, and said they would stay around the clock. That was in place for the next two weeks; that had been all the time, Matthews had been able to get them to sign off on. After two weeks; she should prepare to be on her own, this was simply a temporary precaution. At that point they planned to close their books on the case and her for good.

The two weeks providing her this protection, was only based on the unsubstantiated possibility that her husband had been the victim of a professional hit.

That meant there was no time to waste in her discovery process. Regaining her memory could be a life or death situation. However killer or not, she just needed to know everything and reclaim her life to make sense out of chaos. Diane set her mind to solving in two weeks, what the police department had failed to do in almost two years.

Detective Damon Matthews sat out in front in his car, drawing on memories of his own, regarding the lovely and very brave woman inside the gorgeous Tudor Mansion enveloped warmly in thick ivy.

His eyes were constantly alert, roving the stately grounds and graceful circular driveway. Although a seasoned homicide detective on the force for eight years, he had never sufficiently hardened himself against getting personally involved and caring about the victims of violence. This poor woman had really fought an incredible battle. Over the past many months he had watched Diane Lindsey practically return from the dead. He deeply admired her 'never-give-up' attitude. She was a fighter and a nice woman.

When he'd first been handed the assignment it was practically a fore gone conclusion by police and doctors alike, that she would probably die; then later; that at best, she would be a paraplegic. Instead she had surprised everyone and fought her way all the way back. He respected the way she'd leapt into grueling physical and speech therapy with an indomitable spirit. Persisting without ever a complaint and even with a sincere sense of humor, Diane had impressed him as being an extraordinarily remarkable woman in every way.

In his capacity as the detective covering her husband's homicide, Damon had spent quite some time observing and admiring her bravery as he'd spoken with her over time. Diane had strength, and a tenacity he'd seldom witnessed. He was impressed with her on many levels. That occasionally interfered with his objectivity, which is why he'd insisted on taking her home today; and taking the first 'over night watch' personally, a duty that would normally fall to a much less senior officer.

With the case still unsolved and a motive and suspects as yet unknown Damon felt a tremendous frustration knowing that since her husband's murderer was still free; Diane could still be in serious danger, and for that he held himself responsible.

There had been practically 'nothing to go on' from the beginning. Nevertheless his gut told him it was a professional hit. Drive-by shootings took place in Denver's inner-city, never on a meandering mountain pass. Sadly past experience told him professionals never left witnesses, not even ones suffering from amnesia. To a hired assassin her memory, that might return, would continue to be seen as a threat. Hit men never left any witnesses, and that fact concerned him, even more then the frustration, of being pushed to close the case for good, within the next two-weeks.

Even though the department kept piling more cases on his desk and this case was listed on an inactive status, he had never been able to stop thinking about Diane. She was an extremely compelling victim, and he quite honestly cared what happened to her, no matter how much he denied that fact to himself because it was an unprofessional stance. Certainly his department wanted him to handle it more objectively and they had been pressuring him to close this case for a long time. Now they were adamant about the deadline, leaving no further room for an argument. They'd only agreed to this 'precaution' for two more weeks because of the news covering her release from the hospital and any possible liability for the police department if anyone did come after her. If nothing happened to support his theory about a professional hit, they would simply close the case as random violence.

Damon had been assigned to her case within hours of her being discovered by the car and brought into the hospital. Now he'd seen her nearly every day since, even if only to stick his head in her door and say Hi.

If honesty prevailed, then Damon had to admit to himself a more than professional interest in this beautiful woman with the unconquerable spirit. He admired her deeply and he kicked himself for not catching the killer yet.

This was one of the few cases he'd ever handled without a reasonable conclusion, most baffling for its incredible lack of information about Rand, the victim.

To find a motive and a killer, first you research the murder victim. There had been less then nothing to uncover; and of course Diane was unable to provide any explanation either. It was as if Rand Lindsey's past was erased too, and everything about that pointed to someone who might have been hiding for a reason.

Who Rand had been was as big a mystery as who the shooter was and who might be behind it. Plus the question remained, was Diane complicent before the accident too, or unaware of any danger. Damon leaned toward believing her innocent of any involvement in anything illegal. Her past and history was easy to research and by all accounts she was just a young mother raising her child and running a household and attending the University. There was nothing nefarious there.

He wondered if her first night at home was overly traumatic for her, and if the familiar surroundings of her home would help stimulate her memory and induce recollections about her life prior to the accident.

Damon couldn't help thinking that amnesia was in its way a Godsend to her, as it had, in many ways insulated her from a loss that might have been unbearable. What could possibly be more awful than the loss of a spouse and a child, both taken from her simultaneously? Perhaps if Diane had been forced to deal with all that grief at the beginning, it might have impeded her healing.

They had become friends of a sort during the investigation, but had always kept the professional distance that most victims and police assume. Now sitting here in the quiet, Damon realized he had probably 'mentally' crossed that line.

It was a moral battle, to stay in the car instead of going inside to check on her. After all; in the hospital she was hardly ever alone for a minute, doctors and nurses constantly in and out, and in the beginning a guard at the door full-time, and his own daily visits to check on her status.

Her fight back to full mobility had been all consuming and had kept her fully absorbed while in the hospital. Now as he looked at the house he wondered what she was going through; back in her own home surrounded by solid evidence of all that she'd lost. That couldn't be easy.

Inside the house Diane continued wandering through different rooms, reading book titles, looking at magazines, picking up displayed filigree and sterling picture frames with smiling visages that should mean something to her, but didn't. It was disquieting and disconcerting to feel unconnected to everything, when she knew it must all be very familiar. It was her house and she didn't feel at home in it.

Of course she recognized many of the pictures as Rand and Alexandra or 'Lexie' the name she had given her daughter as an endearment; a piece of information, provided by friends that had visited right after the accident, repeated by the police, and read in newspaper articles.

She picked up a picture of her parents on the mantle, and wished these kind looking people were still alive to help her now. Diane had been shown their picture before and felt no more attached to these people now, than she had the first time it was shown to her at the hospital. These were her parents, damn it, how could she not remember them? It seemed a horrible betrayal to this kind looking couple. She sensed rather than knew that she'd had a happy childhood. But she felt a deep sadness, as she faced the fact that she still didn't remember anything as an absolute.

Diane had always believed in her 'heart of hearts' that the amnesia would miraculously evaporate up on her homecoming. Now sadly she had to accept this void as the 'status quo'. That was painfully disappointing.

So for tonight she decided to get some sleep and tomorrow she would begin her own personal investigation. It was a plan and that was a start.

She wondered, as she had so many times, had the shooting been random or aimed at Rand purposely. Was she meant to be dead too? Most importantly, was there anyone out there planning to kill her now? Until she could answer all those questions, she'd never have any peace of mind.

With a slight smile on her face, she thought of at least one bright spot, Detective Matthews, he'd been there since the beginning and always was when she needed him. Of course it was his job to find the answers too, but she felt that he truly cared about her case and he'd always been kind to her. Somehow it had helped her feel better and not so totally alone, knowing he was on the case. He had been the only real constant in her life since the accident and beyond the hospital, and now that she was home. He'd kindly checked her out of the hospital and brought her home that afternoon. She didn't even know he was the shadow in the car out in front of her house even now.

Diane headed up the stairs to find her bedroom and get some rest. Although perfectly healthy now, she tired easily, and it had been an emotional day. The first day at home had been a disappointment; as no great catharsis, had taken place, upon her arrival.

At the top of the stairs she peeked in from the doorways, into all the upstairs bedrooms, progressing in from the main spiral staircase, until she found the room that left no doubt, it was the master suite.

It had a huge canopy bed draped in antique, ivory lace. The bed was heavily and masterfully carved. It could easily have graced a Czar's bedroom. This was a romantic bedroom and she slowly inhaled a sigh. Not one piece of the furniture in the room matched any other, yet they beautifully complimented each other. Though eclectic, all the furnishings were about the same period, 17th Century and European. As a passing thought, she realized another bizarre fact, with certainty, she knew, the 'history of the furnishings of the bedroom'; even if she couldn't remember her own family. What an incredible irony, the random workings of her mind were.

She was struck with another thought, and returned to the hall. Diane had stopped looking into rooms, upon finding the master suite. Now thinking of her daughter, she suddenly had to find Alexandra's room. It turned out to be the room, just past her own, exactly where she would have expected it to be. Standing in the hallway just looking in from the door she began to shake. Taking a tremulous step into the room she scanned everything, taking in the 'little-girl-four-poster-bed with canopy' nearly covered in stuffed animals. She walked over to the bed and picked up a little stuffed lamb that sat on the pillow.

"Lambkin, her favorite," Diane murmured.

She just knew it immediately, but only that, and no more, just the name of the lamb, with no memory of her child to accompany it.

The tears came very softly at first, as she sat on the bed and clutched 'Lambkin' to her breast and then the tears came harder. The only definite memory so far, beyond recognizing the era of the furnishings, was a small stuffed inanimate object.

Touching other things in the room, she played the little music box with the Ballerina on the top, and glanced at books, reading their titles out-loud; but nothing else spoke to her. Slowly she left the room, pulling the door closed behind her, an overwhelming sadness engulfed her. Tears still scored paths over her face, as she returned to her own room drained.

Exhausted she prepared for bed, not even noticing that she'd automatically put on what used to be her favorite, comfortable nightgown. It was flannel and very soft and feminine and there was an exact match in a much smaller size, in the next room. Diane had enjoyed dressing them in mother/daughter outfits, but for now, she didn't remember that.

Her last thought before her eyes closed was, tomorrow is another day. Then she lightened up a bit, as she realized that was a quotation, stolen from Katie Scarlet O'Hara, the heroine in the movie Gone with the Wind. She was comforted by any memory at all. It was all something, at least a beginning. As the doctors had said it could return in remnants, and random bits and pieces, and even trivia was a start.

Then her mind wandered back to the last flash of memory, and she also actually remembered that 'Gone with the Wind' was one of her favorite movies, and that she'd seen it, in an old theater with balconies in the historical district with her grandmother when she was a teenager, along with Dark Victory, Imitation of Life, The Sound of Music and Enchanted Cottage. I am a classic movie buff, because of my grandmother she thought and could remember the lazy Saturday afternoons and the theater. It was something else to know; which was progress. She tried hard to picture her grandmother's face.

Her name had been Eve, and she died when I was fifteen, unfortunately Diane remembered the coffin at the funeral, rather than her grandmother's face. But she could remember her saying to her once.

"A good old tear jerker movie, is great for cleaning out your eyes and the classics are still better then the new things coming out."

Diane blinked back the tears; she was coming out of the darkness. This was a start, a bit shadowy and incomplete, but it was still progress.

Yes, she would remember everything eventually, every damned thing. She had already remembered a stuffed animal and her grandmother. It might not be all she had hoped for, but it was still a start. Faith dictated there would be more progress tomorrow.

Diane was able to drift off easily and was soon asleep. There were no beeps and monitors here or doors opening and closing all night. Her sleep was dreamless and sound. She was finally home.

CHAPTER 2

Damon had spent a miserable night in his car, staying awake and watchful, which had necessitated his drinking too much black coffee. He was getting too old for surveillance work, and his shoulders ached. Gratefully at seven a.m., his replacement showed up to relieve him, he was now heading home to his own bed and was relieved that the first night had been so uneventful.

Yet, as tired as he was, still he worried about leaving her. The Denver P D had given him quite a fight over putting a guard on the Lindsey residence this long after the original incident. It was very expensive. Never the less, his every instinct told him that Diane was still in danger and it was necessary, even critical, to keep a bodyguard posted. His partner had shown little to no interest, he'd ceased to be interested after the first few weeks.

He was adamant that Rand had just been shot and that with Diane's amnesia, documented in all the news accounts, she would be in no further danger. Illogically to Damon, he even insisted it was a random act, not a professional job. They'd been at odds on it from the very beginning. That theory didn't sit right with Damon. His gut told him this wasn't over. Rand's slate was too blank and he was too wealthy, not to have enemies. In fact even his company records had an amazing amount of holes and discrepancies. Interviews with everyone about him were evasive and shallow. There was no one, anywhere, who seemed able to offer much of a clue about who Rand Lindsey was when he was alive, and his history only stretched back six years and then left a non-existent trail. Only a birth certificate existed up to that point, and no one remembered him or his parents in the neighborhood surrounding the address of his birth. For Damon that was too much dead time, for anyone; to not 'seem to' exist from infancy into adulthood. There were no school records or any prior usage on Rand's social security number, until six years prior to the day of the shooting. But Damon had never found a death certificate, for a young Rand Lindsey either. Old paper records were often only filed locally and could have slipped through all major data base entry systems. Rand Lindsey's parents trail, had moved around, all over six states and twenty or more small towns, and he'd never found anyone who remembered them. Their death certificates were filed in Texas records in the early nineties, a year apart, in Dallas. But there was nothing after that for Rand Lindsey.

Damon didn't find it 'that odd' that no one remembered them. Their employment records reflected a lower class couple with sporadic menial jobs and some periods of unemployment, jumping around after several evictions. The death of the child, belonging to this couple, would create a perfect identity for a person who needed to recreate themselves or come out of hiding about Rand Lindsey's age.

Damon's own inability to tie up the loose ends, made him feel responsible for Diane's safety. He hoped he was wrong, he wanted to be wrong, but he didn't believe he was, even if no one had tried to hurt her in all this time.

He had been working on the follow-up, alone and on his own time, since there were plenty of new and active cases which needed his focus. He was admittedly not totally objective, in a large part, because Diane Lindsey was so horribly and completely alone now. She'd been through enough, he wouldn't let anyone else hurt her again.

Tired as he was; these were his thoughts as he drove home slowly, anxious to crawl between the sheets. The day man was a good officer and the quiet night was a very good thing.

Inside Diane tossed and turned. Part of her wanted to roll over and go back to sleep, another part wanted to get up and commence with her research, on this brand new day of discovery. She had slept very well, after glancing out the window several times during the night and spotting Detective Matthews sitting in his car under the streetlight across the street.

Although their relationship had been kept on a professional basis, she felt in him a concerned kindness. She felt he was someone she could count on and his presence was reassuring.

He had a very likable, self-assured attitude that put her at her ease, despite a handsome face that was reminiscent of an old Marlboro poster. He looked tough and rugged, with very dark hair, not quite black, but nearly and crystal blue eyes, which accented a Colorado tanned, high cheek-boned face. Powerfully built, it was obvious he spent a lot of time at the gym, and everything about him exuded confidence and made her feel safer. Even though he had yet to find the killer, Diane felt sure he would protect her, at least for the next two weeks.

As she swung her legs out of the bed, she looked out of the window in time to see his long-legged frame unfold out of the car and stretch, as he spoke to his relief officer. It was just a bit before seven. He glanced up at her window, as if he could feel her watching him.

She stepped back from the window, so as to remain unseen, in the green flannel nightgown she had slept in. Of course she didn't realize; the way the sun was bouncing off the window, he could not possibly see her.

If he had, he would have thought her remarkably healed and undoubtedly pretty with her shoulder length reddish blond hair all tousled from sleep, and her beautiful, make-up free skin. What a long way she'd come from all the blood, damage and confusion of the first time he'd seen her after the shooting and accident.

She watched him through green wide-set eyes, framed by lovely arched brows, set in a classic oval face. Besides being extraordinarily vulnerable, it was a face with great strength and character.

Her life might be written on a blank page right now, but volumes would need to be researched and rewritten, to restore and rebuild a new life with which to go forward. With that thought in mind, she jumped into a steaming hot shower to begin her day.

She stepped out of the marble shower stall and admired her bathroom, marveling again at the opulence of her house, after so long in a hospital environment. It still seemed surreal to be here.

A sparkling white, seemingly huge, claw-footed tub dominated the center of the bathroom. It appeared antique, but it was just too perfect; it had to be a reproduction. Dramatically dancing on the white porcelain, a myriad of colors from prisms of light, cast down through a domed, stained-glass window, directly above it. The window was gorgeous, made up of hundreds of butterflies dancing among wild flowers and the morning light made them come to life.

Having showered and dressed, she grabbed a glass of juice. Picking up the kitchen phone she opened her address book, ready to begin.

A frustrating, ten phone calls later, no one had picked up a phone, and answering machines and voice mail recordings just weren't offering much satisfaction. She decided that she would continue the phone calling session again that evening.

Instead she would implement Plan B, which by day might perhaps be more productive. She would go to the library and look up all the articles that had appeared regardings the accident on microfiche. She knew that would be as good a starting place as any, to begin her research.

The press had published most of the detailed articles on the murder and car crash, prior to the time she'd been aware of her situation. Admittedly her first weeks and months were a fog of pain medications and surgeries. The intention of a hospital would have been to keep any traumatic news at bay. Now however important that may have seemed at the time, that 'zero information time-window' had deprived her of critical information, that could help her fill in some blanks. Her game plan also involved looking into Rand's business and personal contracts, with the hopes of finding a reason for his murder. Making sense of everything was very important now. After all, her life could depend on it.

What kind of life was there anyway, without a past? Everyone needs a sense of their own history to be complete. She would even check on her own background in order to figure out, if for some reason, she might have been the target. Diane could leave no stone unturned if she ever wanted to feel safe again.

As a survivor of so much physical rehabilitation, it was frustrating to not be able to force her memory to recover too, just as well as her body had. The doctors had all told her the same thing, she could not force memories, or it would have the opposite effect and impede her progress. But that was easy for them to say, she might have a murderer after her. She just had no way of knowing. If someone was after her, 'they', whoever 'they' might be, could come back to finish the job. These thoughts indicated to her, that some urgency was certainly necessary. And though these thoughts seemed melodramatic, they weren't unwarranted given her immediate past.

It was not an easy task to convince the uniformed office on guard duty that it would be proper for her leave the house. But she wasn't a prisoner so he finally just insisted on escorting her.

The public library yielded many details she'd already known, and probably a ton of journalistic speculation as well. Some of the information she guessed had little resemblance to the truth, but had made good copy.

It had been a spectacularly gruesome story to report at the onset, and every legitimate paper, as well as all the garbage-grocery-store-tabloids had reported extensively. It was quite a job reading everything written in the first month after the accident. And photos of the wreck and the scene were hard to digest. Yet she decided that it was still the best possible starting place to unravel everything still unknown to her. She had to start somewhere. The more she read, the less detached she felt.

She didn't feel like the woman she was reading about, more like a detective in hot pursuit on the case. It was the oddest of feelings to be so much a part of this and yet so outside of it all too. She supposed the detached stance was good in a way, it allowed her to be more objective.

I guess I'm playing Pollyanna she thought. The name elicited a random memory; that's what my mother used to call me. It was just a little thing, but it was one more step.

A new thought occurred to her, as she realized she was getting restless from sitting so long. Perhaps one of the reporters could help her. She jotted down all the names of the journalists that had covered the incident. She noted which papers they worked for and then wondered which one of them might be of real assistance and share their findings with her.

Maybe they weren't writing much now, after so much time had passed without new developments, but she was still News. All the papers had reported on her going home. Just maybe one or more of those reporters had leads and information that went deeper than what was reported. It was at least worth a try. She made some notes, noticing that all of the most informative articles and the seemingly best-written ones were by one particular reporter. That's where she would start. His name would top her list of sources to talk with.

Reading the details with at least some knowledge of whom and how much she had lost per se, she felt a detached devastation for the poor woman in the article. Even knowing this was about her; still she only felt the pain, sort of once removed, in a detached and oddly disconnected way.

It was really disconcerting, this feeling of being outside of herself looking in. She'd browsed through family photo albums at the house that morning. Her husband had been a very handsome man, although he had looked very aloof and cold to her now. Her daughter had been an incredibly pretty, cheerful looking child, laughing and happy in all the pictures, a beautiful baby. Although she still couldn't remember her exactly, looking through the pictures she felt a connection to her child and a deep sadness over her death. She'd been in tears after going through Lexie's baby book, and pictures, and touching a lock of her hair, exactly the same color as her own.

She continued to feel nothing looking at Rand's pictures, and that disturbed her. He had been her husband, she should feel something. If they had been close or very much in love, she would have expected more stirring in her heart while looking at him. She stared at the pictures over and over. She didn't know how she knew it; yet glancing once again at his picture she knew without a doubt, that she had not trusted him. Diane knew instinctively, their marriage had been in trouble at the time of the accident. Her intuition told her that he was not a very loving or warm person.

She remembered that friends that had visited after the accident never seemed to be able to tell her anything much about Rand either. As she recalled, they had always been her friends, never his. Few people had offered any insight on Rand. She had gotten the distinct impression that he was a forbidding stranger to everyone they had known, and not particularly well liked either.

What a sad commentary that was, on her choice of husband.

Well, her legs were ready for a stretch and the library was getting too claustrophobic for her.

So complete with her disapproving police bodyguard in tow, she decided to widen the investigation. It was obvious that he thought she should stay home, locked inside, and make his surveillance easier. Still it just wasn't her intent to sit and stagnate. Not now, not ever. It simply wasn't in her nature. That much she did know about herself, she was not passive.

Leaving the library they drove to the downtown district, the vicinity of the main newspaper publications in town.

Upon entering the reception area of the Rocky Mountain News, which was one of the papers that had done extensive coverage. Diane was nearly bowled over by a man walking backwards out of an office, while still yelling frantic instructions back to whoever was still in the office, he had so hurriedly vacated. The man turned and apologized profusely for having stepped accidentally on her instep. Judging by the grimace on her face, he knew she was in pain, although not how seriously. That foot had been the recipient of multiple breaks.

"I'm so sorry, are you okay?" he asked her, showing honest concern.

"Here let me get you a chair," he offered, pulling one over to her from against the wall. He looked down at her contritely, with a winning grin.

Diane caught her breath.

"Fine really. Thank you. I'm okay, but perhaps you should try looking in the direction you're walking. I've heard it said, that can be quite effective, not to mention protecting future innocent bystanders."

They both laughed, as Diane took a seat and slipped her shoe off to gingerly massage her instep.

Mark Roberts pulled up a chair as well, and sat facing her. Straddling the chair backwards and looking at her over the back thoughtfully, he found her very pretty and very familiar.

He took a longer look and noted the police officer right behind her and then he realized who this was and introduced himself.

"Diane Lindsey, I'm Mark Roberts, I covered the series on your tragedy. Please let me tell you just how incredibly sorry I am for your loss and how happy for your recovery. How are you, now that you're out of the hospital? You look just wonderful. No one would ever guess what you've been through."

Diane was touched by his obvious sincerity and tickled at his energy.

"Mostly I'm full of questions, which is exactly why I'm here. I was hoping you'd be able to help me, since you researched my accident for your paper."

She contemplated bumping into just the person she had hoped to see today. Unfortunately it was obvious, he was in quite a hurry.

Diane continued.

"I was actually hoping to speak with you, if you can just spare me a little time now, just to make an appointment to meet again later. I can see you are definitely in a huge rush at the moment."

She smiled, as she stated the obvious.

He too smiled, for it was good to see her looking so well. The last time he had seen her she had been in rough shape. He had thought about her repeatedly, the lovely woman with the will of iron and no past, who had survived the impossible and come back walking. He wouldn't have bet any money on her ever succeeding so well, not based on the doctors predictions. She was a walking miracle, a simple testimony to her own spirit.

Mark had continued to follow her case even though its news worthiness had expired, without any leads in so long. He hadn't worked on the story in months, except the short article reporting her discharge from the hospital. That one he had kept deliberately low key, to allow her more safety and privacy. He hadn't wanted to cover it at all, wishing to allow her some peace, but it had been a non-negotiable order from the editor. Mark thought this woman had been put through enough; without the intrusion of more news coverage. Now he was just very happy to see how well her battle had paid off. She looked absolutely perfect as well as incredibly lovely.

He couldn't stop himself from asking.

"Any luck with your amnesia?"

"Unfortunately no." She replied, touched by the concern she heard in his voice.

"Actually that's exactly why I'm here. I could really use your help, as I mentioned before."

Even though he was extremely rushed, he responded kindly.

"Just name it, I'll be happy to do anything that I can to help you."

"Well I'd like to go over your information regarding the accident and get the sources you used. I need to find out all I can about my own past. Can you spare some time, at your convenience of course, to go over everything you know about me? I know how crazy that sounds, but I really need your help. Please."

"Are you staying in your house?"

"Yes, let me give you the address." She realized how silly a comment that was; he knew her statistics, better than she did. She'd found it necessary to walk outside that morning and look at her street name and house number. It would be amusing if it wasn't so sad.

"Is eight o'clock too late?"

She shook her head and turned to leave, glancing back and up at Mark.

"No, that would be wonderful and thank you I can't tell you how much I appreciate your taking the time to talk with me when you were in such an obvious hurry. I'll see you at eight. Thank you again."

Diane left the building with the police officer, a rather silent shadow following a step behind. She was relieved to finally be accomplishing something, while he was simply relieved to get her out of such a public place. She truly felt that the reporter would be able to help her and point her in the right direction. At least it was a start. Anything was something, at this juncture.

She didn't know how right she was either. Mark Roberts had uncovered much more than he'd written about, more that the police even had. He would turn out to be more help than she could even imagine.

It was close to four-thirty as they left the building. Diane was thinking it would probably be too late to catch anyone else in an office today.

Meeting Mark Roberts had inspired some hope, that there was at least one other person who could help her on the mission of rediscovery ahead of her. She needed more to go on, than what the police had told her.

Detective Matthews had been very kind, but he had asked more questions then he had provided answers, and as the case had laid dormant for some time now, he'd mostly just checked in on her.

Heading home to make more calls out of her personal address book and Rand's seemed her most reasonable course of action. From now until eight-o'clock, hopefully more people would be available to talk with her and perhaps a familiar voice would trigger her own memories.

So, to the great relief of her mostly unobtrusive bodyguard, Diane informed him he could take her home. She knew that he was there for her own safety, but it still felt ridiculously like having a baby-sitter. Part of her couldn't wait for the guard to be gone; yet by the same token it was somewhat reassuring to have one. Life was just full of contradictions.

Making calls after arriving home had been arduous. As the phone rang for the fifth time, Diane prepared to hang up on this attempt too. So far none of the people she had called under the A's and B's had been much help, and the calls had been extremely awkward. People weren't accustomed to talking with amnesiacs, who had once known them; well enough to have their phone number and that now, called as a stranger. She was beginning to feel very foolish talking to people that had once been her friends, asking them to tell her about herself. So far no one she'd spoke to had told her anything new although they had all been very kind and genuinely offered their help anytime.

Now she was on the line to a Joan Phillips, which for some reason she had listed in the B section of her address book. She didn't know that she had a quirky little habit. She listed people under the name she had known them the best. Joan Phillip's maiden name; and the name Diane had known her under, most of her life, had been Brown. The two girls had grown up together and been best friends since second grade. This fact however eluded Diane, in her present state. All she knew was that Joan Phillips name was in her address book under the B's.

Just as she had almost placed the phone back in the cradle, she heard an out of breath voice speaking through the phone.

"Hello, hello I'm here. Is there anyone there? Hello."

"Hello, I called to speak with a Joan Phillips, my name is Diane Lindsey, and the reason I'm calling is…"

"Diane. Di." The response was chock full of happy laughter.

"Since when, are we so formal? I may have lived in Greece for two plus years, but I certainly haven't forgotten my best and oldest friend. I've written and called millions of times and never gotten a response. How the hell are you? I'm absolutely furious with you for never writing or calling me back. I've been worried sick. I finally came home just to find out what was going on with you. I was getting seriously scared."

Joan's diatribe finally ran down.

She spoke like an energizer bunny hopped, staccato bursts of effervescence.

Diane made a mental note to ask the police about her mail all this time. She had never received any, and that seemed very odd.

"Joan, it's obvious to me, we were very close friends. I really would like to meet with you and talk as soon as possible."

"Of course silly, I can't wait to see you either, with my having been gone over two years, we have tons of catching up to do. But why do you sound so strange? What's this obvious we were close friend's stuff, we've always been like sisters. I've been terrified being so out of touch. I thought you had moved or something and lost my address and never gotten my letters. What's really going on Di?"

Joan fell back on her childhood nickname for her friend.

"How is that bastard you married, and my beautiful God daughter? My goodness, Lexie was just a baby when I left, she must be almost five now, and I can't wait to see you both. I flew in last night and tried to call you, but I got a disconnect message. I was ready to call out the search dogs, to find you, as soon as I unpacked and got a little more sleep. I'm terribly jet lagged. I collapsed as soon as I walked in the door. But forget about me, what's going on with you? You sound so distant honey. Boy, I've really missed you."

Diane felt a real familiarity with Joan as her words bubbled out of her, it wasn't memory exactly, but it felt very natural to tell Joan the whole fantastic story. She just felt their connection and friendship on a deeper sub-conscious level; one that made it very easy to confess and explain her bizarre situation. Diane poured out everything she knew up to now, and about her current status. She related the events in chronological order and tried to tell the whole insane story as concisely as possible. They talked and Joan questioned animatedly for over an hour and then Diane realized it was almost eight o'clock, and the reporter would be arriving very soon.

"Listen Joan, I'm sorry to cut this off, but I've got to hang up now. One of the reporters is coming over here at eight o'clock, a Mark Roberts with the Rocky Mountain News. He wrote extensively about all this. So I'm praying that he will be able to enlighten me more, about whatever he may have uncovered, that wasn't in the articles and anyone else I should talk to. I need all the help and information I can get. Could I call you back tomorrow?"

"Are you nuts 'my friend'? You aren't alone anymore! I'm on my way over right this minute. I'm not waiting another day to see you. We'll talk to him together. Perhaps I can fill in some of the blanks that can help. I'm on my way Di, and I won't be long at all."

With that they each hung up. Diane couldn't help thinking that it sure felt good to have someone that cared in her corner, a good friend that had known her well, before. She felt much more hopeful about unraveling everything with so much help. She didn't exactly remember her, but Joan seemed very familiar. It was a warm fuzzy feeling, one that was new and comforting to her.

The circle of people who could help her was growing now. Besides Detective Damon Matthews, she would get additional help from Mark Roberts. As an investigative reporter she felt he could be a huge help by telling her how to proceed from here, and whom she might talk to, and best of all she had a friend, and even without remembering their past, she could feel the depth of the friendship that had once existed, simply from the easiness in Joan's voice, as she'd babbled at her.

For a moment she reflected on something Joan had said, about Rand being a bastard. Did Joan just say that in jest, or had he been? That would be a good place to start. A best friend should be able to tell her much more about herself on a personal level than any news article ever could. Best friends were privy to all kinds of personal confidences, and she knew that Joan was going to be a huge help as well as a solid support system, the thing she needed most of all.

Diane had been in the dark and alone long enough. Anyway, she had a strong impression that she was about to start making sense of things, and that she was at least taking charge of her life again.

Mark drove cautiously for he was a conscientious driver. He was on the way to Diane Lindsey's home and his thoughts registered back to the night of her accident. Unlike so many reporters who doggedly went for a story with little regard for the people involved, he sometimes cared too much, and would rather see the story suffer, than the victim. He was an excellent reporter because his stories were always honest and fair, but he didn't go in for sensationalism. If he unearthed something up that could hurt an innocent person in reporting it, he would rather put a lid on a story, than endanger anyone. In a business that mostly ignored feelings, he dealt fairly and with pathos for his subjects. People came first, not stories. That made him a very rare reporter.

That has been exactly the situation in Diane Lindsey's case. He had dug up quite a story. Something huge that was unreported by anyone else, thus probably unknown. Few other reporters would squelch a good story, no matter whom it hurt, but he had done just that.

Now the question was; should he give the information to Diane herself? If her own subconscious was trying to protect her, perhaps it was better not to give her the traumatic facts at this time. He wasn't sure what was best for her. From the very beginning he'd felt protective of this complex woman who had lost so much in a single night. Diane seemed so incredibly fragile and alone, but he also sensed incredible strength in her.

In the beginning he had worked the case relentlessly, as had the police, but as time went by, he watched the police slack off without new leads to go on. It was often said that either a case is solved in the first few weeks or it never will be.

Mark had been a little more detailed with his investigation and decided to delve into Diane's and Rand's past histories, from the present all the way back to their births. In his search on Rand he'd found a total blank. There had been nothing to find. So as a good investigator he went deeper. The police had stayed in the immediate present looking for a motive, so they had missed what the reporter felt only he had unearthed.

At least that had been his first thought; until Mark had spoken to the Chief of Police, offering up his information, only to be brusquely dismissed. It appeared that the upper echelons of the police department were not interested in sparring in that league and facing those kinds of repercussions. Not with the kind of information Mark had supplied, and the position it could place local authorities in. His research offered proof of collusion and deception at many levels. So instead they had chosen an 'ostrich stance', and buried the information, pretending that they were out of leads. Mark had actually sensed fear in the Chief, and realized they had known everything all along and perpetrated the cover-up. So he'd dropped it there and then. The connection he'd made was a very dangerous thing to pursue, if the police were going to turn their backs.

For Diane Lindsey's safety, Mark had chosen not to report anything he'd unearthed in the paper either, as it would definitely put her in an even more dangerous situation than she was already in. The only thing Mark felt certain was keeping her alive thus far; was her amnesia, because even with around the clock guards, she would not be safe, if the people, who had killed her husband, thought she could incriminate them. This was the big leagues, plus there was an excellent chance that even without amnesia, she'd known nothing regarding her dead husband's past. He was practically sure of that.

She and her husband had met and married only five years before his murder, and people like Rand Lindsey didn't confide in anyone. He may have married Diane in good faith and as a fresh start, or he may have only used her and even having the child as deep cover. There was no way of knowing now.

Mark knew what he had discovered in his research; could prove devastating to Diane, and he didn't want to further traumatize her. Yet if he were in her place, he knew he would want to know, everything there was to know; rather than live in a memory-less vacuum. That was how he felt; he'd have to wait and see how she felt. His intent was to feel his way along slowly.

As he drove up the stately drive to her house he decided he would play it by ear, and find out what kind of answers she was looking for and then go from there. He also admitted to himself, he was truly happy to be seeing her again. She had touched him deeply because of her incredible strength of character, and stamina, which had proved her capable of the perseverance, to return from a deep abyss and achieve a full recuperation. Mark believed there were few people who could handle what she had with so much dignity. Now he only wanted to help without causing any more damage.

Of course Mark hadn't exactly missed the fact that she was beautiful, that was simply secondary to the fact, she was quite a lady and extremely likable at their brief meeting that afternoon. It occurred to him that this was the first time in a very long time that he had even noticed what a woman looked like. That thought rather surprised him too.

He glanced into the visor mirror as he switched off the ignition. He had driven his candy apple red, 1980 Jaguar convertible with the top down. His usually slightly unruly dark blond hair was really windblown now. He tamed it the best he could, combing it with his fingers, yet it still gave his almost handsome, chiseled good looks the wanton abandon of a reckless teenager, even at thirty-nine.

The car defined Mark in a way; it was classy but not pretentious since it was older. It was also perfectly maintained and reflected that he respected its antiquity and was a person who took care of his things. Unfortunately the Jag also showed that he was lonely. The truth was he lavished all his spare time on polishing and maintaining the car, to substitute for not having a person in his life to give that care to.

Four years previously, Mark had lost a fiancée whom he had loved very much on the day before their wedding. Katrina had been hit by a drunk driver leaving the reception hall of the church, just following their wedding rehearsal dinner. He had been a spectator and watched in horror, as her body was thrown over the hood and hit the ground on the other side of the vehicle like a broken rag doll. He'd held her against him and felt her life slip away, in just a matter of moments. There hadn't been time to even say good-bye and he had never forgiven himself, although there was nothing he could have done. He'd never gotten over her. He didn't truly believe he ever would. He'd been angry at the world for a long time now.

In the four years since, time had passed slowly and all he did was work. He had not had the heart to return to dating, he was just incapable of forgetting her. Katrina had been from Sweden, a doctoral student; she'd double majored in medicine and immunology. She was amazing, smart and funny, and completely irreplaceable.

He simply hadn't been ready yet, to reenter the ridiculous world of dating. So instead he threw himself into his work and on off days, of which he took very few, he polished his car and visited a car club in town. It gave him a place to belong that was unimportant enough to save him from any personal involvement. The club was a guy thing, very few women were involved, which made it a sanctuary.

In reality his life was pretty empty, and he was beginning to feel the void. He was somewhat hermit like, and stayed pretty distant from most people, but somehow he felt a commitment to help Diane Lindsey. Her story was about loss too.

As he stepped out of the car, his exhaustion was reflected in his crystal blue eyes. He'd been working very hard and prior to seeing Diane that afternoon had planned the first early evening in a long time, planning to get some sleep. But there had been no way he could possibly have ignored Diane's cry for help.

He rang the bell and admired the old-world etched and stained glass windows. It occurred to him he hadn't eaten all day, and his stomach let out a low growl. One thing was sure, his lean body was certainly in no danger of becoming overweight; Mark had never carried an extra pound on him in his whole life. His body was hard as a rock. In fact he was always fighting to put on a little more weight. He seldom remembered to stop and eat until his body insisted, but at the moment it was suddenly very demanding. Diane answered the door almost immediately. It was obvious she had been anticipating his arrival.

"Thank you so much for coming, please come in."

Diane realized she sounded very formal and stiff, but she didn't know quite how to go about asking a near stranger, to tell her about herself. After fighting so long for physical recovery, her resolve was now equally and stubbornly set to relearning every detail missing from her recall. Limbo was no place to stay so long. She was prepared to do her homework, and this man was a great resource. Nevertheless it was awkward to frame the questions she needed to ask.

She resolved as their eyes slowly spoke, this man would help her dig up the truth. She suddenly had such a strong feeling about him; there was something about this man that made her feel confident, everything was going to be okay. In just the short time together that afternoon, he had given her the impression that somehow he had her answers. She didn't understand why exactly but she trusted her intuition.

Mark glanced around the foyer and up the double curved stairway that climbed from the marble floor, with the graceful rosewood balustrade and the stairs laden with a tapestry runner in subdued tones of roses and grays. It was obvious the house had been designed lovingly by an old-world architect. It exhibited the grace and style of old money, and had that certain grandeur. And now it served to provide a perfect backdrop for this woman standing rather stiffly in front of him.

He saw that she had swept her hair back into a loose chignon, rather than free and flowing past her shoulders in strawberry waves as it had been earlier in the day. With her hair up, she looked less approachable, more serious but still vulnerable. He just wished he knew the best way to help her. He had to figure out the answer to that question fast. Was it to give her the truth in one fell swoop, or should he hold back until she was steadier. After all, she'd only left the hospital yesterday.

"Listen Diane, may I call you Diane?"

"Of course, or Di if you prefer, I just found out that is my nickname, from my oldest friend, whom I can't even remember." she replied ruefully, yet with a smile.

"In fact you will be meeting her very shortly. I just hung up the phone with Joan and she's on her way over. She says she can help fill in blanks too.

Meanwhile why don't we have a seat in the living room?"

"Well actually I was going to suggest that we might go out and grab a bite to eat. I haven't eaten all day, and my stomach is seriously reprimanding me. Perhaps we could all three go, when your friend gets here, if that's okay."

"I have an even better idea. Why don't you follow me to the kitchen instead, and I'll fix you something. No waiting, that way. Someone very kindly stocked my fridge before I got home yesterday. I'll feel less awkward here, instead of sitting in a public restaurant, while discussing something so personal. Plus I can't go anywhere without the bodyguard out front, which makes leaving fairly difficult. He really hates it, and I really pushed my luck dragging him all over the place today."

She gave a sheepish grin, looking like an errant child. Explanation made, he offered no comment, so Diane just assumed his compliance, and turned and walked toward the kitchen, with Mark in tow. He followed relaxing at the thought of sitting quietly in her kitchen and being fed. He couldn't help appreciating the graceful line of her body as she walked away. Diane didn't even walk with a limp after all she had endured. She was truly a woman who had prevailed.

Once in the kitchen it seemed the most natural thing in the world for her to bustle around throwing a salad and omelet together while Mark perched on a stool watching and chatting about ordinary every day things. Then he helped, going through cabinets to find the things they would need for the meal, as he set the counter. It appeared that Diane was as much a stranger to this kitchen as he was. He noticed several times she had to open more than one cabinet, to find the spices or whisk or whatever she was looking for. Mark said nothing, but it was obvious to him that she felt tremendous frustration at not knowing where things were; items that she knew she should know without even thinking. Yet he admired the way she held her head up and even occasionally made jokes about it.

Aside from being very resilient, she also exhibited a very giving nature and an easy sense of humor. The more Mark observed her; the more fascinated he became with this woman, beyond her news worthiness. Diane had beautifully vulnerable eyes that seemed to look right through him. It disconcerted him as he realized that they constantly changed color with the light. Sometimes her eyes were emerald, or gray green or sometimes a lighter blue green. Now in the bright kitchen lighting, they were the color of a spruce tree, they were so deep. It was as unnerving, as it was mesmerizing, and he found himself enchanted by her. He was completely losing all his objectivity. He had an irrational desire to make those eyes laugh and smile and never allow anything or anyone to hurt her or make her unhappy ever again and his thoughts surprised him.

The conversation flowed smoothly, as they each ate right at the kitchen counter perched on stools. Diane joined him. She had been too busy all day and was suddenly ravenous herself. They had delicious Caesar salads with Brie and Canadian bacon omelets, garnished with fresh herbs and big cold glasses of milk. Neither of them seemed in a rush, to get to the conversation he had come prepared for, perhaps realizing on a subliminal level that it would be awkward and painful. In tacit agreement they were letting that part of the conversation wait until Joan arrived.

Mark was fascinated, by the timing that had her best friend gone and living out of the country in Greece all through the entire tragedy, and now had her arriving home completely unaware of what had happened on the exact same day Diane returned home. It seemed to be too much of a coincidence to be real and it didn't set right with his investigators instinct. His journalistic experience told him to be very alert. He was looking forward to meeting this friend himself. His antenna was up.

Diane was amazed at how comfortable she felt with the task of cooking and chatting with Mark. He had an easy laugh and a beautiful crooked smile that was a contrast to his very serious icy blue eyes. Eyes, that seemed to look straight through her. He seemed to hear things that she didn't say, along with things she did. She thought that trait must be a real plus as an investigating newsman. She was finding it a tad disconcerting herself.

While they talked of trivialities, her mind was racing with the questions she needed answered. She wondered if when she reconstructed her entire past she would then remember everything. Or would she simply know about her past in the same way we learn a story we have been told. She prayed it would all come back, even the memories, she knew it would make her grief worse. She felt the void like a hunger. It was a little like being so hungry, your stomach aches, only it was her soul that ached to be filled. She knew it had to be easier to face whatever she learned about her past, rather than drown in the emptiness of not knowing.

As they finished rinsing their plates and setting their things in the dishwasher the doorbell rang announcing the arrival of Joan. Without waiting for them to reach the front door, she swept through it and half crossed the foyer with the bodyguard right behind, since Diane had forgotten to forewarn him of Joan's arrival. Diane assured the officer it was fine and that Joan had been invited and after he looked at her ID, as he had Marks upon his arrival, he left locking the door with a rebuke at it being unlocked before. Diane and Mark stood sizing Joan up, until she closed the gap of foyer standing between them.

She was a bubbly outgoing petite woman, who looked as though she would be completely at ease in any kind of company. Her hair was a massive golden brown tumble of curls falling to her shoulders. It looked as if she spent very little time on it. Although it was graced with a very few God donated silver hairs that even her hairdresser could not influence. She had the kind of approachable attractiveness that would never be quite beautiful, but would always get her plenty of attention. Mostly her countenance was simply cute as hell.

As she reached Diane, she completely enveloped her in a bear hug of an embrace. Until Mark saw them standing together, he had held the impression that Diane was taller that she now appeared. Now standing next to her friend who wasn't all that tall either, he realized just how petite Diane really was, and it served to intensify her vulnerability.

Mark sent up a quick prayer to guide him in telling Diane the right things, in the right time tonight and to help him assess this friend accurately, for Diane's safety. He watched as Diane extricated herself from Joan and led them both into the living area to sit and talk. It was clear she was a bit overwhelmed at Joan's exuberance, and it was equally clear that she hadn't suddenly remembered her, as she had so hoped she would. Joan was still a stranger to her and yet she did feel very comfortable in her presence. She even felt sure that they could build a whole new friendship. It could be based solely on the warmth Joan exuded and Diane could truly feel. Joan was about as lovable as a cocker spaniel puppy and had the unique ability to fill in all blanks for Diane, reaching all the way back to their mutual childhoods. That would be invaluable.

There was an awkward moment right after they all took their seats. Everyone's thoughts were racing, sizing each other up. They had all digested the fact that Diane had not recognized Joan at all.

Joan spoke up first and broke the awkward silence.

"Okay, Di, lets get started. I can see you don't remember me, but that's not a problem, because I do remember you. I know how you think, what makes you laugh, that you love cold pizza for breakfast, can ski at the speed of light, and have the softest heart in the world. You love old sappy, black and white movies that make you cry because of your Nana Eve. Your parents were the greatest people in the world, and I spent more time at your house, than my own, growing up. We've been through puberty, boyfriends, slumber parties and proms. We've made prank phone calls and toilet-papered houses together. We had our first kisses on the same night at a drive-in movie on a double date. I had the back seat and you sat with Bob Teaney in the front, with a Volkswagen gearshift between you. I held your hand through his funeral, after he died in a car crash when you were sixteen. I was maid of honor at your wedding, even though I didn't like Rand and tried to talk you out of marrying him. You stood up with me when I eloped with Graeme too, and three years ago held me together at his funeral, when I buried him and felt like I wished I'd died too. We've been as close as sisters all our lives, and I have billions of pictures, if you want to see them to jog your memory. You will find that you on the other hand, have very few pictures. You never remember to take a camera, and if you do take one, then you forget to use it. Now I've been running off at the mouth long enough, so I'll shut up and give someone else a chance. Please, just believe me when I tell you that I am so sorry I didn't know what was going on, or I would have been here! I was simply lost in my own little pity party after Graeme's death and misplaced a few years myself simply wandering. But I finally came home to find you when all of my letters went unanswered and I'm here now, and I'm staying with you until you are better too. I love you Di, and we will get through this together, just like we did everything else all of our lives. I'm very definitely your friend and you can count on me for anything."

As Joan's second diatribe finally concluded, Mark saw that there were tears in Diane's eyes and something else too, recognition. She may not have recognized Joan on sight, but her heart still knew and recognized her best friend's sincerity.

A breakthrough had occurred, Diane remembered that first date; she could picture Bob Teaney, and remember that first salty, popcorn-flavored kiss. She had spilled her coke all over her new white skin-tight jeans. She remembered that the stain never came completely out. She could remember how pretty Joan had looked that night too. Her hair had been to her waist then, even longer than Diane's own. They had just gotten their ears pierced together that Saturday morning. Diane had picked the gold posts and Joan the silver.

With all the memories rushing in, the tears began to flow freely down Diane's face, then Joan started crying too, and soon Mark was blinking away tears as well. It was a very emotional moment, and in sharing it, they all formed a bond. Even though Joan and Mark had not even spoken to each other yet, they were now all irrevocably bound to help and protect Diane.

Now it was Mark's turn, to bring them both up to date on the statistics. Most of which Diane had been informed of, at least in part, but of which Joan knew only a little, from the earlier conversation with Diane.

Mark no longer had any suspicions about Joan's allegiance to Diane. It was obvious to him that Joan was one-hundred-percent her friend, and had been on target with her feelings regarding Rand Lindsey. She had said his name with obvious disdain that left little to the imagination about how little she had liked him, and how protective she was of Diane now.

Mark recapped a synopsis of all the news that had appeared in the papers and cited police report findings that had been public record. What he didn't do yet was offer any negative information regarding Rand, details that he had uncovered on his own and which the police had conspired to ignore. He didn't want to share those facts, until

Diane could catch her breath from having so much thrown at her at once.

She may have kept totally in the dark. After all she was busy raising her child, as well as carrying a full time class schedule as a student working on her masters. She had been a very active member in her neighborhood community, and church. Her husband had adopted an air of total respectability and appeared a legitimate businessman. He'd had several legitimate companies in which to launder his money through. From what Mark could tell about Diane's integrity, she just didn't fit the image of a wife, who would close her eyes to, or support what Rand had been involved with.

He was convinced that she had been clueless about the kind of man he really was. He made the decision; he didn't think she needed the shock of finding out about him just yet. So he kept to the facts generally known, and answered all of their questions and before they knew it, the antique clock startled them, when it rang twelve chimes. It was midnight and the time had gone by so fast. It was a tough subject, but the company had been animated and they'd covered a lot of ground. Now he could see that Diane looked extraordinarily tired. In fact they all were.

Mark got up to leave, but they all agreed that he would come again the next evening after he got off work. Joan then announced that she had a bag in the car and wasn't going any further away then Diane's guestroom. Mark and Joan went out together, but Joan was back in seconds, complete with her bag and her own pillow.

"I'm so glad you're here. I do have pillows." Diane gave Joan a hug as she locked the door behind her.

"Happy to be here kiddo, but I am compulsive about my own pillow. It's a Joan thing. I used to carry it to slumber parties too. You'll get used to me again."

As it turned out, both Joan and Diane wound up propped up, talking in Diane's big canopy bed. They talked softly and seriously long into the night. Neither of them held back anything and they shared everything about their feelings and fears, just as they had in childhood and adolescence. When Diane finally slept, it was with a sense of well being she had not known since Rand's murder and the loss of her sweet baby daughter and her mobility. She had a best friend and she had pieces of her memory back. It was a start, an excellent beginning, and she knew more would come. The doors for her memories were opened and she truly believed that now that she had begun to remember, it was only a matter of time, until it would all come flooding back.

Her heart knew Joan. She remembered her first date, being sixteen, getting their ears pierced. There were flashes of slumber parties, movies they'd gone to, and a senior trip. It was a start, a big one. They finally both slept, all talked out for one night.

CHAPTER 3

Diane awoke early, the result of living in a hospital so long. Even though she and Joan had talked half the night she couldn't go back to sleep. Joan had groaned and rolled over and gone right back to sleep, having no such compunction to be an early riser.

Diane got out of bed and headed to the kitchen. As she put on a pot of coffee she thought about the events of the night before. She'd found out so much in the last twenty-four hours. It was a tremendous amount to absorb, but she was feeling very hopeful. At least she could remember her sixteen-year-old self, and Joan at that time too. That was encouraging. Waves of memory began to come to her and soak in like gentle surf on dry sand. The foundational pieces of her childhood began to wash up. She could visualize the home she had grown up in; a three-bedroom, middle income house, in an 'Ozzie and Harriet' type subdivision in Denver. There had been only six basic models in the neighborhood of cul-de-sacs, in a neighborhood where all the kids ran in and out of each other's houses, and felt at home in all of them. She had been lucky enough to have a mom, who baked cookies for the whole neighborhood. And a home where all the kids were always welcome, at their kitchen table anytime. Her mom had been the one, all the kids flocked to with their problems, and they were never turned away. She remembered with a smile that even the boys she had broken up with, would still go visit her mother, long after they had quit going out with her. Diane's dad had been equally terrific; he had called her 'funny-face', and could always make her laugh. He was always willing to drop everything to talk with her, and he always paid attention to whatever she told him, no matter how trivial or silly. Her parents had given her a tremendous sense of self worth, for which she was now eternally grateful.

Diane had been blessed with a very happy childhood, and two wonderful parents that had dotingly loved their only child, and given her self-confidence and a strong character; one that had served her well, throughout her entire recovery. How she wished that they were still alive. However they had died six years ago, four months apart. She now remembered everything.

Her father had gotten bone cancer, which mercifully took him very quickly and without a long drawn out illness. Her mother had died four months later of a heart attack, but Diane thought it was really a broken heart. Her mother and father had been so much in love that even after forty plus years of marriage they had still looked at each other like newlyweds. They had given Diane the best possible example of what a marriage and family should be. Yet even though she still could not remember her more recent past, she had the awful feeling that her own marriage had fallen far short of her parent's example.

Joan had confirmed as much to her, the night before. Joan said that Diane had not confided what exactly was upsetting her about Rand, only that she couldn't trust him any more and he had some dark secrets. But she had confided that she was going to file for a divorce, unless things changed. That had been over two years ago, right before Joan went to Greece and about two months before the accident, and the reason why she had wanted to leave him was still unknown to her. What things had to change? She also didn't know. All she had now, were even more questions.

That had been the reason why Joan had figured she couldn't get in touch with Diane. Joan had assumed the divorce had taken place shortly after she had gone to Greece and Diane hadn't received her letters after moving out of Rand's house.

Diane still wondered why the police hadn't given those letters to her; she could have used the communications from her friend. It might even have helped her amnesia sooner, to have been in touch with Joan. So why had they not given her the mail? It didn't make sense.

She suddenly had another memory kick at the corners of her mind. This one was about Joan. Joan's family hadn't been great like hers, it was full of yelling, and step-fathers and families that came and went. Diane could never keep them straight. Her real father had abandoned them when Joan was born. Her mother had made some very bad husband choices, at last count four. At sixteen Joan and her mother were alone again, and both very unhappy. Joan had spent all her time at Diane's house. She had always said that if not for Diane's family she probably would have gotten into big trouble. Her parents had loved her just as they had Diane, and provided a secure second home she was always welcome in. Because of them Joan had grown into a wonderful, loving woman. Diane was happy thinking of her parents and what they had been like. They had been people who touched others, well and often. Kathryn and Lynn Callahan had been very special and she remembered them and the feel of being loved.

As she finished her second cup of coffee and her morning muse, she heard Joan coming down the stairs. She poured another cup of coffee, realizing that she knew Joan would take it black. Little things were coming back, and she felt optimistic that she would have all of her memory back and intact very soon. She could just feel it.

"Good-Morning "Glory!" Diane greeted Joan cheerfully, as a sleepy looking Joan entered the kitchen.

"Hey that's exactly what your mom used to always say in the morning. Do you remember that?"

"Yes, and I also remember that you take your coffee black, and did even when we were kids and not supposed to have any coffee at all. Lots of little things are coming back. I'm starting to remember almost everything up until about the time I must have met Rand. The most current recollection is now your wedding. I think we were about twenty-four. Graeme was prematurely gray and ruggedly handsome. He was a New Zealander; he called himself a Kiwi. As I recall he had a wicked sense of humor, and he was a mountain climber, am I right?"

"Atta girl, let's try something. How about, a little word association, to stimulate your new found memory?"

"Okay let's try. I'm game." Diane was willing to try anything and felt much more positive now, having regained some of her memories. She was now convinced that she was much closer to regaining them all.

"Okay, fire when ready." Diane quipped.

At that exact second, someone did indeed fire, but not questions. A barrage of gunfire was heard and the beveled window of the kitchen exploded, showering them both with shards of glass.

One fragment imbedded itself in Joan's cheek, narrowly missing her eye. She fell to the floor stunned and bleeding copiously from her wound. Diane had been pouring coffee at the second of the explosive gunfire, and one shot had exploded the coffeepot, drenching her mid-section in scalding hot coffee.

Diane too scrambled to the floor and over to Joan.

"Jo, are you all right?" She asked, unaware of even using the name she had always called her friend. Joan simply nodded.

"We better get out of here, and fast, stay down and follow me." Diane ordered as she grabbed Joan's hand, and in a low dash they raced out of the kitchen and into the butler's pantry which had all inside walls and no windows. They still stayed low, running in a crouch.

Now they could hear someone breaking in the kitchen door that led in from the side yard.

"Diane, where the hell, are the police? I thought you had a twenty-four hour guard." Joan hissed in hushed tones.

"So did I, come on, I'm sure they'll be in that door any second."

The two women ran through the dining room and living room over to the front window, but looking out into the street there was no guard, nor his car insight. It appeared that they were totally on their own.

This time Joan grabbed Diane and pulled her toward the front door.

"We have to get out of here, and fast. My car is just to the left of your front door; let's get to it fast while they're coming in through the back. Hurry and stay right with me."

The two women flew out the front door and raced for the car. Once again they were assaulted with gunfire. There was someone shooting at them now that must have stayed in the hedge by the garage. He was right behind them.

They reached the car and jumped in either side. Fortunately Joan had left the keys in the car, and it started in a split second although it seemed like an eternity.

The outside assassin was now running right toward the car from across the lawn, and at the same time two other shooters were flying out through the front door behind them. All three men were now shooting and within twenty to thirty feet of the car. Joan floored the gas pedal and spun out of the driveway, cutting right through the perfectly manicured lawn. The back windshield was struck by gunfire and violently imploded as they fled the property and hit the main road out of the neighborhood.

Diane looked at her friend behind the wheel.

"Oh my God, you've been shot. Joan you're bleeding."

Besides just Joan's cheek bleeding, now there was an ugly bloodstain spreading across the left shoulder of her white silk pajama top and another on her upper right arm and both wounds were bleeding very fast. Joan looked as if she were going in to shock, but still drove like a maniac trying to get them to safety. As they turned a corner they heard a pursuit vehicle right behind them and shots rang out again.

They were on a blank stretch of road that exited the exclusive estates. Joan floored the gas pedal and the Volvo leaped to the challenge. Squealing tires, they flew through the entrance gate, taking with them the barricade bar, across the drive at the security booth. Now it remained dramatically draped and precariously balanced on the hood of the car. They could see the attendant in the booth duck down as they and the car pursuing, accelerated through the now de-barricaded gate. Perhaps at least the man in the booth would call the police, Diane could only hope.

"Quick Joan, make a sharp left on the access road, the fire-station is just up that road." As she said it, Diane also grabbed the wheel and turned it sharply to the left, putting her foot down on top of Joan's on the gas-pedal. Joan was unable to react at all; she'd lapsed into unconsciousness. The car was right behind them as they drove across the fire-station lawn and straight into a bay next to a fire engine.

The pursuit car sped on by and kept right on going at break-neck speed. Diane assumed they weren't ready to take on a whole fire station full of firefighters, several of which were pulling open the Volvo's doors. One young paramedic helped a terrified Diane out of the passenger side, while others helped by getting a stretcher for the driver, now being carried from the car with little sign of life. Diane ran to her friend's side ignoring the questions flying at her from the firemen.

"Will she be all right?" Diane begged an answer of the young firefighter who was checking for a pulse and the other, who was trying to stop the bleeding.

"Will she?"

"It looks pretty bad, but she still has a pulse, let's get her to a hospital. Now!" replied the young paramedic.

Just then the ambulance and police arrived simultaneously in a cacophony of sirens. A gurney was quickly unloaded and Joan gently placed on it.

Diane intended to ride with her friend to the hospital, but instead found herself detained by the two patrolmen who wanted her statement. She quickly explained who she was and told them to contact Detective Matthews, then refusing to accept any other diversions Diane insistently jumped into the ambulance and went with Joan, back to her all too familiar hospital.

It took almost a quarter of an hour to get there, while the paramedic worked continually to stanch the bleeding. Diane had never seen so much blood, and was terrified of losing her friend. She found herself crying and praying with all her heart that Joan would be all right, or she would never forgive herself. She mentally refused to lose anyone else that she cared about. Joan simply could not die. It just wasn't an option. She held tightly to her friend's limp hand and prayed for all she was worth.

The hospital emergency room took over with an air of both efficiency and controlled mayhem, and soon there were wires and monitors all over and surrounding Joan. The attending ER doctor insisted that she leave the room and wait in the reception area, but Diane refused to leave and promised to stay out of the way. When he saw how adamant she was, he left her alone and returned to the business of saving Joan's life.

After finally stopping the bleeding, the doctor explained they would have to get Joan into surgery quickly. The bullet that had entered her shoulder had traveled close to the spinal cord. Those words made Diane's blood run cold, she knew that could mean paralysis. She intensified her prayers as she went into the family surgical waiting area.

Six hours and Joan was still in surgery. Diane was losing her mind waiting, but at least she wasn't alone anymore. Detective Matthews had joined her in the emergency room shortly after the ambulance arrived. She was very grateful that he was willing to wait without pressuring her to go over the story of what had happened again. She had told him all she could. Now for the last three hours he had simply stayed by her side in a companionable silence, occasionally holding her hand or handing her a cup of high-test hospital coffee. His company was comforting and she came to rely upon his quiet but reassuring presence.

Damon was incredibly good looking and yet seemed completely unaware of how striking he actually was, making him even more attractive, plus there was something about him seen in very few men; it was genuine sweetness and a vulnerable shy air that made him even more interesting.

Several times Diane looked up to find his watchful protective gaze resting on her. Her thoughts were predominately full of prayers and obsession over her friend's welfare. Yet she could feel his presence, and it helped.

Damon couldn't help thinking to himself that surely this woman had been through enough. Now her best friend hovered near death. No one person should have to endure so much, and yet he couldn't help admiring the dignity she exhibited regardless of the adversities she came up against. She was one of the bravest and classiest women he had ever come across. He would give anything to solve this damn case and set her free from living in fear. She had experienced more that any one person should ever have to cope with in just one lifetime.

He had called in several times to the precinct for updates on the shooting incident at her house. Uzi's had been the weapons of choice, a fact that definitely signified a serious professional job. Worse yet someone had called the officer on guard duty away from the scene just before the hit. That call had come from the precinct, which would seem to say that there was a dirty cop involved in this case somehow.

Damon also thought about how the Chief of Police kept squashing the investigation, and that from the beginning they had allowed him very little budget or manpower on Diane's case. There had been a huge push from above to just close the file, and only Damon's insistence had made them keep Diane in protective custody this long.

He was in extreme disfavor at the precinct for pushing so hard to continue protecting her. Especially after so much time had gone by uneventfully, but now this proved he'd been right, although he'd rather have been wrong.

Of late the precinct had piled more and more cases on his desk forcing the Lindsey file onto a back burner, yet regardless of that, they had been unable to convince him to close the case completely. That had made him very unpopular. Now he knew that his instincts were correct, which validated him.

Damon was also beginning to admit to himself that somehow the police were involved. That made him both mad and sad. Now he'd have to figure out why and who? He didn't like the thought, that in a way, he was in the enemy camp. Damon made an ironclad pledge to himself that he would keep Diane safe, no matter what, even if he had to leave the force and appoint himself her personal bodyguard. However for now, he thought he could probably learn more about any connection to the force from the inside. So he would wait and watch and be prepared for anything. Naturally he kept all these thoughts to himself. Diane didn't need anymore to worry about. But he was seething, and his anger at the people responsible was over-powering. He just wished he knew who the enemy actually was to have such pull and power.

Damon glanced over at Diane thoughtfully sipping, about her fiftieth cup of black coffee. She looked very weary but she had resolutely insisted on waiting for news of her friend. No amount of coercion or convincing could get her to leave the waiting room.

She sat, head bowed and shoulders weary, staring either into her coffee cup or at the gray linoleum squares on the floor between her feet. She had filled Damon in on all the details leading up to and including Joan's being shot, explaining who Joan was and her whereabouts since Diane's tragedy, and her return from Greece only two days before, and also about how with Joan's help, her own memory, was returning in significant bits. She had described in great detail the events of the previous evening as well as that morning which was vividly etched in her short term memory. Diane had dark circles under her eyes and Joan's blood all over her, including matted in her hair. Yet even with no make-up or rest, since the shooting, she was still wanly appealing, more from demeanor than appearance. She was amazing as far as Damon was concerned.

Not many women could survive everything Diane had with such grace.

Diane had a great eye for detail and had helped the police sketch artist to draw three very good likenesses, that she claimed were very close to the three gunmen. However, so far the department computer had not turned up any matches for the snipers. Damon had a feeling that they wouldn't. He was under the considered opinion that these guys were pros, or they wouldn't have a cop in their pocket.

Damon too felt a wave of exhaustion and hoped they would hear something about Joan's condition soon. The lithographs hanging in the surgical waiting room were all French impressionists, soft pastels, landscapes or Parisian scenes, the places all depicted a wonderful escape from this endless waiting, an escape, that failed to materialize, hour after hour.

Damon sincerely wished he could wipe away all Diane's problems and whisk her away to that lovely French countryside depicted in the Monet reprint on the west wall. He snapped himself out of this reverie and explained it away to himself as fatigue. He knew the truth, he was in danger of being too personally involved to remain objective. This was one incredible woman, and he was determined to protect her.

Shortly after two in the morning, the hospital changed Joan's status from critical to stable, finally allowing her to leave the recovery room and be brought to a room in the critical care unit. Then and only then, Diane gratefully accepted Damon's offer to keep watch outside the room while she caught some sleep on a cot next to Joan's bed. Although she absolutely and resolutely refused to leave her friend's room, Diane's exhaustion was evident. Most of the nurses on the floor knew her well, and had no problem bending rules to see her get some rest. They rolled a cot into the room and tenderly tucked her in next to her friend, since it was obvious nothing would get her to leave.

The doctors had assured her that Joan would be all right and should achieve a full recovery with time and physical therapy for the shoulder. That of course was news she could associate with. She knew that Joan would tackle it like a bulldog and get well quickly, too. Diane just felt responsible and guilty for Joan being in the line of fire in the first place. Frustration and anger overwhelmed her. She was so tired of being afraid, and very angry that someone else had been hurt because of her by nameless monsters pursuing her, for yet unknown reasons. She wanted answers to some tough questions."Why are people trying to kill me? And when would the lunacy all stop?" she thought in abject frustration. Diane sent up a single prayer, "Please don't let anyone else get hurt because of me." Then gave in to exhaustion, at last falling asleep, safe, knowing Damon was outside the door watching her back for her.

Somewhere during the long night he had ceased to be Detective Matthews and they had gotten comfortable with each other. For two years he had been a constant in her life as the detective on her case. Tonight with all the shared worry over Joan, he had also become her friend. So Diane's last thought before closing her eyes was of Damon.

Before lapsing into a near comatose like sleep she graciously thanked the nurse in the room very much for the cot, asleep before she'd finished speaking. Diane gave in to a deep dreamless oblivion.

Damon on the other side of the door in the hospital corridor had to fight off his own weariness. Yet he was adamantly determined that no one would get to Diane again, at least not as long as he drew breath. Since he didn't know who else he could trust on the force, he was determined to guard her himself. He intended to be constantly vigilant on her behalf. Only he had a big problem, he was about ready to drop from exhaustion himself. That came with the territory though, he'd been here many times. After all, his line of work was often not conducive to sleep; he drank another cup of hospital high-test coffee that the nurses had so kindly provided. Yet he knew he could not stay sharp enough to be useful much longer, he needed someone else for back up that he was sure he could trust with safeguarding Diane and Joan.

As Damon sat drinking the coffee and thinking, he jotted notes about leads from the recent shooting. At least he now had fresh leads and a hot trail, not to mention the link to the department. He followed the chain of command from the patrolman who was told to cease watching Diane, back to Detective Sergio Santorine, his own ex-partner.

He and Sergio had been through many disagreements as partners. Once lukewarm friends, they now hardly spoke. Sergio never let procedure or the law, stop him; he was a bully pure and simple, using his position to his advantage, always bending regulations. He would do just about anything he could get away with. He and Damon had barely spoken in the last six months. Now Damon decided it was time to visit his old partner, as soon as he could get someone trustworthy at the door for Diane and Joan. He felt responsible for the two women now, and was going to make absolutely sure they stayed out of harm's way. It was personal now, intensely personal if someone on the force was a traitor. After a lifetime with the force he had to face that he could no longer thrust the department he'd given his last twelve years to.

By seven a.m., Damon had figured out exactly who to call to keep watch, someone he could absolutely trust. Even though the department had once again assigned twenty-four hour police guards, for Diane after the recent attack, Damon wanted someone to guard the guards, since he had no idea who-else might be on the take, someone that could keep an eye on things without being observed themselves.

When he had been in the military, his bunk mate and best friend in the Green Beret was a superb martial arts expert and a born hero. He had undeniable common sense and could be trusted absolutely. He had received a medical discharge after mortar fire had made him deaf in one ear, and that had pretty much canceled his plans for the police academy too. So in order to make use of his criminology degree and work at what he loved best, investigation and surveillance, he had become a private investigator for several law firms. He was quite simply the best. No run of the mill detective, Chase Nealson was a man full of honor and scrupulously honest. He was a "Yes" and "No", kind of man who used words at a minimum, but whatever he said could absolutely be depended upon. He was completely incorruptible and someone Damon would not hesitate to trust in any situation. Damon and he had kept a close friendship over the years. When he gave Chase a call and explained the situation, Chase had replied without any question, "Give me an hour and I'll be there." As simple as that, problem solved, no questions asked.

CHAPTER 4

At eight a.m., Damon stuck his head in the door and saw that Diane was awake and sitting in a chair looking concerned as she held Joan's hand. Joan had been restless during the night, but had still not awakened fully.

Diane was getting very worried about her friend and would not leave her side even to get a cup of coffee. Tired as he was himself, Damon went down to the hospital dining room and got her a tray with a healthy breakfast, coffee and juice. When he took it up to her he absolutely insisted that she eat it, and would accept no excuses. She had only been well such a short time, and he didn't want her to have a relapse.

At his insistence she took a few half-hearted bites, but drained the coffee with no urging. They spoke softly taking care not to disturb Joan.

Damon described Chase and explained to her why he felt having him there was necessary. Diane looked frightened at the inference that the police might be involved. But she had decided to put her faith in Damon and by extension in Chase also. She was accustomed to her life having bizarre twists and turns, and this one seemed no more unusual then any of the others, that made up her recent history.

It seemed to her that in the couple of days since her release form the hospital, time had escalated at warp speed, so much had happened. As she reclaimed more of her life back, there were others just as anxious to take it away from her.

She and Damon were of the definite opinion now, that this had never been a random crime. Someone wanted her dead now too. That eliminated any possibility of a random act of violence, especially with the police guard called away.

Soon Chase Nealson arrived sticking his head in the door; Damon waved him on in, inviting him to come meet Diane.

Chase walked very slowly over to them, his every step slow and measured. He walked as a hunter walks, without making a sound but also gracefully. He exuded calm and his appearance was peaceful too. A once darker head of hair was now salted with a distinguished amount of gray, and gold-green eyes with a mysterious gray ring around them gave him an offhanded sex appeal. He had a decided, unidentifiable magnetism. In any other face those eyes might have been sinister, yet Chase's eyes just made her feel softly observed and exuded a protective calm.

Damon had made a good choice. Diane instantly felt an easiness settle over her. This man would be hard for anyone to get by or around. She knew instinctively that Joan and she were in great hands. Chase exhibited a visible confidence; and between he and Damon, Diane knew, Joan and she couldn't be safer.

Damon briefed Chase on the case to date. The three of them worked out a strategy of sorts, a time schedule for Damon and Chase to change shifts, etc. As they talked quietly in the corner of the hospital room, they were surprised when an anesthetic influenced, very husky voice rang out.

"Hey you guys, can I play too? I always thought whispering was sort of rude. How about including me in all this plotting going on."

Everyone turned to Joan, and walked over to her bedside, Diane reached down and took her hand again, and her face lit up as she smiled at her friend.

"Glad you deigned to join us. You scared us half to death. I am so terribly sorry, that you were hurt, it should have been me." Diane looked at her friend with compassion and sorrow. "I'm so very sorry, Jo."

"It's okay my friend, I'll do almost anything to get out of unpacking all the junk I brought home from Greece. That's precisely why I stayed over last night, avoidance and procrastination are my strong suits, and the only thing I like better is a chance to play *Camille*. Now I've managed all of the aforementioned, and believe me I can be a regular *Sara Bernhardt*. You'll see, I'm going to nurse this thing for all I can get, count on it."

Now she had everyone laughing, and the somber attitude in the room dissipated completely. Joan could always work a room, and she was not unaware of the new good-looking men in this one. Her eyes took in Chase from head to toe, and she found herself wondering, just how bad she looked? It was suddenly of great concern to her.

Damon introduced himself and Chase to Joan, and Chase assured Joan and Diane in his quiet reassuring way, and with a minimum of words, that he would indeed keep them safe. "You ladies have nothing to worry about; no one gets through me. Nobody; and you can count on that."

The sincerity in his voice convinced both Diane and Joan even more than the words he'd spoken.

A nearly imperceptible spark flew from Joan to Chase, and was returned in kind. Diane saw it and smiled inwardly, somehow she absolutely believed that Joan would be watched very carefully from now on.

Damon felt comfortable slipping out of the room as the two women spoke of inconsequential things along with the obvious and Chase took a seat quietly in the corner of the room, facing the door, like any other visitor.

CHAPTER 5

Mark was half out of his mind. He'd picked up the teletype the second he got in that morning, in shock he read about the shooting at Diane's home the previous morning. Now he was reading with great concentration, not only had there been a shooting, but a victim had been taken to the hospital with two gunshot wounds and in critical condition. All that had been yesterday.

He had been given an out of town assignment the previous day on a big story and had just arrived back, fighting a huge case of jetlag. He'd tried to call Diane last night to apologize for being unavailable that evening, and wound up leaving a message on her voice mail when she hadn't answered her phone. He'd had no idea what had gone down in his absence until now, nearly twenty-four hours after the fact.

Frantically he called his police department source and got the details. He was relieved to find out it was not Diane who'd been shot, but very sorry that Joan had been. She was a bright, funny lady, and a wonderful friend; even only having met her once, he had liked her very much.

Mark threw his story together in record time and turned it in. He couldn't get to Diane soon enough. He knew she must be feeling frightened, and beyond anything reasonable, and having nothing to do with the story angle, he just had to go to her. She had consumed his thoughts, and he hated to admit it even to himself, but he was way out on a limb, the thoughts he was having were not all professional.

She was beautiful inside and out, courageous, and about every other adjective he could think of. No matter what he was doing, he kept finding his thoughts returning to her. Diane Lindsey had endured more that anyone should be forced to in any one lifetime, and didn't deserve any more tragedy in her life. Yet it just seemed to keep on coming.

At the hospital reception desk they informed him, no admittance was allowed and no information could be made public on Joan Phillips and wouldn't even tell him the room or floor. When he insisted on speaking to someone else, they calmly left him to cool his heels in the waiting room.

Impatiently he paced. "Why the hell did hospitals use such a disgusting shade of green anyway?" Mark wondered, having random unconnected thoughts out the frustration of simply waiting. "And why wasn't I there with them?" a thought even more to the point.

There were no answers to any of these rhetorical questions, but he knew that the people that were after her were not ever going to quit and go away, until they had terminated any witnesses. These were serious people and virtually unstoppable. It was time he prodded the police into doing something, and made them stop this cover up. That would mean it was time for the information that Mark was holding back to surface. The police would not be thrilled that he had unearthed confidential police records but it would force them to take some action.

The truth was Rand Lindsey had been a thug named Anton Savion up until seven years ago. Granted, Anton came from old money and had an Ivy-League education, but he was still a thug. He had run in some pretty elite company, some serious Mafia types, soldiers of fortune, and heads of drug cartels. Then when he was in too deep, he turned informer, to save himself a prison sentence and was placed in the witness protection program to turn state's evidence against a really serious Mafia Boss.

Diane had not met him until he was Rand Lindsey, charming and legitimate. Mark felt fairly certain that she didn't know anything about his checkered past. She just didn't seem like a woman who would build a life with an Anton Savion. In fact it was Mark's educated guess that Anton had chosen Diane as the perfect wife for a perfect cover, and perhaps Alexandra had been an extension of that too.

For a time Anton had been a consummate actor and convincing in his new role, acting the part of the responsible suburban business and family man. However reports from neighbors and acquaintances just preceding the accident showed chinks in his cover. His facade had been wearing thin and the real man was beginning to show through.

From the information he'd compiled on Anton, he had been a completely ruthless man and wouldn't have hesitated to manipulate others for his own devices. Mark felt Diane had just been a pawn in his deadly game and cover-up.

His dossier read like an overly dramatic crime novel; a basically amoral man, who thoroughly enjoyed using others and getting away with murder and mayhem, usually just for the thrill of it. He appeared to have been completely devoid of a conscience.

From what Mark had been able to uncover, as Rand he had not been able to keep his nose clean either. He had returned to some gun running in South America, and played a part in a few mercenary coups as well.

He had been one of those people that craved the danger and excitement of living on the edge. His finances were awesome, so he didn't do it for the money. To blow a perfect cover, after turning traitor on the cartel was simply idiotic, either he had a death wish or he'd thought he was invincible. He'd been a true excitement junkie. His personality profile pointed to a megalomaniac sized ego. Either one, it had cost him his life, as well as his child's and provided two years of hell for his wife.

Mark felt no pity for the loss of a man who could have put his wife and child in such danger. As far as Mark was concerned, Rand Lindsey a.k.a. Anton Savion had been a real bastard and had gotten exactly what he deserved. Death was actually too good for him, considering what Diane had been through, and the loss of beautiful little Alexandra. Mark had seen all the pictures, and Lexie as Diane had called her, had been the spitting image of her mother, from all accounts a sweet wonderful child, and too difficult a loss for her mother to face, hence the amnesia. Even withstanding all Diane's own struggles to recover. It was hard for Mark to muster much more that disgust for Rand Lindsey.

The problem with Rand having been in the witness protection program was that the police usually let transgressions slide. Because the person was virtually a ghost, without a past, minus any records, it was the government's job to protect them. Consequently if you were in the witness protection program you could get away with almost anything because you didn't technically exist.

Rand Lindsey had been quick to take advantage of that, but it had eventually gotten him killed. The man he had testified against, had been given life without parole. Nicholas Pappas had been one of the top three drug traffickers in the world, and he made a very nasty enemy. When Rand became active again it was only a short time until the Pappas' family caught up with him. Now they were after Diane, and it would be a mammoth job to keep them achieving that goal. These men were very accomplished at eliminating obstacles. So damned if Mark was going to allow the Denver police department to sit on their hands, until Diane was just another horrible statistic.

All this information had been left unreported and Mark had kept the lid on, feeling it would further endanger Diane if it got out. Now he just didn't know what was best for her. Maybe putting a spotlight on Pappas would send his goons into hibernation. Although somehow he doubted it, Nick Pappas would probably be more likely than ever to make sure, that his message got across, that he couldn't be crossed without evening the score. After all, he wouldn't ever be a free man again, but he had successfully managed to keep running his empire from the inside for years now. One little cog in his revenge cycle was all that remained for him to send a clear message to his enemies that crossing him was a death penalty. Leaving no witnesses was a given.

Pacing like a caged animal up and down the small waiting room and hall, Mark lost his patience. He returned to the counter and demanded to talk to someone who could tell him where to find

Joan Philip's room, because he knew that would be where he would find Diane. Even knowing her such a short time and only professionally, he knew without a doubt he would find her at her friend's bedside. Diane had lost so much already. It was inconceivable that she would lose her friend too.

Finally the receptionist talked to the police guard on the job, outside Joan's room who then asked Diane about Mark. He finally received admittance to the sealed end of the critical care unit where the women were being protected.

Mark felt somewhat reassured, that it had been so hard to get in, as he definitely wanted them to be safe and secure. As he headed down the final corridor he realized how much he was looking forward to seeing Diane.

As Mark came through the door Diane looked up from the chair beside the bed, and made a soft shushing sound and gesture, pointing to a sleeping Joan. Then she arose and came toward him signaling that they should step out in the hall to talk and not disturb the sleeping patient.

Diane looked completely exhausted but still unbelievably beautiful to Mark. Once again it crossed his mind that he was looking at her with his heart and not just the eyes of an objective newsman. With everything that had happened he had made a decision, it was time to tell her what he knew; at least then she could wrestle with a demon that had a name. He felt, that were he in her place, he wouldn't want to be in the dark about who was after him. Although the truth would probably upset her; finding out the kind of man she had married. It might also set her free of a spouse she couldn't even remember, but probably still felt some loyalty towards.

"How is she?" Mark asked with concern in his voice.

"She lost so much blood and needed a transfusion, she's really weak, but she'll make it. She's a fighter."

Diane offered up a weak smile, "Would you believe she is still cracking jokes about it? She's really been terrific. Even if she hadn't been my best friend before, I'd want her for one now. She's actually been cheering me up. Go figure."

The hospital corridor took on a conspiratorial air, as they whispered quietly back and forth.

"I feel so helpless and I hate it. I knew what to do when all I had to do was concentrate all my effort on recovery. I could tackle each day knowing with hard work, I had control of my own progress. I managed to wake up each day feeling hopeful. Unfortunately, this, I have no control over, and optimism doesn't appear to have any influence over the outcome. People that I care about, but can't protect, keep getting hurt. I hate feeling out of my depth and helpless to change things."

There was such deep sadness in Diane's voice, Mark hurt for her. On impulse Mark's arms surrounded Diane and she laid her head against his chest and felt his heartbeat against her cheek.

Several moments passed and Diane pulled away and raised her head, to gaze questioningly into his eyes. Neither of them spoke, neither of them needed to. This wasn't the time for them to deal with their still emerging and undefined feelings. Other things were far too pressing, life or death things; survival type things.

Mark saw how tired Diane was, and decided maybe it wasn't the best time and place to go into what his research had unearthed. The truth could wait a little longer. Maybe she needed to know, but right now he honestly didn't feel that she could handle much more. He determined to talk to Detective Matthews next instead.

From what Diane said about him; as she'd explained how Damon had gotten the private investigator Chase to be a double safety, Mark could believe he was a good cop with Diane's best interests at heart. So after their brief conference in the hall, Mark exacted a promise from Diane that she would eat and lie down. She looked ready to keel over. Then Mark left, to search for the detective, and fill him in on all he had unearthed. He had tried to talk to someone else on the force over a year ago, a Sergei something and been up against a brick wall. Now he had no intention of being stonewalled; not with Diane's and Joan's safety at stake.

CHAPTER 6

Damon had been butting his head against the proverbial wall all morning, computer files had been dumped, and paper files had disappeared. It was as if Rand Lindsey had never existed."What the hell was going on?" he pondered.

He finally pounded up the corridor to the commissioner's office, where he was informed by the commissioner's secretary. "Sorry he'll be in meetings all day, I'll have him call."

Damon had the distinct impression this was just a run around, but he determined he would find out what the hell was going on before the day was over regardless of stone-walling techniques. Diane's life was at stake and he would not be put off any longer.This last incident proved it was never a random shooting.

When he got back to his desk, he saw Mark Roberts waiting, albeit impatiently, pacing like a caged animal. Mark was a man who absolutely exuded raw energy. A lean man with intense ice blue eyes, he appeared to hypnotize with a glance. Yet he gave off an air of total self-confidence and detached strength of which it was obvious, he was completely unaware. He was a man women would be drawn to, and other men would automatically like and admire. His looks were unremarkable but his demeanor was commanding and dynamic. He was solidly contradictory, detached yet kind and caring too.

Damon reflected that Mark in his past interviews and articles, was one of the very few reporters he respected. He felt Mark used truth and integrity religiously. His reporting style was concise, fair, unbiased and honest, sometimes brutally honest when uncovering wrongdoing, but always totally compassionate of the victims of his stories. Damon felt that it was damn seldom reporters let the truth get in the way of a good story. Yet Mark's articles were always checked and double checked and completely accurate, and he had never sensationalized a story that might have put Diane at risk. So now, as Damon approached him, he did so with a genuine interest in hearing whatever he might have to say.

As Mark saw Damon returning, the two men extended their hands for a firm handshake, and greeted each other hurriedly but with a mutual respect. They had met multiple times briefly, always in a professional context, but felt they knew each other a little better now, since each had heard about the kindness of the other through Diane. They also felt some camaraderie at being on the same mission, the one to protect Diane and keep her safe. Perhaps there was a little competitive spirit as well, since both were beginning to look at Diane as a woman, and not just as a case or story.

Mark didn't waste any time. "Is there a private place we can talk?"

"Come with me." Damon also got to the point and turned and led Mark over and into the interrogation room.

"Okay what can I do for you?"

Without any preliminary small talk, Mark just launched into everything his research on Rand Lindsey a.k.a. Anton Savion had turned up. Damon listened without interruption until Mark finished and then asked several pertinent questions. When the conversation was through, both men fell silent for several moments.

It was Damon who finally broke the silence.

"Well this sure explains a hell of a lot."

"So, are you part of the cover-up, or are you going to help me protect Diane and be willing to go up against this conspiracy if you have to?" Mark got straight to the point.

Indignantly Damon replied, "I'd give up my badge before I let anything happen to an innocent woman. Now that I know who the enemy is, I'll pursue them to my last breath. Damn that 'creep of a husband', of hers, for putting her in this position anyway. If the son of a bitch wasn't dead already, I'd ring his neck for the position he put her in and what he's cost her."

Mark concealed a smile, it was fairly obvious to him that they could count on Damon, he was definitely willing to put Diane's welfare ahead of his job or the department.

As a side thought, Mark wondered if Damon wasn't just a tad over zealous to be totally professional? Of course that was a question he'd been asking himself often lately too. It crossed his mind that things would become even more complicated than they already were, before everything was said and done. Both men were about to choose Diane's safety over their jobs.

The two men conferred a while and then Mark left, to get back to the paper. They agreed to keep each other informed about any developments, but keep everything close to the vest for now, since they didn't know who could be trusted. Both of them felt Diane was pretty safe at the hospital, with both the police guard and Chase.

Damon now understood all the closed records and missing files, but not why someone in the department would accept a pay-off that allowed an innocent woman to be killed. Yet he also knew his ex-partner was a money-hungry bastard without the burden of scruples, so he was pretty sure where the leak was, especially since Mark had hit a brick-wall when he'd approached him.

For now, he would try to use that leak to his advantage, and use Chase as an 'ace in the hole' to keep the women safe. He had a really 'off-the-wall-shot-in-the-dark-idea' forming in his mind. He decided to go home and sleep on it. He was beat and needed a few hours of down time, if he was going to be any good to anyone.

After a few hours sleep and several cups of coffee Damon was ready to go back to work on this giant puzzle.

Damon had many things to check and recheck. But at least he knew where to look for the enemy and the answers. Nick Pappas was alive and vengeance was a rather strict code among his type, but maybe Damon could get to him and convince him, that Diane posed no threat to him. It was a long shot to consider trying to reason with a Mafia boss. But Damon knew that no matter how many hit-men he stopped or took off the streets, that Pappas would have an unending supply to keep sending out. And eventually the odds would be in favor of the bad guys, and Damon just couldn't let the odds take Diane out. Of course he'd be stepping into the line of fire with any confrontation too, so he had to weigh the advantages against the collateral damage and any good that it could possibly accomplish.

He knew that the department would only protect Diane for a while longer after this attempt and then she would just be a sitting duck again. And innocent people around her, like Joan, could be hurt or killed in the fallout. Then too, within the force, there were traitors who would hand her over for forty pieces of silver, "Damn Sergei anyway." So there were a lot of backs to watch, and consideration to give.

But desperate measure though it was, and probably one of the most unorthodox methods he'd ever conceived, he decided to find out what facility Pappas was being imprisoned in, and at least take a shot at reasoning with him. He realized he was getting way too close to this case to remain objective. And going to a penitentiary to talk sense into a cartel boss was an idiotic idea for a cop to even consider. But for Diane's life and safety, he would consider even the insane notion of talking with Pappas. After all Pappas had a wife and two children, and it was almost an unwritten code to leave women and children out of vendettas. If he could be convinced that Diane had no memory and no knowledge of her dead husband's business dealings regardless; if her memory returned, and thus posed no threat, maybe he would leave her alone. It was a ridiculous idea, but it was something. After all, the cartel boss had an ironclad alibi, prison. It's not as if he would admit anything to Damon, a detective. It was a ridiculous last-ditch effort, but it was worth a shot. Probably he would simply set himself up as an additional target.

Yet Damon headed to the computer inquiry desk, and put in a request for the files and final trial transcripts on the Nicolas Pappas' trial and his incarceration records. That was about all he could do at the precinct, then he headed back to the hospital to relieve Chase.

CHAPTER 7

Joan was sitting up in bead and feeling her oats. She was teasing Diane unmercifully.

"Well Miss Femme Fatale, give? Which one is your favorite, the handsome detective or the sexy newspaperman? If you can spare our earnest bodyguard outside the door, I'll take him."

Diane couldn't help giggling, Joan was so outrageous and so much fun, it was impossible to sustain a solemn mood, even given their circumstances.

"I'll just bet you will take Chase, and the sentiment appears to be mutual. I saw the goo-goo eyes you two were making." Diane smiled.

They maintained good spirits even if the hospital room was beginning to close in on both of them. The doctor was expected in anytime now. Both Diane and Joan were desperately hoping for a pardon, and to be able to check out of the hospital soon. Although where, they would go from here, they still didn't know. Despite Joan's urging Diane had refused to leave the hospital or even the room, since they had arrived. But then going back to her house certainly didn't seem like such a red-hot idea anyway. In truth this was the safest place for her.

They felt very safe and protected with both the police guard assigned and Chase guarding the guard. The whole thing seemed a little unreal and melodramatic. But considering Joan's condition, they both knew it was all too real.

"Listen Joan, perhaps it would be better for you to stay away from me for a while. It would certainly be better for your health. You don't need to be mixed up in all this, and as you pointed out, I'm surrounded by protectors, big strong sexy protectors." Diane tried an upbeat tone but it fell a little flat.

Joan's reply was a quick one, even a little snippy and didn't even miss a beat.

"No, you listen! You aren't going to cheat me out of the most adventure I've had in ages, or in being around a best friend who still remembers me as a teenager. Now just answer my question, which one do you like better, Mark or Damon? Please stick to the important stuff, would ya?"

Joan banished the serious note with her light banter. She always seemed able to lighten the mood and make Diane smile, or in this case crack up laughing.

"I'll plead the fifth, you nut. You'll never get it out of me." Diane and Joan dissolved into healthy giggles; they really did act more like teenagers than mature women who had just been shot at. The human spirit was a true survivor, and even in the midst of such a serious situation, Diane and Joan managed to keep a sense of humor.

About then Damon stuck his head in the door, amazed to find the two women dissolved in giggles.

"Okay, what's going on here?" He demanded in mock seriousness. "Have you two lost your minds?"

"Absolutely." they replied in unison, and then Damon found he was laughing too, it was contagious. They had all lost their minds, and it was a welcome break from the seriousness of the situation.

When everyone maintained a semblance of control, Damon toke a more official note and decided to brief both women as to what was planned to date, and where the department stood, and what they were willing to do, as far as guarding Diane and by extension Joan well. He began by telling them about his plan to talk with Nick Pappas, head to head, and only then seeing the shocked look on Diane's face did he realize what a blunder he had made.

He now realized that Mark might have told him everything, but hadn't told Diane anything yet. He had assumed that Mark had explained everything before coming to him. Now that thankless job fell on him. So as quickly and as succinctly as possible, Damon related to them everything that Mark had told him that morning and then his follow up from there.

All the sordid details about Rand definitely had a sobering effect on Diane. "Good heavens," she thought, "I married a mercenary and never had a clue", and then she suddenly remembered everything. It all came back in a torrential downpour of memories.

She suddenly remembered, she had begun to lose all faith in Rand, and was seriously considering leaving him just prior to the accident. She had not known all these details about him, but she had begun to catch him in too many lies, and had also begun to see a dark side to him. He had exhibited an occasional cruel streak that scared her where Alexandra, her 'little Lexie', had been concerned.

The thought of her daughter, brought about a flood of poignant memories, which came crashing down on her like a tidal wave. Tears flowed unrestricted down her cheeks in torrents. Pain threatened to engulf her. Both Damon and Joan could see from her apparent and immediate misery that her memory had returned like a slap in the face, making the accident and her death, two years ago painfully fresh at this moment.

Joan reached out in silence and just took her hand, silently communicating her compassion and that she was there. Damon put an arm around her and also found that there were no words, so the three shared her fresh grief in a shared silence, until there were tears in all their eyes.

Eventually the tears ran out, yet a deep hurt put Diane into a sort of delayed shock. Eventually Diane looked up and exhaustedly thanked them both for being there for her. Then Joan and Damon listened as she broken-heartedly spoke of her lost baby. She spoke eloquently and piteously about her beautiful only child, for hours she brought *Lexie* back to life in stories and verbal pictures; that were now painfully fresh, and throughout the recitation she cried; for the agony those memories rent on her heart. The other two could only listen as waves of memories threatened to destroy her, until Diane was silent once more. Then the quiet sat like a pall in the hospital room.

There was a cursory knock on the door, and Joan's examining physician came in and looked at her chart and then at her wounds, and told her she could go home in about five days, as long as she took it easy. Joan switched the solemn mood with a forced light response.

"You betcha Doc, I'll take it real easy." Joan assured him.

"I'll try not to get shot at anymore, till these are all healed, deal."

The doctor gave her a wry smile, not quite sure what to make of Joan.

"Just you rest young lady, that's an order."

After the doctor left, they all felt some of the emotional tension in the room dissipate and felt relieved that Joan was doing so well. Of course that started a whole new dialog on where the women would go in so few days.

It was a useful topic for switching the gears away from the pain that the interrupted conversation had brought on. It was an unspoken agreement to change that subject. Diane needed a break from old wounds made fresh by memories flooding back.

Thus they debated on a plan of action following Joan's release. They all had different ideas, but they also had some time to decide. So with no need for an immediate decision they tabled the discussion. It was all pretty stilted and forced anyway with all the fresh pain hanging like an apparition in the room. Diane was very quiet; and neither of the others pushed her.

It seemed like a good place for Damon to take his leave.

"Goodnight, you two. I'll be right outside if you need me. Sleep tight."

He left to return to his post, wandering the halls and safeguarding them through the night.

As soon as the door closed behind him, Joan winked at Diane. She was determined to change the mood and lighten Diane up.

"I'm telling you Di, he's attracted to you, and that's obvious."

Diane sensed her effort and tried to reciprocate, although slightly resenting not being allowed to wallow in her grief. She forced herself into a normal banter.

"Jo you are impossible, and you have a one track mind. But I think you may also be right. He does seem to be going above and beyond the call of duty for us. But how do you know it's not all because of you?"

"Don't try reverse psychology on me. So back to my earlier question; pick Mark or Damon? And don't look all innocent either, you know exactly what I mean."

Diane ignored the question and countered with one of her own, she was trying to lighten up, even while deep inside she was still devastated.

"What about you? I noticed you perk up every time one Chase Nealson stuck his head in the door today too, and I'd bet money that I saw sparks fly between you two."

"Well at least we know whom I'm interested in! You have a choice, the serious detective or the sexy newsman. I'm putting my money on Mark. I know your type. You couldn't go wrong with either Damon is great looking, but Mark exudes sexy, and his smile could melt icicles. And he's chattier then Damon too."

Joan laughed, but Diane saw that she was looking pretty worn out. They were both faking it, and it was exhausting work.

"Enough talk for tonight, you need some sleep and so do I. Quit teasing me for a while and let's both get some sleep. But I really want to thank you for everything. I couldn't have a better friend."

Diane kissed Joan goodnight on the cheek and turned out the light, then curled up on the cot next to Joan's bed.

"Good-night kid," a sleepy voice responded out of the darkness, "I love you, you know."

Diane actually fell asleep rather quickly after Joan spoke such a comforting sentiment. She would choose to think both optimistically, and to stay in the present. She reminded herself that getting her memory back had been the goal and that she had wanted it, so she couldn't think of it as any thing but a blessing. And things could certainly be much worse. After all she had a great friend who had just escaped death as she had herself and she now knew who the enemy was. She had the protection of both a police detective and an ex-Green Beret and she could walk, talk and thanks to Joan, even laugh. In a typical *Pollyanna* attitude, she decided she was really pretty lucky. Her memories didn't change the facts. Nothing was essentially different. She simply had to face remembering Lexie and trusting that she was now in a glorious heaven, happy and eternally well. Lexie would always live deep inside her and she would make a choice to see that memory as a gift and a comfort. Diane would never get over the loss of her baby daughter, but at least she could mourn her and remember all the sweetness they'd shared.

As Diane finally drifted off, her last thought made her smile.

"Damon or Mark, which is it going to be? Darn Joan for planting that question anyway, now she was pondering it herself. Interesting choice though, they were both terrific men and both concerned and able to help her."

Sometimes life left you with nothing but the beating of your own heart, but even then it could offer hope too. Sleep ended any more thought and she slept dreamlessly and deeply.

The sun poured in the hospital window. Diane awoke from her very hard and lumpy cot and stretched as her feet hit the floor and she stood up.

"Good morning Glory."

Joan greeted her looking as if she had been up for hours, although it was barely six a.m.

"Watch it, the last time we spoke those words, people were chasing us and trying to kill us right afterwards."

Diane laughed wryly.

"Okay, you are absolutely correct, let's not tempt the fates. It really doesn't feel real though, does it? I mean none of this should actually be happening to two such ordinary women. I feel as though we have been cast in a bad movie, and I wish the writing would get better."

Joan looked serious for just an instant and then fell back on her usual nutty sense of humor.

"On the other hand at least the cast includes some real hunks."

"Well at least I'm not wandering around in a fog anymore. I always thought amnesia was a crock, strictly used in fiction for high drama, so I'm certainly glad not to be such a cliché anymore and at least I know who the bad guy is, even if it's too crazy to believe. It's just illogical that they are still after me, now that Rand is dead. I'm no threat to them and I had nothing to do with the things that Rand did. I thought there was some sort of gangland code of honor about leaving women and children out of these revenge things. But then I'm getting all my pseudo knowledge from Godfather type flicks."

Diane said all this very tongue in cheek.

But Joan felt that she was probably whistling in the dark, trying to keep things from seeming as serious as they were.

"It does seem pretty nuts for them to come after you. Seriously, after all this time and with your amnesia, why for heaven sake, are they after you? It really doesn't make sense. Are you sure you don't know anything, some secret that could hurt someone? Or maybe they think you know something that could, but you don't and never did. Or they could think you were in on the double-cross with Rand, maybe they even think you were a mercenary too."

With that Joan stopped talking because Diane burst into uncontrollable laughter.

"Yea, that's me, hit-woman and international gun runner. You've go to be kidding, how could anyone think that? For heaven sake I was a mommy, involved in the Mommy and me swim group, a weekly bridge player in the neighborhood card club and I sing in the choir at church. How could anyone see me as a criminal or as any kind of a threat? I'm about as likely an enemy to the cartel, as you are!"

"Well as a matter of fact...."

Joan didn't need to finish, they were both laughing again. As serious as the situation was, it was also ludicrous and defied explanation. Maybe when Damon saw Nick Pappas, he would make some sense out of everything. Although it seemed like quite a stretch that Nick Pappas would give any information to Damon at all. Mob bosses weren't known for their cooperation with the authorities or for 'confessing it all' to cops.

CHAPTER 8

With Joan in the hospital, doing so much better, on this, her last evening of incarceration, Joan practically shoved Diane out her hospital room door. She knew she'd be safe out with Mark, and that the police guard would follow close behind them. They were both feeling claustrophobic in the little hospital room after six days there. They had talked through much of Diane's grief and it had been an intense time, now Joan was pushing Diane to lighten up and get out. The truth was Joan needed an emotional break herself from the closeness of the room, and the seriousness of having been shoot at, it had been a strain to always be peppy after all that had happened.

"Don't you two worry about me at all. I have Chase for company, and he can keep me entertained quite nicely."

She winked at Diane which made Chase look a tad uncomfortable.

Like everyone else he found Joan's sense of humor infectious, but he was unused to it being aimed directly at him, and he was also just a little bit in awe of this gutsy lady who took a bullet and yet never ceased cracking jokes. And although he wasn't ready to admit it, even to himself; he kept finding more and more excuses to visit her room and check up on her personally. He was very attracted to Joan, although he truly liked both women. They had strong characters, both of them and he really admired the strong friendship the two of them shared and how they both persevered no matter how tough things were.

Chase had to admit to himself just how evocative he found Joan. She wasn't the drop dead gorgeous that her friend Diane was, but she was bubbly and cute and more fun to be around than any woman he had ever met before. He looked forward to the evening of guarding her and getting to know her better too.

He verbally helped shove Diane and Mark out the door too with the encouragement to go grab a bite and leave things to him.

Although Chase felt a pang for his friend Damon, who he felt cared for Diane, he knew Mark was more than just professionally interested in her too. And he'd also seen the sparks fly from Diane's side of things, even if she wasn't aware of them herself. He had keen abilities when observing others and had seen the obvious attraction they each held for the other.

So at the insistent urging of her friend and Chase, and recognizing their interest in also being alone, Diane allowed Mark to convince her to go outside the hospital for a simple dinner. That, of course, being as simple as dinner with a bodyguard in tow could be.

They had dinner at a little bistro famous for it's ambiance and seafood chowder. They began the evening talking about recent events, but in tacit agreement slowly turned to the soft recitation of each other's lives, that usually happens on a first date. After half a bottle of excellent wine they were both completely relaxed and the conversation took on an intimacy of its own. Pretty soon they even forgot the guard sitting one table over and covertly watching the room, and their backs.

Mark told her of his recent heartbreak, and talked quietly about his retreat into being a workaholic since the death of his fiancée. Of course he knew her story, but now she talked softly about how she felt about everything going on, and she shared some happy memories of her daughter. They talked softly and shared their feelings quite easily. It seemed there was nothing they couldn't talk about.

They danced to soft, live music played by the restaurant's quartet. Diane's head fit comfortably into Mark's neck when they danced. He wasn't a very tall man, and it was nice to fit so well against someone. Rand had been very tall and rather stiff and had hated dancing as Diane recalled in passing. It felt truly sensual to feel so one with Mark's body on the dance floor. The entire evening was a welcome respite from all the recent stress and horror, and it felt so completely natural to be with Mark.

At 1 a.m. the band stopped and they looked around, realizing everyone else had left, except them and the bodyguard. So, they gathered their coats and headed out, regretful to end such a pleasant evening. Realizing how late it was, they were reluctant to go straight back to the hospital and disturb Joan's rest, and the truth be known they were also hesitant to end their own evening. It seemed they still had so much to talk about.

They went over and asked the police assigned bodyguard if he would follow them to Mark's house where they were going to go for a while and talk. The sergeant didn't look happy about it, but said, it was up to them.

"Diane wasn't his prisoner, it was just his job to keep anyone from killing her."

That comment went a long way toward sobering them up, but not enough to keep them from still wanting more time together. So ill-advised as it was, they headed for Mark's house.

The inevitable was quick approaching, despite possible danger, or perhaps even in part, because of it. Diane and Mark's attraction was now palpable. It had started out working towards the common goal; of clearing up, the mystery that was her life. But now it was so much more. It was a pressure cooker of all the ingredients of fear, drama, survival, good memories and bad, followed by a powerful evening of pure relaxation and this heady exploration of a new attraction, as a distraction from all that had gone before it.

The dramatic events that had preceded this intimate evening only served to intensify the pleasure at now being alone together and a powerful sexual energy took hold of them both.

Two people who had experienced so much loss and pain in their individual lives were now thrown together, under dangerous circumstances, with stress that was a living presence, and a feeling of their own mortality, with a joint concern over Joan. The evening of good food and wine had made their conversation more and more conspiratorial and also more and more intimate. In the back of Diane's mind she giddily realized that she and Joan had childishly talked of which man she liked better only a few days ago and she'd laughed at Joan then.

Now in the back of her mind she was asking herself the same question.

Earlier in the day, her answer might even have been different. Damon had been so good to her. She knew he'd even gone against his own department for her. He had called Chase in to keep her doubly safe. His every thought had been for her safety, with little regard for his own position. She thought the world of him and knew he had feelings for her too. But Mark, with his flashing eyes, sexy grin, and the honorable way he had handled, what could have been a big story for him, had also made an impression on her over this last week.

Two terrific men wanted her, and no matter what else was going on in her overly-dramatic, real-life soap-opera, she was enjoying all the attention. She wouldn't be human if she didn't. Her last two years had been unbelievably difficult.

Now she just wanted to be in this moment, thinking languid sensual thoughts and not thinking of anything serious at all. Just feeling wanted and caught up in 'just this moment' and feeling outstandingly, fabulously and gloriously alive was delicious.

These thoughts swirled lazily through her mind as they drove up the winding drive to his house, both of them ignoring the thought of the car that parked on the curb and the disapproving officer who observed them approach the house.

The evening had been perfect and romantic: good wine, food, candlelight and conversation. So, though it was probably very unwise, Diane knew even with her life still in danger, and her past and future, extremely uncertain, she wanted him. And in that instant she also knew, that on this night she would deny him nothing. This was a night to simply rejoice in being a whole woman again.

Mark walked her to the door, and without a word walked her inside, to escape the guards eyes upon them.

Had this been a normal first date he would need to say a hasty goodnight and get out quickly in order to remain a gentleman. He didn't want to cross a line that would make her life even harder and more complicated; and yet it was practically a physical pain, wanting her so much. In the last week he'd found her consuming his thoughts, his heart and his dreams. He could hardly think of anything else but Diane.

As they faced each other in the dimly lit foyer, no words came, but their faces spoke volumes as Mark's nearly crystal blue eyes met Diane's, which had small tears glistening in their corners, from the emotion she was feeling. She looked so unbelievably beautiful and incredibly vulnerable. Mark could barely catch his breath. He reached out to gently remove a strawberry and golden tendril of hair from in front of Diane's eye, the wind had blown it on their drive home, with the top down on his convertible. As he tucked the hair gently behind her ear, her hand came up to rest softly on his chest, where she could feel the rapid beat of his heart in her palm. Neither made a move to go further; they stood like that for what seemed an eternity, answering unasked questions with their eyes. Each saw the need in the other and in one natural motion, Mark swept Diane up into his arms. As if it were the most natural thing in the world he carried her up the stairs to the bedroom at the top, a room that would be the backdrop, for an incredible night of lovemaking. A night that had been inevitable from the first time he had met with her after she'd been released from the hospital, because her vulnerability accompanied by her sheer grace, had struck a chord in him that no one had in four long years.

In return, Diane had been drawn to Mark, because from the very beginning he had put her welfare ahead of everything else. He'd suppressed a great story to protect her even before they had known each other. Now being in his arms felt right and comfortable, and she knew that she wanted him on this night.

She didn't know if she was in love with him yet, since she also had very strong feelings for Damon; and even though his professional demeanor never allowed him to express any feelings for her, she knew that they were both feeling something, perhaps just friendship and respect, but something.

But as Mark slid the straps of her pearl gray silk dress off her shoulders and it slid sensuously to the floor, the time for thinking evaporated. It was replaced by pure animal passion, as the lace slip and stockings joined the dress, making a gray silk puddle on the floor around her feet.

Mark stood back, still fully dressed himself and very slowly admired her body, then reached behind her and undid her bra and slowly removed her panties until she was completely naked in front of him. Her nipples hardened, and he reached out to gently stroke them with just his index fingers in a circular motion that caused them to go so rigidly taught that it almost hurt.

She could see the lust and raw need in Mark, yet he was so exquisitely slow that she was beginning to fear that he might drive her completely crazy before he even got undressed himself.

Boldly she reached out and began unbuttoning him now, unzipping the trousers, through which she could already feel him, rise with wanting her. It seemed quite natural to her to undress him and stand completely naked before him, even though they were practically strangers a week ago.

Now they'd shared so much, and life felt so fragile and tenuous, that Diane didn't want to consider being practical at all. She just wanted to hang on to this feeling, the one of being exquisitely alive, as long as she could. There would be time enough for practicality in the morning, she'd think then, not now. Now was just for feeling, not for thinking.

She gasped as his lips touched her neck and slid down to the hollow between her breasts as his hands languidly stroked her thighs and gently found the warm wetness between. She let instinct take over and found herself running her tongue gently around his ear and then down his neck. She placed little butterfly kisses across his eyelids and then their mouths found each others in a kiss that set off internal fireworks of such magnitude that they were both stunned by the intensity of their desire.

Diane felt very bold and wanton as her lips traveled down the length of his body and took him into her mouth. Oh, but the salty taste of him was heady. He moaned very softly, and she felt powerful, knowing the ability she had to give him pleasure. After an indeterminate time, for time had lost all meaning, his mouth found her as well, and she shuddered, as waves of pleasure totally consumed her, in a heat that radiated from her very core. It felt incredibly decadent and decidedly delicious to just give into the lust and pleasure that was their inner heat, finding every way possible to give pleasure and consume each other.

As the sun came through the lace curtains, Mark and Diane were still gently stroking each other and muttering the things that lovers do after an incredible night of passion and lovemaking, like a favorite song they had played again and again that night, trying to memorize each other's bodies and rhythms and never tiring of the mysteries of that discovery process.

"My darling it is 5 a.m. We should get up and get presentable and get back to the hospital."

Mark spoke quietly while making lazy circles with his finger around Diane's bellybutton.

"Joan will be waking up soon and today is check-out day, so there are arrangements to be made. Coming back here was pretty foolish. We could have put you in real danger. I wasn't thinking straight last night. I fear that I wanted you so much that I risked your life."

Mark stood and looked out the window happy to see the guard still in his car out front.

"After all we don't really know if we can even trust the standard issue, police bodyguard considering the last night you spent in your house and what happened to you and Joan then."

Diane stretched, and sat up reluctantly, hating to come back to reality.

"Okay, just let me hop through a quick shower. Want to joint me?"

She flirted and teased him just a little. She didn't want the evening to end yet.

Mark grinned, he didn't either. They could stall the return to reality just a little while longer; he wasn't about to turn down a shower with a beautiful, very wanton woman. It was, after all, only five a.m. They'd still make it back to the hospital by seven. Meanwhile that shower, especially with Diane in it, sounded pretty darn irresistible.

Diane and Mark headed back to the hospital, with the police shadow right behind them. It felt pretty strange to be followed by a total stranger that knew they'd spent the night together. They found that in the light of day, being followed by the police guard, and returning to a Joan that would look knowingly at their being out all night, served to make them feel pretty transparent.

Diane was quiet on the ride, the night had been wonderful but she felt a little awkward now, a little like an errant teenager and very vulnerable. She knew Joan well enough to know that nothing would get by her. Joan would pick up on exactly what had taken place almost immediately. An even more uncomfortable thought came to mind, as she wondered if Damon would be at the hospital when they got there. She wouldn't want to hurt his feelings or be insensitive and her own privacy issues were at stake too. Diane felt like a kid who had to go home to parents that might be waiting up for them. It was 6:30 a.m. as they entered the room quietly.

Sure enough, they were in hospital room for only a few minutes before Joan was looking probingly at Diane and Mark, arching one eyebrow knowingly. Chase was still at her side and Diane gave her friend an equally questioning look.

Diane was thankful that for once Joan kept her mouth shut. Because exactly five minutes behind them, Damon also showed up, ready to plan Joan's discharge. Luckily, he didn't seem to sense anything unusual, and everyone's comfort level returned to a precarious equilibrium.

Damon explained to them all that he had arranged a safe house for the women, because he didn't feel that they were safe at either of their own homes.

The police were still unreliable, because of what had happened before, and could happen again. So he wanted to discuss with them, having just he and Chase as their bodyguards, with just disappearing completely from sight, being their best defense. He wanted to keep their whereabouts totally unknown to anyone else, even the police. But he needed to know; if they would put all their trust in him and go along with this plan.

It was a sobering thought that they would be totally cut off and should trust no one. But the plan made sense to everyone.

Mark then volunteered to also take a shift as bodyguard. He had been in the Air Force Special Services and was no stranger to weaponry, and he argued that three eight-hour shifts, divided between the three men, would be much easier on everyone than two twelve-hour shifts, with Damon still on the force. Which for now, they all decided was the best place for him to stay, even given his willingness to resign, since that way he would always know any developments in the case.

He made it clear though where his allegiance was. Damon's intent was to make it look, as if he too, had lost Diane and Joan, and that they had given him the slip and gone into hiding, all totally on their own.

Of course the police department would be glad to let it go, relieved of the expense of twenty-four hour surveillance. For a short time they would pretend that the women were at Joan's home, and keep the police guards outside of her home there.

It would work as a double blind, while they were really safe elsewhere. Joan's place would also be a barometer of activity surrounding their actual safety.

Damon knew Pappas wouldn't give up, but with so few people involved, and those few totally trustworthy, and with Joan's house as a clay pigeon, there would be no leaks and they would be invisible. Naturally Diane and Joan weren't thrilled with being virtual prisoners in order to remain unharmed, but the plan made sense for now and everyone was in agreement.

With the hospital checkout all arranged within the next few hours and after a final check-up by the doctor who wrote her discharge, a nurse arrived, pushing the obligatory wheelchair that all hospitals always insist evacuee's leave in. And with a minimum of fan-fair they got Joan all loaded up, and the five of them and the nurse pushing the chair went down a back corridor and out a service elevator. Damon had just rented a car from Hertz that was untraceable and had tinted windows. The standard full-size run-of-the-mill rental car was one nobody would give a second thought to. It was parked in the alley at the hospital's kitchen entrance. He would take Joan and Diane with him.

Chase was to follow way back and watch for any possible tails. The police department guard had been told to go home and get some sleep, Damon would take over.

The current plan now was that, Damon would supervise guards at Joan's home for about a week, and then would check the house one day, and discover that Diane and Joan must have slipped out the back door while the guards were guarding the front of the house.

The police would probably drop it, relieved, figuring they were grown women and had a right to go wherever they wanted. There was always more caseload than manpower. So the police would move on quickly. Anyway that was the current plan. Now he just had to get them unnoticed to the safe home he'd arranged, keeping them out of harm's way was the only thing that was really important. All three men were united in that goal.

Joan put her head back against the seat on the drive from the hospital to the house. It frustrated her to no end, just how easily she wore out. But then she and Chase had talked quietly into the night until almost 2 a.m.; pretty late for the 'walking wounded'. Yet the mere thought of their conversation, caused a gentle smile to turn up the corners of her mouth. That infused her with the energy to now quiz Damon on the drive.

"Damon, tell me about Chase, how long have you two known each other? And how did you two meet? Spill it Bud, I want the straight skinny. And I want it yesterday!"

Damon smiled and told Joan all he could about Chase on the winding mountain drive to the house he'd arranged, that seemed to be taking them down every small dirt road in foothills of the State of Colorado, well out of Denver now. Diane relaxed considerably, grateful that Joan was carrying the conversational ball, and keeping Damon talking.

Damon shared with Joan all the facts about Chase that he felt Chase wouldn't object to, but tried not to give out too much information of a personal nature. Chase was like he was in so many ways, they were both pretty closed off and private, with work that absorbed most of their waking hours. Neither man had ever been married, because their professions were too hard on wives. They had talked about all the police and detectives that had failed marriages, and why?

Now as he listened to Joan bubble out question after question about his friend, he smiled wondering if Chase was about to change his loner status. This would be a pretty irresistible woman if she set her sights on even the staunchest bachelor. Damon had certainly noticed their mutual interest the last few days. He had been fighting a battle of his own, not to be too drawn toward Diane. She touched so many chords in him, and made him realize just how empty his life really was. But he knew that to keep her alive, he had to keep it professional. It was too text book dangerous, for the detective to fall in love with the victim, and he had determined that wouldn't happen. The last few days he had distanced himself from her, and he knew she had gotten the message too. The police guard had told him where he had guarded her last night, and who was with her.

He couldn't say it didn't cause a little sadness, but he knew it was also for the best. Early in his career he had suffered a broken heart he almost didn't survive, he didn't need another one. The truth was he'd never gotten over her. She had been the love of his life.

His reverie was interrupted by another question from Joan.

"So, you've recited some statistics, but how about some good stuff. Any women in his life I should know about, like ex-wives, a 'witch of a mother', a girlfriend, even a casual one? I don't care much about his military training, more his availability status."

Damon rolled his eyes, and laughed.

"Those questions you'll have to ask him directly. I'm just a tight-lipped cop. I couldn't begin to talk about any of that personal stuff, I'd turn to stone."

He answered, only half -kidding.

Diane decided to jump in and save him.

"How long, until we arrive, at wherever it is, we are going? Tell us about the house where we'll be staying. It seems like we've driven more than was necessary to get here. I'm sure we've made some pretty big circles. Was that to make sure we weren't followed?"

"Bingo; and we haven't been, so all is well. And actually, we are almost there. It's the home of an artist friend of mine, who is studying in Europe. I have the key to keep an eye on things and get out of the city occasionally.

The original structure of the house was built about eighty years ago out of imported river rock granite. It's sort of an eccentric castle-like structure, but it is very charming too. I think the original builder was an Englishman, and he recreated his ancestral castle. My friend's grandparents built on a huge atrium that floods it with natural light, so it's a terrific home for an artist. It has sixty acres, and a long private drive with a locking gate, which makes it a perfect safe house for you two. We are actually, not very far out of the city, however at 8,100 feet, and in the mountains, so it's never too hot in the summer, but the roads can be treacherous in the winter. I trust that will mostly work to our advantage. It's in a very small community of 'privacy nuts', people who moved to Colorado; as a 'get-a-way; so no one bothers, or pays any attention, to anyone else. The house is mostly surrounded, by very substantial horse properties and you can't even see your nearest neighbors. All of those things should make it perfect, and there is nothing to connect either of you to it. No one else, but my friend in Europe, even knows I have the use of this place. I've never mentioned it to anyone. I never really thought I'd be using it to keep two such lovely women safe from the Mafia, although it should, certainly serve the purpose well."

About then he pulled to a stop, and stepped out of the car, fortunately wearing his Sorrels, since there was about a foot of fresh powder on the ground, and the snow was still falling. He walked to the gate and inserted a key in the big padlock and swung the gate open, got back in the car and drove through. The other two cars followed and then he re-locked the gate. They followed him up the long winding drive, recognizable only because of the beautiful blue spruce, lining both sides of the road.

The snow was really piled high back in the trees, and made it nearly impossible to see the drive at all. Finally, they came through the trees and glimpsed the house. It was spectacular. Castle-like on the sides and back, and turrets could even be seen on the roof, but the front was this amazing all glass structure, through which a practical jungle of greenery could be seen, a tropics inside, with the snow coming down outside, it appeared somewhat surreal. For once even Joan was speechless.

Diane uttered a hushed, "Wow."

Joan turned around in her seat and looked deeply at Diane.

"Can you believe this?"

Amidst all the bullets flying and mayhem, life was still looking pretty intriguing as far as she was concerned. Looking searchingly at Diane for a split second, she knew that they were having exactly the same thoughts. It was uncanny what good friends they still were. Despite time lapse or amnesia or anything else, they were still as close as the two fifteen year olds that had spent nights in each other's houses, talking about and sharing everything.

Now that they had arrived at the safe house, everyone visibly relaxed. Getting out of all the cars respectively, Chase and Mark hurried over to the Hertz rental and everyone solicitously helped Joan up the slippery front steps.

Damon took Diane's arm and went ahead to open the huge double doors, with what looked like an ancient skeleton key. His considerate nature showed further as they entered a foyer and great room with a raging fire already burning in the fireplace, proof that Damon had preceded their arrival prior to coming to the hospital, simply to make their arrival more comfortable.

Diane gave him an appreciative glance, and thanked him with her eyes. He really was an unbelievably terrific man, who always seemed to be going above and beyond for them.

Then she glanced over at Mark, and her heart caught in mid-beat. Her cup indeed ran over, a great friend and a new lover, both protecting she and Joan.

Joan was watching her, and practically read her mind. Now Joan almost couldn't wait to shove Mark, Chase and Damon out the door and catch up on last evening. It was extremely obvious to her, that there was much to tell, on Diane's end, and she also wanted to tell her all about Chase. So, after they were warmly ensconced on the big divan in front of the fire, luxuriously covered in lap robes, the men left to walk outside, and talk and plan, and unload supplies out of the rental car trunk. Damon had picked up tons of food and miscellaneous comforts. It seemed he'd thought of absolutely everything.

The men left only after being assured they were fine alone inside.

"Of course we are. Go on," they spoke almost in unison.

Damon intended to stay and take the first watch, but needed to be back to Joan's house in time to be replaced at 11 p.m., by the police surveillance guard to uphold the charade that the women were at Joan's. Chase had been up all night and would head home now and get a little sleep. Mark volunteered to take the next eight hour shift after Damon left, and Chase would be back after that. It was a schedule they could all manage. Although if truth was known; not one of them actually wanted to leave at all. They were personally involved in one way or another by the eventual outcome, whether by honor or growing feelings. There had never been such an enthusiastic group of unpaid bodyguards. Both women deserved to be safe and these three men had determined to take that responsibility very seriously.

Damon walked back in the house with the groceries, after watching the other two men leave. He had given each of them a gate and house key so he didn't need to follow them back to the gate and lock up. Of course their safety here wasn't dependent upon being locked in, but rather in the secrecy of their whereabouts. Nothing could truly stop the mob if it became known where they were hidden.

Chase would be driving Damon's car back to Denver and leaving it parked in front of Joan's house as a decoy and Mark would drop him back at his own car in the hospital parking lot.

Damon would do his level best to keep everyone believing the women were elsewhere. He headed inside intending to make Diane and Joan feel as comfortable as possible, for as long as it was necessary. Everything was arranged to create the illusion that they were being taken to Joan's, and he knew with certainty that they had not been followed, not this time. And everyone knew the precautions to take every time, plus Chase and Mark were not connected as far as anyone else knew.

Diane and Joan were catching up on the previous night, neither holding back anything, curled up on the comfy sofa, in front of a roaring fire. Joan was tired but had taken half a pain pill, so she was not in pain.

Naturally, within hospital confines, and with nurses coming and going, Joan's evening hadn't been nearly as romantic as Diane's, but she had very high hopes for where it was heading. It was obvious she was crazy about Chase.

"Who would ever believe amidst bullets flying, we'd both find love?"

A melodramatic, *Camille*-like, Joan exclaimed, back of her hand flung to her forehead.

Diane had to laugh.

"Don't get carried away, It may just be shell-shock,a war-zone romance,and wind up amounting to nothing. Everything is too crazy right now to think straight."

Damon came back in the room about then and they both looked up guiltily like two kids caught talking in class.

"So you pulled first guard duty, huh? This place is gorgeous, how about a grand tour?"

Joan rebounded.

"Damon, it really is terrific of you, to take such good care of us. This place is wonderful."

Diane spoke gratefully.

"Sure if you're up to it, I'll show you around and where your rooms are, it really is a great place. I bought a few things you might need, and put them on your beds, later you can give me a list of whatever you need or want from your own places, but I think I picked up enough to get you each through the next several days. Joan, take my arm and we'll begin your tour, but be sure and tell me if you get tired or need to rest."

"Boy I'm going to get spoiled with all this solicitous treatment. Lead on, sir."

Damon led them from the family room into the atrium, brim full of exotic plants. It was a magic room with the snow visible all around them, yet hot house warm and humid on the inside. All varieties of incredible green flowering plants and even full size trees thrived in and amidst the winter wonderland surrounding them on three sides.

"There is a central sprinkling system in here and a thermostat that keeps it tropical in here all the time." Damon explained to them.

Next, he took them through an equally sunny (or rather today) snowy, eat-in kitchen, with windows everywhere and hand hewn rustic cabinets.

There was a massive antique mahogany bakers rack and workstation in the middle, and a huge brass and copper rack above, holding every conceivable kitchen pan and gadget, new and antique all thrown together, a wonderful eclectic assortment. There were even dried herbs and flowers all mixed up in the charming clutter. It was one of the warmest-coziest kitchens Diane had ever seen, she definitely liked it better than the one she had in her house. It made her anxious to cook up a storm in this wonderful place. She suddenly remembered that she really loved to cook and bake, and shared that thought.

"You are both in for a treat tonight, just let me in here, with whatever is in those grocery bags."

The tour continued to the formal dining room, sort of *Vincent Price Gothic*; heavy slab table, with benches, and even two suits of armor. It was a little too primitive to be taken seriously, and so far the only room that didn't feel cozy, just dramatic. The chandelier was actually candles. It fit the castle atmosphere, but somehow seemed more amusing than intimidating.

They moved on back to the great room and entry, and then around, but not up the stairs. It was obvious that Joan was fading.

"Next stop, your bedroom Joan, it's time for this patient to return to bed-rest."

Damon stated with authority.

For once there was no argument, or even a response from Joan, indicating his instincts were correct.

Damon led them into the only bedroom at the bottom of the stairs.

"Here you are Madame. Can I have the butler, run your bath?"

Joan had to laugh; it wasn't often that Damon kidded around.

"No, that will be all sir, the room is beautiful." It truly was. A huge canopy bed was the focus of the high-ceilinged spacious room. The furniture was all deep-red cherry, rich with hundreds of years of care. The canopy and bed were covered in yards and yards of Chantilly lace in rich ivory. There was a gorgeous little sitting area all done in royal blue

Queen Anne, a small settee and two delicate little chairs. Joan sank down gratefully on the bed. "I hate it that I wear out so easy."

"It's to be expected. Stretch out and take a little nap. I'll come in and check on you in a little while."

Diane lovingly tucked a throw from the end of the bed around her friend and kissed her lightly on the forehead. Joan's eyes were already closed, the Darvocette had done her in.

"Now you can show me to my quarters, too, please."

She teased Damon enjoying discovering this amazing house, but pretty tired herself after her amazing sleepless night.

They walked up the stairs, then and further down a gallery type hall they entered a second terrific suite.

This one was clouds and clouds of pale blue and peach, all either satin or antique lace. It was the most feminine room Diane had ever seen. The bed was also a canopy but, so delicate as to look like it might have been meant for a fairy princess. The room possessed an aura of such daintiness; every detail was exquisite, as if it had been decorated for a much-loved daughter.

"Unbelievable, Damon I feel like I've walked into a fairytale."

Diane exclaimed. Icing on the cake, there was even a fireplace in the room, and thanks to Damon's preparedness, it was even already ablaze. Diane was touched, a quick glance around the room also showed caring, in several fresh flower arrangements placed around the room.

Diane walked over to one of them, and gently stroked a petal.

"Gardenias in Colorado in January; you are truly amazing."

She spoke very softly.

An embarrassed Damon, flushed slightly and charmingly, hung his dark head.

"Amidst all these troubles, I wanted you to at least be comfortable."

Blue eyes looked deeply into hers for just a second.

"Make yourself at home. I'm going to walk the grounds and check on everything."

With that he ducked his head and was gone, fleeing from the room, embarrassed by her compliment.

CHAPTER 9

Diane went into the bath adjoining her suite, it was splendid. A mammoth antique claw foot bathtub, that had been adapted as a whirlpool tub, sat on a Persian carpet.There were double sinks that appeared to be floating in the air, with no bases of any kind; they were of striking cobalt glass of some kind. A bidet, as well as a toilet, again in cobalt blue offered a mixture of antique and ultra-modern that looked like an Architectural Digest set, it was very striking.

"Wow", she thought, "exile is certainly romantic here."

Still the thought of not going out at all, Joan's present condition, and that they were still in danger, remained a dark cloud.

"Even in a fairytale setting, hiding out was still hiding out!"

Was her summarizing thought.

Suddenly she felt pretty tired her self; after all she had gotten very little sleep last night, maybe she could use a little rest too. So she went in and lay down, and before she knew it, she was out like a light.

Diane's eyes sprang open, as Joan settled herself down next to her on the bed.

"Hey, sleepy-head, we've slept most of the afternoon away. If we don't want to get our days and nights mixed up, we'd better get up."

Diane blinked, and sat up looking at her watch.

"Good grief, it's almost 7 p.m., you're darn straight we should be up. I'm going to go start a decent dinner, no hospital food for you tonight."

They both headed downstairs and found Mark in the living room,

"I came back early."

He informed them when he saw the confusion on their faces.

"I figured then Damon could head to Joan's house and make the cover look better by being there sooner and until his relief came. And I don't have anything going at the newspaper, so I won't be missed, and I preferred to be here rather then just worrying about you two from my place. So let me know if there's anything you need, this guard is at your service."

He bowed deeply and his eyes twinkled as he took in a sleep tousled Diane, and gave her a wink.

Diane still felt a little self-conscious being back around Mark in Joan's presence, with Joan having pried nearly every detail out of her. So she decided keeping busy would be her best defense against awkwardness.

"I'm off to the kitchen to rustle us all up some dinner, I haven't looked to see what there is to work with yet, but I'm willing to bet I can come up with something edible. Are you two hungry, because I'm actually starving."

And with that she exited to the kitchen, leaving Mark smiling at her awkwardness..

Joan followed her into the snow-surrounded kitchen and plopped onto one of the comfortable padded leather chairs pulled up to the work station.

"Need any help, or do you remember I'm hopeless in the kitchen?"

"Just keep me company; that would be great. Boy it's awkward, the day after, the night before! I'm still a little amazed at myself, and a bit afraid of what he must think of me."

Diane sighed.

"It would be for you kiddo, you've never moved so fast, you've always been so slow and cautious, but I think you have to trust your instincts here, he's really a good guy, and I can tell he's crazy about you."

"Damon is a good guy too."

Diane said quietly.

"And right now I have no right getting involved with anyone. I feel as if I am in a world spinning completely out of control. Aren't I supposed to know for sure if I'm in love, before I go to bed with someone? "

"It doesn't always work like that Di, sometimes sexy counts, and sometimes nice isn't enough. We don't always fall for who we think we should, but just who we do. You can't be sorry about Mark, he's really terrific too, and your chemistry is tangible. So, don't fight it, explore it. To help you do that, I'm going up and take a nice hot bath, and rinse all the hospital off me, and while I luxuriate, I'm going to send Mark in to keep you company while you slave over a hot stove. Don't argue with me either. I'll be back down in two hours, so cook very slowly."

With that Joan flounced dramatically out of the room, leaving a bemused Diane giggling.

"It was impossible to be too serious with Joan around." She thought.

True to her word, Joan sent Mark in to join her, and from then on they never had a difficult moment. They immediately fell into comfortable chit-chat, while she bustled around throwing dinner together. When she'd pass close by, it seemed the most natural thing in the world for him to reach out and take her in his arms, and culinary skills were forgotten in the interim.

Yet somehow when Joan rejoined them in two hours, Diane had managed to produce quite the feast, passion aside. There was a fresh Caesar salad, mushrooms stuffed with crab and brie, a glorious Chateaubriand in a flaky pastry crust, steamed sweet-pea pods, and even a meringue shell filled with fresh strawberries, wreathed with homemade whipped cream.

They all ate gluttonously in the cozy kitchen, deciding against moving into the medieval dining room. The conversation flowed smoothly, and everyone toasted the cook and the larder for being so luxuriously stocked.That made Diane once again aware of how considerate Damon was.They finished eating and Mark insisted the cook shouldn't do the dishes, so he sent the two women into the great room while he took over the clean-up duties.They went without much argument and left him to the task at hand.

"Truly great dinner, Di, you can work magic in the kitchen. He's really a sweetheart you know."

Joan switched gears.

"Yes, I agree, but is this really the time to get involved?"

"Things have a way of picking their own time, it's not always negotiable. After everything you've been through, maybe it's about time for some good stuff. I know you've always been cautious, but look where that got you, married to the worst guy of all time. Sorry, I don't mean to rub it in, but he was one big bad deal. Now along comes the sexy reporter, a man of real integrity from what I can tell and you drag your feet.Well stop it Di. Life is really too short. We've recently had a lot of proof."

"I know you're right. I will quit dragging my feet as you put it. I would just feel better if I was sure it was love, not just lust, perpetuated by living in constant danger."

"Only time will tell, friend. I don't know exactly what I'm feeling for Chase either, but I sure want to see where it leads. He's a doll, a quiet one, but a doll. I will draw him out, even if it kills him! Then I have every intention of catching up to your exploits of last night."

Joan teased a now blushing Diane.

About that time the cuckoo clock in the hall chimed ten, and there was a simultaneous knock on the door. Mark came running out of the kitchen, a pistol drawn.

"You two go upstairs. Now! We aren't expecting company."

Mark ran to look out the atrium, to see the front porch clearly, and breathed a sigh of relief.

He hollered up to the women halfway up the stairs.

"Don't panic, its just Chase, a day early. I guess he couldn't wait to see someone."

He opened up the door and let Chase in.

Chase peeled several layers of clothes and shook the snow out of his hair.

"The storm is getting worse by the moment, I was afraid if I didn't come up early, you might not get out of here at all tomorrow. After all, you punch a time clock and still need to work, so I figured I'd let you get going, before you're snowed in. I got plenty of rest and had nothing else I needed to do. So feel free to shove off."

Diane and Joan joined them in the entryway, and Mark looked at Diane with disappointment in his eyes at being shoved out the door, but what

Chase said made sense and he didn't want to embarrass Diane by saying he simply didn't want to leave her yet. Fortunately, a more perceptive Joan realized they could use a private moment and suggested Chase come with her to the kitchen and she'd fix him a plate."

"You wouldn't believe the dinner Diane made. So come and feast my friend, it beats any sorry sandwich you may have made yourself."

Joan made it obvious there was no room for disagreement, half dragging Chase with her. He didn't seem to mind her holding his hand.

They left Diane and Mark alone to say a passionate good-night, although neither of them wanted him to go anywhere, except upstairs for a repeat of the last evening. But they erred on the side of reason and said a long delicious goodnight. Then Diane locked the door behind him and went to join Joan and Chase in the kitchen.

As she entered she saw that they were talking animatedly while Joan served him his plate and poured him some ice tea.

Diane could feel the closeness in the air.

"I'm worn out you two, so even though I know I'll be breaking your heart by leaving you two alone, I'm going upstairs and read for a while. I just wanted to say goodnight, so, good-night."

With that she winked at Joan and was back out the door, and gone before they could insist she stay.

Chase looked at Joan, intently.

"I guess it's no secret that I find you pretty special. I honestly couldn't wait to get back here."

He spoke holding nothing back, when normally he tended to be pretty reserved.

Joan kept her response simple.

"Ditto!"

Joan replied as she stepped in close and put her arms around his neck and kissed him very lightly. Despite the pain in her shoulder from lifting her arm so high, she stayed like that for a long time, until he reciprocated and they were both left breathless.

Dinner was suddenly completely forgotten, and they moved into the great room and Chase put more logs on the fire and they cuddled up on the couch.

"This is not my usual on-the-job demeanor. You've blown my professionalism all to hell."

"Shut up and kiss me again. Believe me it makes me feel very safe and protected. So you are doing your job."

Morning found Chase still holding a sleeping Joan against him on the couch. They had kissed and talked long into the night again. They shared pasts and touched and held each other. He admitted he had always thought something was missing in his life, having never been truly in love before. Now he admitted, that was exactly what he was feeling for her, and that she was the woman he'd always wanted, but didn't think existed.

Then she admitted to him, that after her husband died, she had never expected to find love again, but now she had. Neither played coy or held anything back. However due to Joan's still sore wounds, he had refused to rush things; hence they just enjoyed kissing and sharing.

At 8 a.m. Damon returned to take over, and found Joan and Chase in the kitchen having coffee. Chase got up, and poured him a cup of black coffee with one sugar; he knew how Damon took his coffee. They'd been friends a long time. Joan gave him a big smile, as she swung off her stool.

"I'm going up and grab a morning shower and get human, I'll be back down in about half an hour, will you still be here?"

She asked looking straight at Chase.

"Yea, I'll be here. I'll just finish my coffee and keep Damon company."

Damon was too good a detective not to read between the lines, and the looks, and he was happy for his friend and a little sorry for himself.

"Was it a quiet night?"

He inquired as Joan left the room.

"Very, what did the department have to say, when you claimed they gave you the slip?"

"I haven't told them yet. Right now the department is convinced that they are in Joan's house, with all the blinds drawn, and not planning to go out at all, for the next several days, while Joan recuperates. There is a twenty-four hour guard out front. That keeps everyone from looking for them for a while, and allows us to see what the bad guys will do next."

Damon stated, looking pretty happy with this plan.

"Plus I have repairmen, per orders from Diane, through me, fixing all the damage at her house from the last shoot out, as if she will be returning there in a few days. Of course, I figured that regardless, all that must be fixed up anyway, for whenever she can finally go home. Bullet holes make a bad fashion statement, in such a gorgeous home."

Chase burst out laughing, that was such an unaccustomed comment coming from Damon.

"I can see you haven't missed a beat. You are the best, and you are thinking ahead, and keeping these ladies safe. For that, I personally thank you too. I guess I'm not very subtle about how I feel about Joan. So, I can't thank you enough for calling me in to help on this case. Thanks to you, I have met a very special woman. I'm in love with her, Damon. I can't explain it myself, but I know it's the real thing. I now have a very personal interest in watching over them."

He stated with a candor that amazed Damon. Damon had known him for years and never heard him speak of any woman, as more than a casual date.

The unexpected truth blurted out, seemed to ask for an honest response, so Damon gave him one.

"You're a lucky man. She's quite a lady; spunky, funny, and easy to look at too, I wish you nothing but happiness. I'm a little jealous myself. I have been admiring Diane for the last two years, but kept it so professional that now I've blown it. I know about Mark, and it's probably all for the best, but still I envy you your romance."

Chase wasn't surprised by the admission, but by the fact that Damon had made it. Having no words of wisdom, he just reached out and squeezed his friend's shoulder, choosing to retreat into a comfortable silence.

At that moment Joan burst back into the room. She never just walked, she burst, she bubbled, she flounced, and in tow was a much more sedate Diane, looking rested and very young and innocent. Her face was freshly scrubbed and her hair pulled back in a haphazard ponytail almost on top of her head. It gave her the appearance of a high school cheerleader. She was wearing loose blue sweats she'd found in a bag in her room, and Damon thought she was unbelievably appealing. He turned his back and poured himself another cup of coffee, and some composure.

"Good morning. Boy, did I sleep well, and late. Can I fix any or all of you some breakfast?"

Diane entered the kitchen already feeling comfortable there after making dinner the night before. A kitchen always made her feel at home.

"As you well know, I'm completely out of my element with anything more then heating up 'left-overs'. So all I did was watch while Chase made the coffee, and I'd just love something to soak it up with. I bet Chase could eat too."

Joan piped up and then swept Chase along by the arm as she left the kitchen to wait to be called for breakfast. He was willingly swept; happy to have her alone again.

That left only Damon for an audience. Diane looked at him and waited for a response.

"That would be great, I'd love anything you want to make. I didn't have time for much this morning; I went into the precinct at five, to check on some things while it was quiet there. Then I went by Joan's and checked on the surveillance at her house."

He filled her in on the fact that everyone believed she was staying with Joan, for the time being, and that the plan was working well.

"I do believe you think of everything, how can I ever tell you how much I appreciate you?"

Diane spoke in all sincerity and with a catch in her throat. She felt there was so much more, they never said, than what they actually did.

She busied herself cooking up a storm, which made her feel less haunted by the things they couldn't say. As she sliced up granny-smith apples for fried apples, seasoned pork-chops and prepared quiche, she wondered if she was crazy, attracted to two men, and wondered what to do about it.

Joan kissed Chase good-bye at the door, and teased him, "I'll sure miss you today. Midnight seems a long way away. Or are you going to show up early again, because you'll miss me too. I didn't buy the bad weather excuse last night. I know you just wanted to see me."

"Right you are, I won't even try to deny it. I do have another case that I have to either wind up or assign to someone else though, so I don't quite know when I'll be back. However, when I do return, you will be my only concern. Until you and Diane are safe for good, I'm not going to accept any other clients. I have to admit that I care very much about ending all this lunacy, so we can plan a life together. I never thought I'd ever feel this way and I never want to lose you, now that I do."

Joan had tears in her eyes at how genuine his words were, and her answer was simple.

"I love you, too, hurry back to me."

CHAPTER 10

The day passed pleasantly enough. Diane and Joan made lists for Damon of things they would like from their own homes. Both felt a need for some of their personal things and Damon understood, he'd brought them each one bag in the hospital, but that had been of his choosing not theirs. Lists would make things much easier, then his having to guess again.

Then Diane brought up a valid thought. She needed to get an idea of her finances. There was no need for Damon to be footing all the bills here. After all, wasn't her deceased husband supposed to have been filthy rich? Couldn't she access those funds as his widow?

Damon realized the logic behind her thinking and decided as soon as he left, he'd check all that out for her.

They shared a great brunch and a walk through the rest of the house, the parts they hadn't seen yet.

There were three more beautifully appointed bedroom suites, each with private baths and an unbelievably lavish, upstairs library, complete with rolling ladders to reach the top shelves. It looked very used, loved and oozed rich, with its dark walnut shelves and desks, and more books than most small town libraries even dreamt about. Both Diane and Joan were enchanted. The library also had three huge leather armchairs and a grandiose pigskin sofa. They immediately settled down there to further absorb and take in the room.

"This room is simply amazing, tell us more about your friend who owns this place."

Diane questioned Damon, and Joan eagerly seconded.

Damon sat down and acquiesced.

"Mary Jane grew up here, raised by her grandparents. She lost her parents in a horrible accident when she was very young, so this was the only home she ever really knew. Her grandparents were my parent's very dear friends and when Mary Jane didn't have a date to her high school prom, I was called upon by my mother and her grandmother to save her from teenage disgrace. I was three years older and in college, but my mother was quite a saleswoman, so I found myself being a dutiful escort on a blind date, assuming of course, that Mary Jane would be a dog, since she hadn't been able to get an escort on her own."

Joan couldn't resist.

"Well was she?"

Damon laughed and smiled.

"Absolutely not, just quiet and a little reclusive, a trait I certainly understood, since I was pretty quiet then too. Actually, Mary Jane was and is very pretty, actually very, very pretty and we have been good friends now for about fifteen years."

Both women looked at each other and raised an eyebrow, there was more to this, than he was telling, they thought.

Damon continued unaware of their speculations.

"She is a fabulous artist and many of the paintings throughout the house are hers. Her grandmother died five years ago, and then her grandfather followed about a year later. She found the house so lonely without them, that she decided to take some European art classes and travel a while. She really has an incredible talent, and paints in the style of the Old World masters, which probably stems from growing up here."

It was obvious he had left out volumes. So ever the inquisitor, Joan pounced.

"Any romance Damon?"

Diane couldn't believe how Joan put him on the spot, but found her self very interested in the answer too.

"About ten years ago Mary Jane got serious about another art student, he left her pretty broken hearted. I guess I was her transitional man. It lasted for about four years, it was the happiest time in my life, and then she decided she couldn't handle the fears and uncertainties that went along with being a cop's wife. I was new on the force and very excited about my career. I couldn't even consider quitting. My whole life all I'd ever wanted to be, was a hero; a good cop. I had asked her to marry me. She said no, it's as simple as that. But we've always remained friends. That's something, right?"

But to the two women listening, it didn't sound at all simple. They knew the sound of a broken heart.

Damon continued his story.

"We broke up. I took it pretty hard but I was also a realist, and I knew from watching other cops, that she was right. I was determined not to get close to anyone again; I am first and foremost a cop. Most of the time that's enough."

He said softly looking directly at Diane.

"But we've always stayed good friends and we are still both loners. Over the years I've come to believe she is very wise and still a very good friend, that's enough. End of the story."

Both women were amazed at his candor, in fact he was pretty surprised himself, and a little uncomfortable now that he'd revealed so much.

But Joan being Joan smoothed everything over by just being her perky self,

"Well, you must have stayed friends, right? Or you wouldn't be here, and then we wouldn't be here; in this great palace. I sure do love this house and I can't think of a better place, to be a fugitive from the mob."

She finished dramatically, breaking the tension and cracking them all up.

Everyone relaxed.

Soon, after they'd gone back downstairs, Mark arrived and Damon took his leave again, promising to get some answers for Diane on the state of her finances.

Joan discretely headed upstairs for a nap. Then Mark proceeded to devour Diane, as soon as they were alone. He was the most sexual, sensual human being she had ever known, he brought out an energy and passion in her that she didn't believe she had ever felt before. He didn't just kiss her, he covered every part of her face with gentle lips that couldn't seem to get enough of her, and he did it with an intensity that left her weak. He made her feel all the emotions expressed in old fashioned romance novels. Feelings that she'd never thought real people truly felt, and that she hadn't come close to feeling since those sixteen-year-old kisses with Bob Teaney in the back seat at the drive-in. However this was far beyond the innocence of a sixteen-year-old. Mark made her feel totally and completely a woman. It was intoxicating and frightening all at the same time. Was it love so soon? Or just lust? Whatever it was, she surrendered to it completely, because it made her feel so incredible, too wonderful, to even think any more, at all. She took his hand and quietly led him up the stairs to her room at four in the afternoon, and it seemed the most natural thing in the world.

Once again, time had elapsed, and they had been almost unaware as they pleasured each other. They made love joyously, and totally uninhibitedly. It was probably over an hour, before they slowed enough to even speak.

"Hi, there….." Diane said very softly as she rested her head in the crook of his neck, where she seemed to fit perfectly.

He answered tenderly.

"Beautiful, just so beautiful…." Mark said so little and yet so much.

He stroked her hair tenderly; looking so deeply into her eyes, it was like making love to her all over again. Every look and movement spoke volumes.

The depth and intensity of his feelings was a tangible thing. She looked back into his eyes, the clearest blue eyes, and the most radiant smile, she'd ever seen in her life. Then she knew without a doubt that she did love him.

It didn't matter that it was so soon; or what the circumstances were. It simply was. Diane loved him, completely and without reservation. It was as if she'd known him forever, and fate had intended them to be together, now and always. She reached out and put her fingers around his neck and grasped the hair at the nape of his neck and pulled him over on top of her and kissed him deeply, wordlessly telling him of her realization.

Mark responded in kind and miraculously made love to her all over again. His stamina amazed her and excited her beyond anything she'd ever felt. This man was the most amazing lover she could ever have imagined, and she gave, as good as she got.

Sometime later they heard Joan up and about and realized it was now well past six.

Diane jumped up guiltily.

"I need to start some dinner, look at the time."

She was already throwing on her clothes and pulling a brush through her tangled hair.

Mark laughed.

"Some guard I am. An army could have marched in here, and they'd have caught me with my pants down."

"But certainly with other things up!"

Diane returned, surprising herself, as she threw him his pants.

They both went downstairs and joined Joan in the kitchen. She was foraging rather aimlessly in the pantry and looked up gratefully as they entered the room.

Diane immediately took over. As had become their habit, the other two sat, and watched, talking animatedly while she made dinner. It was amazing how comfortable this all seemed already. None of them really felt in danger here. Damon had assured them, they'd not been followed, and everyone was still under the impression that they were at Joan's house. They were all beginning to feel pretty removed from all the worry, that had been so prevalent just the week before, as well as becoming extremely comfortable in each others company all the time. Funny how you get used to anything, and after while; it just becomes the way it is.

Once again, Diane created an Epicurean masterpiece, roast lamb with a mint and apple chutney, tiny potatoes tossed with fresh parsley and rosemary in a butter sauce, and asparagus steamed and served with toasted almond slivers in a hollandaise sauce.

"It's a little hard to feel sorry for myself, wounded wing or not, when I'm staying in a palace, being fed gourmet feasts, and falling in love with a handsome palace guard."

Joan quipped as she ate the last bite.

"I tend to agree, my friend."

Diane winked at Mark.

"Time for this guard dog, to start the dishes, that was a terrific meal, gorgeous, thanks."

Obviously Mark felt pretty contented and at home too, as he busied himself cleaning up.

Pretty soon they had company. Chase arrived early and no one was surprised. Joan pulled his plate out of the oven and they sat down together at the counter, as if it were the most natural thing in the world.

Mark and Diane finished up the dishes quickly and headed out to the great room, but before they settled down to sit, she changed her mind.

"You haven't seen the library yet, come with me, it's a wonderful room, I want to show you," and once again today she was taking his hand and leading him, this time up the stairs.

"This feels vaguely familiar, my dear."

Mark teased her holding her hand.

Her response was to turn on the stairs and put both arms around his neck and kiss him resoundingly.

They did make it to the library eventually, and he agreed it was a terrific room, as he pulled her onto his lap on the pigskin sofa. They really felt like two teenagers. There was a massive TV built into the shelves across from the sofa and a remote control on the table at Mark's right. Out of habit, being a news junkie, Mark switched on the evening news, then went right back to snuggling Diane.

But suddenly a familiar name spoken in the broadcast caused them both to bolt upright and focus on the telecast.

"Nicholas Pappas murdered in his cell at Rockland Prison today, former mob leader and inmate for the last six years. It was believed he still managed a large crime family on the outside, and had never truly given up the reigns of the underworld network. Police are questioning one of his so-called associates, one Mario Corielli, once his right-hand man. It seems of late there had been some serious power struggles within the walls of the prison and in the cartel as well. So much for; 'honor among thieves'. We'll be back with more on this story, as it becomes available, and now to our sports desk. Good-night, from the crime desk."

A sports commentator began reciting the day's statistics while Diane and Mark continued to stare at the screen. Finally Mark clicked the TV off and they looked at each other.

"That means it's all over, right?" Diane asked in a semi-shocked voice.

"I just don't know. I'd love to believe that, but things are seldom as simple as they seem, especially woven into the fabric of a crime syndicate. We never knew for sure that he ordered the hit, and even with him dead, it may not be called off. We need to still proceed with caution, for sure. Let's go downstairs and tell Chase and I'll bet we hear from Damon very soon too."

Back in the kitchen Mark quickly recounted what they'd heard, and told them he was going straight to the paper and pull up everything he could find about the Pappas' murder and the ramifications in his organization. This wasn't just a big story, but one that intimately affected someone he had come to love with all his heart. He was gone in minutes, but not before holding Diane tightly and promising her he'd be back as soon as he could.

He had only left the driveway by a matter of minutes when Damon came bursting in the door.

Chase greeted him with a cursory nod. "We heard about Pappas, now tell us what you know."

"Well, at this time, I've got more information than I can process thoroughly. But, I think what you all want to know is, does this mean Diane is safe, and that she and Joan are out of this vendetta. Unfortunately, the answer is; Hell no, it's so much worse than we even imagined."

I took a look at Diane's bank account, when I left here this afternoon. What I found was that in Rand's personal account at the time of his murder there was less than $28,000. But, in trust for Diane in the event of his untimely death, untouchable by anyone else but him, unless he was dead, there is slightly under a billion dollars. Even he wasn't nearly that rich, so my guess is he somehow managed to steal major mob money, or double cross them somehow in a very big way. That is an offense they would be highly unlikely to forget, much less forgive. Now all that money is accessible only to Diane. I don't think they were out to kill her. Not yet anyway, but they will definitely want their money, so she is in grave danger. In death, Rand put her more at risk than ever. Of course, he never counted on dying, megalomaniac son of a bitch. He just used the trust to her as a cover, never intending to actually die and leave her that money. Now that he has, he's put her in the worst danger of her life. Mario Corielli makes Pappas look like a 'kind old man', by comparison. Word on the street says there is no doubt, he personally had his mentor killed as a major move to take over the business. Corielli is totally ruthless and ready to take over not just

Pappas' organization, but a couple of other families as well. Two other old dons were murdered today, within one hour of the hit on Pappas. His statement is clear and irrefutable. Now, my guess is he's the one coming after the money. Corielli is, unfortunately, still very much alive!"

They all sat quietly and absorbed the information.

"We'll give them back the money. I don't want it, this crazy, we just give it back."

Diane spoke emphatically.

"It's not that simple. These aren't people you can just reason with, there is no such thing as trust. Believe me; the answer just isn't that easy. Besides do you really want to fund; drug trafficking to kids, murders for hire, and more mayhem? We aren't going to help animals. It wouldn't matter anyway, they would still kill you. I intend to make sure you live a good long time. We do need to get you out of here though, in fact, you need to totally disappear. Joan, I'm afraid that goes for you too, or they can use you to get to Diane. Since they know that, you aren't safe either."

Joan interrupted.

"Well, of course I go too, I'm with Diane all the way, whether or not they were after me or not."

She reached out and grasped Diane's hand.

"Disappear how?"

Diane asked very softly.

"I've got the beginning of a plan, but it will take me a few days to put the whole thing together,"

Damon was thoughtful as he looked directly at Joan.

"How are you doing, do you think you can travel?"

"I'm fine, really, almost as good as new. I don't even have to go back to the doctor. I have the stitches that just melt away eventually all on their own. Why?"

"Aren't you supposed to do some physical therapy for the arm and shoulder?"

"Oh yeah, but I'm sure I can do that anywhere. Travel where?"

Joan wasn't much for being put off.

"I have an idea, it's a little avant-garde but I think it would keep you safe, without keeping you all holed up in one place. It's expensive, but we know that for Diane, that's certainly not a problem now. Money has its advantages."

"My friend, the Billionaire." Joan quipped.

The others couldn't help but laugh, as usual Joan managed to break the tension.

Damon continued patiently.

"Like I was saying, there are some preparations to be made. We need to get you each clean identities. It's just too hard to hide you as yourselves. In this computer age; anyone, can find anyone, so it's time to transform you into two women that nobody is looking to abduct or kill. Diane, tomorrow I'll need a letter to your lawyer, giving me permission to draw out $150,000 on your behalf. We are going to get you and Joan the best safe identities that money can buy. Then we'll have passports made. You will open a new account in the Cayman Islands and transfer all the existing trust money into a numbered, unidentified account. Then the two of you are going on a luxurious round-the-world cruise."

"Damon are you out of your mind? A cruise now and take all that money, I don't want any of that money. Not ever."

Diane was emphatic.

Damon reached over and took her hand.

"Please Diane hear me out. Okay?"

"Okay, but this is sounding pretty crazy so far." She gave him her attention.

"Like I explained before, we don't want the money back in the hands of the mob; where it would be used for more crime. Once you move it and they lose it, I don't care what you do with it. You can give it all to charity if you want. However, for now it can be instrumental in keeping you both safe and out of harm's way. That's the most important thing. Why a cruise? Lots of reasons; one, it is almost impossible for anyone not on a ship's manifest to board a ship, thus, no one can look for you there. Second, no one would, because it is a crazy thing to do. That's very much the point. Doing the totally unthinkable is a safe course, exactly because no one else would think of it. Who takes a cruise when they are frightened for their lives? And here are some other considerations, there will be a full gym on board, for Joan's new and your continued rehab,

Diane. Hell how can you argue against great meals, terrific ports of call; where with safe identities, you will be free to go out and about normally. With just a few cosmetic, surface changes to your appearances, you will become invisible. That's exactly what we are after. Then I can go to work with a task force here and try to end this mess. I know it's hard to consider leaving everything you have, and totally starting over, but it is the safest thing for now. Now, please just consider it, okay?"

Damon was so earnest and it was so obvious he cared, that they both did sit and think about it, and let it sink in.

Chase had been quiet up until now, but now he spoke. "It's an excellent plan Damon, and just to make it even safer, if the ladies will have me, I'm going along. I'll still feel better if I'm watching over them, no matter how safe it will probably be. I've got some money put away and I can afford the time off, so if it's a go for them, then count me in too, although I've never been much of a sailor or very comfortable with the lives of the rich and idle."

Diane was so touched by everyone's concern and help and she knew Joan would be happy if Chase was along.

"This is all turning into quite a plan, and it all makes perfect sense in a crazy way, but let me make one point perfectly clear. No one here is to suffer for this crazy mess, all finances needed for everyone will be covered out of the money from the mob. It may be under my name, but you are all in this mess with me. I'll accept no arguments of any kind. You are all welcome to whatever is needed to finance this insane coop and to cover all expenses here, while we're gone too, and that is not up for discussion."

Diane was emphatic, so no one argued about it.

Everyone was in agreement. Chase and Damon would take care of creating three safe identities in the next few days, so they could proceed. Money would be moved, arrangements made. The mood was pretty serious as each pondered what was just ahead of them.

CHAPTER 11

The next afternoon Joan and Diane were sitting in the atrium surrounded by luscious plant life, while watching still more snow come down. They were discussing the changes they could make with their hairstyles and colors and teasing each other about radical possibilities. By tacit agreement they had decided to keep it light.

"I think you should go truly red, Di, I mean deep, deep red, it would still go with your coloring, and maybe a real short cute cut, sort of Jill St John, like in the old *'007'*. You would be adorable. I thought I might go very dark, almost black, like my Italian grandmother. I always loved her hair, it was almost a blue-black."

"No Jo, you should be the redhead, and I should go dark and sultry, to be the most drastic change, if we really don't want to look anything like ourselves."

"I can't imagine you dark, Di. It just wouldn't work."

"I'm inclined to side with Joan."

A grinning Mark spoke from just inside the doorway. They hadn't heard him arrive with the sound of the inside waterfall and brook babbling in the atrium.

"Oh, would you now? When did you get here?"

Diane said, jumping up, to run and give him, a welcoming hug and kiss.

"About an hour ago, I've been with Damon, he filled me in on the new plan; it appears you two are going on the lamb, in real style. He's already left to put everything into motion and I need to talk to you, Diane. Joan, please excuse us, okay?"

"Sure, no problem, I know the drill, it must be time for my nap. Night, night…"

Joan left them with a wink.

"Diane I'm just going to say this. As crazy as it is this soon; I can't give you up now. I'm in love with you, and if you'll let me, I want to go along too."

"I'm so glad. I wouldn't want to go anywhere without you either. By the way, I love you too. But, what about your job, you can't just leave, can you?"

"Where is that written? I'll quit. Nothing else is more important than you are."

Mark couldn't resist any longer and pulled her into his arms, devouring her face, and inhaling deeply, his face in her hair.

It was several minutes later, when he held her away from him and spoke again.

"Besides two couples traveling is a much better cover. I'm in agreement with Joan, by the way, I can't see you with dark hair either."

Diane laughed, "Okay, I'll go dark red, very short and sassy. I do love you, I can't help but feel a little guilty to be going away on a fabulous trip with my lover and friends in the middle of what should be a terrible time. I'm deliriously happy and filthy rich. If it weren't for a slight problem like hired killers on my trail, things would actually be pretty wonderful."

Mark was glad she was being so upbeat, but he knew that she was not as brave as she sounded. He planned to always be there for her, even when she wasn't feeling as brave. When memories of little Lexie threatened to break her heart, as they often would. He realized that all he ever wanted was to protect and love this woman.

"But can you really just walk away from reporting, I thought you loved it."

He answered her question seriously, he didn't want her feeling guilty.

"I am a writer, not just a reporter. With a laptop, I can write anywhere. In fact, my love, I can live a dream and finally write a book. I've always wanted to. So no guilt allowed on my behalf, I will be the happiest man in the world with you and time to write the great American novel."

With that said, he gave her another long lingering kiss, putting an end to any further discussion.

CHAPTER 12

The next few days flew by, with all the preparations. Joan's hair was now very dark, and Diane was a saucy auburn, short and framing her face in soft tousled curls. Chase had compared her to a young Ann Margaret, and Mark to a saucy Jill St. John in her hey day as a Bond girl, both comparisons were pretty darn flattering. She had to say she rather liked all the compliments and the new her, although she had hated cutting her hair. It had taken it, a long time to grow out, in the hospital, after they'd shaved it all off upon her arrival for a brain pressure plug.

Joan looked very striking, the dark hair made all her features more defined, and not nearly as bubbly somehow, more mysterious and a little aloof which definitely made her look very different. Anyway it was a very good look for her, and she accentuated the whole effect with dark smoky eye makeup. Then she winked, and she was once again her bubbly self, despite her new, very sophisticated look.

The men teased them; about having whole new women to fall in love with too. They had all adopting the attitude, of two couples planning a fabulous vacation, rather than people forced to hide to stay alive. It was easier on the nerves that way.

Damon had taken passport pictures with a special camera and left again. He said they were very close to being documented with brand new identities.

There was every likelihood Damon would have everything they needed by the next day, or at the latest the day after that. Not wanting to trust or involve anyone else, he had miraculously managed to handle everything himself, pulling only a few official strings to expedite the timing of the documents. He had gone to four totally different sources for the fake identities, deciding it was best if Chase and Mark also went incognito. The key was not to connect any of them in any way.

He had transferred the entire trust, with Diane's power of attorney, into bearer bonds for her to deposit in various offshore accounts. Just discussing that made her crazy; it was so much money. Finally, he calmed her down explaining a plan, where by only $150,000, went into her personal account, which would keep the four of them solvent on the run. The rest would go into a separate account that could later be set up as a charitable trust. To that she added her own stipulation too, which was that everyone present be on the accounts in case anything happened to her.

At the roundtable-type discussion where she raised this indisputable condition, she startled them, as well as deeply touched them all. However, to that plan; Damon suggested yet another safety valve. That it take any two of them to withdraw any amount over $50,000. That way if any one of them fell into enemy hands, it would keep them alive, if they couldn't be used to get at the money alone.

They all marveled once again, how he thought of everything. But he declined being included, as a police officer it would be a serious conflict of interest. Even being Diane's power of attorney had been one in these last few days. But as soon as they left he would destroy those papers.

"When all of you leave tomorrow, or the next day, I'll return to police business as usual, I don't want any paper trails that lead to me, for all your sakes. As Chase knows, I have had him make all your travel arrangements so I can honestly say I don't know where you've gone. As far as I'm concerned you are still at Joan's house."

Spoke a very adamant Damon.

"We are all so grateful for everything Damon, you have been a wonderful friend, thank you from the bottom of my heart." Diane had tears in her eyes as she spoke, "I will never forget all you've done. Never!"

Damon shrugged it off, but felt a lump in his throat as he spoke, soon they would all be gone and he would never see them again, or at least not for a very long time.

"Well I need to get back. I still have some last minute things to take care of, and I'm going by Joan's to visit you two, for appearances sake."

He finished and took his leave.

After Damon left, they all felt subdued for a bit, as they realized how much he'd put himself on the line for them all. But then so had everyone here. Each of them was giving up their very homes and identities because of something completely out of their control.

"How can I begin to tell you how sorry I am, that all of you have to go through all of this, for me. Joan you have always been my best friend. Now I can't believe that because of me, you've been first shot and now exiled. Mark, I can't understand why you are leaving your job and your life for an extended period. Or you either Chase, when just two weeks ago we were virtually strangers. I am so lucky to have such good and loyal friends. This whole thing would be awfully lonely and frightening all on my own."

Diane's voice cracked.

Once again an effervescent Joan changed the tone.

"Oh yea, Di it's just awful. You're putting us through the adventure of a lifetime. A world cruise, with men we love, I don't know how I'll ever forgive you. After all I could be home wandering my lonely house, eating bon-bons and watching the soaps for entertainment. How I'm going to miss that, while seeing pyramids in old Algiers. So get off the pity party kiddo, we are going to have a ball!"

As always Joan could chase away the blues, and make her smile.

Mark put his arm around her, and assured her how happy he was to have her in his life, no matter what the circumstances. He too would get to live a dream because of her. Really write, the way he'd always dreamed of, with the added bonus of terrific fodder for the novel.

He teased.

"Perhaps I'll write about a woman on the run from the mob, with a ton of money and three terrific friends who all care about her and are happy to go along. Maybe the writer will fall madly in love with the heroine. I think it could sell, what do you think?"

Now Diane was laughing out loud, and they all joined in.

Even Chase in a few words assured her that all this had brought him more happiness than he'd ever known, and he was looking forward to the trip too. If not for Diane, he would have never met Joan. For that alone he would be eternally grateful.

When everyone had their say, the holiday mood returned and they all turned to Chase and demanded to know the itinerary.

He went to get a brochure to show them all what he had booked, and laid out the map of the world in front of them that charted the course.

"We fly from here to Miami and board one of the most beautiful ships ever built, from there we make several stops in the Caribbean. That will allow us to open some offshore accounts and get rid of all that pesky money. Grand Cayman, is the key spot for our necessary banking business, but then we will see all of the beautiful ports of call in that vicinity, before going on to South America, where we will travel all down the eastern coast and then across to Africa. We follow the coast towns again around the Dark Continent, and then move on to the exotic Far East, then the South Pacific, hitting every tropical paradise. Then the inside passage in Alaska, to Canada and down the Western Seaboard to Mexico. Where circling Mexico we go through the Panama Canal and back up the Eastern Seacoast, to New England and Nova Scotia, then over to Scandinavia and through Europe into the Mediterranean where we end our romantic odyssey in the crystal blue waters of the Greek Islands. All total having hit all four hemispheres, and every major continent. We will be busy and well fed for 185 days and glorious nights of fabulous shows and starlit nights, and moonlit dancing. How did I do?"

Chase couldn't help it. He looked rather proud of his plan, and he had talked more at once, then any of them had ever known him to do continuously, ever.

They were all a little awestruck at this amazing plan. Boy, were they ever hiding out in style, and six months should allow for a good cool down time for the mob, maybe even time to put Mario Corielli away and end this whole mess.

It was indeed a trip of a lifetime. And a trip that allowed for the possibilities of a continued lifetime. It should serve the two-fold purpose of keeping Diane invisible and the money out of reach of the bad guys.

But it was impossible to completely ignore the tension everyone was under, despite the upbeat appearance. This was a huge step, leaving everything and disappearing for six months and might still end with them all having to start completely over again, in yet another place; if it still wasn't safe to return to Colorado when the cruise ended.

They had all gotten pretty comfortable in Mary Jane's snowy mountain palace and Mark and Chase had long since quit relieving each other of guard duty. They were both, pretty much always around, not wanting to leave Diane and Joan at all, if they could help it.

The four of them had a comfortable pattern set up, and Diane always cooked them great meals, the men did the dishes, then they settled into the library to watch the news, and keep up with the outside world.

On this, their second to last night here, they looked around a little nostalgically, since they were all pretty at home here now. The library was everyone's favorite room.

Once again a newsbreak grabbed their attention, as it showed Joan's house on the screen. The front of the house still smoking as firemen worked on the TV screen, to extinguish a firebomb that had reportedly gone off about ten minutes ago.

The newscaster continued with his report as they all were glued to the screen in horror.

"It appears Detective Damon Matthews had just arrived to see Diane Lindsey, who is under police protective custody following the murder of her husband and child two years ago."

Then the screen was filled with photos of the car wreck, and then a picture of Rand, Diane, and Lexie. Diane gasped.

"Almost two weeks ago unknown assailants shot at Diane Lindsey in her home, and wounded her visiting friend, Joan Phillips."

Now they flashed a picture of Joan and Diane as they looked when they had been taken to the hospital after the shooting, it showed Joan's stretcher being pulled from the ambulance, Diane standing next to her, holding her hand.

"Funny," Diane thought, "I never even noticed the press there."

The commentator continued giving statistics about how after Joan's release from the hospital the two women had been under constant guard at Joan's home.

"Now the policeman out front has been found killed, execution style with one bullet through the head, slouched over in his car. Detective Matthews, having just stepped in the door as the bomb exploded; has been rushed to County Memorial Hospital in critical condition. He remains unconscious at this report. And the biggest mystery is; the women aren't anywhere to be found. They have disappeared without a trace."

He concluded his story melodramatically.

"We will return to this story after a commercial break."

"Oh my God, Damon has been hurt. We have to get to the hospital." Diane exclaimed.

"No, he wouldn't want that, everything he's done has been to keep you safe. You can't just be visible again or it would all be for nothing. Be sensible, that was meant for you."

Mark's voice trembled as he thought about the lengths these people would go; to kill the woman that he loved. He had lost one woman to a drunk driver. He didn't want to lose another to a different breed of maniac.

Chase spoke up calmly, "Damon would want you safe. We are getting out of here immediately. My guess is they were watching your trust fund. When that money disappeared out of your account, by way of Damon, they threw a major tantrum, figuring you were about to bolt. Thank God, Damon was clever enough to keep up the charade that you were both really at Joan's house. But now they'll be looking all over the Denver area. We need to move fast, and get out of this state. I know where Damon has all our new identification. It's in his safe at his house and he should have gotten the passports today. With those we should have all we need. I have a key to his house and I know the combination to the safe. I'll run over and get them, and the bearer bonds and get right back. Meanwhile, Mark, call and find any flight leaving Colorado Springs, not Denver, going anywhere out of this state, anywhere, but preferably an early morning flight when the airport will be at its busiest. It doesn't matter where we are going, but make sure it is a flight with plenty of availability. Because two couples are going to show up without any reservations, and I don't even know our names yet."

He grabbed Joan and pulled her to him.

"I'll be right back."

It worried him that she was being so quiet, it was so unlike her. It had all the signs of shock, after all it was her house that she'd just seen one policeman murdered in front of; and they knew from the news report, that Damon might not make it either.

"Joan, are you all right?"

"It's not all fun and games, is it? If it weren't for Damon, Diane and I would be dead now. He has to make it. He just has to."

"He will, baby, I know him, he's as tough as they come, and he'd want me to keep you both safe. This is what he'd want us to do."

"Go on Chase. Get going. I'll take care of everything here. And I'll call the paper and keep up to the minute reports, on Damon's condition, and I'll find us a flight, to catch in the morning."

Mark said putting an arm around both women protectively.

The whole night was a blur. Damon's condition was critical, but at least he stayed alive, although he had yet to gain consciousness.

Chase got everything out of his safe, and left him a letter saying almost nothing, yet making it very clear, that he'd been the one in the safe. Then praying a silent prayer for his friend's quick recovery, he said a cryptic good-bye; that wouldn't make sense to anyone else but Damon, if he ever got well enough to read it.

True to Damon's reputation there were four perfectly laundered identities represented in a large manila envelope. Four sets of perfect documents. Each of them had a birth certificate, a social security card, a passport, and Colorado Drivers Licenses.

There was even a Visa in one of the men's name and a MasterCard in one of the women's name, probably secured cards with huge deposits, if he knew Damon; one for each couple, to validate authenticity, and make things like reservations and car rental possible. There was also $10,000 in cash, he'd thought of everything.

He smiled as he noticed that Damon had made them two married couples. Convenient, since that's how he had booked the two penthouse cabins onboard the ship, although they were still just prepaid to the travel voucher, for as yet unnamed recipients. He had explained to the travel agent that it was a trip for VIP's who didn't wish to list their names until boarding. At $298,000 per cabin, for a total of $596,000 paid by cashiers check to the travel agent, the agency hadn't uttered a word at that irregularity. When dealing with clientele of this caliber, with that kind of money, they deferred fairly easily.

⁂

Mark had tucked the women into bed against weak protests, since he felt they needed some rest. They were planning to leave for the airport at about four in the morning.

It was well after midnight now. He had found three different flights leaving between seven and eight a.m.; they would grab luggage and some clothes in Florida. They had plenty of time to shop, before boarding the ship in three days. Now they were in flight mode and traveling very light.

Chase returned and he and Mark briefed each other, over a pot of coffee. They were both too wired to sleep.

"You can go ahead and call and book the flights, since we now have credit cards, thanks to Damon's good planning, and we know who we are."

Chase slid all the ID's over to Mark, to make the arrangements.

"You and Diane fly into Miami, and book Joan and I into Ft. Lauderdale. I know Florida very well. So I'll rent a car, and pick you two up at the Miami International Delta luggage pick-up, outside carousel number seven, about an hour after you get in. Since our flight leaves a little earlier from Colorado Springs, you shouldn't have to wait too long, the airports are only about an hour and a half apart."

Mark looked down at the ID's, everything looked perfectly normal, except now he was James Vann, Diane was Janice Vann, Chase was Chaz Mayer, and Joan was Susan Mayer. Starting tomorrow, they were all going to have to get used to being complete strangers to themselves. They would all have to become accustomed to and familiar with these new names immediately, and not hesitate to answer to them. Their lives depended on it.

Mark called and booked all the reservations. In a few hours they would be leaving. As an added precaution he and Chase would just leave the cars here. They would take an airport transport, from a nearby hotel, after first taking a cab from the castle to the hotel. He was trying to think of everything.

He made another call, for a status report on Damon. They would all feel much better about leaving, if he were at least out of intensive care. Funny, although he had been an unspoken rival for Diane at first, Mark still admired and liked Damon.

He was a good man and a caring one, and to keep Diane safe he had put himself in major jeopardy. The mob would be ruthless trying to find the money, and he had made himself the last link to it. They would be aware of that. Damon had made sure they would be safe, never thinking of himself.

A sleepy but tension-riddled Diane entered the room, and sat down across from him, and idly flipped through all their new paperwork.

"This all looks pretty official. I couldn't sleep."

She seemed very lackluster and defeated.

He covered the telephone mouthpiece.

"I was checking on Damon."

She nodded, and waited.

"Please let him be okay." she muttered softly.

Mark listened for a while to who ever spoke on the other end of the phone, than hung up.

"He'll make it. They have changed him from critical to serious. There is no doubt he will live. He's a tough guy; he regained consciousness about fifteen minutes ago. He'll be all right Diane."

Diane felt better but she still felt terrible too.

"He's hurt because of me and we are all just going off and leaving him, without even a good-bye, it just doesn't seem right."

Chase, reentered the room, and heard Diane's last comment.

"But it is right. What he was working for; and what he would want us to do. You can't forget that, Diane, and you can't feel guilty either. He's a cop; it's always part of the job to walk into tough situations.

The possibility was always there, and he knew that. And he chose to be who he was."

That suddenly reminded her, that Damon had lost Mary Jane, for exactly that reason, and it also made her realize, that since they were still good friends. Mary Jane might want to know, what had happened here to Damon, she would if it were her. And since they were all about to leave him, she suddenly wanted to make sure, someone close to him would be there, to help and just to care.

She didn't share her thinking with the men, but just got up and excused herself, and left them alone together to finish their plans.

She dashed up the stairs. She had seen the number by the phone in the upstairs library, scrawled in a beautiful artistic handwriting.

'*Numbers to reach me*' Followed by two international phone numbers, and signed by *Mary Jane*.

When Diane had first read it, she had felt like an eavesdropper, but she had gotten the impression, that Mary Jane had written that note, hoping for a call that would bring her back to Damon. It was just a woman's intuition thing, but now she was counting on it.

Without hesitating she dialed the first number.

A sleepy voice picked up the phone.

"Hello."

"Is this Mary Jane?"

"Yes, who's calling, do you know it's the middle of the night?"

Her voice didn't sound angry, just a little confused.

"I'm very sorry to wake you, but it's very important. Who I am doesn't matter, I'm calling for Damon Matthews…"

Mary Jane cut in.

"Is he all right?"

Her voice sounded suddenly very wide-awake.

"I hope he will be, but it's very serious right now."

Diane proceeded to give her all the details and it was obvious to her that Mary Jane cared very much. She asked all the pertinent questions and got all the hospital information, and finished the conversation by thanking Diane for letting her know.

"Just tell him I'll be there, as soon as I can get the plane connections. Take very good care of him, there at the hospital. Thanks so much for calling."

Mary Jane hung up before Diane could correct her that she wasn't with the hospital. Then on reflection, she decided that assumption, was probably perfect.

Diane smiled as she replaced the phone on the cradle; it would be best if she did think Damon had asked for her to be called. And it would be great for him too, when she flew all the way here to be by his side. Perhaps they'd pick up where they had left off. Diane felt much better knowing he'd have someone in his corner. He was a terrific guy, and she wanted him to have someone too. She hadn't bought all his nonchalance, about their breakup.

Diane felt pretty pleased with her matchmaking, as she headed back down the stairs. As she walked into the kitchen she found everyone up at 3:45 a.m. and guzzling coffee.

Joan had come down while she was on the phone. It looked like no one was having any luck sleeping.

Mark looked at her self-satisfied smile, and knew something had changed since she had left them. He queried her, and she told everyone what she had done, and they all looked pretty happy about it too. It perked them all up, knowing they weren't leaving Damon all alone, and that Mary Jane had been so quick to want to run to his side. The news woke them all up, much better than the coffee. Good news is pretty therapeutic.

On this much happier note Diane fixed one last breakfast for everyone in this kitchen she'd grown to love. Then they left, a little sorry to leave this beautiful place. Now they just hoped Damon and Mary Jane would heal and find happiness here too.

CHAPTER 13

It was an uneventful day's travel, but they were all totally exhausted when they were rejoined as couples, together at the Miami International Airport. Everything had gone according to their plans and without a hitch.

They had traveled 'very light'; the only bag any one carried was the briefcase with the bearer bonds; which by silent majority, had been placed in Chase's or rather Chaz's capable hands.

On the way to the airport in Colorado Springs, everyone had agreed, that from that point on, new names only, in all circumstances, even if they were sure they were alone. It would just be safer and simpler. Halfway wouldn't do, they had to accept their new identities wholeheartedly and never stumble over it again.

Although only mid-day upon arrival in Miami, they were all totally incapable of any shopping, having virtually no sleep the previous night.

They would have two more days in Miami, before boarding the ship, so there would be plenty of time to shop for cruise clothes. Plus they could add to their wardrobes on the ship and in different ports of call too.

So for now, they opted for just a quick trip to a drug store, for some toiletries, toothbrushes and such and then they checked into a beautiful two-bedroom suite at a brand new luxury hotel on the Miracle Mile.

Once settled into the lovely rooms, with a fresh breeze blowing in from the terrace off the beach they all relaxed. Naps, it was unanimously agreed upon.

So Janice and James went to one bedroom, and Chaz and Susan to the other, everyone intent on getting some rest.

When Janice first laid down, she tucked her head into the crook of James' neck with every intention of getting some rest, but the mere smell of him, the touch of him, and all their tensions gave way to a passion that neither of them could, or wanted to resist. No matter where they went; or who they now called themselves. One thing couldn't be denied – they always wanted each other.

They reveled in the strength of their mutual desire. They loved the taste, and smell and sounds of each other. It seemed they could never get enough of this new intimacy. But finally, fulfilled and spent, they slept. James uttered only one word before he closed his eyes.

"Beautiful."

Janice responded with.

"How I love you."

And they were both out like lights.

Susan and Chaz reacted much the same to being alone, but after some snuggling, Chaz insisted she sleep, or he would leave. She was still not completely healed and he was so scared of hurting her.

"You know for two grown-ups we are being very innocent, I'm not made of glass and I won't shatter. I'm a woman and I love you, and you tell me you love me."

Now she teased him a little.

"According to our drivers license's we are married. So isn't it about time we consummated this union and Chaz made love to Susan? Because you have told me you loved me, but you are keeping me at a distance; as if I were made of fine porcelain. I really do want you and I love you Chaz ,'sexy name by the way'. I like it. But forget everything else right now except that you love me too."

She winked at him and pulled him close for a passionate kiss.

After the kiss, Chaz pulled back and looked down tenderly into her eyes,

"You know, I've honestly never even felt anything close to this before, in my entire life. I used to half believe I was missing something, some component human part, a soul perhaps, because I never felt more than casual sexual interest, with any woman. Whenever I was with one woman, I was always half looking around for a better one. With the exception of Damon, I've never even had a really close friend. I grew up in a series of foster homes, most of them, with too many kids, to even be sure, which of us was which. You learn to quit feeling, so you'll quit hurting. I went into the military and became an accomplished killer, it may have been for Uncle Sam, but it's still killing. Special Services are pretty solitary, you keep to yourself and you stay alive. Damon is the only man I've ever called friend. Yet we've always kept it pretty distant too. I've never shared much of myself with anyone. Then he called me in to help on this case, and there you were. I felt more than I had ever felt before. It was difficult for me to understand. I felt like I could see you, with eyes that had never been opened before. I cared so much, so fast, it just astounded me, and those feelings scared me too. My first impulse was for flight, but I knew I could never leave you. Especially when you told me you loved me too. But it is all so new to me, so very special, so fragile, and I want so much for it to all be perfect. Believe me I've never been a patient man, and I want you more than I've ever wanted anything. But I want to wait. I want everything to be perfect. Can we wait just a few more days? We'll board the ship, and it will be as if we are on our honeymoon, because in my heart I have truly taken you for my wife."

Tears coursed down Susan's cheeks, she had never felt so cherished in her life.

"Yes my darling, I love you with all my heart, we will wait, but hold me close."

He did so happily, and eventually they fell asleep in each other's arms.

"Chaz and Susan would have one hell of a honeymoon."

That was the last thought in Joan's mind as she slipped into a glorious slumber.

CHAPTER 14

There was a glorious sunrise over the ocean the next morning, as they all relished the big room service breakfast, served to them on the terrace.

"Wow, snow yesterday, now 78 degrees with a nice ocean breeze today. I could really get used to being a jet setter. I love room service, this weather, and all of you, and I just know today is going to be terrific. It's been so long since I've gone shopping or been out among the living, it will be great to just get out and walk. I guess I was getting a little cabin fever. No matter how attractive the place, if you can't leave, it becomes a prison."

Some things never changed, Susan was, as always everyone's enthusiasm booster.

After such a restful night's sleep they were all feeling pretty great. They'd finished breakfast, and headed down to shop the Miracle Mile, a hot spot for the rich and famous.

The men of course were not thrilled about shopping, but stoically admitted it was a necessity. Janice and Susan on the other hand had a ball as they picked out item after gorgeous item, clothes, accessories, shoes, and bathing suits. Whether choosing for themselves or the guys it was lots of fun, as they piled James and Chaz higher and higher with packages.

The men were resigned early, about having any real choices and just accepted whatever boxes they were handed. Although even they seemed to enjoy picking out Tuxedos and formal wear. After all, it was to be an elegant cruise. Neither of them had ever owned their own tuxes, and in this one selection, they each showed that they had a sense of style, and really got into it. In fact they each wound up getting two tuxes, one set with tails and one without, and although neither wanted to admit it, they did have fun.

Janice and Susan insisted on picking out their formal outfits in the privacy of the dressing room, since they wanted to surprise the guys, when they wore them onboard. They had the best time, picking designer originals, one after the other. Although both women had been financially comfortable before, neither of them had ever experienced this kind of decadent shopping spree.

By three, the men begged for a reprieve, suggesting lunch and a swim, which they enjoyed thoroughly, after returning to the suite to dump all the loot.

That evening, they dressed casually in new sun-dresses, slacks, shirts and had an unbelievable Italian dinner, sitting outside on a balcony, with a three-piece band playing soft calypso music.

"Life just doesn't get any better than this."

James said reaching over to kiss Janice lightly.

Everyone was of the same opinion. But unspoken tension still came along wherever they went, sometimes it was forgotten for a time but it was always there. They were still worried about Damon, and wondered if Mary Jane had made it to him yet, and how that would go. It was sad not to be able to just call and find out. But they all agreed to wait until they could reach Damon at home, for safety sake. Calling him at the hospital, people might overhear, and hospitals only gave information to families.

Nevertheless it has been a good day, and the four of them thoroughly enjoyed the dinner, the music, and each other's company. They found themselves dancing under the stars, with the soft music and sea breeze blowing gently, long into the night.

The next day dawned as perfectly as the last. This was their last day in the hotel. Tomorrow, James and Janice Vann and Chaz and Susan Mayer would board the fabulous new *'My Fair Lady'*, a ship built strictly, for round-the-world cruising in the most lavish style imaginable. She was the largest, most luxurious, and most expensive ship ever built. And this was to be her maiden voyage, so everything would be gleaming and brand spanking new. *'My Fair Lady'* had seven restaurants, two grand showrooms, nine different cabarets, nightclubs, and dance clubs, a piano bar, two libraries, a lecture hall, a movie theater, bowling alley, billiard room, full gym, world class spa, tennis courts, skeet shooting, a climbing wall, four pools, one Olympic size, one a wave pool, and hot tubs and saunas by the score. The promenade deck had thirty-four stores and a full Casino with its own shows. It was equipped with every amenity and luxury available, intended strictly to fulfill the every desire of the rich and famous that were to be *'My Fair Lady's'* guests. She was built to pamper and spoil the world's most already spoiled citizens, and lacked nothing for accomplishing that goal.

Last minute running around had included getting luggage to pack away their new wardrobes before boarding, so they would look like normal cruise passengers. They could hardly be seen boarding, with all shopping bags and boxes.

It all still felt, just a little unreal. Diane had checked out of the hospital, after two years of major surgeries and physical therapy, yet still had been an amnesiac when she'd gone home not quite a month ago. With Joan's help she'd now also beat the amnesia. Then, just a few days later, Joan had been shot, and they had run through a barrage of bullets only to wind up back in that same hospital. Within that short time, they'd met and fallen in love with Mark and Chase and gone into hiding at Mary Jane's castle. Damon had been nearly killed. They had gotten he and Mary Jane back together, been on flights from snow to paradise, under all new identities, indulged in the shopping spree, to end all shopping sprees. Now tomorrow, Janice, James, Susan, and Chaz they would sail into the sunset for a six-month unbelievable luxury cruise.

It was enough to blow anyone's mind, and it had all taken place in twenty-seven days. It was very definitely surreal, and tough to comprehend how they could be anticipating such a wonderful time, out of such a devastating tragedy. Yet they were all in high spirits, healthy, happy and passionately in love.

Janice, of course, still mourned 'Lexie' and always would, but she also knew realistically that it had been nearly two years. So she reveled too in all the joy that new love brings, and she was deliriously happy every minute she spent with James, even when doing practically nothing. She marveled that she could be happy just being with him. They never ran out of things to talk about.

Now that she had her memory back, she couldn't even understand how she had lived with Rand's coldness. They had hardly ever even had a conversation in the last few years, and there had been nothing tender or loving in their relationship. In retrospect, she questioned why she had been content to be so unhappy for so long? Had it been fear of failure? Or what she feared most, that she had cared too much, what other people thought, to admit a mistake. She remembered she had been a bit of a phony, acting to friends and neighbors as if everything was perfect. She had *'Pollyanna'd'* herself into being a fake. These recollections didn't make her like herself very much.

Now she thought that she'd never experienced anything as wonderful as the closeness and intimacy, James and she shared, or the friendship she had with Susan either. It didn't matter so much what anyone's names were, only that they were all safe and together. In fact it was all so incredible, she kept being afraid, that it couldn't last, and yet it just got better and better.

Susan was looking forward to the Bon Voyage with even more excitement. She wasn't so young, and not really a virgin, of course. Her husband had been dead three long years. With his death she had stopped really feeling. She had loved him very much and there had been no one of consequence since, no one she had felt anything for beyond just being casual.

She was crazy about Chaz in a way that went very deep. However, she was also struggling with some guilt feelings and some questions about whether or not to tell him some pretty ugly truths abut her self. While in Greece the last two years, she had worked out her grief over Graeme's death by being pretty amoral. She had gone from grieving to being a party animal. She had been self-destructive in a multitude of ways. Some drug experimentation, some drinking, and some very indiscriminate sex with some very young, beautiful, meaningless men. She had fallen back into a childhood coping mechanism of lying to herself and everyone else. She had tried and tried to justify her actions. When ultimately she couldn't anymore, she'd straightened up and ceased all of it, cold turkey. Eventually she'd really put it behind her, and older and wiser, she returned to the States to pick up a semblance of normalcy.

Instead, all these unbelievable events had taken place and Chaz was in love with her and she felt unworthy of him. He thought of her as just a nice widow and she didn't know whether to tell him the truth and risk losing him or continue to lie by omission. Part of her wanted to confess and the other part couldn't bear to take the chance.

She was so deeply touched at his wanting to wait and make this special. He was so sweet and so vulnerable. Joan wanted him with all her heart. Quite simply, he made her heart come alive again. But the fact, that he was treating her so special, just served to intensify her guilt about her past. She just didn't know what to do. Leave the past in the past or tell him all the things she was so ashamed of?

James was completely and thoroughly in love with Janice, and now in a crazy way because of her; he was reborn, he could love again, write and travel. Those were all his dreams rolled into one, and he felt a little guilty and a little like a gigolo that all this was made possible using Janice's money. If he could ignore that niggling at the back of his mind, he was the happiest he'd ever been, when they were together. She was a breath of fresh air, she was always up beat and the strongest woman he'd ever met, a real fighter with an indomitable spirit, and he loved her beyond all reason. He didn't even mind leaving everything else for her, she was worth it to him, she filled his life, and he wasn't lonely anymore.

Chaz was also looking forward to the launch date, but he was nervous beyond belief. He had been with women, of course, and sex was good, but he had never experienced intimacy, he had honestly never really cared enough to even stay the night. Now he never wanted to leave this woman for even a minute. Being in love was new to him, and totally foreign. He'd never planned to marry, and had never wanted children. Now he found himself in totally uncharted territory and part of him was petrified, as he found himself thinking picket fences. What had started out as a routine assignment to help Damon, had turned into a completely life altering situation. Now he couldn't begin to imagine a world without Susan in it. He only wanted to make her happy, keep her safe, and love her for the rest of his life, and all that, even before they'd had sex. Tomorrow night would be incredible but it came with some honest trepidation.

The last day in Miami passed uneventfully; packing the new luggage, a great lunch, a swim, a walk on the beach, a very pleasant dinner. They were all so comfortable in each other's company, and everyone felt extremely relaxed, all things considered. They had an early evening, and went back to the suite.

Over dinner they had discussed it and decided they needed a status report on Damon, there had been nothing in the local news. They had decided to call Mary Jane's house and see if they could reach her after the hospital visiting hours were over. Janice called, and got no answer. They debated calling the hospital, and decided it was worth a try. They'd all feel better if they knew Damon was out of danger.

Chaz called from a payphone in the lobby, on a calling card, and they actually put him directly through to Detective Matthews' room. A woman picked up the phone and he asked for Damon, saying he was a friend of his from the force, and identified himself as Chaz. He heard the woman relay the information and Damon came on the phone right away.

"How are you, and your lovely wife?"

"More to the point, how are you? We are all just fine, not a hitch."

"Couldn't be better friend. Mary Jane came all the way from Europe, and hasn't left my side, she hasn't even been home yet. Funny, someone from the hospital supposedly called her, but we can't figure out how, they would have had the number. Anyway, if you should happen to talk to the nurse or nurses who thought to call her, thank them for me, would you."

Damon was very obviously happy as he spoke. Chaz couldn't see that he was sitting holding Mary Jane's hand, as she sat on the side of the bed.

They spoke cryptically, but found out all they each needed to know. Damon knew they were safe, and Chaz knew that after a concussion, a broken collar bone and some third degree burns healed, he'd be fine physically. Even better, it sounded as if Mary Jane was the best medicine of all. He knew that would please Janice and Susan. So the two friends wished each other the best and hung up.

Everyone back in the suite was glad to hear the update and headed for bed, guaranteed sweet dreams now that they didn't have Damon to worry about, and Janice looked positively smug after hearing Mary Jane was with him.

CHAPTER 15

Not every day can dawn brightly. Cruise day dawned rainy and dismal. Yet, nothing could really affect the up beat mood in the suite. The terrace wasn't an option in the downpour, so they went down to the hotel dining room and enjoyed a light breakfast, knowing that there would be incredible food to experience for the next six odyssey months.

They were all in a party mood, and so glad Damon was out of danger and not alone anymore. Janice couldn't help but be a little proud about having called Mary Jane. She just wished she could be a fly on the wall and know what was really happening between the two of them.

In Denver that was a question in Damon's mind as well.

No one could have been more surprised than Damon when Mary Jane walked through his door in ICU.

It was the day after the bombing at the Phillips home, and the murder of a fellow policeman to which he had assigned watch duty. He could think of little else since he'd come to, beyond the coldness of the man who had ordered the execution of that officer, and the fact that he'd also meant to kill Diane and Joan with a bomb. Damon had suffered a concussion, but as he had drifted in and out he'd thought of very little else other then Mario Corielli and the lengths to which he would go to get his money. Then it occurred to him that the bomb was probably meant to cover the tracks of a search or to smoke them out, he would have needed Diane alive, until he got the money back.

All of the reflections of the crime evaporated from Damon's thoughts as he did a double take on the realization that Mary Jane was here.

He felt an involuntary joy at seeing her; and concussion or not, recognized that certain feelings had never died at all, just gone into suspended animation. Suddenly he knew just how much he had missed her, and had to remind himself with a sad jolt that they were only friends now. His concussion had confused him for a moment and thrown him full throttle back into feelings of their past romance.

All this ran through his mind in a flash as she walked from the door to the side of the bed and took his hand, looking down sweetly at him. He saw then that she had tears streaming down her cheeks.

"This is what I was always afraid of. This is exactly why I left you. Yet, when I heard you were hurt, I could think of nothing more than getting back to you."

She said without preamble. Suddenly the years disappeared and it was as if they had never been apart. Damon also felt tears fill his eyes.

"How did you know?" He wondered out-loud.

"A nurse called me, didn't you know? Didn't you ask them to call me?"

Suddenly Damon knew exactly who had called her, he remembered Diane commenting on the note in the library one day. He sent a silent grateful message to her. Even with all the rushing to leave, for her own safety, she had thought of him and done this wonderful thing. She had called Mary Jane back to him, something he might have wanted, but never would have done.

He realized in that instant, that his attraction to Diane was only that, and came from loneliness, because the only woman he had ever loved or ever would love, was standing right in front of him.

But he wondered.

"Is she only here as a friend?

He needed to keep his emotions in check until he knew. He was still a cop, and her being here, might not mean she had changed her mind.

Damon answered her, after thinking a moment.

"No, I didn't ask anyone to call you, but I am very glad they did."

And for the next several minutes talking wasn't very important, as they just looked deeply into each others eyes.

Damon's torso was heavily bandaged from the broken collar-bone and burns. But, his handsome face was only a little scraped. It only made him look vulnerable, like a kid who had fallen off a skateboard.

The concussion made it a little hard to concentrate but he was able to see that Mary Jane was a beautiful woman now, rather than just a pretty girl. She had matured since the last time he'd seen her. Her hair had grown long, almost to her waist, but multi-layers of golden hair wisped casually around her face, framing a unique heart-shaped face. Her lavender-blue eyes as big as saucers, looked steadily into his. The years apart evaporated into a non-issue.

A major cosmetic company had once asked her to be their exclusive eye model. Her eyes defied reality, they captured hearts at a glance and yet she was totally unaware of how gorgeous she was. She had laughed at the cosmetic offer, and never even really considered it. She had always been so shy and so quiet, before Europe. Now Damon noticed a self assurance and a poise that she had acquired with maturity and her success in the art world. He wasn't even aware that she had already had several exhibitions and one-woman-shows. She was a rising star in the European art scene, a scene that disallowed amateurs. She was a truly talented artist with a distinctive style that was unique. Collectors recognized Mary Jane as a valuable person to buy early in her career before they wouldn't be able to afford her work. But Damon had always believed in her talent and loved her shyness and poise.

Damon looked at her perfect lips. They were very full, sensual, and naturally deep pink. She wore no makeup at all and she never had. As he drank her in, he felt himself fall head over heels all over again. But, he was afraid to hope. She might have come strictly as his friend. However, he was hoping, hoping with all his heart that it was more than that.

Now, two full days had passed with her barely leaving his room. They had talked about his injury, her trip, how her artwork had flourished, the shows she'd had and every other inconsequential thing in the world, except her feelings. It was driving him crazy.

She held his hand when sitting on the bed next to him, and she kissed him hello and goodbye, lightly, but with warmth, each time she came and went. More and more his joy at seeing her faded, as he realized that she wasn't returning his feelings, but then he realized, he wasn't showing his either.

They were both being very careful, and he though about taking a risk and telling her he wanted her back, that he wanted *them* back.

But, he only thought it, and they just continued to converse casually, never really saying anything.

CHAPTER 16

The sun came out at two and they were to board the ship at two-thirty. It would appear that the vacation Gods were smiling upon them after all. It had turned from a dreary deluge into a glorious day. The pier glistened with puddles from the rain, now drying in the bright sunlight.

Porters took their bags from them as they stepped out of the cab and they checked in and approached the gangplank. They were all in high spirits. It just didn't seem possible that Janice had gone through so much and Susan had just been shot, and that they'd all been forced, for their own safety, to adopt alias' and hide out. Real life had become a melodrama and yet today was the beginning of a dream trip they were all looking forward to. By a common consensus, they had unanimously agreed, not to think of this trip and their new identities, as hiding or running, but rather as an amazing adventure which would never have come about, if not for the amazing circumstances that had precipitated them.

With only a few slips, they had all gotten used to the new names. By doing it completely and even in private, it had become natural fairly quickly, like actors become their characters in a play. It was amazing what the human spirit could accept, when lives depended on it.

It was hard not to be excited about this method of hiding out Chaz had chosen for them. In many ways they were all happier and better off than they'd ever been in their lives. It seemed somewhat bizarre considering recent events, but true never the less.

However, no one was doing much evaluating at three that afternoon as they were fed unbelievable amounts, of beautifully garnished appetizers, served on gleaming silver trays, by a gracious wait staff, parading delicacy after delicacy under their noses, while keeping their champagne glasses full to the point of over flowing.

None of them had ever felt so decadently spoiled. This was worlds away from the events they had just weathered.

"I do believe that I'm about the luckiest woman in the world."

Janice commented, relaxing back into her deck chair.

Susan's snappy comeback cracked them all up but made them look over their shoulders to make sure no one overheard, it was classically, outrageously Susan,

"I'd have gotten myself shot sooner if I'd known where I'd get to recover."

Chaz had a perfect way to shut her up, he swept her into his arms and kissed her resoundingly. As he let her go, he admonished quietly.

"Let's keep some information hush-hush, my love, or I'll make you stay in the cabin."

"Actually I'd rather like to have you keep me in the cabin."

She winked lasciviously and everyone laughed.

"You two be good now; the honeymoon starts tonight."

James teased them. He had no idea how true that was.

As James, life felt much lighter, than Marks had. No solitary car club, no depressing news stories and deadlines to make. He was in love and he had the time to explore just how amazing that all felt.

Janice shot Susan a look that said, "I didn't tell him, I swear."

Susan rolled her eyes and communicated that she believed her. No harm done.

Chaz looked slightly sheepish.

The four friends decided to tour "*My Fair Lady*."

"Why is it they name ships for ladies, and princesses and queens anyway?"

Janice queried.

"Chauvinist isn't it? I think it dates back to Viking days when the men were in love with their ship, and the sea was their mistress, and manly men would never carve a man at the bow it had to be a gorgeous busty woman."

Susan parried back.

Chaz laughed.

"The tradition is centuries old, don't shoot the messenger. I chose this ship for its timing and itinerary, not for her name."

The ship was dazzling. Every salon, game room, shop, restaurant, lounge and atrium was more gorgeous than the last. The grand atrium was nine stories tall, crystal and gold, with waterfalls and lush greenery. The plants were exotic, flowering and full of tiny white twinkling lights, shaped like miniature teardrops that made all the trees look as if they were dripping in dew. On closer inspection, Susan exclaimed that there actually was water, inside each and every little light. It gave an amazing effect, the twinkling lights refracting through the water droplets.

Janice stopped to study them more carefully.

"It's amazing how the refraction of light; or in our case, place and circumstance can so completely alter the initial illusion. In a way that's exactly what this trip is doing, it is a refraction of our fear and flight into paradise. We are all very lucky to be experiencing this refraction at this moment, together and in such a beautiful setting."

Janice had captured them all with her observation, but after a moment they continued on even more appreciative of their glorious surroundings.

There was a grand curved stairway, made out of glass and the stairs were also filled with white lights that created the image of twinkling, diamond stair runners. It was magical everywhere they looked.

The piano bar was classy and whimsical, with keyboards in ebony and ivory everywhere, weaving across walls, ceiling and floor all in inlaid onyx and alabaster marble.

The library, beautifully appointed in rich mahogany, had windows interspersed all throughout, with big cozy window-seats to read in. It held every well known classic in at least three languages. The books all had burgundy rich, matching, leather-bound spines, obviously made especially for this library.

The casino made Caesar's Palace pale in comparison, it was elegant, all in dove gray and deep plum, and it looked like the plush inside of a genie's bottle, which is how all the wait staff dressed. It was both exotic and whimsical.

The gym was high tech and fully equipped with 'state of the art' shiny, chrome and black work out machines, facing windows full of a fabulous view of the sea ahead, would become a spectacular incentive to use the treadmills. Set at the bow of the ship, they would always be entertained while they exercised, by the ever-changing panorama in front of them.

The spa was a grotto, and the caves looked real. Every possible form of pampering was available, and it would be perfect for the massages after the physical therapy needed on Susan's shoulder and for Janice to continue her strength work outs.

For that matter both James and Chaz were pretty impressed by the gym and spa too and they would certainly prefer this gym to their own minimal home gyms. Both men did regular work-outs but certainly not in this kind of style.

Everyone laughed and enjoyed each new discovery, this ship was a small town unto itself and nothing was lacking for making it spectacular. What an incredible experience this was going to be. Each had commented in one way or another that this was a surreal dream.

The shops that filled the entire eighth and ninth landings felt like a magical Champs Elysee, and the shopping was equal to the most fabulous shops in Beverly Hills. In fact, some of them were the same ones seen found there, and in Monte Carlo and Paris. Fountains filled the center isles and glass domes speckled the ceilings as if full of twinkling stars at night and filled with sunlight during the day.

Finally, after poking around the ship from stern to stern, they decided to go and see their respective cabins. At check-in they had been asked to wait until after five to go to their rooms, or they'd have gone sooner. That was to allow for smooth baggage delivery, that the sleeping floors had been kept clear.

Now they anxiously went up to the penthouse floor, where they had the top category deluxe suites. They were interested in seeing their homes for the next six months. At the hall they split up and each couple went to their own suites.

When Susan and Chaz got to their cabin, Chaz unlocked the door, then turned and swept Susan up into his arms and carried her over the threshold.

He set her down very gently on the sofa, and went down on one knee at her feet. He took her left hand reverently in his and slid a wide gold band with an antique canary diamond on the third finger.

"This was my mother's and my grandmother's and now I want it to be yours. I went by and picked it up that last night, because I want to truly be your husband. Our ID's have already married us, but I wanted our hearts to marry us as well. Will you marry me? I love you as I never thought I would love anyone."

Chaz finished as if he had run out of air. He seemed to be holding his breath, waiting for her answer.

For once Susan was speechless, her heart was so full; tears of happiness and completeness ran down her face unchecked. She simply nodded, and kissed him so softly it was as if a butterfly had briefly settled on his lips. It was solemn and sweet and a lifetime commitment, all at the same time. Finally, she looked straight through his golden eyes and into his soul, and in the softest of voices, audible only to the heart, she said.

"I do."

With that she dismissed her past and embraced their future. She decided some things were just best left unsaid. Greece had been a different lifetime, a grieving time and of no consequence to her future. Nothing would come out of thinking about it or by sharing it. This moment was about futures together. They were each brand new and now was all that mattered.

He responded.

"I do too, forever and always."

Then Chaz stood and took Susan's hand and kissed it gently, just above the ring then said.

"I love you with all my heart."

"I know, I can feel that with all my heart, and I will love you all the days of my life."

Then she kissed him again, but not softly this time. This kiss held heat and hunger and passion. Chaz returned it with a wonder he had never felt before. It was like the first time for him. Nothing else before this could even be counted; he quite simply, had never made love before. Now he realized just how different and empty just sex had been. The emotions were powerful and tender, as he slowly took Susan's clothes off and shed his own.

His lips went from her earlobe, tentatively down her neck; he kissed the now nearly healed bullet wound at her shoulder, then traveled to the hollow of her throat. He felt her pulse under his lips, than moved to envelop her left nipple, which instantly stiffened, as he rolled his tongue ever so slowly around it with wider and wider circles, until the cleavage brought him back to the middle. Then, he found his interest traveling toward her bellybutton, sensuously going lower. She intertwined her fingers in his hair; letting passion overtake her, she guided him still lower.

When pleasure became so consuming that she could stand no more, she pulled him up on top of her, where she could kiss his lips again. They kissed and kissed for what seemed like an eternity. The slowness making it all seem more delicious, more wonderful, and profoundly special; as if no two other people could ever have felt this way before.

Then Susan gently ran her hand down the length of his beautiful strong body and found that which she so wanted. She desired him so much; to taste, to hold, to envelop and so she did, lovingly, teasing him with moans of such pleasure, he thought he would explode.

Finally, mouths found each other again and bodies had come full circle from pleasuring each other. They once again lined up, one on top of the other, joining miraculously, tenderly, even fiercely, as they sealed their love in a physical union, that defied all reason, and ascended to a place of such heightening pleasure, that all reality faded away, and only pure joy existed.

They never made it to dinner that evening. But, then again they were never missed because Janice and James never made it either. Four very happy people spent their first night aboard the ship as lovers.

About ten p.m. Janice and James discovered a room service menu, and availed themselves, but the newlyweds, never seemed to need any sustenance, other than each other.

CHAPTER 17

Mary Jane came every morning and sat next to Damon, and spoke of trivialities; it was obvious that keeping it light was her goal. She held his hand, brushed errant hair out of his eyes, and even kissed him lightly, hello and goodbye. He napped now and her mind wandered. She wondered how long she would straddle the fence between old friend and one time lover. She was unsure of her own feelings, and had chosen to avoid thinking to much about it. When she had gotten the call initially, all he years disappeared and she was once again admittedly in love with Damon. But, on the flight here she began to talk herself out of it, after all this was exactly what she had run away from. She hated his being a cop.

She had grown up without her own parents because her father had been a cop. He had been on a big case and made some very important people angry. Her father had been shot down on a public street; in downtown Denver at ten in the morning. Her mother had unfortunately been standing next to him since they had just left the obstetrician's office together. They were chatting and happy, they had just been told that they were expecting their second child. They couldn't wait to get home and tell Mary Jane that she would soon have a little brother or sister.

It was at that moment that the car spun around the corner and a gun was pointed out the window to mow down her father. They hit her mother too. Her father died instantly. Her gentle, sweet mother lasted almost a month in a coma. Then she too died. Mary Jane was seven when she was orphaned.

She went to live with her grandparents. They told her what had happened very minimally, and then never spoke of it again. But, when she was older she had gone to the library and read all the articles herself, hoping to try to understand the senseless violence that had taken her parents and the baby that would have been her sibling.

Mary Jane had a good life with her grandparents and she had loved them very much but her loss was never forgotten, and she still missed her parents, even to this day.

Mary Jane had been in love with Damon since that first meeting set up by her grandmother. She was so happy with her arranged prom date, and so proud of her great looking, college-age date. It was the only time at school that other girls had envied her. She had been so shy back then. He almost treated her like a younger sister in the beginning; it was obvious he was fond of her, but not the least romantic. After a couple of years she gave up on him and found another boyfriend, a fellow art student. It was pleasant enough, but nothing special. They broke up when he found someone who was special to him, someone who could really care about him, as Mary Jane never had.

She'd made more out of the breakup than she really felt, because Damon was being sympathetic, and also seemed to be treating her like a woman for the first time.

As time went on he really began to treat her like a woman, and finally as his own woman. Their romance was wonderful, magical and sweet.

When her grandparents left her the house they moved in together. Life was terrific; it was like living in paradise. They were unbelievably happy. Then Damon graduated Law School, and that's when everything fell apart. He decided to enter the police academy, instead of the prestigious law firm that had offered him a position. He said that now that he knew the law, what he really wanted was to uphold it. He was very ambitious and smart. With a Law degree, he was determined to make detective quickly, and there was little doubt that if he set his mind on it, he would do it.

Mary Jane was inconsolable. They fought; she was immovable, but explained nothing. He knew nothing about her parents except they were dead. Without any explanation he felt she was being unreasonable. He stubbornly went into the academy, and finally on to the force. He thought surely she would stand by him, since he didn't really understand the pain hidden behind her adamancy. Finally, the fights ended because Mary Jane left.

Damon couldn't believe she was serious, they had been so happy. They'd tried staying friends, they'd said they would always remain friends, but finally it hurt too much, to accept so much less from each other than what they had been. They drifted apart.

She threw herself even more seriously into her art, and went to Europe to study. It had kept her busy and she'd forged out quite a career. She was a success, but there had never been anyone else. She could never quite quit loving him. Now here she sat, but nothing had changed. She still couldn't live with what he did for a living and the fear of always losing him, if not this time, the next time. Yet she still loved him. She knew that too, had not changed. Her only small hope was that just maybe his love affair with the force had dimmed.

Naturally, he couldn't give specifics on this recent case. But she knew what she'd read in the paper. She could also tell he felt betrayed in some way by his old partner. So as they spoke about inconsequential things, she wondered what the future held. She wondered if he would quit the force. He still had a law degree. Could she leave Europe? She had worked so hard, and come so far, and was just beginning to benefit from the fruits of her labor. But, as she reached over and once more pushed his hair back on his forehead while he slept, she also knew it would break her heart to leave him again. She did still love him; he was even more handsome than she remembered, kinder, and sexier too. Damon still made her melt, merely with a glance; she was still intensely in love with him, whether she admitted it or not.

"Hi there, my sweet girl, where were you? You were daydreaming."

His voice startled her out of her reverie, and for a second she was terrified he had heard just what she was thinking. She bolted from the room with an excuse about getting some coffee.

It left him a little taken back, and then he started wondering most of the same questions that she had just contemplated. He had been so happy from the moment she walked through the door. He had mentally thanked Diane or rather Janice a million times. He realized in retrospect that he had never quit loving Mary Jane. The feelings he'd thought he had for Janice were admiration, loneliness and transference.

Diane had known what he needed when she placed the call that brought Mary Jane back to him. He realized that it was time for them to talk seriously; they had some of the same problems to work out that they'd had before. However, he hoped they were both more mature now, and could deal with it all more reasonably. Because Damon knew one thing for sure; he wanted her back with all of his being.

CHAPTER 18

Janice woke first, she had her head on James' shoulder, and she inhaled the warm musk smell of him. It was sexy, so uniquely him. She could never remember a time that she had enjoyed another person's smell, but she sure loved his. She loved everything about him. She was so happy it scared her. It seemed somehow wrong to be so completely happy, considering their circumstances and the need for false identities, this cruise, all that money that wasn't really hers, a bad guy (a really bad guy) named Mario Corielli looking for her, and Damon still in the hospital. Yet still she felt such an unbelievable sense of security, as long as this incredible man lay beside her.

He stirred now, and rolled over toward her. Then without a word, gently began to make love to her. They were so natural together, so special, so erotic yet with an overlying love so tender and pervasive it was a part of everything else.

In the next suite, Chaz was also awake, propped up on one elbow, tenderly watching Susan still sleeping. He thought her the most beautiful woman in the world. He luxuriated in the memory of their lovemaking that he had only ended just before dawn, a few hours ago. He had never known anything even remotely like last night. It had stripped him of every defense; it had made him vulnerable. Some of that had scared him. He'd always been the tough guy and these were such new and foreign feelings. But, he wouldn't give up a second of it, and he would never give up this incredible woman, and all the feelings she evoked, even if sometimes it scared him. This was now his wife in his heart.

He had told her over and over in a multitude of ways throughout the night of his love for her, and still, he knew he hadn't even begun to describe the depth of his feelings. Even more wonderful, he knew and felt that she felt the same intensity of love for him. Chaz looked down tenderly and felt so lucky, and so incredibly happy.

Though no one made it to the next morning's breakfast seating; four slightly sheepish, well-satisfied people did meet at their assigned table for lunch, in the dining room at noon. After just a moment of awkwardness, they were all laughing and talking at one time, busy planning the day.

It was an extraordinary day; crisp, clear and delightfully breezy with an incredibly robins-egg-blue sky, which determined that the day would be a joyous one. They were docked in the Bahamas but had all decided to stay on board. Nearly everyone else had evacuated the ship for an island excursion and they rather liked the feeling of having their own personal yacht. Although no one mentioned it or the reasons; they were all pretty tired too. There was a generally languid lassitude of the thoroughly happy, and totally sexually exhausted. They easily reached a common consensus to just soak up some sun and enjoy the aft pool deck all to themselves.

The next few days were spent at sea and allowed for lazy, sun-filled deck days to become a habit. Janice and James and Susan and Chaz swam, made love, ate, and danced, and they all fell, more and more in love with each passing day.

James was writing everyday, too. No matter how much the others begged and cajoled he wouldn't tell them a thing about the book he had started, and was working feverishly on it in spurts. He'd always thought it would be easier to write a book. Now he realized stories and articles with deadlines were much easier. It was a kind of mental torture; up against a project that had to go four hundred pages and had no specific parameters. It was tremendous pressure even if he was enjoying the process. Every time he stopped writing he feared there was no more in him, and that he was a fraud. But, then he would sit down at the laptop the next time and miraculously more would come. He didn't even know where it came from, but thank heaven it did keep coming. Each day the story grew and the pages added up and he saw the progress.

He became ridiculously superstitious though and wouldn't even tell Janice what it was about, afraid of jinxing the book. She accepted his eccentricity, although it didn't stop her from cajoling him on occasion for hints.

They all fell into comfortable patterns, of being all together often, and then breaking into separate couples, or going in separate directions as just the girls together. Everyone worked out in the gym everyday, so they were all getting very fit. Janice and Susan always went together, that and the massages after each session, gave them girl-chat time. They loved sharing their new found happiness and both could still hardly believe, all that had happened to put them here.

The four socialized very little with the other passengers. Both because they were so happy with just each other, and because they still weren't completely comfortable introducing themselves with their new identities. It still felt like play-acting in an ongoing role, using these names. They had all stuck to the rules though and they never lapsed, not even in private. But, it still felt like a charade and a bit wooden when introducing themselves to other guests.

They were seated at a table for four in the dining room, and they mostly, happily, had kept to themselves.

They had observed the other passengers though, and had spotted many faces that could be seen in a People magazine. Those passengers were all pretty private too. There were more than a handful of the rich and famous on board. Movie stars, politicians, big business types, and even one astronaut also enjoyed sharing this ship with them. It was ideal and still a bit unreal too.

The days were mostly beautiful, but occasional rain and thunderstorms were greeted with delight too, for they incited long periods of joy in their cabins. All in all; they were four very happy people, cruising the Caribbean, eating, dancing, laughing and making love all with great enthusiasm.

The one worry they had was getting rid of the briefcase with nearly a billion dollars worth of bearer bonds inside. One or the other of them was constantly baby-sitting it as it wouldn't fit in the room safes provided mostly for jewelry. That was a cumbersome responsibility. However that burden was thankfully almost over. Tomorrow they'd anchor in Grand Cayman.

For once Janice was being very stubborn, and was not accepting any arguments. She had given it considerable thought and she didn't want all the responsibility of all this money. She insisted that they split it in half, and that each couple have a separate account. She wanted everyone to have access to the money; just in case they got separated, or anything happened to anyone. She trusted these people with her life, and knew each had risked their own safety because of her.

She would not listen to any arguments to the contrary either. Later when this was all over, she hoped to use the money to help inner city youth, and she figured each of the others would have ideas and causes equally compelling. Whatever they did, she knew it would be the right thing; each of them had a spirit of generosity and exhibited no greed whatsoever in spirit or any other way.

In the meantime, by mutual consent they were all to use whatever they needed on this trip, which although extravagant, would still only be a drop in the bucket to that kind of money.

It was still almost inconceivable to Janice that she had married a man like Rand, and not known him at all. But, the time had come to let all that go. Now, there was James, and he was everything to her, her friend and her lover, indeed her life. She could ask for nothing more.

As Diane and now again as Janice she had accepted the fact, that her baby was gone, and that was the only really sad part that she still carried with her. It would always hurt, but it would dim too. She remembered Lexie's smile, and the bell-like sound of her laughter. It resounded in her memory time and time again. She remembered the way her baby had smelled fresh from her bath, wiggly and wet against her. Remembered, that her feet and tummy were very ticklish, and how she loved stealing bacon off her mother's place at breakfast. She thought of the silky baby hair, soft against her cheek, when her daughter crawled in bed with her after a bad dream. Janice remembered everything now, but wouldn't want to be deprived of any of those memories ever again. She would never be sorry for the time she did have her precious little daughter. She treasured those memories even with the pain that wrought.

James often held her, while she told this baby story, or that one, and more than once his tears joined hers, as she finished a memory. Susan could also be counted on in her bad moments. Janice felt that despite her loss she was still a very lucky woman to have such wonderful friends. True, they all fought with a little guilt over this incredible trip, funded by dirty money, but for the most part they felt safe and very happy and lucky. Although she knew that they would all sleep better, when the money was banked in Grand Cayman and no longer in their cabins in a briefcase.

CHAPTER 19

Damon was finally being released from the hospital. He couldn't wait to get home. He and Mary Jane had decided that he would go home with her, to the castle. She felt it would be more restful for him, and her studio was there. She needed to paint, it calmed her, and it would help her reclaim her composure; seeing Damon every day and remaining casual. They still had not spoken of their feelings for one another, and it was driving them both crazy. It was progress though, that at least they both assumed she would stay with him, throughout his recovery period.

Despite their inability to have a serious discussion about where they were headed, neither of them could give up being together either. So, the plans were in place that he would go home with her. They had always been so happy in the castle.

Now, without discussing it, they both clung to the immediate future, that at least would be together.

The department told him to take all the time he needed, and he planned to do just that. He had lost some of his allegiance. He hated the deceit and the cover-up that had nearly cost Diane everything. Damon hated feeling responsible for the dead officer, who had been murdered that night in the car, all because he had assigned him to guard Joan's empty house. No one should die protecting an empty house.

And a witness protection program, should never have been used for the likes of a criminal like Anton Savion. Thanks to his being made 'persona non grata' by the authorities, it had given him a license to cost the innocents around him their lives. These legalities had given Damon cause to question his life's work. He was a whole lot less gung-ho about his whole career choice at this juncture. More and more, he was considering that maybe it was time he pursued his law degree.

He knew that he would have a much better chance of rekindling the life that Mary Jane and he once shared, if he chose to leave the force entirely. Whether they spoke of it or not, he knew they were still capable of working it out. The love was still there, he could feel it.

He planned to talk to her that night, when they were away from all the glare of hospital lights, annoying monitor beeps, announcements and nursing staff intrusions. They'd get serious and cozy in front of the fireplace in the library, and he would tell her, how much he still loved her, and that he would do whatever it took to be together again. He wanted to marry her. Wanted to be together always and he didn't fear telling her anymore. Without the police force between them, he knew her answer would be yes. He was willing to go anywhere she wanted to go. He would be the lawyer, she had always wanted him to be. Now, he just couldn't wait for her to pick him up so they could get out of this hospital, back to the castle and on with their future.

By ten o'clock in the morning Damon was pretty concerned. Mary Jane still had not arrived, which was beyond strange. She had arrived every other day, no later than nine. Today, she knew he was leaving, and they had told her to be there between nine and ten. Now, she was late and there was no answer at her house. It just wasn't like her to be late. Not like her at all. He was getting seriously concerned.

At four he called a cab and headed to her house. He was sick with worry. There was definitely something wrong, his fear was a tangible presence. It walked right beside him a large dark apparition, making its presence loom bigger than life. Damon's heart was pounding, it was loud in his ears, and it was an echo that blocked everything else, as the cab pulled up Mary Jane's drive. The gate had been wide open. He couldn't even make out sounds, when the cab driver turned in his seat, faced the back of the cab and matter-of-factly told him the fare. He could see the cabby's lips move, but heard no words, as he looked up the driveway and noted her car still in the driveway, the front door wide open too and looking quite abandoned.

All his instincts told him this was bad; even if he hadn't been calling all day without an answer.

The cab driver spoke again, louder, more pointedly, still he didn't hear. He was praying to see her bound out the front door, having just run back inside for something she might have forgotten. Finally, woodenly he reached in his pocket and threw a hundred at the cab driver. Not waiting for change, Damon got out and headed through that front door, knowing somehow exactly what he would find.

Snow had blown into the entryway; enough snow to know, the door had been open for quite some time, hours and hours. The fire had gone out, probably a long time ago, there were not any hot embers still glowing, no sign of life at all. Her purse sat still open, on the entry table, the way it always did when she was home. As he approached it, he saw a folded note set haphazardly under the edge of her handbag. With increasing dread, he took it and unfolded it, somehow already knowing what it said.

Your girl for my money.
Don't fuck with me!

That was all. That was enough. Simple and to the point, deadly cold, it had no signature, it didn't need one.

Damon felt the pulse pounding at his temples. They had her. They had Mary Jane. He had just gotten her back, and now Mario Corielli, a cold-blooded, murderous butcher had her.

Damon couldn't even think for a few moments, so great was his panic. He still suffered from post concussion symptoms which caused some confusion in this agitated state. Time froze. Tears stung his eyes. He loved this woman, he couldn't stand the fact that she was in danger because of him. It was all her worst fears realized and it was all his fault. He would never forgive himself. Corielli must have followed Mary Jane home after she'd left from visiting him at the hospital. Damon had made himself a target when he'd moved the money, now so was she, only she knew nothing. What if they didn't believe her?

He had to think. He didn't know where they money was, or where the four of them were either. But, he knew their new names and the original plan. He could find them. But even if he gave Mario the money, he didn't believe Corielli would let anyone live. His type, were all about revenge. He had to make an example out of any one who dared cross him, that was where his power would show itself.

No, the answer wasn't that simple. He knew they were watching. He knew they wanted him to lead them to Diane and the money. Just as surely, he knew, if he did; they would all be dead. If he didn't, Mary Jane was still at risk. He was definitely between a rock and a hard place. Yet logic dictated that at least for now, they would hold Mary Jane as a bargaining chip, and for a short time at least that would keep her alive.

In exactly the same time frame Damon stood blackmailed for the money; and Mary Jane was held hostage, it was finally being safely deposited in two different accounts by two happy couples, in a Grand Cayman bank. The relieved group in Cayman didn't have a care in the world, as they left the bank with new accounts instead of the briefcase full of bearer bonds. They were finally completely at ease and content, to no longer be in possession of it. They were completely unaware of Damon and Mary Jane's plight.

Mary Jane was just coming to, from whatever had been on the cloth those men had held over her nose, when they grabbed her just inside the doorway of her home. She had been getting ready to leave for the hospital to go pick Damon up. Had that been this morning or yesterday? She wasn't sure what time it was now. She was disoriented, in a room without a window, so she couldn't tell if it was day or night. She still felt pretty fuzzy in general, finding it was impossible to concentrate. And she had an awful headache.

Unfortunately, she also was able to feel that her hands were numb and cold and tied behind her back. Mary Jane had rolled from her side facing the wall onto her back to look around the room, but, with her hands tied behind her, that position soon became intolerable.

She now rolled up to a sitting position, swinging her legs over the side of the bed. Her ankles were also tied. But not so tightly, and it wasn't too difficult to get upright and set her feet on the floor and her back against the wall. She was on a twin bed shoved in the corner in a very small room. In fact, judging by the size, and a bracket on either side that looked like it had once held a bar, she decided this was actually a large walk-in closet, not a room at all. That explained there being no window. The twin bed almost totally filled the space.

She could hear voices on the other side of the door. Three, she thought, but they were muffled and she wasn't positive. But, if there were three men outside, and no window on her side of the door, and since she was tied up rather tightly, escape seemed pretty unlikely for now.

To remain sane, she back-tracked over everything she could remember about the abduction. They had grabbed her from behind and slipped a hand over her mouth with something on it, ether maybe. A hood had covered her head almost immediately. With her eyes cast to the ground as they grabbed her, she remembered two sets of shoes and pants cuffs. Expensive dress pants, designer patent leather loafers, the touch of a cashmere sweater grabbed by one of her hands before she passed out. It was something. Mary Jane tried to figure out who might kidnap her and why. Who were they? Well dressed and the fact they came prepared with ether or something like it, was her only clue. They had been calm, spoken very little and although efficient in capturing her, had not been overly rough. She didn't remember being hit or hurt in anyway, beyond the fact that being tied up, had caused her arms and hands to ache.

Was it random or connected somehow to Damon? It had to be. She could only guess, but would bet money, it had something to do with the case he had been hurt on. It always came back to that; the damn police force. Then she calmed down. What good would all this supposition do? Her best bet was to keep a clear head.

The doorknob turned, the door swung inward. Now there was barely any room at all, the door actually bumped in to the bed.

A bright light filled the room. There had only been a small night light bulb on inside before. The bright light really caused her head to pound. For a moment her eyes wouldn't, or rather couldn't focus. Her headache exploded.

Finally, she was able to see, and that scared her even more. The man in the room had not bothered to wear a mask, or cover his face in any way. Her immediate thought was that if he wasn't afraid of her seeing him, then he never intended for her, to be able to identify him. The ramifications of that thought were very sobering.

He was short and powerfully built, like a wrestler, his neck almost caricature thick, heavily corded. He was cast perfectly as captor and intimidator. Just one look, told her, escape was impossible, it would be useless to even try.

Several seconds passed, while each appeared to calmly size up the other. Neither spoke. Mary Jane looked much calmer than she felt and the man was impressed with, at least, her facade. She took in the expensive clothes, the very good haircut. He was a thug, but appeared to be a well paid one. She knew that Damon's case had involved a mob connection, and that her home had been used to hide a Diane Lindsey, that they were after. She wondered if this was just a case of mistaken identity. Maybe they thought she was Diane Lindsey.

Somewhere in the back of her mind a random quote ran through her head.

"He who speaks first loses."

She couldn't remember where it came from. But, she continued to maintain her silence and look right back at him, refusing to show any intimidation. It was an effort though. Inside, she was feeling as if she would be sick at any moment. He was not a bad looking man, though certainly not classically good looking either. Rough and strong but with some polish, and in a contradiction to the situation, he looked like he might even be capable, of being kind. Maybe he was when he wasn't holding people captive. Somehow, she got the impression he was not the one she had to fear. Just as a Doberman, is not a problem to a non-threatening person; unless its 'master', commands it to be. So, she continued to portray an outward calm, she absolutely did not feel, picturing him as a Doberman without orders to attack.

He was thinking that hostages usually spoke in rapid-fire panicky spurts. They questioned, cried, begged and generally fell apart. But, not this woman, she was showing dignity; and an amazing calm she couldn't possibly be feeling. It made him admire her in an unbidden flash. Which was out of the question, he knew he couldn't afford to feel anything. He was getting too old for this, he couldn't afford any sentimentality.

The last several years he had helped Mario climb to the point where no one questioned his take-over. An organization couldn't successfully be run from behind prison walls. So, the take-over and murder of Nick Pappas hadn't really been a surprise to anyone, in any of the families. Only the ruthless attack on the supporters of the old don had shocked anyone. Yet it also gained the respect of all the other syndicate families.

For centuries, and from Europe to America, nothing ever really changed. New lions devoured old ones and took over the lead, until they too grew old. Someday, a long time from now, another young lion would try to take Mario out and history would continue to repeat itself. In many ways, they all really had no choices, except to live out their designated roles.

Jason had grown up on the streets. He'd run with Mario since he was thirteen. He'd gone home with him at fourteen and been raised by his parents thereafter, no questions asked. He had watched Mario's father act as a major player, in the old regime. He remembered when the man who was like a father to him, was shot down in the street in another power struggle. A then twenty-year-old Mario hardened and angry, took over for his father.

Jason had cried at the old man's funeral. But, his own son stood like granite next to his mother, dry-eyed. He took her home, kissed her cheek then took over his father's job as an enforcer in the Pappas organization. By twenty-five he was a major player. Now ten years later, no one would question the fact, he had taken over as king, of the corrupt world he now ruled. Jason had climbed that ladder with him, always one rung beneath him. He'd never questioned Mario and his loyalty was unwavering. This man was his brother and

Jason understood loyalty. He held the respected second chair, and perhaps was the only man in the world Mario did care about and trust. Nevertheless Jason was tired, and he hated it, when women were involved.

He liked the old rules that left women and children out of the business. Two years ago he had agreed that Rand Lindsey – the re-manufactured Anton Savion deserved to die. Yet, he had always felt it should have been away from his family. Jason felt his wife and daughter should never have been caught in the fall out. He was glad, not to have been involved in that incident.

A younger Mario had handled it himself and hired from outside the organization, and had lost the money in his haste, along with killing an innocent child and injuring that poor woman. Mario had been so enraged at Anton, and the theft and his betrayal, that Mario had let revenge make him react irrationally and too quickly, when he'd finally been found.

Mario had admitted that, just once afterwards to Jason. Then neither of them ever mentioned it again. Mario wasn't sorry about the innocent being hurt, only about losing the money. Jason knew that Mario didn't really have a conscience.

Now, still in search of the stolen billion dollars; here was yet another innocent woman, being involved unfairly. Jason realized he was beginning to have questions, too many questions and was very conflicted. A commodity that he could not afford and one Mario would view as a weakness. Weakness could never be tolerated; because weakness could make him hesitate.

Money and power had lost their sparkle for him. They controlled so much money now; that a billion dollars didn't even seem to make any difference. Mario's life style and even his own wanted for nothing, except the peace of mind to enjoy them. The organization's tentacles were so long and far reaching; that they had control over more money than most third world countries. Because of the sheer scope of their empire, they had more power than most any other person, living or dead on the earth. In a way, they were monarchs of a small country, a very powerful and rich country that made up its own rules. Yet Jason accepted that he was no longer very excited by any of it. He loved Mario like a brother. Yet he was losing his heart for this business. Jason had no life, no family, and he had the beginnings of a conscience, that he didn't really know what to do with.

Mary Jane was still just looking at him calmly; he had a sudden horrible feeling that she had read his mind. He spun around on his heel and left the room, closing the door again behind him, still having never spoken a word.

Mary Jane felt as if her bones had been liquefied, all rigidity went out of her body, she slumped now. It had taken every ounce of strength and reserve she had ever possessed to appear so calm, and not speak, when all she felt was panic.

Now she still knew absolutely nothing and wondered what she had expected to gain with her bravado. Tears came and slipped quietly down her cheeks and with them so did all of her faked calm.

She just wanted Damon, she wanted to go home, and she wanted to know why she couldn't, where she was, and why she was there. But it looked as if it would be a while before she got any answers. Her tears came faster. Her hands were still tied behind her and her bravado had escaped her. Tears came and slipped quietly down her cheeks, with all of her faked calm sliding away with them.

With her hands still tied behind her she couldn't do anything to stop the flow of tears and had a moment of panic, where she feared, choking and drowning in her own tears and mucus. She rubbed her face against the coarse blanket, to wipe away the tears that had threatened to clog her nose and mouth. Then, she got a hold on herself. They couldn't beat her. She wouldn't allow it. She pulled herself back up to a sitting position, and by sheer force of will, ceased crying.

CHAPTER 20

Damon took Mary Jane's car, her keys had been left in her purse. He drove the dark green Cherokee like a mad man down the mountain road from Mary Jane's house. Colorado had been having terrific snowstorms this winter. Even in a place known for its snow, this was record breaking. It seemed as if the nearly white-out conditions on the road would swallow him up. Yet a combination of terror and determination had him flying at break-neck speeds back toward town. He wanted to talk to someone he could trust, and sadly realized there was no one.

Chase would have been his best bet. However, he was gone, and not even Chase anymore. With the concussion and under such stress he couldn't even remember his new name.

He felt distrustful of the police department. Corielli was a very powerful man, and could afford to buy all the brass he wanted. Damon knew that he already had some of the department in his pocket, from the incident that had culminated in Joan getting shot. And he hoped that his lousy ex-partner was the only snitch, but basically knew that in his position, responsible for Mary Jane's life, it was best not to trust any one at all. He would rely only on himself.

He needed to have a clear mind, and he needed to be able to out-think Corielli. After some thought he decided his own house was the logical place to wait for their next communication. Damon would be at the mercy of a waiting game, until they contacted him.

He would trace the others in a second and bring the money back, if he felt for even one moment, that it would really be the end of all the danger to Mary Jane and Diane. But, he had been a cop too long. He knew these kind of criminals minds all to well. Corielli would feel the need to make a statement, and it would be an ugly one. Now it was up to Damon to think of a way, to keep it from being either Mary Jane or the others.

He couldn't think, he couldn't find any answers, as he drove into his own neighborhood and up his drive. Now the waiting and the agony would begin in earnest.

CHAPTER 21

The banking had been completely effortless, in Grand Cayman at The First National Bank, an amazingly easy and uncomplicated procedure considering the amount of money involved. No wonder, the new power moguls were all banking here now, instead of Switzerland. It was quick, painless and very private. That weighty task behind them, they were off to seize the day.

Janice, James, Susan and Chaz were now on motor scooters on their way to *Hell*, a uniquely named town and probable tourist trap.

It proved to be not much more than some lava formations mysteriously growing out of a bog, a post office featuring 'post marks' from *Hell* and T-shirt shack also determined to commercialize *Hell*. They all had a good laugh at the adventure that flopped.

Then they were off to a sea turtle farm, followed by Stingray City, a world famous sandbar and National Geographic site, where they could get up close and personal with hundreds of gracefully, beautiful stingrays.

That turned out to be the highlight of the day. After a boat ride to the sandbar, they all hit the water. Janice was thoroughly charmed by feeding them and with the help of a local boy, even got to hold one. She laughed out-loud every time one of them took eel from her hand.

"It feels like suction from a vacuum cleaner. It's really incredible. You all have to try this."

The others declined, laughing at her pure enjoyment, as she fed the creatures until they swarmed her and she was completely surrounded by them. The sea around her, was a black and gray swirling mass, of leathery-velvety-sensuous-sea-creatures, part flying and part swimming all around her. She was as delighted as a child.

Susan felt it would panic her to have them all around her like that.

"I think you're out of your mind, what if they sting you?" Susan expressed her concern."

"That only happens if you step on them, silly. Haven't you ever heard the saying, don't bite the hand that feeds you? Besides you heard them explain all that on the boat ride here. This is really too cool!"

Okay, Di, I'll take your word for it."

Everyone froze, Susan had slipped and used Janice's real name. They had all been so careful. Since their lives depended on it, they had been religiously diligent, even in private. Now they heard it as if it had been shouted from the rooftops. It caused a moment of pure panic. Everyone sobered visibly. Janice quit feeding the rays and they dispersed slowly, moving on to the next tourist with a bag of eel morsels. It got very quiet around them.

Finally James laughed.

"Lighten up everyone, no one is paying any attention to us. They came to pet the Stingrays too. I don't even recognize any other guests from the ship. It's really no big deal."

It wasn't either. No one was anywhere around them. If they had drawn any attention to themselves at all, it was only in growing quiet now.

Everyone relaxed, and the moment passed, but it had served as a reminder to them all, to be careful. The day had been wonderful up until the sobering reminder, of why they were on this unbelievable odyssey.

Now each of them in their own way bolstered themselves back up and put the incident behind them. After all, they'd escaped all the bad guys and they were safe and having a ball.

If they only knew, what had taken place in Denver that morning, they wouldn't have been able to enjoy anything at all.

CHAPTER 22

It had grown very quiet, on the other side of the door. Mary Jane couldn't see her watch, since her hands were still tied behind her. Her impression was that it was night, but she didn't know why she thought that. Perhaps it was quiet, because they were going to sleep in the other room. It was so hard to grasp how much time had elapsed. She didn't know how long she'd been here, or how long since the man, had come in the last time.

It felt like forever and yet she couldn't have actually guessed definitively. Time was judged by things you did, reading, a movie, or a conversation. But, in a void, with no intellectual stimulation, it became very abstract, and thus very hard to measure.

It was beginning to drive her crazy, so much nothingness. The truth was people spend very little time, not being involved in some activity or other. When absolutely nothing is happening, it becomes impossible to gage the time. This sensory deprivation was driving her crazy. At this point, she wanted something to happen, anything at all. She decided to quit waiting and push the envelope.

"Hey out there. Someone, please, I need to use a bathroom."

Her voice came out like a frog, it was really weak and sounded unnatural. But, as she'd spoken, she realized, that was a way to judge the time frame. If she hadn't had to use a bathroom yet, it probably hadn't been more than eight hours, since the abduction. Her bladder was a measuring device. Eight hours was pretty much her outside limit, between bathroom uses. It was amazing how reassuring just figuring this much out was to her. When you have no control over things and don't know what's happening, any revelation helps you feel more in control. Using deductive reason was very satisfying.

The door opened again. The same man stood in the doorway. He had a sardonic smile on his face.

"Well, you can speak."

He crossed the space in one stride and reached down to untie her.

She stayed perfectly still while he undid first her hands and then her feet. She was grateful that the restraints were gone, but still resentful that they had been there in the first place.

"Please, may I use a bathroom now?"

She asked politely, but a little angrily as well. Boy, she hated having to ask for basic human decency.

"Absolutely, follow me. You can have something to eat too, if you're interested. We aren't monsters, and we don't intend to hurt you. We will make you as comfortable as possible."

"Will you tell me, why I'm here?"

"No, it's not really important that you know that. But don't worry; I don't think you will be here very long."

He took her through a main room, which looked like an average apartment living room, into a small inside bathroom, again with no window. He let her go in alone and pulled the door closed behind him.

She was alone again, this time at least untied, but there was definitely nowhere to escape. It was humiliating having someone, a stranger waiting right on the other side of the door. She ran the water in the sink and splashed her face with the cool water. Then she took care of other things, all leaving the water running. It gave her a modicum of privacy. There were no vents or attic access she had noted.

She considered a shower, it would make her human and more alert, but there were no towels, except one small used hand towel. Plus, she didn't really feel comfortable taking her clothes off, with strange men on the other side of an unlocked door. That would have to wait. Splashing her face had helped. She rubbed her wrists, trying to return some circulation to her hands. She questioned making an attempt to knock, or see if anyone might help from the other side of the bathroom wall, but determined that her chances were slim, and it would only anger her captors.

She had been correct. There were three men. She wouldn't stand a chance of escape. She had noted only one window in the main room, but they were several floors up, and it didn't appear to open, at her cursory glance. She thought about screaming for help. But, she figured if that would have done any good, they would have gagged her. Since they hadn't, it probably wouldn't accomplish anything, other than to piss them off. Why make them angry for nothing. She was determined to maintain calm at all costs. A model prisoner would have a better chance as time went on, or so she hoped.

"Thank you. I am thirsty. There was no glass in there, may I have a drink to take back in with me, please."

"We have food if you want to eat, pasta, bread, salad, wine."

"I don't feel very hungry, but maybe just a little, thank you. At least I won't starve to death."

She decided to be charming if she could manage it. Thinking, her abductors were more likely to treat her better that way, and maybe even tell her something that could help her figure out what was going on.

Jason knew all the things that were running through her mind, he knew hostage mentality inside out, a fact which made him more than a little ashamed. More and more he found himself questioning the quandaries in which his job put him. Yet a lifetime of following Mario was a tough habit to consider breaking. Who was he, if not an enforcer for his friend?

"Come on over and sit down."

He indicated the small dinette table. He was serving a wedge of lasagna from a pan in the oven while he spoke. He also pulled a salad bowl from the refrigerator and threw some antipasto in a small wooden bowl. Next, he set a bread basket containing breadsticks on the table. Then the plate and bowl in front of her; complete with some silverware and a linen napkin. He did it all with such ease. It told her he was comfortable, here in this kitchen. He had reached into every cabinet with familiarity, and linen napkins were not a temporary place item. It all signified to her that this place was not new to him. So Mary Jane deduced that screaming probably would accomplish nothing but an adverse reaction in her captors. She dismissed that option again for good.

The two other men sat in the living room concentrating over a chessboard. They appeared to be ignoring her, however she was pretty sure they were alert to everything going on and just chose to look laid back. Quite honestly the whole thing reminded her of an old James Cagney movie, except it was all too real, and she couldn't just turn off the TV; and wake up in her own bed at home, safe with Damon beside her. She knew he must be worried sick, but also thought somehow he would find her. She had to believe that.

As she was thinking, she took a few bites of the food and realized that she really was hungry, a fact which seemed incongruous given the situation. It was also surprisingly good. She found herself saying so out-loud.

"This is excellent lasagna."

It seemed so odd to speak a normal sentiment in such an abnormal circumstance, that she froze after saying it, a little confused. What was the proper etiquette when kidnapped anyway, she thought again. Oddly enough, it all felt more awkward then frightening; sitting here eating a hot meal. The men seemed fairly non-threatening, they were feeding her and treating her humanely. Maybe they meant her no harm after all and it would all be over soon. However Mary Jane feared, she was probably 'whistling in the dark'. Yet, for now, that was better than letting the fear she felt take over at the glaring fact that nothing had been done, to keep her from being able to identify them.

A hood over her head or keeping her blindfolded might have been initially more unnerving, but it would also signify that there was some small chance that she would someday be free again. This total lack of concern with being seen, indicated a much more sinister final outcome.

About half of the food on her plate disappeared while she was thinking. She was surprised that she'd eaten so much.

The man sat across from her, maintaining a steady inscrutable gaze, and not uttering a word. It unnerved her a little, so she broke the silence and got straight to the point.

"Why am I here?"

He answered her without hesitation.

"You are simply a bargaining chip to get to a large sum of money that belongs to my boss."

"I'm not Diane Lindsey."

"We know that, but your cop friend took the money out of her trust for her. So he knows where she is. By the same token, he knows where the money is. That money was stolen from us. We want it back. It's simple really. If your friend gives my boss the money back, then you'll go free."

He said it all so matter-of-factly that Mary Jane believed him.

"What if you don't get the money back?"

She asked so softly, he almost couldn't hear her.

He shrugged. It was a chilling answer. She was suddenly very tired, as if deflated. All her energy escaped her. She set her fork down and folded her napkin.

I'm ready to go back to my room." She said quietly.

"Please don't tie me up again. I can't do anything, not in that cubicle and without a window."

"I wasn't going to." Jason replied not unkindly.

They crossed the room again and she went back to confinement. This time at least she knew what to think about. But once inside Mary Jane found that she was too tired to think at all. She thankfully fell asleep. Sleep was the best way to cope with such close quarters. It was a welcome escape. In sleep her dreams took her back to Damon; where she most wanted to be.

In her dream she and Damon were walking along a beach, a beautiful white sandy beach, seagulls called out loudly. The sky was blue and clear. There were no waves and the water was like glass. Far out on the horizon an old wooden sailboat with oddly shaped sails moved along slowly and slightly keeled over. It was a lovely tranquil scene. Damon was holding her hand and they stopped to kiss; a light, gentle, happy kiss. Then suddenly the clouds turned dark and lightening cracked loudly, hitting the ground jaggedly at her feet. Damon was gone. Waves pounded the shore violently, threatening to pull her out to sea. More lightning and thunder struck practically at her feet. The next wave curled over her head, and drowning, she couldn't breathe.

She awoke in a panic from the dream. The night light bulb still lightly illuminated the closet. Not being tied up, she could read her watch. It was eight-ten. She had come in and gone to sleep around midnight. She had slept eight straight hours and yet it seemed like minutes.

She couldn't bear the thought of a whole day cramped up in here with nothing to do. She would lose her mind. She stretched and called out through the door.

"Please can I come out, and use the bathroom?"

The door was opened almost immediately. At least they were considerate captors, she thought idly.

A fact proved even further a moment later. As he walked her back through the living area to the bathroom, he handed her a small drugstore bag.

"I thought you might need some things, and there are clean towels and a new sweat-suit in the bathroom. I thought you might like some clean clothes."

"Thanks."

She nodded and went on into the bathroom. She was irrationally grateful for this consideration. Perhaps just grateful they weren't monsters. Yet shouldn't she be angry? It was hard to know what to feel. Her heart seemed to be protecting her from abject fear, allowing her to see the little indicators of humanness on their part, as a positive sign. It was probably just a coping mechanism to ward off a panic that lay right under the surface. But it helped.

She stepped under the hot shower and stopped thinking for a while, and just enjoyed the hot stinging spray. She used the shampoo and conditioner that was in the bag and then the mousse and comb when she got out. The sweats were a little big, but soft and clean, and she was happy to find a toothbrush and toothpaste too.

When she finished she felt revived, and able to shake the bad dream.

"Now a cup of coffee would be great." Was her only thought.

As it so happened, he poured her one, as soon as she came out. He was part criminal and part mind reader. These little side thoughts helped her keep it together. As long as she kept a sense of humor she felt she would stay sane. He broke into her daydreaming.

"I make a pretty decent omelet, if you're interested."

He said matter-of-factly.

"I'm not much of a breakfast person, but thanks, do you have any fruit?"

It all seemed so normal, but of course it was anything but. Yet they continued to converse relatively, comfortably, considering she didn't even know the name of the man who was making her breakfast.

"We have a cantaloupe and some yogurt if you'd like them."

"That would be fine, thanks."

It was crazy, how normal the conversation sounded, but it made it all a little less frightening. She thought about everything that had happened and realized she was adapting. A person could get used to anything really. It was all a survival mechanism. Mary Jane was a survivor. She had never realized that before. She was rather proud of how calm she was; and how well she was handling everything. What she didn't know was that Jason was thinking the same thing.

He was totally impressed by how coolly she handled being abducted and held captive. He would have expected panic, anger, or fear; not this total calm. She was amazing, unlike anyone else he'd ever seen handle this stressful situation. She was polite, even casual with him. He didn't even know if he would handle the situation so well, if the roles were reversed. Probably not, he was a lot less naiveté about how these things usually turned out. That thought made him a little sad. He wished he was able to believe in happy endings. The truth was, he couldn't because he'd never seen one.

That fact alone, made him think again, just how brave she really was.

CHAPTER 23

Damon spent a few hours running checks on the identities that Diane, Joan Chase and Mark had left with. He used a brand new cell phone, avoiding his own home line which no doubt would be bugged. He made his calls in the attic sure no one would have planted any devices there, and eventually he hit pay dirt.

James and Janice Vann, and Chaz and Susan Mayer had sailed out of Miami on the ship, *My Fair Lady*, less than a week ago. He could catch a flight tonight and meet them at their next port of call, St. Bart in the Netherlands Antilles. Considering that there was little doubt he was being watched, and he wasn't about to lead Mario Corielli straight to them, he also knew he would have to be very careful to make sure he wasn't being followed.

Mary Jane meant more to him than anyone in the world. It was hard to even think straight, with her life in the balance. Yet he had to consider the others too.

Damon cursed the mob, the situation, his vocation and everything else that had placed him in this position.

Not normally a drinker, suddenly he felt like really tying one on. However after only two scotch and waters, his head was pounding to such an extent he couldn't even think. It had been a long day, and he was still weak. Despite his despair, he fell asleep on the couch, the phone on his chest, still willing it to ring.

CHAPTER 24

In Grand Cayman the day had been unbeatable, azure blue skies, stingrays, boating, just another incredible day in paradise. The four of them were totally, happily, sun soaked, and exhausted as they re-boarded '*My Fair Lady*'.

"Home again, home again, jiggity jig."

Susan mumbled softly as they got out of the transport boat, returning them to their ship.

"It is good to know there is a nice cool cabin, with a big bed in it, that my key fits. I could definitely use a nap before dinner. I am the laziest slug in the world, but I love it all. And I love all of you. What a day!"

Janice spoke contentedly.

James replied.

"You go on and get a nap my love; I need to write a while. I'll grab the laptop and head to the library for a few hours of work. And I'll catch up with you in the shower before dinner."

James raised one eyebrow and winked.

Chaz teased him back.

"More information than we need to know, buddy."

Then he directed his next comment to Susan.

"As for you my love, I think you could use a nap too. How about it if I tuck you in for a couple of hours too?"

"No argument here."

Susan rested her head on his shoulder.

"How about you joining me?"

"Absolutely, just try to stop me."

So each couple went their own way and planned to meet at dinner again in three hours. Life was good. In a week, life had evolved from running for their lives in to a vacation in paradise. They were all so at ease. They couldn't have even imagined the trouble that was brewing back in Denver.

Trouble, Damon had to deal with all alone, and that put Mary Jane in such a frightening position. None of them would be enjoying themselves at all if they'd only known.

Susan stepped through the cabin door and turned to face Chaz, pushing the door gently closed, behind him. She slipped both arms around his neck and kissed him so softly, it was as if a butterfly had brushed his lips with its wings, which was her most endearing feature and uniquely her. Then with the same concentrated softness and very, very slowly, she proceeded to kiss his eyelids and cheeks the same way. Deliciously she tantalized him, until he could barely stand, the nearly not touching sweetness of her.

She kissed his ears and then his neck all with a slow fiery trail of butterfly softness, a gentleness that was almost torture. As she reached his collarbone, she began to take tiny nibbles. Whenever he tried to return her attentions she held his hands down to his sides and continued to take all the initiative. She would allow him no reciprocation at all.

Eventually, still never uttering a word, she led him to the bed. There gently and in slow motion she lay back onto the mattress, pulling him down beside her, still holding his hands captive. She raised each hand singularly, and kissed and sucked each finger, tantalizing him so exquisitely and slowly, that he thought he would lose his mind. He tasted of the ocean and salt, and his skin was warm from the sun. She loved the taste of him, the touch of him, and she loved that he was allowing her all this time without pushing for more or taking over. His body was beautiful, hard as a rock, finely defined, but his skin was so soft and smooth that she couldn't imagine anything ever feeling better to her, petting him was a delight. Susan slowly undressed him and kissed every inch of him ever so slowly and as gentle as a breeze. No part of him was exempt from her exquisite torture, not toes, knees, thighs, or buttocks, back, and shoulders. Soon he was moaning softly in a frenzy of want, almost purring at times, his body quivering with need.

Then when she had left no part of him untasted, unloved, unexplored, she quit, indicating he remain still for her.

Susan stood at the foot of the bed and with his eyes looking at her lovingly, she shed her clothes very slowly and then lay back down beside him, pulling him over onto and into her. Yet now he extradited himself from her, and proceeded to enjoy her body with the same thorough slowness that she had shown him. He stroked every inch of her passionately, part gentle massage, part kissing, part tiny nibbles, until she begged him to enter her.

Her fingers entwined in the back of his hair. Filled with want, she sucked his tongue into her mouth and pulled him onto her, and with one smooth simultaneous motion he was in her, and she enveloped him in a passion that grew deeper with every passing moment and movement.

They spoke loving, sweet words, as all lovers do, meaning every word. Unconcerned with repetition or what they actually said, but rather fueled with the feeling that everything was completely and totally right because they were together. Hours had passed and still they could not get enough of just the closeness, and they were still tracing lazy fingers over each others nude bodies when the announcement came over the speaker that dinner would be served in fifteen minutes.

Laughing, at where the last three hours had gone; they scrambled through a shower and glowing, with still damp hair, Susan wearing no make-up except an afterglow. They headed in high spirits to the dining room. They were grateful it was a casual evening. As they slipped into their seats sheepishly, and looked across the table at Janice and James, they all found themselves laughing. They were also hastily thrown together; and equally contrite-looking and soon they were all chatting and laughing about everything and nothing. They all delighted in simply being alive. Another fabulous dinner, a show and some dancing awaited them. Life couldn't get any more perfect.

Their dinner was incredible. Each of them enjoyed a different masterpiece. The ship's chefs were indeed culinary artists, as interested in making the plates beautiful; as making the food delicious. Janice had a broiled, stuffed salmon, filled with crabmeat and crowned with decorative vegetable curls. Susan's plate was painted with an apricot glaze, on which rested butterfly shrimp toasted in fresh coconut. James had a Chateaubriand in a gorgeous flaky crust, topped with a pastry rose and intricate leaves. Chaz had chosen the chef's pasta with lobster and scallops. It was served in an exotic looking pasta woven bowl that looked too pretty to even eat.

The four of them pigged out and even had decadent desserts. Strangely all of them were ravenous. They were becoming very spoiled on this cruise. It was hard to even imagine a time, when they hadn't all been together. This voyage had taken them away from reality and transported them into pure joy.

"Was it really such a short time ago, that I didn't even know who I was?"

Janice wondered out loud.

"I just wish I'd come home sooner, to help you."

Susan said still feeling badly that she hadn't known her friend needed her.

"It's all water under the bridge now, all's well that end's well. Right? Everything has worked out now."

James wanted to get the less serious mood back.

Chaz chimed in, "Everything happens for a reason, if it hadn't all happened exactly like it did, we might not all be here, so I have no complaints. Beside me is the lady who makes me the happiest man in the world. And I know you two are as happy as we are. So I say, let's drink to all of us, and to right now, this minute. The past is gone, and best forgotten."

"Here, here!"

"Cheers."

Everyone headed out of the dining room to go see the show in high spirits.

CHAPTER 25

There was certainly no celebrating going on in Denver. Damon was awake now, rabidly willing the phone to ring. Surely Mario Corielli would make contact soon. However, he seemed at the moment, intent on making him sweat. Damon was losing his mind just waiting. He wanted a chance to talk to Mary Jane. He needed to know she was all right. He paced the room for about the millionth time. It was ten a.m. Something had to happen soon.

Finally it rang, and for a second he was frozen, unable to reach out and take the receiver out of the cradle. He said a quick mental prayer and answered the phone.

"Matthews here, go ahead."

"I like that, straight to the point, so I'll be the same. You have one week to bring me a billion dollars. I'll call you here exactly one week from now. You better have the money!"

"What assurances do I have that you won't hurt Mary Jane?"

"None!" The voice was flat and as cold as ice.

"Not good enough, I want to talk to her or there is no deal."

"That's not going to happen. But she is alive and safe now. And when you give me the money in a week, I will return her to you in the same shape. I have no reason to hurt her, unless you give me one. I am after all, a businessman, and this is business. I'm ready to close this chapter when I get my money back. Anton got what he deserved, so keep that in mind, you can't cross me and get away with it!"

"I don't want any more innocent people to die, if you get your money will you leave everyone else alone?"

Damon pushed again for assurance.

A deep chuckle resonated over the phone. "Just get my money, detective. No promises except on your girlfriend, you're damn lucky that I'm giving you that much. That's the deal, take it or leave it."

The phone went dead in his hand, he continued to hold it anyway, until a recording sounded, announcing that, "This phone is off the hook, please hang up and try your call again."

It startled him, and he did as it requested and hung up.

Mario had as good as told him he would still kill Diane if he got a chance. Could he trade Diane's life for Mary Jane's?

He knew he had to get to the money without leading them to Diane, or rather to Janice. Damon had to make sure he lost any tail they had on him, and then get to the others without leading Mario to them too. Then he had to get the money, and he had to get back in a week. He had to, in order to save the woman he now realized, he couldn't live without. Hardest of all, he had to do it all praying that Mary Jane was still all right now, and that they would keep their word, even though the money would come up a little short.

He remembered that Diane had never wanted the money, so he knew that she would have no problem giving it back. But where would that leave all of them. Even if he managed not to lead anyone to Diane, there was every possibility Mario would kill him, when he handed over the money. He'd promised Mary Jane's safety and no one else. That both reassured him and chilled him.

If he couldn't get to Diane, there was every chance that killing Damon would be his next revengeful choice, to make a statement. Someone would have to die to make a point that Coreilli was in charge of the situation. The money wasn't really the issue, control was.

All in all, Damon had few choices, but to get the money within the week, what ever the outcome after that turned out to be didn't matter; he had to make every effort to keep Mary Jane alive, even if it meant letting a monster win.

CHAPTER 26

Mary Jane had spent a very long morning, in what she had begun to think of as; her room. She looked at her watch every couple of minutes. Time went by so unbelievably slowly. It was beginning to drive her insane. She hated so much 'nothing' time. She desperately needed something to occupy her. She would have given anything for just a sketch pad and charcoals, or even a child's cheap watercolor set and a pad of watercolor paper, or some clay and a couple of sculpting tools, absolutely anything. It had been years, since a day had gone by without some artistic expression. She needed the release, especially now, under so much stress.

Being alone with nothing but her thoughts was a uniquely odorous sort of torture. She fluctuated between fear, anger, and boredom, uncertain which was worse. She wanted to see Damon again, and alternated between the desire to tell him she loved him and that she hated him. She had no way of knowing, he'd already decided to quit the force for her. So her age-old hatred of his job, raised its ugly head. First her parents and now maybe even she would die as some criminal's vendetta reigned. And she couldn't stand to think of Damon at risk again too. After all she'd already deducted that if they were holding her hostage, it was because, they still needed to manipulate him, to do something. So he must be alive; at least for now. She clung to that thought.

She remembered the way the man had put it.

"You are just a bargaining chip, my boss just wants the money."

So until they got the money; she and Damon would be kept alive. But after they got it, would they really let her go? Would they let Damon live? Maybe she'd read too much Mario Puzo, but she didn't think the whole thing could just end with them getting to live happily ever after. These were serious bad guys, and she had seen their faces. Damon had crossed them, just by being the honest cop he was and doing his job. So there was probably no way in hell that they would ever be free or together again. The saddest part was she would never be able to tell Damon, how much she still loved him and how sorry she was for the wasted lonely years. There had never been anyone else for her. Damon had been her first love and now she would never get to tell him, he would be her last.

Her reverie was interrupted by a knock at the door and then it opened.

"Would you like some lunch?"

Mary Jane glanced at her watch, surprised to see it was now thankfully noon. Time had finally passed while she was thinking. A break from claustrophobia was a welcome respite. She needed to stretch and moving around would be a blessing.

"Oh yes, please."

She followed him out and back to her seat at the table. Anything to break the monotony and the worrying; was a blessing. She took note it was always the same man who came to get her, and talked to her. The men in the other room were like furniture, just there. They never spoke to her, or came into the same room. One of them was even different from before. Did they really think they needed three big men to contain her? The thought tickled her, macabre though it was. Maybe it was in some sort of gangster handbook of protocol that it took three men in a hostage situation. Her thoughts helped her relieve some of her tension. She decided to try to charm her captor a little, to get something she wanted. He didn't seem like a monster, and she wouldn't ask for very much.

"Listen, I know this is an odd request, but I am going stark raving mad with nothing to do. I am an artist. Could I possibly get a sketch pad and a pencil from you, before I get put back in my cell?"

She asked with pride and also a humility, in a way that showed strength, not in anyway begging; her head was held high, yet not arrogantly.

Jason had to admire the request and the way in which it was made. He tossed her a sheet of notebook paper and a Bic pen.

"Just make a list of the supplies you need, and be specific. I'll send out for what you need from an art supply store."

He set a Caesar salad in front of her with grilled chicken on top.

"Now eat."

Then he poured her an ice tea from a pitcher on the table.

"Thank you. This looks delicious."

But she didn't rush to take a bite. Mary Jane was still excitedly making a list, like a child at Christmas.

She wasn't back in her room very long when he opened the door and set a large bag down inside on the floor. Like a kid she rushed to open and examine everything. She had been specific and he had gotten her everything she'd asked for and more. She was still laying it all out, when she realized the door had closed and he was gone, not even waiting for a thank you. She returned to setting up a small portable easel, something she hadn't even put on the list, the need had just been anticipated. There was even a very small mini drafting board, although the bed would have to serve as her chair. There seemed to be a basic starter set, for every media. She had canvas and oils, water color paper and watercolors, sketchpads, a charcoal set, and even basic sculptor tools and clay. At least four times more than what she had requested, she couldn't help but be a little touched and grateful. Although she knew she had to beware of hostage syndrome, she couldn't help but be pleased.

Surely a man who treated her so well, wouldn't kill her, she uttered a silent prayer.

CHAPTER 27

Damon had given it serious thought and he had an answer of sorts, though still in the formative stages. He knew that he'd be followed, so he had to lead them on a wild goose chase and then lose them. An embryonic plan had formed in his mind. He would leave on a flight scheduled for Seattle, because it would be best to head the opposite direction. Then if he chose a Seattle flight that touched down briefly in Reno, he could get off in Reno, watching for a tail. It was his guess they wouldn't be on the actual flight, but rather planning to pick up tracking him in Seattle. At least that's what he could hope for. From that point he'd use a phony I.D. he had for undercover work. He could fly anywhere, watching carefully behind him. If it looked safe by the time he reached that next destination, only then he would head for South America. That was the ship's next stop after St. Bart. He couldn't make that port of call, what with the diversion in the wrong direction first. But he figured he could catch up with them in Devil's Island, French Guyana in two days time and still allow himself several decoy flights.

Then Diane would have to fly with him back to Grand Cayman, give him the money and he would head back to Denver. She could catch up to her cruise in Guayaguil, Ecuador. He felt it was still the safest place for her – to stay on the cruise. As long as he didn't lead anyone to her, she would still be okay there.

Then he alone would have to contend with an angry mob boss. He could only pray they would keep their word and let Mary Jane go. He wouldn't place any bets on his own life after that. The odds wouldn't be good.

He threw a bag together without much thought. He hoped to be gone no more than five days if he could manage it. One day headed the wrong way, one to reach the right destination, a day to find Diane or rather Janice, he had to quit slipping. He was the one who had drilled pointedly into them, before they'd left.

Then it would probably be the next morning before he could fly with Janice back to Grand Cayman, where he was sure they would have banked the money, since that had always been the original plan. He hoped they could make it back to Grand Cayman, that same day and before banking hours were over. Then Damon would try to start home that night, and if not the very next morning which would be day five. Worst case scenario he would still be traveling day six, yet home late that day. If he got really lucky, and he and Janice could get a flight out the same morning she disembarked, then they'd save a day. He was trying to figure out every eventuality.

He thought about calling ship to shore now, to guarantee expediency, but that would be foolhardy. He could count on the fact that he was being watched and most likely listened to. His place was almost definitely bugged and his phone tapped. His cell phone if confiscated, would give them all the numbers that had been called on it, so until he was out of danger he couldn't give anything away on it.

He might try a ship to shore call somewhere in transit after he was sure he wasn't being watched or followed anymore.

Damon had booked the flight to Seattle from his phone and paid on his credit card. The flight would leave in two more hours. He didn't need too much, so he was out of his house very quickly, driving his car to the airport. Leaving Mary Jane's car in his driveway, as he passed it he'd felt a lump rise in his throat. Before he'd even left his block, a car fell in right behind him, making no secret of the fact that they were tailing him.

Then at the airport check in counter, two men flanked him being totally obvious. Then one of them stepped up to the counter and boldly asked to buy a ticket on his flight. They weren't even trying to be subtle. Damon froze. This was going to make it much more difficult. Then he heard the agent tell the man the flight was already overbooked and the next flight was in one hour, if he wanted to buy a seat on that one. Relief flooded over him.

Damon turned and headed to the gate. They fell in behind him, even without having obtained a ticket but were stopped at airport security without boarding passes. He never thought he'd be grateful for 9-11 precautions. They could no longer intimidate him and make sure he boarded that plane. Yet, he had no doubt that they would have someone else waiting at the other end. He just prayed they wouldn't have anyone watching in Reno.

CHAPTER 28

The light in the closet presented a problem at first, so after struggling for a short time, to see what she was painting, in so much shadow; Mary Jane exasperatedly knocked on the door. As before, he responded quickly, and the door was opened.

Forgetting to be polite, her artist's temperament kicked in.

"I can't see worth a damn in here. I promise I won't make a break for it. May I please come out and work by the window? I must have natural light."

She practically stomped her foot every bit the temperamental artist.

He smiled, and then he laughed out-loud.

"I see I've intimidated the hell out of you."

"I'm sorry."

She surprised herself, laughing too.

"But when I work, I can't think of anything else. I wasn't very tactful with my request. You so kindly brought me all these things, now I just want to be able to see and move about, so that I can use them. I really won't try to escape. When I'm working I think of nothing else, and that's the truth."

He believed her. She showed such passion talking about her art. He wished he felt that kind of passion for anything in his life. He admired her and realized he wanted to give her whatever she wanted, even if the others would grumble. There were unwritten rules that said he shouldn't let her out, except at brief times; just to eat, etc. A person in his position couldn't afford to get to know their captives, it was important to stay strangers, because.......

Jason put an immediate stop to that unfinished train of thought.

"Okay, we'll let you work by the window for a while and see how it goes."

He had stopped any hint of a smile and said this almost gruffly. He turned his back and walked away, but he left the door open.

A bit taken aback by the abrupt chill emanating from him ,Mary Jane was still quick to grab the easel, a canvas and her palette and set up by the window, turning her back on the two other men, sitting in their chairs over their customary chess board. She missed the disapproving, grudging looks the men in the living room shot at the man, who had let her out.

She only saw the way the natural light hit the canvas. Soon she was completely absorbed in her painting, watching the work materialize out of some amazing secret place in her imagination. The men tried not to be caught watching, from across the room, through hooded disinterested eyes. They begrudged her intrusion and didn't wish to humanize their hostage in their own minds.

A scene soon emerged, first softly as if out of a thick fog, and then with more and more detail. It was a ruin, maybe Roman, maybe Greek but definitely mysterious and very gothic. Soon the leader couldn't help but just stare openly. An ethereal woman wearing a diaphanous garment appeared in the picture, she was crying quite openly, in a way that affected the viewer. He could almost feel her sorrow. Jason realized he felt connected to and even felt somewhat guilty, as if he had somehow caused the pain, being projected onto the canvas. Of course he had to accept the very real fact that he was responsible for the artist's situation and that it would be quite frightening to be her. Of course the woman in the painting, was a reflection of the artist in front of him now, and he had caused this sadness that was emotions being vomited onto the canvas, straight from her fears.

His eyes caught Michael's and he sensed the disapproval, he knew that Mario would be hearing about this. Never getting involved was a cardinal rule. He couldn't afford to be human; and he couldn't afford to practice empathy or sympathy.

He couldn't feel or care, or have any real interests outside the business. He shook his head hard, holding an internal argument with himself.

"So what was the point of his life any way. He was tired, weary of a life that played over and over, the exact same scenarios, except with different players. How many Mary Jane's had there been?"

Maybe three other women had been used over the years to make men do something they didn't want to do; innocent women, that had little to do with anything.

"Why."

He questioned himself now?

"Why did he always do what he was told? What would he have been if not this? Maybe he'd have had a normal life, an honest job, a family even. What had happened to those other women?"

He tried to remember, than he blanched. Jason remembered; two of the three, were returned dead, as a lesson. He had returned them to Mario alive, after their 'whomever', did or didn't do 'whatever', had been demanded of them. Mario had still killed two of the three! Mario had no conscience and maybe for way too long now, Jason hadn't had enough backbone to resist doing whatever he was told. But, he knew he had a conscience himself, no matter how unpracticed; because right now it seemed to be slapping him in the face. It was a bold revelation. He didn't want any more regrets to live with.

Jason had never really gotten over the death of Alexandra Lindsey. He had seen all the pictures in the paper, and he knew all about the horrible effect, that the accident, had inflicted on her poor mother, Diane Lindsey; and then what a long awful recovery she had survived. He finally felt, 'enough was enough' and now the detective's girlfriend; another innocent, was victim to Corielli's lust to win. Jason knew it wasn't really the money.

Anton and Mario had once been close; they'd grown up together. They'd had youthful recklessness in common, had liked the same kind of trashy women, and had partied together; all when Jason was still too young for any of that. But, he remembered Anton, and how cool he had seemed. Only Jason knew, that taking all that money from Pappas, had been a joint effort between Mario and Anton. Only Anton had made the terrible mistake of double-crossing Mario too.

When Anton got away with all the money, it enraged Mario. He became really cold and truly cruel after Anton double-crossed him. From that time on, he hadn't been able to let it go, or put it behind him; not with the money still out there. Anton and Mario's deal, had been a pivotal episode in Mario's life; and had helped fashion the monster and cartel boss that Mario had become afterwards. Jason felt until Mario got the money back, he would never get over Anton's betrayal. But Jason couldn't ignore the fact, that so many innocent people were becoming involved. He suddenly felt much older than his twenty-nine years, and was bone and soul weary with vendettas. And more than anything else, he felt sorry, for this passionate artist, painting frantically in front of him, pouring out her own emotions.

Jason wished he had anything he felt as passionate about. He wished he cared that much, about something. He didn't even have a hobby, unless cooking counted. That was the one thing he did, that he really enjoyed, and so did everyone else.

If not for Jason, the men would have to make do, on take-out food. He took pride, in the fact that everyone seemed to love his cooking. But then why not, he had learned it all from Dottie Corielli, in the warmth of her home and kitchen, where he had grown-up from fourteen on, treated like a son by Mario's mother.

Mama Dottie was still the most wonderful woman and cook in the world. Yet in typical old-world style, she knew nothing of the business and never asked. She had even buried her husband without questioning why he'd been gunned down. She went to church everyday. She baby sat her grandchildren, Mario's sister's kids. She cooked, she gardened, and she never asked Mario; as she had never asked his Father about the business. He supposed she came from generations of women who played 'ostrich' well.

He'd been thinking a long time. Lost in thought, he was startled when Michael shook his shoulder.

"It's after one boss. How about we eat? Huh!"

"Yea, okay it will just take a few minutes."

And he headed for the kitchen.

Both men were looking at him strangely, but neither said anything else. Jason was the boss. They had little interest, as long as they were fed. But they were definitely not happy about Mary Jane in their midst. It was uncomfortable. They never wanted to humanize a hostage, and it was disconcerting having her in their space. They couldn't totally ignore, how beautiful her painting was, which made her more real to them; not just any nameless, faceless woman, on the other side of a door.

CHAPTER 29

The show had been outstanding. *My Fair Lady's* theater productions could rival Broadway. The talent was phenomenal and absolutely first-rate. Tonight had been *Phantom of the Opera*. The music was so beautiful and so haunting, and performed by Michael Crawford himself.

Janice was still singing softly as she and James entered the suite. He was holding her hand as he had through the entire performance. She literally felt dizzy she was so in love with him. Even just sitting beside him and feeling his hand in hers made her happy. She thought back to her years with Rand and felt terribly sad. She unfortunately remembered everything now. She and Rand had shared nothing, although he'd been charming in the beginning that had ended almost immediately after the wedding. She'd obviously been in love with the idea of matrimony more than the actual man had warranted, and motherhood had fulfilled her even when he didn't. But knowing now, what she knew love could be, she knew what a travesty their marriage had been. She would never settle for a marriage like that again. What she now shared was amazing.

At the point in her life when Rand had come along, she had begun to think that there was something seriously wrong with her. She hadn't felt anything for anyone since her first boyfriend, Bob Teaney. He'd died in a car wreck when she was sixteen, and she had blown the memory of him up to proportions, that only teenage angst could. So no one else had ever measured up.

When Rand came along, he at least appeared perfect. He was so good looking, and although a little aloof, he was very attentive, at first. Of course, she was also influenced by the fact, that all her girlfriends had swooned and declared him a real catch. When you are an innocent, that can be enough, silly as it seemed now. Although she remembered clearly; Joan's (oops Susan's) opinion had changed rather quickly and she'd advised her to reconsider just before the wedding. Now she wished she'd listened to that advice.

After they were married she got wrapped up in being a perfect wife and homemaker. He did provide a lovely home. She decorated and cooked, and figured that if they were not very close, well that was just the way real life was.

She kept so busy and had so many friends and in the beginning at least Rand was always polite, even if not particularly warm. Then she'd become pregnant and was so caught up in the pregnancy, followed by being absorbed with the counting of fingers and toes, when her beautiful baby girl arrived. She stopped worrying about him being distant. She was an ecstatic new mother, completely immersed in the role, and loving every moment with her baby daughter Alexandra, her little *Lexie.*

But when her baby was fifteen months old and very ambulatory and would delightedly hug her father's legs, or try to scramble up on his lap, she watched in despair, as he would push her off, like so much lint on his pant leg. He had never wanted to hold her, never helped with a diaper change. She had always believed that he would come around, when Lexie wasn't such a baby. Self delusion had been a coping tool. Diane had so wanted to have the successful marriage that her parents had once shown her.

Instead, as time went on, he showed only slightly veiled distaste, which broke her heart to watch. She tried to talk to him, and he walked out and stayed gone for several days. So she started back to school intent on getting her degree, and being able to support herself and Lexie someday. The last year of his life, before he was killed, they were two complete strangers; each knowing that it was only a matter of time.

Then the morning of the drive he acted very agitated, like a man on the edge. Rand told her he was leaving for a while; and that when he returned he would try harder, that everything would be different. Not a quitter, she hoped he was right. Rand explained they needed to drive to a private airstrip in the Keystone, Arapaho Basin Area. He asked her to ride along, and to bring his Rolls back home after he left, but then they wound up taking her Mercedes, because Lexie's car seat was already in it, and he was in such a hurry.

On the drive he had chosen to take Loveland Pass rather than I-70. That struck her as very odd, since it was a windy, scenic, touristy, back-road and he'd said he was in a hurry. All her efforts at any kind of conversation fell flat, and at one point he even snapped at her to "Shut up!"

Lexie had started to cry and she undid her own seatbelt to turn around in her seat, and settle her child down, in the back seat. It was at exactly that moment the other car had pulled up beside them and a dark-haired, black-eyed man, raised a gun, leveled it at her husband and pulled the trigger. The last thing she really remembered was his ice cold smile as the gun went off..

It all seemed to happen so rapidly, yet at the same time in slow motion. Then the other car rammed their car, and sent it careening over the ledge. She remembered that her scream, had been joined by Lexie's gulping sob, as the vehicle was airborne.

Then there was a crash, and at the actual impact, she'd been ejected through the shattering windshield. There was a very loud noise; and then a blinding flash of fire and she blissfully passed out.

James had been watching her face; he knew she was remembering something. Now, as he saw tears run unabashedly down her face, he enveloped her in his arms and sat down in a chair, pulling her down onto his lap. Susan buried her face in his neck and gave into the torrent of emotions. When she had cried enough, she told him everything she remembered; and he told her it was all consistent with the facts, the partially open seat belt explained how she had been flung from the wreckage. No one had ever quite understood that, since it was pulled out as if she's been wearing it. It had evidently not had sufficient time, to totally retract before impact. He held her a very long time, sort of half rocking her, as he might soothe a small child. They didn't speak for quite a while.

"I can identify the man who shot Rand,"

She finally uttered, making that single declarative statement.

"I can see him clearly, I will always remember that face!"

James froze. He wasn't sure if this was good news. But then she was already in all the jeopardy she could be, and for now she was completely safe, with him and a new identity anyway. Remembering could only help the healing process, couldn't it? He could only hope so. He wanted so much for her to quit hurting. She had lost so much and come so far.

Fear caused him to snap.

"You just forget what you saw. Erase that monster's face from your memory. I don't want you to remember. It's too dangerous."

Then seeing the look on her face he stood up and cradled her against him and carried her like a child over to the bed. Pulling back the covers, he laid her down gently, and began to undress her gently. He wanted to put her nightmare far away and offer her sweet dreams for the rest of their lives.

She seemed lost in her own thoughts and paid little attention as he undressed her, until his fingers touched her breast as he was removing her bra that hooked in the front. Then as if coming out of a deep sleep she looked directly into his ice blue eyes. In that flash, she rejoined him, one hundred percent with him, in the here and now. She was no longer in a past that ended tragically, but his lover once again, right here and in this moment.

Janice reached up and gently ran one finger over his cheek-bone and then over his lips too. She lightly traced his temple, than entangled her fingers in his hair, slowly bringing his lips to hers.

He kissed her back thoroughly, than buried his face in her hair and neck, inhaling deeply. It was an incredible turn on, the way he sniffed her, telling her all the while how good she smelled, and how beautiful she was. She didn't think it was even possible, to love and want someone so much. This man was the most important part of her life. She could feel to the depth of her being, that she would love him forever. Each moment that they were together, she loved him more than the last. His lips had found the hollow at her throat, then a nipple, which he sucked greedily, with more and more intensity. Her breath caught in her throat. His tongue grazed her belly-button then outlined her hip-bone. She felt as if she couldn't breathe at all, so ballooning was her passion. As his face dipped still lower, she actually lost consciousness for a tremulous few moments of unparalleled ecstasy. When her eyes opened, he was looking into them. He'd felt her slip away. He had such a look of love and ten derness on his face, as he tenderly pushed her hair back from her forehead.

"Do you want to talk about it?"

He asked her ever so gently.

"I relived the accident in such detail it was almost as if it was happening all over again. It just shook me up for a moment. That's all. I'm okay now."

She smiled impishly.

"Actually thanks to you, much better than okay."

He relaxed and laid on his back, pulling her over onto his shoulder, his arm around her, his hand toying with a curl of her hair.

They were so completely happy together, and everything felt so natural, despite all the sad things in both their pasts. This was a miracle, a wonderful, constantly unfolding, exceedingly happy, miracle. Janice and James fell asleep in each other's arms murmuring how much they loved each other.

CHAPTER 30

Damon was comfortably settled in his seat, glad to have left the two goons behind at the gate. Extremely relieved this had been a full flight, he shut his eyes a moment and rested while people boarded and stowed their luggage. Of course, he only had the one carry-on duffel bag; he hadn't bothered to go through airport security to clear a gun. With his badge he could have checked his regulation police revolver and picked it up at the other end. But, as much as he would have liked to have it, he had decided he couldn't allow the slow down it would cause at each gate, nor the complications when he switched identification.

Now he rested his eyes, during the stewardess spiel that no one ever really listened to. After all, he thought randomly, not even an idiot needed help fastening a seat belt and a floatation device was rather inept in any crash over land. Life was so full of repetitious, ridiculous rhetoric, things we were told over and over again, throughout our lives, that we either already knew, or didn't really need or want to know.

Then something so momentous comes along, like having the woman you love abducted by the Mafia, and mundane things, were all still happening all around him. There was still a stewardess droning the same silly instructions as any other flight. Something probably done by rote, with no one else, even recognizing the insaneness or repetition. But in the face of all the serious things he had to think about ridiculous and annoying.

His life was balanced on a precipice, and yet everything around him went on exactly as usual; it was indeed a crazy world. He knew that even if he pulled this whole thing off, brought the money back, and gave it to them. They could still probably kill Mary Jane; and if not her, then him for sure. They couldn't leave a cop to testify against them. The chances were he'd never see her again, no matter what he did. Not unless somehow he could manipulate them, better then they did him. It was all a big, complicated, and very dangerous game. One he no longer wanted to play. He was tired of seeing people scared and injured, he was no longer an effective cop if he wasn't detached, and he was definitely no longer detached, this was personal, intensely and agonizingly personal.

The left over concussion trauma, shadowed by worry, a lack of sleep and last night's scotch, all made it really hard to concentrate at all. Fortunately, he drifted off and slept. Considering it was a plane seat, he slept amazingly well. He slept so soundly, that he never noticed the man two rows behind who got up and walked up the aisle twice and looked at him sleeping, with a sardonic interest. Unfortunately, Damon slept unaware that the obvious tail back at the airport was a decoy. The phone tap on his home line had already alerted Mario to his flight plan and they had a man booked on that same flight, five minutes after Damon had made his own reservation. With the concussion, he had been lax and booked the flight on his regular phone line, rather then using the cellular in the attic.

There was nothing obvious about this man either; he looked much more like a bookkeeper than a thug. Vince Pardrone was a nondescript, mousy sort of man, partially balding, with thick glasses, but he was also a master of disguise and often wore wigs or contacts. So few people would ever be able to identify him after an assignment, but then there were very few people left behind anyway. He looked nothing like the expert martial artist that he was, and Vince was trained in all kinds of weaponry as well. He could have been deadly in the military, but he had come up through very different ranks. First he had served under the old don, Nick Pappas, and now under Mario Corielli.

Vince was a little bulldog, loyal and mean as hell; he followed orders to the letter. His motivation was difficult to fathom though. No one really knew anything about him, not even Mario. Vince was 'commissioned labor'; a very special kind of hired killer; someone who had just always done, what ever was ordered of him, on a commissioned individual basis. His specialty was murder and he was very good at it.

He had no personal life; that anyone knew of, no vulnerabilities at all. But he had never failed on any assignment. When Mario had assigned him to this one, he had been clear, and his instructions had elicited a cold, frightening smile of satisfaction from Vince. It was exactly the kind of job he lived for.

Mario had told him to be discreet and invisible while following Detective Matthews and to follow him to the woman; Diane Lindsey. Then wait and watch until she gave Damon the money. Then and only then, after the detective had left; he was to follow through with the rest of his assignment.

His instructions were simple and the kind of assignment he lived for.

"Make an example of her! Do anything you want to her; just make it gruesome. I want her to be a lesson to anyone who ever even considers crossing me. Make it obvious and go very slowly, and then, and only then, kill her. Leave a note that gives graphic details of what preceded her demise and then send her head to the Denver Post Newsroom!"

It would put Mario on a level, that few had ever aspired to; and it would gain him a respect; no one would ever question and a fear that would make everyone bow to him for a very long time. However, for Vince, it was just all in a week's work, or should he say pleasure. Vince smiled chillingly, thinking of Diane, he had her picture, yes indeed; this would be pure fun and games. Then he too, shut his eyes and drifted off. It was a long flight from Denver to Seattle.

CHAPTER 31

After dinner, Mary Jane was once again, back in her little room. But, it was easier now. She was tired, from a successful day's work. It had felt good to paint again. And yet, as completely absorbed, as she usually was in her work, she had not been unaware of the undercurrents and disapproval in the room. Mary Jane realized that the man in charge had broken unwritten codes today. The other men had expressed displeasure, in very covert glances at him. Throughout the day everyone had remained deadly quiet, flipping through magazines, playing chess and watching TV, but barely talking to each other. Yet, she had heard them talking animatedly when she was in her little contained area, before, even if it had always been muffled.

Nevertheless, she was grateful for a day that found her working again, no matter how strained it had been. Once, she was lost in her work, she was unaware of her surroundings anyway. The painting was a good one. It would go with her series of ruins. The crying woman had been a surprise to her though. In the series, up to now, there had been no figurative depictions. She assumed that the woman came from her own feelings of desperation and entrapment. Her paintings always reflected her own inner turmoil. In that way, they were her bringing her truth forward. That's what made her work important and was making a name for her. Mary Jane's work was always the truth.

After she and Damon had first broken up, she had been touted as a genius for her '*Ladies Alone Series*'. It had been poignantly sad, and the critics had loved it. It had been instrumental in her healing. Every time she painted a different broken hearted woman, she'd shed a little of her own sadness. By the end of the series, she hardly cried anymore herself. The series had done that for her.

Until running back to Damon's side in the hospital, she had even begun to think, that she was all over him. Now, she knew she never would be. From the moment she had first arrived at his bedside, she had known, that she had never stopped loving him. He was the only man she wanted. If she got out of here alive she would tell him that. Cop or not, she loved him. She realized now how stupid she'd been. Love doesn't make conditions, it doesn't demand anything, it just is, and it just gives.

The more she thought about it, the more she knew for sure, that she finally had all the answers she needed, about her future, if she ever got out of here, to have one; then a future with Damon was it.

Deep in thought himself, in the other room, Jason was having a hard time getting Mary Jane out of his thoughts. Her painting still stood on the easel by the window, although one of the others, Michael he thought, had pushed it back toward the corner of the room, out of the way. It was so mesmerizing, so sad and alone. He wanted the woman to stop crying, but she never ran out of tears. The painting seemed alive whenever shadows shifted, or with any change in the light. He thought it must be incredible to create something so real and capable of evoking feelings in whoever saw it. This was a gift, and he envied the woman behind the closet door. Mary Jane had a talent and a life. Someone loved her enough, that it had turned her into a pawn in a deadly game. But the point was, someone loved her.

Who loved him? Who would even care if he were in her shoes?

Maybe Mario would buy him his freedom, but it would be more about his machismo than about Jason. He knew in his heart that Mario had gone power mad. Jason knew that he, no longer had a heart, staying on top had become his addiction. Unfortunately, Jason still did have a heart, and it was getting harder and harder to do the things that were asked of him, especially when he couldn't sell himself on it being for family. His adopted parents were dead and if Mario was his brother once, that was over; it just felt wooden and empty now.

It was now well after midnight. Michael and Thomaso were sound asleep. The place was very quiet, he got up and went into the kitchen and heated up a cup of coffee. He sat brooding and thinking hunched over the cup.

All he kept thinking of was; that he didn't want to be part, of that very talented lady's fear and anguish, her anguish so boldly visualized, in her artwork. He didn't want to be a part of the organization, at all anymore. It was all he knew, but he also knew, it was wrong. It was time to do something right.

Without any further thought, he got up and strode across the room. He opened Mary Jane's door very quietly and put a hand over her mouth. As her eyes fluttered open, he shushed her quietly, signaling her to come with him quickly and not to make a sound. She seemed to understand. He locked her door again, and led her out the front door, locking that behind them too. Next, they entered a fire and emergency stairway and headed down a couple of floors. They came out and took the elevator the rest of the way to the garage level. He signaled her to get in a black Mercedes sedan and they drove out of the garage and into the night.

Only then did she speak.

"What's happening?"

"I'm letting you go. I don't want to be a party to anything happening to you."

He looked very strained as he said it, and a little surprised at what he was doing himself. Since he'd been thirteen years old, he'd never disobeyed Mario. Now he had just written his own death warrant, and he knew it.

"Oh my God, thank you, I don't even know your name."

He smiled.

"It's Jason, but please don't remember it."

He pulled over to a curb, next to a phone booth. He handed her a quarter.

"Call 911, they'll send someone to get you. Good luck, Mary Jane, and good-bye. Have a nice life."

He smiled weakly. It was a smile that never really reached his eyes; sad eyes, eyes full of pain.

"What will happen to you?" There was very real concern in her voice.

His answer was a shrug, as he nodded for her to get out of the car.

She nodded back, understanding that he had just made his own life very difficult. Then she stepped out on the curb with a sigh of pure relief.

Mary Jane had survived and this man had made that happen, even when his job had been to do exactly the reverse.

CHAPTER 32

The flight was descending now as it approached Reno. Damon locked his seat into an upright position, as the stewardess walked by checking seat belts. He couldn't wait to land and make sure that he was in the clear. He prayed there were no more goons waiting at the Reno airport. With any luck at all, they would be at the gate in Seattle and bypass the connection in Reno.

He knew Mario was many things, but certainly not stupid, so he had to expect someone to be watching the gate in Reno. He just prayed they'd be as obvious as they'd been in Denver, so he cold spot them; and then having done so, lose them.

The plane sailed onto the runway. Then, a few minutes later, after some passengers disembarked and more passengers began to board, he stood and nonchalantly went to the men's room at the back of the plane. He didn't want to disembark until the last possible minute, so anyone watching at the gate would quit watching. Finally, just as the last person boarded for the continuing flight, he quickly returned to his seat, collected his bag in one smooth move and headed for the hatch door. The stewardess looked disgruntled that he was so slow to exit the plane. She had been just about to close and lock the door. However with a frown, she stepped aside and let him exit. Then, just as she once again starting to close the door, a second man, a man who for some reason gave her the creeps, also came up to leave. She happily stepped aside, glad to see this passenger leave. It certainly was odd, the way he seemed to be following the first man. He hadn't even been carrying a bag. And she was sure his ticket had been a through one, and that all the Reno departures had been accounted for.

Oh well, you couldn't keep someone on a plane if they wanted to get off, the plane was still at the gate, yet that man still gave her the creeps. When she had served his ginger ale he had stared at her with a smile that made her, at best uncomfortable. Anyway, she finally got the door closed and locked, putting the last minute departures out of her mind, and got busy getting the new bunch of passengers settled. Soon she was completely immersed in the same old speech she made at the beginning of every flight.

"The curse of being senior stewardess was the redundancy." She thought.

Damon went halfway up the covered walk that attached the plane to the gate. He saw them closing the door at the other end and decided that he'd lay low in the walkway. Anyone at the gate would then watch the plane leave in about twenty minutes and leave. He settled down cross-legged, a quarter of the way up the walkway, and leaned his head back against the wall, shutting his eyes again to wait.

Vince was now trapped in the little elbow that joined the accordion walkway to the plane; he couldn't round the curve, without being in plain sight of the detective he was tailing. But the plane door was closed now, so he wasn't obvious just standing there either. His concern was that when the plane pulled away from the accordion-like connector, he would be in full view to anyone on the tarmac. He didn't want anyone to draw attention to him, or yell up to him, causing Damon to become aware of his presence. He knew at this point, Damon was still oblivious to him and only concerned about who might be watching outside the door. But how long could that last, with them both in the same thirty-foot enclosure and the plane about to leave, and the door closed on the other end?

CHAPTER 33

Mary Jane was insistent now.

"I mean it, what will happen to you?"

He hadn't answered, the first time she asked, so she repeated herself.

Still, no answer was forthcoming. She was exasperated now.

"Listen, I know what you have just done for me, and it can't be a good thing for you. I'm not an idiot. Let me call Damon, I mean Detective Matthews. Then you can take me to him, and we'll all work this out. I'll explain how you helped me! Then you can get some help too."

He smiled, at how sweet and naïve she was. 'Not good for him,' was certainly a massive understatement.

"Mary Jane, people like me don't get help from the police. You wouldn't understand my world. Now get out of my car and make that call."

He added as an afterthought.

"By the way, you're in Chicago. We brought you here in a private plane while you were knocked out. I thought you might like to know, since nothing will be familiar to you. That's why I suggested you call 911. Chicago's finest can call Denver for you. I'm sure they'll have you home before you know it."

He reached across her and closed her car door.

She pulled it open again, indeed, with some force, to keep him from just taking off.

"Not good enough, Jason, you will get yourself in big trouble by letting me go, won't you?"

"You don't know the half of it! It's not your problem, now go on, make that call."

Jason was getting more and more frustrated, but he was feeling something else too, maybe a little touched. He cleared his throat gruffly.

"I'm not going."

And then she plopped back into the passenger seat slamming her car door behind her.

"Now you listen to me, get on a highway and put some distance between us and this town, before your buddies back there wake up. We aren't done talking. And don't argue with me anymore. They'll be other phone booths; I'm not getting out, on a dark corner in Chicago, wearing nothing but a sweat suit, in the middle of the winter. You want me to freeze to death?"

She said all this derisively and slightly bossy, too, and he found himself amazed at her, but also putting the car in gear and doing as she said, just the same. Neither of them was safe in Chicago; that much was absolutely clear.

Thomas or Michael would awake and sound an alarm by 4:30 in the morning. By then he would need to desert the car. They should be as far away from it, as possible by then. She was a bright lady.

That gave them not quite four hours to distance themselves. He had to admit, he was rather glad that they'd to be sticking together, a little longer. She was quite a woman, standing by him; a practical stranger, and her abductor. Even though now he was also the man who was helping her escape.

He was now a little uncertain which way to head. "Well you seem to be running this show."

Jason only half teased.

"So which way, or what is your plan?"

"This is your town, what's the best way to leave without a trace?"

"Bus, I guess. The Greyhound station is in the worst part of town. So if we leave the keys in the car, we can guarantee, it will get stolen."

He was thinking out loud now.

"No names are needed for a bus ticket, so we are out of Chicago, without a trace."

"It's a plan, head there."

"We can go two different directions at that point; it would be for the best."

He looked pretty stubborn on this point.

Mary Jane thought a while before speaking.

"Listen, I don't know why you were doing what you were doing, but I do know this, you are a good and decent man. You saved my life, and probably put your own, in a lot of danger. I'm sure your boss is a very nasty man, and he isn't going to forgive and forget your change of heart. Please, at least let me call Damon, from the station, and get his advice for you. Maybe there is someone you can turn yourself into here in Chicago; that can help you."

She was so sincere and it was so obvious she cared, he knew for certain that he had done the right thing.

"I will never forget your offer, but my best bet is to just disappear. I have some money put away with my passport. If we swing by my place now before they are looking for me. I can grab them and then just disappear. I'll leave the country from some obscure airport tomorrow morning, after taking an untraceable bus tonight. Let's just head two different directions at the bus terminal, okay? It really would be the best plan. But, I'll never forget you cared."

She answered resigned, but understanding, too.

"And I will never forget what you spared me at the expense of your allegiances and perhaps even your own life. You are a 'good man', prove that to yourself from now on, with everything you do."

He fell silent and absorbed what she'd said as the drove.

CHAPTER 34

The plane rolled away from the gate, and the noise was deafening, standing essentially, right next to the plane, as it pulled away. Vince clung to the accordion-like ripples in the elbow section that he was hiding in, trying not to let Damon see him. When the plane had completely rolled away, he looked down, very relieved to see no one, on the tarmac nearby. Staying as close to the edge as he could, and out of Damon's view, he worked to remain invisible. Finally after a time he peeked around the corner cautiously, he'd heard Damon stand up, groan and walk up closer to the door that opened to the terminal.

Both men stood quietly, for several long minutes. It never even occurred to Damon to look behind him. He'd only been concerned with any men waiting inside the terminal. The ruse at the

Denver airport had served the purpose it had been intended for; he had never guessed that Mario had booked someone on his plane with him. Damon was still not as sharp as he would normally be. A concussion and Mary Jane's abduction had taken a toll on his clarity in this situation.

Damon hadn't even considered Vince's presence and now here they stood, not thirty feet apart, Vince invisible.

Vince was getting quite an adrenaline rush out of this whole cat and mouse, hide-in-plain-sight deal. He was as high as a kite, this was a kick; and he lived for exactly this sort of excitement. Outwitting the cop, and then getting to torture and murder a woman, he couldn't ask for any better than that; and to think, on top of all that, Corielli would pay him to do it.

About twenty minutes after the plane pulled away, Damon felt it was safe to enter the airport. Any spies should be gone by this time. He knocked on the door lightly and then with some vehemence and urgency.

In seconds a very confused gate clerk opened the door very surprised to find a man behind it, so long after the plane had left the gate. Nevertheless, she let the door swing open and let him enter, leaving the door open for a moment while she walked over to confer with a senior agent about the oddity of a man staying in the walkway, for so long.

Damon followed her over to the counter; and while Damon was explaining, no one paid any attention to the thin, nondescript man who unobtrusively zipped out also, quietly merging into a group of people standing directly behind Damon.

Vince had gone completely unnoticed, and he was feeling unbeatable and totally euphoric; an invincible feeling that persisted when he followed Damon to the next ticket counter and bought a ticket on the same flight; from Reno to Miami, and Miami to Devil's Island, French Guyana.

"What a piece of cake!"

He thought.

"As an extra added bonus; I not only get to have fun and games with a beautiful woman, I'll get to do it in an exotic paradise."

Within the hour, they were both settled in their seats on the flight to Miami. Unfortunately, Damon was completely unaware of Vince Pardrone tailing him. He was totally relaxed now or as relaxed as he could be given the seriousness of the situation. But he thought he was in the clear. Unfortunately, with his defenses down, he wasn't watching for familiar faces from the last flight, and Vince sat well back. He felt pretty confident he'd gone unnoticed, and he had also picked up on the alias Damon was using for the tickets so he didn't have to worry about anything until Devil's Island.

Vince couldn't help but think it was a fitting name; for a place to catch up with Diane Lindsey, his assignment, and do what he came to do. Following Damon, after all, was only a means to an end.

CHAPTER 35

The bus terminal in Chicago was one of the dreariest places that Mary Jane had ever seen. European public transportation was always far superior to the U.S. She had really loved Europe, her artistic temperament flourished better there.

They had stopped by Jason's building. She'd waited in the car. True to his word he was back in a matter of a few minutes. Maybe in his business you always kept a bag packed. He'd returned with only one, small leather duffel, but it was obviously packed to capacity. Part of her wondered how much cash he had shoved in there. He was in a curious business, for a man who seemed so truly kind. She flashed on all the art supplies he had gotten her.

After they picked up his stuff, she asked him questions to that effect, about how he'd gotten involved in all of this.

Surprising even himself, he answered her honestly. He had nothing to lose now in telling her and it actually felt good to share his story. No one had ever cared enough about him, to even ask before.

He didn't use names but he told her how he'd met his present day boss, a high level criminal, when he was thirteen.

"I'd run away from home. My mom was a junkie and a prostitute and I never knew my dad. I was living in an alley, eating out of the trash, behind this one Italian restaurant, when I bumped into this tough seventeen-year-old punk. His aunt owned the restaurant.

"First he beat me up. Then he took me in and fed me a big plate of spaghetti!"

He laughed at the memory of the young cocky Mario.

"I don't know why he beat me up, and I don't know why he took me in and fed me. But that night he got his aunt to let me do the dishes and sleep in the back of the restaurant. So thanks to him, at least I was inside at night. I did that for about three months. Then one day, he took me home and introduced me to his Mother and Father and then showed me to my room, at his house. Just like that, no discussion, no explanation. That's just the way it's always been. I've always been there for him, because he was once there for me. But, I swear, I've never killed anyone and Mario knew me well enough; that he never asked me to. I swear that

Mary Jane. The truth is I just can't do any of this stuff anymore. It just seems utterly senseless."

His voice just trailed off. It was such a sad and lonely comment. He knew that there was no excuse for any of it, and he thought that there was no way someone like her could possibly understand. But he was wrong.

Mary Jane's heart went out to him. She reached out and put her hand over his. She didn't say anything, she just understood and forgave, and he could feel it and appreciate, the kindness and compassion in her.

Now it was time to part ways. She gave him her phone number if he ever needed her.

"I'll testify for you, if you ever turn yourself in, or get caught, okay?"

"Okay."

He answered, surprised when she reached up and hugged him.

"That's not going to happen, you know?"

She nodded solemnly.

"I know."

He spun on his heel and walked away very fast, but not before he felt his eyes sting. He would always be glad he'd helped her get away, no matter what happened to him later. It felt good to do the right thing for once.

CHAPTER 36

In Miami International Damon made an uneventful plane change. He was feeling better all the time and making better time than he'd expected. He hadn't lost a night in Reno as he'd anticipated. There had been a flight leaving for Miami within less than an hour of his arrival into Reno, and thankfully a seat available. He knew now, that not bringing his gun had been wise. That always involved so much time and paperwork and local red tape. Nevertheless, he rather wished he'd have one when he arrived in South America. After so many years as a police detective; he was not used to being unarmed. It was like walking the streets naked.

There was no time between flights, to attempt a *'ship to shore'* call, but based on his flight schedule, he'd be in a full day and a half ahead of the ship anyway. He could be on the dock when it arrived, and if they didn't disembark early, he would have a message delivered to them on board, in case of any inability to reach them prior to their docking by phone.

Using the extra day that he would proceed their arrival; he would make flight arrangements for them to go with him to Grand Cayman, and then for getting them all back, where they belonged, after all the transactions were over. Damon had decided to make those plans including Chaz, that way Janice wouldn't be traveling back alone, just for safety's sake.

Of course, he couldn't know that the money, was split in half, and he'd need one person out of each couple, to access it anyway. Just as they couldn't know, the hell he'd been going through, or about Mary Jane's situation.

The thought of her made his heart ache.

"They had better not hurt her." He prayed with his whole soul.

Damon put some stock in Mario's promise not to hurt her, only because he couldn't even get him to pretend, any leniency for Diane. Which was why he had to protect her location at all costs.

But there would be a problem when he returned with the money. One, it would be short, a drop in the bucket short, to the original billion, but a quarter of a million more or less, was still a major deficit, when it stood alone.

Then again, he consoled himself; it was possible that some of the money was actually Rand Lindsey's own and had never even belonged to the mob. Damon hoped that was the case.

Damon was deep in thought on this, and felt he had to leave some of the money behind with the others. Although a cruise included most things, it would eventually come to a close, and they would need to settle quietly somewhere. All those plans demanded money. Staying out of harm's way was an expensive proposition.

They were all in an impossible situation, with very insecure futures. Diane would be hunted until Corielli found her. If Damon didn't lead them to her or give her up with the money, then vendetta could not end. Mario wanted her dead and probably Damon would pay with his life too.

Damon was weary of thinking about it all.

"Where would it all end? Could he spare Diane and survive delivering the money in exchange for Mary Jane? He thought so. But, please God, just don't let Mary Jane be hurt. Keep her safe, and take me if you must."

Little did he know, how things had shifted, and where the most danger, now lay.

Damon couldn't know that Mary Jane was free now, and frantically calling him over and over, wondering where he was. Nor could he know that she was on her way back to Denver right now.

Meanwhile the most immediate danger, sat eight rows behind him, in the menacing mask of a nondescript, benign-appearing, little man, most dangerous of all, because he was invisible, casually looking out at the wing from his window seat.

Vince was feeling very self-congratulatory. For a big shot detective, Damon hadn't been so sharp. On the other hand, Vince had to give himself credit. He was the best. He pulled a picture out of his pocket and stared transfixed at a picture of Diane Lindsey.

"This was one gorgeous broad."

He thought.

It was seldom he was given Carte Blanche on a hit. Usually he had to rein himself in, and follow orders to the letter, and he always did. There were always his little escapades on the side, that no one dictated, and which he did for pure pleasure.

But this time it was so simple; after the transfer of money over to the detective, he could do whatever he wanted with Diane.

Vince's directions were minimal but delicious.

"Go slow, so every gory element of the torture will show up in an autopsy."

It was to be, the most obvious case of premeditated evil possible. Then at the end, his instructions were very specific; decapitate her, package the head and body separately and very well, then ship them back to her hometown newspaper. It was to be a graphic example, a brutal, horrific, very tragic example. The news would have a hey-day.

Corielli would be reviled, respected and feared. All thanks to the mastery of Vince's work.

Vince was practically salivating as he thought of lots of exotic torture methods, some he'd read about, some he had proudly come up with, all on his own.

He slid the picture back into the inside pocket of his jacket, rested his seat back and relaxed completely. He daydreamed, a slight smile on his face. If the business woman in the seat next to him, could read his thoughts at that moment, it would make her physically ill. She would probably drench the little pervert in projectile vomit. Luckily for him, his thoughts were not transparent.

People like Vince were rare.

Whether one subscribed to the theory of nature or nurture, creating such monsters, he could not offer up proof, on either side, or maybe for both, depending on your point of view.

His birth had been uneventful, unwanted and unheralded, to average lower-middle, working-class parents. He was a middle child of three nondescript kids, born to insignificant, not very happy, or terribly unhappy people. His parents just got by the best they could. His brother and sister had grown up as complete carbon copies of their parents.

Vince had found a finer destiny, as he thought of it.

When he was very young, maybe as young as two or three, he started with bugs, then rats, then cats and dogs. By the time he was seven he killed his first human victim. It was an incredible high, and he was never caught or even suspected.

He had simply taken a toddler out of the playpen, in a sunny back yard, when he saw the mother carry in her basket of laundry. Then he'd taken the child directly to the creek and drowned it, just for fun. But it was over too quickly.

So the next time, three weeks later, he took the local drunk's child away, from right under her nose while she lay passed out cold, on her sofa three feet away, from the babies playpen.

This time he took the little girl into the nearby woods, to a cave he knew of. Amazingly its little life lasted three days, without food or water, and with him practicing all kinds of ideas on it. He knew the sound of a crying baby upset most people. He, on the other hand, decided it was pretty cool.

He turned eight a month later.

He learned caution, and timing well, it was a necessity.

The first child was assumed to have climbed out of the playpen and drowned by accident. But when the second one was found, the town was in a mad hunt for a psychopath. People were all watching their children a little closer, to say the very least. Of course he was in no danger — no one was looking for a scrawny eight-year-old, with his glasses taped together on one side with masking tape.

That's when he first realized he was invisible.

The tinkling bell sounded in the plane cabin, announced a forthcoming descent. Damon righted his seat automatically without waiting for the canned speech.

It was funny, an odd sixth sense, was tingling around the back of his head. It was going so smoothly, so far, yet something, just felt wrong. The feeling was strong and unshakable.

"Maybe I'm just anticipating my own impending doom."

He thought.

"I hope if they are going to kill me, that they just make it fast and get it over with. As long as they let Mary Jane live, I don't really care what happens to me."

Of course he knew that he was lying to himself. He did care, in fact he cared deeply. Damon wanted a chance to live a future, with Mary Jane. He wanted the home, the hearth, the kids, and the dog. He wanted to live, and then watch, their kids, have kids. He'd just rediscovered their feelings again, and now he desperately wanted time to explore them and grow a future together.

However at least he was happy knowing; he wasn't leading any trouble to Diane's door. He had given Mario Corielli's men the slip. It had gone so smoothly, he was still amazed.

CHAPTER 37

The Caribbean breezes were gentle and fragrant, as *My Fair Lady* sailed away from Saint Bart's and into the South American waters.

"So many, unbelievably beautiful places to see; its still so hard to believe that we are here."

Susan remarked casually, sitting in her deck chair, a book face down on her lap.

"Does anyone else feel like, we are stuck in the dream of someone who should be interviewed, on *Lifestyles of the Rich and Famous?*"

"Just hope they don't wake up then; or our ship could turn back into a Pumpkin! Sorry, I'm paraphrasing *Cinderella*, badly!"

Janice laughed, and Susan joined in.

The girls were alone on the deck, reading and sunning.

James was writing, because as he said so often.

"Writers, write."

Chaz had accepted an invitation to play some poker in the casino.

Janice and Susan were using their time to catch up. Everything was so perfect that it almost seemed impossible.

They shared, in whispered confidence and easy laughter, how terrifically happy they were with James and Chaz. They were both so newly and happily in love with such good men.

"Maybe the only shadow on this whole thing is ..."

Janice hesitated, then stopped.

Susan nudged her.

"Go on, you know you can tell me anything"

Still Janice hesitated. Susan waited her out.

"This is going to sound silly and so petty. But here goes. I miss our old names. I fell in love with a Mark, now he's a James, I've known you all my life as Joan or Jo and now you're......."

Susan interrupted.

"I know, I know exactly what you mean, I feel almost schizophrenic sometimes."

She reached over and grabbed Janice's arm.

"Remember the day I slipped and said Di. It made me feel like I'd committed some mortal sin. I think I was waiting for the sky to rain bullets, and if it had; it would have been 'all my' fault."

They both laughed.

It helped, to talk about it. There wasn't another soul anywhere near them, so they could talk openly.

"As long as we are excusing our whining and complaining; may I also voice the fear; I worry about what happens at the end of our fantasy exile? I want to settle somewhere eventually. We can't drift and hide forever, no matter how much money we have. People need a place to be home."

Susan was nodding sympathetically.

"Of course I think about that too, but I don't think it will be as hard for Chaz and I, we aren't in anyway the main focus. I'm probably already forgotten, and they never even knew of Chaz. By the way, I like *his* new name."

Susan said crinkling her nose at the sun.

"I think it's pretty sexy!" Susan tried to lighten up the serious tone the conversation had taken.

Janice continued.

"This whole thing is more of a negative for James. As James, he has no contacts and no one knows his past reputation. That will make it much more difficult, for him to get a book published. Publishing is a very competitive business. Yet as Mark Roberts, he probably could have been guaranteed a contract on his book, before he ever even typed the first word. I hate knowing what I've cost him."

"What about what you've given him? He's happy, in case you haven't noticed, very happy with you. And if the book's any good, and I'm sure it will be. It will get published, so stop worrying, and relax a little. He'll be prouder, when it succeeds on its own merits anyway. By the end of this cruise, your trail will be stone-cold-dead. The bad guys will give it up, and pack up their guns and go home, and the four of us will go somewhere we've always wanted to live, and start over, and settle down there. Then a year from now you'll come through my kitchen door, and I'll put your cup of coffee down in front of you, in my Wisteria Lane type kitchen, and you'll complain that life has gotten dull."

When Susan finished her monologue they were both laughing again.

They didn't even notice as James came up behind them and put his hands over Janice' eyes.

"My creative juices have taken a break, mind if I borrow some inspiration?"

He directed his question to Susan, as he pulled Janice to her feet and with him, toward and into the pool.

Janice barely had time to pull off her sunglasses and shoes before he dragged her in splashing and laughing.

Susan leaned back and smiled, happy for her friend. After observing them for a moment, she started to feel like a peeping Tom as they kissed, and she looked away and out to the sea and caught a glimpse of some dolphins playing.

Susan's mind wandered. Everything did appear to be wonderful, but she still carried tremendous guilt feelings, over the truths she had not told.

Chaz loved her now, but she wondered how he would feel if he knew about her Greek tragedy. She wondered again whether to unburden herself and take a chance on losing him. Once again she settled on silence, as her best solution. Yet it was a sad feeling, knowing that she felt like damaged goods. Guilt and deceit made very uncomfortable companions.

She picked up her book and returned to her story. It wasn't long before Chaz rejoined the group and they played a rousing game of pool volleyball, until they all got ready for lunch.

This day and the next, were sea days, then they would be arriving in an exotic port called Devil's Island, it was in French Guyana.

Although breathtaking, the island had a dark and interesting history. It had been a notorious penal colony. Although a beautiful paradise now, for former prisoners put there, never to leave again, it must have felt very different. The ruined prison buildings were still there and reputed to be haunted. Evidentially, escape from the island was extremely dangerous and nearly impossible, because of the way the island's tides worked over the islands ragged coral reefs. And because of those tides, the ship would be dropping anchor out past the reefs, and shuttling passengers in on the tenders.

The sea days and shore days were so well divided up, that they always seemed to appreciate which ever kind of day it was. They were all wonderful anyway. Bad weather never even seemed to cross the ship's path. Yesterday had been spent in St. Bart.

Each and every place they had been so far; was even more beautiful than the last, and unique in its own way. The itinerary had been chosen with great care, and it did its level best; to make this the best world cruise that had ever been put together.

The days at sea, were filled with ship's activities, even lectures for archeologists and history buffs on each port. The meals were unbelievable, but dangerous to the waistline, if you didn't pace yourself. The shows and entertainment opportunities on board still managed to keep surprising and amazing them with their variety. Last evening had featured '*Lord of the Dance*', with the original Celtic cast flown in just for the two shows of that evening.

Dancing and quiet walks on decks were their usual ending to the perfect evenings they all shared. The four of them, found excellent and boisterous good fun, within the confines of their own small group. The men had become good friends too. They had a multitude of interests in common and also shared many of the same values. It was a very compatible pair of couples who truly enjoyed each other.

Only James still had parents alive and he called them regularly, so they weren't worried, they just thought he was on an undercover assignment.

Chaz had never been close to anyone except Damon, and he thought of him often and prayed he'd recovered and hadn't been under too much pressure from the police force, orr worse yet, the mob.

He still feared ramifications from Corielli. He wasn't a man who would accept being bested.

So Chaz wisely worried about Damon, standing alone, without anyone to watch his back. He knew the women reveled in imagining a happily-ever-after ending; in which he and Mary Jane rode off into the sunset. But he was much more realistic. Mary Jane made him vulnerable, and that worried him.

He thought about checking in with Damon, when they put in to the next port, Chaz would feel much less guilty enjoying paradise, if he knew Damon was safely ensconced in the castle with Mary Jane, and that they were both fine.

Unfortunately his intuition told him everything was just running too smoothly, and if things looked 'too good to be true' then they might be, 'too good to be true'. This thing wasn't going to just go away, no matter how much they all wished it would. And Damon was the one still out there, 'swimming with the sharks', while the rest of them sailed away on this fabulous ship.

So Chaz was understandably concerned about his friend. Tomorrow he'd call Damon, from port. That would be virtually untraceable and would both help relieve his mind, and thrill the women here, to get an update on Damon and Mary Jane's progress.

CHAPTER 38

Mary Jane was frantic. She had called Damon's number and her own, and then the detective desk. They told her matter-of-factly that he was on medical leave. They didn't know anything else. They didn't even have a report that she'd been kidnapped; which she'd discovered in an indirect fishing expedition.

Damon had vanished, and she didn't know what to do or where to go. Jason's ex-boss was without a doubt on her tail and she couldn't find Damon. It certainly wasn't her intention to be abducted once again. Once was definitely enough. She had to stay out of sight.

Denver was probably not a good idea at all. That's where they would be watching. But she had to find Damon and stay close.

Mary Jane had to think with a clear mind. She had to rid herself of panic. Than she knew just where she could go, she'd thought of the perfect place to hide while continuing to try to reach Damon.

Claire was a good friend, a fellow artist, with a place in Steamboat Springs, Colorado. It wasn't very far away from Denver, but it was remote enough to be safe, and out of the way. She would just keep calling Damon's number until she reached him, and pray they hadn't kill him; because she'd disappeared. She hoped that they would just let him keep thinking, they still had her, to manipulate him.

Then Damon might still do; what they'd taken her; to make him do for them.

She was sure that's where he was now; getting the money that Jason had told her about.

If only she could let him know she was safe. Then he wouldn't be at their mercy. His 'cell phone' had droned that, it was no longer in service. Of course he might have canceled it so as to not be traced by its signal. Mary Jane couldn't risk leaving an obvious message on his, or her own answering machine, so she left a message in her grand-parents name that they had called and were feeling well; she knew, he would know it was her since they were dead.

She also sent out a prayer out for Jason's safety, wherever he was now. From what he'd said, he would be dead, if he were caught. She owed her freedom, to his bravery and to his deserting everything he'd known and a man who was like his brother.

Now, that same man was quite likely to put a contract out on him. What a sad world to live in. The Mafia used words like honor and loyalty. But they had everything all twisted around. She thought it appeared pretty lonely and desolate. Funny, how they called it a family. What a dysfunctional family it was.

It seemed that suddenly her life was spinning out of control, on a non-stop course to lunacy. Mary Jane desperately wanted the peace of working daily in her studio back, but, she also knew; that she had to play this hand out here in Colorado. She was in love with Damon, and she wasn't going to run away from it this time. Mary Jane planned to share a life with Damon. So he simply had to come back for her.

Her decision made, she called her friend from a phone booth in a little strip mall just off of I-70 near the Genesee exit. She wasn't taking any chances. She wouldn't going to go home for anything, her place wasn't safe. She was still in the slightly too big sweat suit, with only a little bit of the money left; that Jason had given her. Mary Jane had very little left, after buying her bus ticket back to Denver and getting off here.

Since she and Jason had walked out, without any of her things, at all, in Chicago. She didn't have identification of any kind with her, and now only

$62.75 left. She'd been forced to take a bus for twenty hours from Chicago, what a grueling and dismal trip that had been. The blessing was the bus hadn't required identification. Plus, the plan had called for being untraceable. That had made Greyhound the only logical choice since 9-11. Every other means of transportation was documented. She didn't know what bus, Jason had taken, but she hoped he was safe now too.

Now she'd decided to get off at the Genesee exit, rather than going into downtown Denver. No purpose could be served by going further into Denver, and some sort of sixth sense, told her not to go to the police after her call. If Damon hadn't trusted them; then neither should she. It was an awful feeling that there was no one to turn to. Then she'd remembered Claire. With a flood of relief she dialed her number.

The phone startled her out of her wandering thoughts as some one picked up.

"Hello, hello, is anyone here?" It was a man's voice, and he was starting to sound exasperated.

"Oh I'm sorry, is Claire there?"

"Sure, hold on just a minute."

He'd set the phone down, and the mechanical operator's voice came over the phone, demanding she deposit $2.75 cents more; which she did. Then she could hear the man telling Claire the phone was for her.

Finally Claire was on the line.

"Yes hello, this is Claire."

"It's me, Mary Jane. I'm in trouble, Claire, I need a place to stay."

"Well of course, where are you, and what can I do?"

Claire was just as she remembered, no nonsense and matter of fact.

"The phone will go off in a second, and I need to get more change. I'll call you back if it goes dead."

"M.J. stop and take a deep breath and calm down, give me the number there. I will call you right back."

Mary Jane relaxed, and smiled at her friend's use of only her initials. Claire had always called her M.J. even though no one else ever had. Usually it slightly annoyed her, now it filled her with relief.

She quickly gave her the number written on the phone booth's phone and hung up.

"Of course that makes sense."

Mary Jane thought, while she waited for the phone to ring, glad there was a phone booth at all. There were damn few of them left around anymore. Even in Europe everyone had a cell phone.

She picked up the phone before it had even completed a full ring.

"I'm at the Genesee exit on Interstate 70, where the Chart House is. I'm right across the street in a little strip mall diner. I wasn't dressed well enough to go in the Chart House. Do you know where it is? Just up from the buffalo herd?"

M.J.'s tone of voice sounded a panic alert, so Claire didn't ask any questions.

"Okay, M.J. I know where you mean. It's approximately a two and a half hours, to drive there from here and I'm on my way right now. Hold tight, okay? I'll be there as fast as I can. I don't know what's going on, but I'll be there."

"Thanks Claire, and I'll be here."

She hung up the phone feeling drained, but relieved. Now all she could think about was a shower; she must look like a bag woman. She ran her fingers through her hair tiredly.

Then she left the phone booth and went into a little restaurant in the strip mall owned by a Greek family and ordered coffee and a sandwich and waited.

As tired as she was, the time crawled while she waited for Claire to come and get her. Mary Jane felt very lucky and grateful, that she had reached her easily and she was coming so quickly without even an explanation.

She thought back; they'd met six years ago in a show in Paris. They had been the only two American artists invited to exhibit at the very prestigious show. That had been ample enough reason and 'in common', to make them bond for the week.

It turned out they were very compatible, at first because of their artwork and then, because they truly, took a sincere liking to each other. They understood each other, and that grew into an fast and durable friendship, and although their personalities were worlds apart, their friendship grew.

Mary Jane was shy, and had grown up 'a lonely, only child' in her grandparents beautiful, but very isolated home.

Claire Cane had been the middle of a brood of eight. She had grown up in New England, and proudly referred to herself as an '*Old Mainer*'. She dropped the R's out of words that had them, and added them onto words that didn't. It had always cracked Mary Jane up, to hear her say Linda as Linder and Florida as Florider.

But, as Claire explained good naturedly making fun of herself.

"*Mainer's* don't waste a thing, we may take the 'R's' out of some places, but we always use them some whea.. else!"

Mary Jane had found Claire outspoken on nearly every subject and they'd had so much fun running around together. Her French was flawless though, and that had proved to be a huge help, as the two young women toured Paris together building a friendship.

Mary Jane had still been stinging and saddened, from her break up with Damon, and she had spilled her sorrow out to Claire who listened sympathetically. Claire was still unmarried and a free and open spirit then and nothing had daunted her. She would do anything, and say anything to absolutely anybody. She never met a stranger, and even Parisians liked her, which was unusual, considering their inexplicable distaste of Americans as a whole. Claire had such an infectious good-humor that everyone loved her, M.J. especially.

Mary Jane enjoyed the week immensely, and afterward they became avid pen pals.

Through out the years; they'd met at a few other art shows; but mostly their bond was forged, with a very personal letter writing campaign. In their letters over the years, they had shared everything, and probably saved themselves on outside therapy. In many ways they were closer than people, who saw each other every day; because they always wrote about important stuff and the trite and inconsequential never invaded their letters, as it tends to in conversation.

Claire's description was that they wrote 'meat and potatoes', and left out, the 'decorative parsley' and 'dessert'. It was a friendship that had grown very deep; even allowing, that they only had a minimum, of face to face visits.

So actually, Mary Jane shouldn't have been surprised, that Claire was on her way to pick her up, without even a question.

She also knew; that she would be welcome to stay, as long as she needed to, even given her circumstances.

It was certainly fortunate, that just last year, Claire had moved to Steamboat, Colorado. She'd met and married a man who was, a 'big wig' with the world famous Steamboat Springs Ski Resort; and she'd written that she loved it there, even though she still missed the autumns in

New England, and her large family, left behind in Maine.

It was damn lucky that she had moved to Colorado, because right now M.J. really needed a good friend and a hideout. She couldn't wait to have a long hot shower, a little nap when they got to Steamboat, but on the drive there they would have a 'marathon' catch-up session.

She knew Claire would have some solid, no-nonsense advice, on this frightening quandary in which she found her self. She had always been able to count on her, for common sense, and had relied on her, in the past, for things that no longer seemed so important. Now she was bringing life and death decisions right to her doorstep. Yet Mary Jane knew, she could count on Claire not to panic. In her own calm way; she would give her all the support she needed.

The long bus trip had been grueling, and her fellow passengers depressing, but she knew she looked pretty depressing herself. Claire would have a hard time recognizing her, but she didn't have anything to touch up with, not even a comb.

The best she could do, and had repeatedly, was run her fingers through her hair. Now it just felt greasy and dirty. She felt revolting, but there was nothing she could do, but wait to get to Claire's house.

She rested and may have even dosed. The next thing she knew she felt a hand on her shoulder, giving her a gentle shake.

"M.J., are you okay?"

Boy was she ever relieved to see her dear friend had arrived.

"Just unbelievably drained, I'll catch you up on the drive."

She arose wearily but immensely relieved to see her friend, and followed her to the Land Rover parked out in front of the phone booth. It seemed an eternity since the phone call.

With supreme effort she climbed in the passenger side of the car. Claire reached over and held her hand, her eyes conveyed her concern.

"Just rest kiddo, there will be plenty of time to talk later. You look beyond exhausted. Put your seat belt on and your head back and sleep. I'm patient and we have all kinds of time, 'to get down to' whatever the problem is. But not now, I can see you've been through something awful, so just rest. That's an order!"

No argument was forth coming either; at that point she was too tired to answer. A weariness like she had never known before rolled over her. Mary Jane felt herself slip into unconsciousness, as the car backed slowly out. See didn't see the overwhelming look of concern on her friends face.

CHAPTER 39

The plane taxied in for a landing at Devil's Island. It was a primitive airstrip. The plane sat on the tarmac, as they rolled the metal stairways up to the front and back doors for passengers to disembark. Then they would walk across the pavement and board a second set of stairs into the terminal.

Damon was in no real hurry, since he had a whole day to kill.

'My Fair Lady' wouldn't arrive in to port, until nine in the morning, the next day.

He'd have time to check into a decent hotel tonight and get a solid night's sleep. He could also place a ship to shore call, so Diane would meet him first thing in the morning on the dock. With any luck at all, she could be on the first tender with Chase.

He would make all the flight arrangements in the terminal now; for them to fly out with him, as soon after eleven, as he could get them on a flight, to Grand Cayman.

Depending on the time the three of them arrived, they might possibly, even be able to conclude all the banking and be done, returning on the same day.

Things were going much smoother than he could have hoped for. Damon thought, that if it wasn't for such dire circumstances; it would be good to see them all again. He'd felt very alone, since Mary Jane had been taken.

It would be a relief to talk to Chase and share how scared he was, he'd felt pretty isolated worrying alone, and Chase might have some good ideas.

The more he thought about it, the more he looked forward to Chase going along with himself and Diane to Grand Cayman. It would give him a chance to get some much needed feedback, before Chase escorted Diane back here safely. It would help tremendously to confer with Chase, about the best way to guarantee Mary Jane's safe return and then his own survival. It all came down to making the transfer of the money for Mary Jane, without walking into a trap himself and winding up dead.

Damon wanted more than anything in the world to see Mary Jane again and spend the rest of this life loving her.

There had to be a way to keep them both alive.

Vince fell in to step, practically right behind him. He was feeling very bold and even reckless, on his 'invisible', head-trip.

Unfortunately Damon was still completely unaware of the tail on him, which would have been very unusual for him, under normal circumstances. He was so naturally observant, but he had failed to notice the man on the trip to Miami, or at the gate change, and now in the Devil's Island terminal. His guard was down now; and that was a very costly error.

Vince was feeling omnipotent and very confident now. He was practically rubbing his hands together in anticipation, feeling that they were closing in on his prey.

His hand stroked the pocket which held Diane Lindsey's photograph, and he smiled chillingly, thinking about the fun he would have with her, before he put her out of her misery. He planned to make her, beg him to, 'kill her!' What fun he was in for, the mere thought, practically had him salivating.

Damon was at the Island Reservations counter, checking on future flights. Vince stayed back enough that he couldn't quite hear everything, but he thought he'd caught the word Cayman. He wondered why they had overshot the Caribbean and wound up in South America, if they were now going back to Grand Cayman.

But, when Damon finished his reservation and walked away, he stepped up to the counter, and indicated with a pointed finger, aimed at Damon's retreating back.

"I need a ticket, with my friend on the same flight that he just booked."

With that he flipped his 'platinum card' out on the counter, and the agent didn't seem to find anything unusual in the odd request. He ticketed Vince Pardrone to Grand Cayman the next day, and passed over his paperwork.

Vince hurriedly followed, in the same direction Damon had disappeared, frustrated he couldn't find him anywhere in the terminal. The detective had already caught a cab to a nearby resort hotel.

Yet giving it some thought, Vince relaxed, he wasn't too worried, since he already knew Damon's next move. He'd be right behind him again tomorrow. He had his ticket too.

The 'check-in' at the Devil's Club Resort went quickly, and Damon was relieved to reach his room and finally relax. It was nearly six o'clock and he was exhausted. Since they'd fed him on the plane, he'd be fine till morning.

He didn't do much more than shed his clothes before slipping into the cool gardenia scented sheets. What a relief, to know that he was going to make the time frame, they'd set him.

However, just as he was drifting off; he realized he had to call the ship, to guarantee they would be on the first tender tomorrow. He had the operator at the hotel agree to place his call and call him back as soon as he was connected, then turned on the television, in the room just for the noise.

Paying little attention to it once it was on, he wandered across the room and opened the fruit basket on the table, biting into a very juicy, delicious plum; he distractedly wiped the juice off his chin, as the phone rang.

"Sir we have your party on the line, we are putting you through now."

The island sing song of the hotel operator said before he plugged in the connection.

Next, he heard Chaz's voice.

"Hello, is anyone there?"

"Yea, it's Damon."

Chaz recognized the tension in his voice and he didn't waste time with small talk.

"What is it?'

Damon was quick and succinct as he explained everything.

Chaz asked a few pointed questions, than expressed his deep sorrow at what Damon must be going through, but neither man wasted any words.

"We will be on the first tender. I guarantee it. Janice and I will have all the paperwork to travel back with you and get the money. You can count on us."

"I know. I'll see you both, tomorrow morning, on the dock."

With that, they both hung up the phones.

"Poor Damon," Chaz though, "He must be going through a living hell."

It had been lucky, that the cabin phone had caught him in; they were all out of their rooms so much. As it was, he had been the only one in, at the time of the call. Now he headed up on deck to find Susan, Janice and James.

He had to tell them what had happened. It seemed so unfair, that they had all been having such a good time, while Damon and Mary Jane, were going through this nightmare.

CHAPTER 40

It was so wonderful to be tucked into a warm bed. There was even a fireplace in the guest bedroom, with a roaring fire lit.

Claire coddled M.J. as if she were a child. She tucked her in, fixed her hot chocolate and started the fire, all without any questions, just like the drive. She made it obvious that everything could wait, until Mary Jane had a good night's sleep.

"M.J., I want you to get some sleep. Whatever is going on, it will hold until tomorrow."

She smoothed her hair off her forehead, as if she were a child, and gently kissed her on the forehead, planning to leave the room.

"Claire, please wait, I need to talk. I want to tell you what's going on. I need to talk to someone."

"Okay, if that's what you want. I'm here and I'm listening."

Mary Jane loved Claire's matter-of-fact calmness. She was so steady, and so undemanding, she was like a human sedative. Being around her just naturally helped her to relax. Even now, she held her hand and patiently waited for her to speak, in no way rushing her.

Finally Mary Jane did begin to explain.

She began her story; with getting the call in Rome about Damon, and how she had rushed back to the States to be with him, and sat by his bed while he was hospitalized, but that they had both, 'stupidly', not spoken of anything important. Yet, she still knew, that love was still in both of their hearts anyway.

Then she told Claire about being kidnapped, and Jason, and how she had been freed.

Trying not to leave anything out, she described what she knew about the case Damon had been involved in, and how that tied into her abduction, and the money.

She was as detailed as she could be and laid it all out consecutively; regarding the sequence of events, right up to her call for help.

Then she explained her panic at not knowing where, or how to reach Damon.

Claire listened without a single interruption and then responded calmly. But only after it was obvious Mary Jane had run out of steam.

"You've been through the ringer kiddo. But it's going to be all right. It seems to me the most important thing we can do, is to reach Damon; he has to know you are safe, than they will lose the power to make him bring them the money. He can just disappear too and join you, and you'll both be safe here."

"You make it sound so simple, but I don't know where he is!"

Mary Jane sounded desperate.

Claire appeared to be thinking seriously, and when she spoke it was obvious she was still thinking out loud.

"The media is a real circus, and usually a pain in the ass, but maybe we can use them, to get the news to Damon, wherever he is. We just have to make sure we don't give your whereabouts away, in the process. But it is a thought."

"How do we know, who to talk to that will 'get the news out', yet be willing to keep my whereabouts secret? If they were to get me again, it just makes Damon more vulnerable again. Trust and the media, are tough to put together."

Mary Jane responded seriously.

Letting Damon know she was safe would free him from being blackmailed, they just had to figure out the best way to leak the story.

"My husband knows the publisher of out local paper, maybe he can help get this on the wire service, where it will be picked up nation wide. Can I call him in here and will you let me tell him what's happening?"

"Of course, I trust whatever you think is best. I just want to do something; before they kill Damon!"

"M.J., I understand, why don't you get dressed and I'll explain everything to Paul, and if he thinks it's a good idea, we'll call our friend at the newspaper, okay?"

"Okay."

She answered with renewed energy, glad to be doing something that might help Damon.

Within the hour, Paul had the publisher of the Steamboat Journal, Lynn Kennedy in their living room, and Mary Jane was telling her unbelievable story once again, this time to a gray-haired reporter, who looked like a man that would be much more comfortable on a horse than at a newspaper.

He asked lots of questions and took copious notes, and promised to keep her location a secret.

Lynn seemed like a kind man, a good-guy. In fact, as good a story as it was, and as much as he wanted to write it for their own small paper. He made the gallant decision to write it and fax it to a reporter friend in Denver instead.

He would rather give the story away, than jeopardize this woman's life.

If the article originated in Steamboat it would be a dead giveaway where a search for her should begin. So he would sacrifice a byline, to assure her location not be given away. Steamboat was a very small town, let the bad guys turn Denver upside-down.

Paul, Claire, and Mary Jane all expressed their gratitude, and when Lynn left they all thankfully headed to bed.

Now Mary Jane could finally sleep, knowing that tomorrow, the story would come out and warn Damon. She just had to pray that he would see the article before Jason's boss did.

That would be one enraged bad guy, when his whole blackmail plan fell apart. Mary Jane also prayed Jason was a long way from his grasp, somewhere he would be safe. So many people were tied up in this thing; it was like handling an octopus, there were tentacles in every direction.

Mary Jane finally managed to fall into a troubled sleep. She had done all she could for now. She just hoped that she would get the chance soon, to tell Damon just how very much he meant to her.

"Please God, keep him safe, and bring him back to me."

She fell asleep with that prayer on her heart.

CHAPTER 41

The morning sun came through the still open blinds, with a fiery vengeance. Although it was only seven thirty, it was already bright enough to beat Damon's eyelids into wakefulness.

He awoke groggily, and called for room service.

"Bring coffee and a continental breakfast; no, make that a full American breakfast, and a full pot of coffee, please."

A mechanical, bored clerk responded that it would arrive in about twenty minutes.

Figuring that was perfect; be jumped up and padded to the bathroom for a hot shower. The shower spray was invigorating, sharp and hot almost to scalding, with that irritating staccato change of temperature, that always seemed a given in hotels, probably unavoidable, with so much plumbing interfacing between multiple floors and corridors.

Nevertheless it was a satisfying experience, and he rapidly dried off, shaved and dressed, which choreographed beautifully with his breakfast arrival.

He no sooner buttoned his last collar button, then room service arrived. He signed, added a tip and sat down to what looked like an excellent breakfast. The plate was decorated with flowers giving it a festive air. Damon relaxed for the first time, since his discharge from the hospital.

He was beginning to feel a little more confident and in control. For the first time he let the thought cross his mind, that maybe it would all go smoothly. Maybe, he would give them the money and they would let Mary Jane go. That was really all he truly cared about. If they let him live that would be a bonus, but he wasn't thinking that far ahead. All his thoughts were on Mary Jane.

Secondarily, Diane was his concern, although, now he felt certain, he had kept her out of harm's way. As soon as he got the money from her, she would be back on her odyssey cruise for another 'five-plus' months. She couldn't get any safer than that.

The ship would begin to run the tenders, at nine a.m.; in slightly over an hour. He was only minutes from the pier, so there was no hurry.

Damon could enjoy a leisurely meal, and make it in plenty of time. It would be good to talk to Chase; he would probably have some good ideas, for making the safe exchange of Mary Jane for the money, and maybe even manage to elude death himself. He hung on to the thought that he and Mary Jane might still have a future.

Also awakening that morning, on Devil's Island, but in a much seedier room, Vince was shaking off the effects of the absinthe, an addictive drink he'd had too much of, the night before.

He lay fairly still for a while, the effort of lifting his head up off the pillow, seemed too strenuous with his hang over. He ran his hands over the sheets next to him, until his hand touched a bare flaccid thigh.

He groaned inwardly; '*the mess*', was still there in the morning. Vince had really tied one on last night, reveling in the delicious forbidden liquor, which had been offered in the dive, on the waterfront. Either Devil's Island bars were unaware of the ban on the precious addictive liquor, or they just didn't care about the law. Most likely, it was the second option.

The bar had charged an outrageous eight dollars a shot for it. He'd lost count after the first fifty-dollar-bill was gone. By the look of his wallet at the end of the evening, he had pulled out several others; but then money was never a problem. There were always jobs for him to do.

Vince enjoyed his work, he'd even do it just for fun and without compensation; which explained the body in the bed beside him; just some hooker, from the bar; he had used, then abused, and finally snuffed out. He loved watching the last breath go out of their lungs, as he stared into their eyes while they died, full of fear and agony.

It was a beautiful thing; that final grimace, as the realization hit them; it was really all over, their unimportant little lives, gone.

Death was an amazing metamorphosis to watch, much more interesting than a caterpillar to a butterfly, was a human being as their soul left the body and their lights went out.

Now of course came the tough part, getting rid of the body. They were cumbersome after rigor mortis set in. As he remembered she had been a tall statuesque, dark island beauty. He was a slight man and very tired. He didn't want to be bothered with her now, or have to carry her very far to hide the body, especially in an unfamiliar terrain.

Then Vince thought about it some more. He would be gone on a flight at eleven thirty that morning, just a few hours away. He'd paid cash for the dive room and given a phony name, he'd just keep it simple and extend a day over the phone, and tell them no need to clean the room today. It certainly wasn't the kind of joint to look for extra work. Then they wouldn't find the body, until check out time tomorrow. He'd already be long gone.

"Simple plans were usually the best." He thought.

After his call downstairs and a promise to drop by the payment before checkout time tomorrow, he stuck the ***Do Not Disturb*** sign on the door just to be safe.

He rolled last night's 'fun and games' remnant, over onto her stomach and covered her up to the neck with the sheet. Satisfied, that it just looked as if she were sleeping, he didn't give her corpse another thought.

Vince took a shower and got dressed for the day.

He was already mentally looking forward to his next victim, for two reasons. Killing Diane Lindsey was a two pronged thrill; first of all it would be a paid gig, enriching his bank balance admirably; and there was the added bonus of being told, to stretch it out as long as possible before the final big finale'.

So often he was instructed to curb his natural talent and enthusiasm for his work and cut straight to the end result. But it was much more fun, when handed some creative license on a commission. This was definitely a plum assignment, he thought, nearly rubbing his hands together in anticipation, even if the Lindsey woman hadn't been so beautiful. That just sweetened the prospect even more.

CHAPTER 42

It had been a tense night on shipboard, after Chaz briefed everyone else on the recent events regarding Damon's and Mary Jane's plight. No one felt like go out to dinner in the main dining room. They all went to Chaz's and Susan's suite and talked and talked.

James and Susan felt as if they should all get off, and accompany Damon back to Grand Cayman. But Chaz explained with a cool voice of ultimate reason, that it was better if they stayed aboard, and that he and Janice would rejoin them in only two days in Galapagos, Equador. He actually wished he could do the whole thing himself; he would have preferred not to include even Janice, she was the one both recognizable and earnestly hunted. But to access all the funds, they needed one from each couple.

Over the last couple of weeks they had all gotten very close, so he didn't try to keep any of his concerns secret.

Chaz explained his biggest fear.

"Damon says he lost the tail in Denver, and avoided one in Reno. But the truth is; that just seems too easy to me. I think they'd have been more thorough than that. These are serious men and they aren't generally obvious unless it's a decoy display. Damon was tired and fresh out of the hospital with a concussion, as well as scared half to death about Mary Jane. Normally I'd say he's the best cop around, but this just doesn't sit right with me."

Chaz finished and James jumped in.

"Your point being; you think Corielli is sharper than Damon at this junction, and maybe Damon has missed something."

"I'm afraid so. I can't believe that they aren't tracking him somehow: to get to Diane."

Chaz reached over and patted Janice's shoulder as he spoke. He'd lapsed by saying 'Diane' in this instance, because the mob was looking for Diane not Janice.

James answered, still thinking about what Chaz had just said.

"Then she stays on board. I'll go with you instead; I can access the money in our joint account too."

"I already thought of that myself, but that would leave she and Susan unprotected, while we are gone for those two days."

Chaz didn't like that idea at all either. Not if Damon had led them to the ship by his phone transmission.

Janice spoke up.

"This whole thing is my problem, it always has been. We will follow Damon's instructions to the letter. I'm going, and that's that, now quit talking about me as if I'm not here. I'm the center of this whole mess and I want to fix it. I always wanted to give the money back anyway. Now let's just do that and free Mary Jane."

Susan had been unusually quiet and had been thinking about everything that was said. Now she spoke.

"I think the best defense is a good offense, isn't that how the saying goes?"

They all looked at her, she had their attention.

"Chaz is the expert here on surveillance, protection, and well bad guys. Isn't that right? So I think he should be utilized in that capacity. And not appear to be with Damon and Janice/Diane at all. Chaz can 'fall back and follow', and watch for anyone else doing the same thing. He can be the 'eyes in the back of their heads'. Get it? No one knows or expects him, to be with or behind Diane Lindsey when she meets Damon on the pier."

Chaz looked at Susan with admiration.

"You aren't just gorgeous, you are smart too. It's a good idea, a very good idea."

Now he directed his remarks to Janice."As Diane, you get off alone, and head straight to Damon.

Explain to him quietly, that I will take a separate cab and go to the airport alone. Tell him to leave my ticket with the counter attendant, at the baggage drop station. It won't be suspect for him to stop there, if you check a bag. So grab one and throw a few things in it. I'll pick the ticket up by myself, and I will board separately, but right behind you. I'll never be very far away, but we won't talk at all, okay? Make sure you stall and talk, at the pier cab stand, until there are two empty cabs at the cab stand; so I can stay right behind you both, at all times; then I will see, exactly who you hand my ticket to at the counter. Loiter there, after checking in yourselves, until you see me collect the ticket and get through check in too. Don't ever proceed beyond my sight line. Whisper these things quietly to Damon as we proceed through each place, he'll understand the protocol, but don't ever look directly at me. Okay? We have a plan."

Chaz finished and James responded.

"Right; that is a good plan, but this is the woman I love, and I can't just wait here in the lap of luxury wondering what's going on for the next two days. 'Four extra eyes' are even better than 'two', how about if I disembark as well? I can also travel alone and watching. If this is a trap, you'll need me. If it isn't, then there is no harm done. I'll buy my ticket at the counter. I'll take my own cab. I'll watch you and them from even further back."

James was very assertive as he finished, but it all just stemmed from the fear that he could lose the woman he felt was his life; if they found Diane Lindsey now. Everyone seemed to understand.

"Okay, that's what we'll do."

Now Chaz directed his conversation back to Susan."Well it looks like we are leaving you all alone, will you be all right?"

Susan forced a laugh, though her heart definitely wasn't in it.

"Sure just bored, without all of you, while you go have all the fun."

As always she relieved some of the stress of the moment, by taking a light tack. It was her gift, to try to lighten the strain, everyone felt, whether she was Susan or Joan.

"We better all get some sleep, tomorrow could be a long day."

James suggested, as he took Janice's hand, and they went to their own cabin.

When the door closed behind them, he pulled her almost roughly into his arms.

"I hate having you in danger again. Janice and James have been so safe and distanced from the Diane Lindsey case. *My Fair Lady* has been a terrific cocoon. It is as if we are being thrown out of a play that was all romance back into a fear based nightmare, where you are always hunted."

"Darling don't be silly, Damon is a good detective, and with Chaz and you there, I'll be the safest woman in the world. Mary Jane is the one we need to worry about."

It was hard not to love, a woman who always thought of everyone else.

James pulled her into his arms again, and kissed every inch of her face, her eyelids, temples, each beautiful ear, and her neck. He felt so full of love for her, as she took his hand, and guided him to the bed.

They tenderly undressed each other, voicing over and over their passion and desire for each other. The more they made love, the more special it all seemed. Though they were beginning to know each other's bodies very well, it was still always as magical and seemingly new, as that first time. He kissed her until she was breathless with wanting him. He sniffed her delicately and stared deeply into her eyes, adoring her, and wanting to give her all the pleasure he could. She loved it; that he never hurried their lovemaking. He waited so long sometimes, that she would beg him to enter her. She wanted him more everyday and felt she would never tire of his body. Silken skin under her finger tips, over solid muscle. He felt like velvet, spread tautly over steel; and she loved to touch him, to taste him, to smell him, and hear his voice. Making love to him always felt more like a dream than reality. She wished tonight would never end.

Much the same thing was going on in the next cabin.

"Are you really going to be okay?"

Chaz still sounded concerned.

They were curled naked, under the sheet; Susan's head was on his chest.

"Darling, I'll be fine, it's all of you I'm worried about, just keep Di safe."

She immediately realized her slip, but neither of them said anything, letting it go.

He kissed her deeply, pulling her over on top of him, he looked into her eyes.

"I love you, you know?"

"I do know, and I love you too. Everything's going to be just fine, wait and see."

She was always the cock-eyed optimist, and he adored her.

No more words were spoken, but then none were needed.

Chaz ran his hands gently over Susan's body, tracing lovingly, every curve and angle. Then his lips traced where his hands had been until her back arched begging for his body. He teased her tenderly with lips and tongue, and then passionately returned, to kissing her deeply, she tasted herself on him and found that intoxicating. Susan honestly felt, that no one else could possibly know this kind of happiness. They had to be the two luckiest people in the world.

Eventually they slept.

CHAPTER 43

As Damon approached the pier he scanned all the faces. He had taken several glances over his shoulder, and felt confident that he was not being followed.

Of course he wasn't.

Vince Pardrone was still in his motel shower, with no plan to follow again until the flight to Grand Cayman. It was a shame that Damon hadn't been as observant yesterday.

As Damon looked off toward the sleek, gorgeous ship anchored out about a mile. He wondered what the trip had been like so far for Diane and Chase and their significant others. He imagined that it must have been pretty incredible and couldn't help wishing that he and Mary Jane had been forced to endure the same fate, instead of the one they were experiencing now. It wasn't jealousy exactly, he just experienced a wistful, slightly fervent wish, to change the present circumstances and relax and be happy, among friends with Mary Jane holding his hand.

If only Damon were in back the states now; he would be able to relax.

The morning Denver News headlined with the story of a kidnapping victim. It featured a photo of Mary Jane, stating that she had escaped her captors and made it safely back into her home state. It cryptically requested that a certain unnamed police detective get in contact with the paper, at her bequest. It further stated that the victim was in seclusion, for her own safety.

What a terrible twist of fate that Damon was not where he could see the paper.

CHAPTER 44

Chaz awoke long before anyone else, went up on deck, and poured himself a cup of coffee. Taking it with him, he thoughtfully strolled the deck. He worried about today, the whole thing just didn't feel right to him. He was getting danger signals constantly. Damon was good, but he was distracted too. Chaz hadn't believed, from what Damon had told him; that the two goons, at the Denver airport, would have been Corielli's only attempt, to follow him.

Mario was too smart and too cool, to be that unprepared. Damon was normally very sharp, but in his confused state; and in a panic after the kidnapping. He might have used his cell phone, home phone or Mary Jane's house phone for reservations; and been tapped or traced.

If Mario Corielli already knew his flight plan, then the airport display was just for show, and there had been men placed on his plane following him, or men that followed after the connecting flights each time.

Every morning, the ship went out of its way, to cater to its rich and famous clientele. Aside form the incredible selections of international coffee served, they were kind enough to set out an international selection of newspapers too.

He remembered James's excitement, realizing he could keep up on his hometown news no matter how far out to sea they wandered.

"Once a newsman; always a newsman," had been his comment at the time.

So as Chaz watched the steward set out that day's papers, he wandered over to peruse the headlines, and grab a paper to take back with him. Approaching the large selection, he glanced down at several, and then his eyes halted on the Denver paper, as he hastily read the headline story. He'd never seen Mary Jane's face before but the article struck a chord immediately.

He grabbed the paper almost violently, threw a twenty dollar bill down to pay for it, then dashed off with it like a madman, not even waiting for change.

Arriving back at the cabin, after running almost the whole way, he burst in to his and Susan's room. She was awake and in her dressing gown, sitting at the vanity, combing her hair. Upon his dramatic entrance, she spun around surprised and happy to see him.

The look on his face startled her, and she rushed straight over to him.

"What, what is it?"

He pushed the paper into her hands, and pointed at the article.

"Thank God." she exclaimed, "I wonder if Damon has seen this?"

"I hope so. I have to show Janice and James."

He was already halfway to the door.

James opened the door quickly in response to Chaz's staccato knocking.

He and Janice were both dressed and ready to go ashore, it was almost time, to go to the tenders.

As he had done with Susan, he now shoved the paper into James's hands. James read quickly and silently while Janice read over his shoulder.

"This means she's safe and Damon is free of their blackmail, doesn't it?"

James directed his question to Chaz.

"That's how it appears. Can you make a call to the paper, and see what else you can find out? I'd like to be able to tell Damon all the good news, when I see him. Maybe they'll give you the contact number for Mary Jane. I know that would make his day. He has been worried sick about her, and I'm sure, now she's going crazy, worrying about him too. It will be wonderful to put them in touch with each other and relieve both their fears."

"I'm on it."

James was already flipping open his cell phone, it was prepaid and not traceable to anyone. He dialed the Denver News editor directly on his personal line.

Janice felt such relief for Damon.

"We go ashore in fifteen minutes, right?"

"Wrong, there is no need to put you at risk now. You stay on board, where it's safe. I'm going alone to give Damon the news, no one knows me, and no one will pay any attention to me alone. Don't worry about anything. If Mary Jane is safe, then Damon is off the hook. If there is any kind of trap set, we aren't going to walk into it. I'll see Damon alone and make sure he's safely on his way back to Mary Jane, without a tail. You can count on that."

James hung up the phone.

"I have a contact number for Damon to call Mary Jane. They weren't to give it out, only get a number she could call him back. But since I knew the reporter who had the byline and my boss was also his, he gave it to me."

He passed the written number over to Chaz.

"You know it's still not a bad plan to watch your back. Why don't I just go to shore with you now and be that extra pair of eyes for the two of you, while you explain everything to Damon. Janice and Susan will be safe here, they are the only familiar faces?"

James added, making sense.

Chaz responded with a terse nod and then added, thinking out loud.

"As I rethink all of this, it occurs to me Damon will need to 'lie low' for a while too, with Mary Jane. Or this whole thing could repeat itself. I think I'd still prefer to fly with him to Grand Cayman. We can share the wealth, so that he has the funds for he and Mary Jane to disappear like we have."

"Absolutely, that's a great idea and I can still go too. I was looking forward to getting rid of all that money, it's brought nothing but pain and suffering. Maybe it's still the best plan to give it back and stop this lunacy."

Janice was adamant now.

Susan had entered the room, while they were all talking, and stood quietly listening, looking for the most logical answer from a detached point of view. Now she listened carefully as Janice spoke tentatively figuring it out as she went along.

"There is enough money, to hide us all forever. But, although I hate seeing it used; for 'whatever' the mob may use it for. It might be worth it, to end this 'craziness'. Surely the fact that we gave it back, even without them having Mary Jane, would end this ridiculous vendetta. Someone has to call a cease-fire so we can all quit hiding out. We can't run or hide forever, no matter how great this cruise has been so far. You all need the chance to live normal lives. Everyone here has sacrificed normalcy for my sake. Damon and Mary Jane could hide too, but I think it should stop here. If we all hide out this last five plus months onboard as planned, after they have the money back, they will move on."

Susan had tears in her voice and there was no mistaking her sincerity. She walked over and hugged Janice.

"You are strong and brave and I love you. But don't blame yourself for any of this. We are all exactly where we wanted to be. And as scary as some of it has been, most of it has been amazing. If not for this situation; we might never have all found each other, and Damon wouldn't be headed back to Mary Jane. Love has found all of us, in the midst of this mess, so 'all things have come together for good', and we all need to trust that it will continue to work out."

Chaz took over, shaking off the sentiment.

"This puts us back into our original positions then, so back to our original plan. Let's all prepare to go, just like we were, before we read the paper. I sure wish there were ways to lock those creeps up instead of reward them, but this is Janice's decision. I can respect it and her. Let's go now. Janice will go up to Damon alone when we get off the tender. I'll follow them. James can follow us all, to the airport and wait and watch until we all board the plane."

James broke in.

"Wait, I've got the best solution. There is no need to take Janice at all. I can fly with Damon and I'll get to money. I'm on our joint account too, then Janice can head back to the ship and stay with Susan until we rejoin them in Equador. It makes the most sense. It will work and lead any trouble away from the women. What do you think Chaz? Can I go in place of Janice?"

They all had to admit, it made sense.

"We'll all tell Damon the good news then we men will go ahead and fly to Grand Cayman. Janice will leave the airport and come back to the ship. It's a plan. Now let's get going."

James recapped and Janice nodded her ascent.

There was nothing left to do, so they went to the tender boarding area and got on the first tender. Only with the plan changed Janice didn't bother to bring a bag. She'd be back soon enough, she thought.

Of course none of them could know of Vince Pardrone and his evil plans!

CHAPTER 45

The headlines had seemed a wonderful way to get the message to Damon. How could he miss them? It had been on the front page. Now Mary Jane just anxiously awaited a phone call, assuring her that Damon was safe too.

Claire and her husband had been wonderful about everything, she was so glad to have such a wonderful friend. Mary Jane would always be grateful. They had opened their home and their hearts to her, in this crazy situation, even when it wasn't safe to have her here. Yet they had made her so completely welcome. Now the newspaper would screen the calls and when Damon called in, get a number for her to call back. Very soon she would be in his arms again and she couldn't wait to tell him, all the feelings she could now openly admit to.

Claire came into the kitchen, joining her at the table, where she was sipping her coffee thoughtfully; the paper still at her elbow.

"Did you finally get some sleep?"

"Yes, thanks to your solution. After the interview, I slept like a baby. It was such a good idea, but I was too close to the problem and never would have thought of it alone. You've both been so terrific. Please thank Paul for me too. He's a wonderful man, you are very lucky to have found someone who's wonderful enough, to deserve you. You have always been so special to me. I can't begin to tell you how grateful I am for everything."

Claire looked a little embarrassed at all the praise; so rather than respond verbally, she just reached over and squeezed her friend's hand.

It was nearly eight-thirty, Mary Jane was praying the phone would ring soon with some news. There was still a deep-seated fear she couldn't even articulate, that given her escape, and Jason's desertion, that the man who'd ordered her taken, might have simply gone ahead and killed Damon. So until she heard something she was sitting on pins and needles. For now, she was just grateful to have her friend sit and hold her hand.

Neither felt any urgent need to speak, for quite a while.

Claire was saying a silent prayer for her friend too. She prayed for this whole crazy thing to end happily and soon, getting M.J. and her long lost love back together again.

She also said a further blessing, thanking God that she did have Paul and that their life was so simple and uncomplicated. Until something like this happened to someone you actually knew, you simply couldn't fathom these type of circumstances. Life was truly fragile, and you never knew what it would hand you next. There was a definite lesson to be found here. It was, to truly appreciate life when it's going smoothly, because in a blink of an eye, that can all change. She squeezed Mary Jane's hand once more, and then stood up and let her go.

"How about some breakfast as I recall, you love waffles?"

Sensing the argument about to ensue, she put her finger to her lips and made a schussing sound, and M.J. complied, so she went on.

"I even have some fresh blueberries, so you are in for a treat."

Claire was intentionally chipper trying to allay all the tension of the waiting.

Mary Jane recognized her friend's effort, and matched it with a false enthusiasm, but at least she tried.

"That sounds great, thanks."

So Claire cooked and Mary Jane tried to keep up pleasantries, while never taking her eyes off the phone.

Then somehow they actually ate the waffles with thick Canadian bacon slices, and carried on a semi normal conversation for the next hour. Paul had already left for the resort. It was ski season in the Rockies, a busy time for him. The women chatted nervously and waited.

Finally Mary Jane's composure slipped.

"Damn-it, I wish he'd call; this waiting is killing me."

"I bet, but you have to give it time, why don't you go take a shower and get yourself together. You'll feel better. Help yourself to my closet. We're still about the same size, and I know you have to be, 'sick and tired' of that sweat-suit."

"But what about the phone, he could call?"

"Listen if he calls you, or I hear anything from anyone else, I'll bring the cordless straight into the shower! Okay? Now go on. It will do you good."

Claire aimed her out the kitchen door as she quit talking.

Mary Jane headed for the shower. It would help to pass the time and she wanted to look nice when she saw Damon, which she hoped would be very soon.

CHAPTER 46

The tender came smoothly into the dock, and the crew pulled her expertly into the slip. The gate and ramp were pushed into place in one effortless move, making it obvious that it was 'second nature' to the tender crew. It was always nice to watch people work that really seemed to enjoy what they were doing and worked with such choreographed precision.

Damon watched the passengers begin to disembark. Diane, or rather Janice, was the third passenger coming down the ramp, he saw her immediately. And she saw him and waved, but she appeared to be alone. He didn't see Chase, or rather Chaz. He had to get used to their new names too. After all he had been the one to drum the importance of not slipping, into them. But he had not been with them, since their metamorphosis, so their names were still foreign to him. Nevertheless he gave himself a quick lecture to be diligent and careful about only using their new names.

Now he just wondered, why Janice was alone, and then he thought like Chaz, and figured it all out for himself. He was dropping back so as not to appear with her. He was most likely not far behind, planning to watch their backs.

In retrospect it was a good plan, he wished he'd thought of it sooner, although he was having a hard time thinking of anything but Mary Jane. Anyway he was glad Chase was the best. Damn it, he thought mentally correcting himself again, Chaz.

Now Janice's foot touched the pier, and she and Damon closed the distance between them rapidly, and embraced like two old friends. She stood back and looked kindly into his eyes.

"It's going to be all right. Have you seen the Denver Paper?"

He didn't know what she was talking about. He answered simply.

"No. Why?"

"How much time have we got? Can we sit down somewhere? I have some very good news to tell you."

Janice looked elated and intense at the same time.

He led her off the pier onto the dock and over to a bench; with no one around. They sat. He turned to her expectantly.

She didn't utter a word, but instead pressed the folded, cut out, front page of the Denver paper into his hands.

Damon unfolded it and glanced at it, and then read it thoroughly, before looking at her again. When he did he had tears in his eyes.

"She's safe!"

Now Janice just as simply handed him a phone number written neatly on a ship's notepad.

"This is her number; there is a phone booth right over there. Why don't you call right now?"

He just took it gratefully and went strait to the phone booth. No other comment was necessary.

In the meantime, Chaz had observed everyone on the pier, and pretty well determined that no one was watching Damon or Janice. But he continued to watch them from a distance anyway.

James did so as well, also pretending a disinterest in anyone else on the docks. The tender was untied, and headed back to the ship.

Soon the only people present were Damon in the phone booth, Janice on the bench outside and Chaz and James standing idle and separately just looking around.

Finally as they all looked around and realized everyone else was gone. Chaz gave an imperceptible nod and he and James walked over to join Janice and wait for Damon to finish his call. It was obvious that he was relieved and talking animatedly to someone. They all hoped it was Mary Jane. They all waited together, relaxing at the fact that there was no one watching Damon. Glad all their paranoia had been for nothing.

There was no way they could know that; as they let their guard down, Vince Pardrone was enjoying a huge breakfast with a hearty appetite.

Left behind, like so much garbage, was the prostitute's corpse in his hotel bed. He on the other hand, was whistling lightly at the airport diner counter while anticipating a very tasty Caribbean Quiche he'd ordered. Not only was he looking forward to his upcoming task, but he was relishing his thoughts of the night before. Things were going just as he'd planned now. Vince hadn't imagined that the lay over would have provided such an entertaining evening. The hooker had been quite talented in several areas. He'd enjoyed her in every way, some of it at her invitation. But then she hadn't known how it was going to turn out. She had even willingly consented to being bound, laughing and teasing him to; "Do his worst!" And he had, too…

The fun had really begun after he gagged her and slowly, very slowly caused her pain, in every way he could think of, and a few he just stumbled on to; while she was gagged, and could hardly make a sound. He had seen the exact moment; after he tied her up and gagged her, when her eyes mirrored her pure terror as she recognized his power. That very first second, when she realized, while looking into his face, that she had made a serious error in judgment; thinking he was just any ordinary customer.

He'd spent the next several hours inflicting pain creatively, until she would thankfully pass out. Then he would bring the helpless woman to, with smelling salts, and delight in the sheer agony in her eyes, while he tried yet another new technique. It had been a terrific evening, and provided great foreplay for his real assignment.

Vince hated to rush, but last night, that had been a necessity. After all he had to get some sleep; the real job should start today. His plan was to draw Diane Lindsey's ordeal out at least three days, there would be no hurry, it simply had to be executed with exactitude at the completion.

Surely that stupid detective would lead him to his target, before this day was out. He'd obviously had no clue, that he was being followed; he'd never given Vince a second glance. Once he had his prey, then he could take all the time he wanted with her. His anticipation was excruciating.

Vince reminisced with a smile. He had discovered the diaries of the *Marquis de Sade'* in the library when he was in junior high, 7th grade if he remembered correctly. It had been the most fascinating book he'd ever read, at that stage of his life. Since then he had thoroughly researched any and all writers which specialized, in the areas of inflicting pain creatively and the great art of sadism. He'd even kept a journal for several deviations and innovations of his own devise. He prided himself in the fact that one day he would be read and worshipped as the best of his genre' and would become even more famous then the Marquis. Vince fancied himself quite the writer and with great care; he had documented in detailed depth, every single detail, of the tortures of his considerable victims.

With last night's conquest, he counted his unfortunate lab rats at eighty-seven women and fourteen children; bringing his grand total over the hundred mark. He felt a certain pride at his prowess, it took quite a man to come so far, and still be invisible. And Vince had never even been questioned. His self-satisfied smile, as he thought this to himself, was chilling.

Yet all around him, people ate their meals, but took no notice of him. They never did.

CHAPTER 47

With great relief and tremendous happiness; Claire pressed the phone receiver into her friend's anxious hands.

Damon had identified himself and asked for Mary Jane. Who was just at that very moment walking into Claire's studio, where Claire had been working while waiting for Mary Jane to dress; after her shower.

M.J. answered the phone shoved at her, tentatively.

"Yes." Just the one word was enough.

"It's me, my love. I got your message. How are you?"

Although she'd been praying for the call, it was still a surprise to hear Damon's voice, which reflected all his concern and she melted. There was no resistance left in her, just relief and joy.

"I'm fine. Where are you? Are you safe? I've been so scared."

His laugh rolled through the receiver and warmed her.

"You've been scared! I was frantic. I just thank God you are safe. You are somewhere safe?" He questioned.

"Perfectly, but where are you?" She queried again.

"Would you believe South America?" He laughed again, so relieved to be talking to her.

"But, I'll get to you as quickly as I can, can you wait there for me?"

"Please hurry Damon; I have so much I want to tell you." Then she couldn't contain herself any more.

"I still love you. I've never stopped, and I don't care about anything else."

His answer was simple.

"I love you too and I'll be there as soon as I can get there. I'll make arrangements and call you back the second I'm done; I promise you my darling. I love you with all my heart."

He had disconnected, yet she still held the phone in her hand. Mary Jane felt hesitant, to replace the receiver, back in the phone cradle, and forfeit their connection. Finally, she set it down and turned around to see Claire, still watching her and smiling. They both had tears in their eyes.

"I heard M.J.; I'm so glad he's safe. Where is he?"

"Can you believe South America? But he's heading here right now; he'll call back, as soon as he has his reservations."

Mary Jane was so openly happy now and couldn't help acting like a teenager.

"He loves me, Claire. And it's all that matters."

"Of course he does, he'd be nuts not to." Claire laughed, back to being her no nonsense self.

"All's well that ends well. Now, I'm going to get some work done. There are blank canvases or anything else you want on my worktable. Time moves faster when you're busy, so help yourself; if you feel like it."

"I sure appreciate everything you've done for me Claire." Mary Jane said with real sincerity.

"You can make it up to me, if I ever get kidnapped! Okay? Now, let's get some paint on canvas." Claire laughed and shifted her concentration to the acrylic wash she was working on.

Mary Jane followed her lead, and set up her work area, her mind floating back to the painting she had left in the apartment in Chicago, idly wondering what would happen to it. But, more importantly, she wondered; where and how Jason had managed so far. She prayed that Jason was safe for a long while, until the canvas consumed her energy, as she forcefully and joyfully applied bold color and a sunrise formed out of the blank whiteness.

CHAPTER 48

Hiding wasn't any kind of a life. The truth was; that when he thought about it, he'd never had any kind of a life. He'd simply shared the Corielli's lives.

Jason had never been much of a drinker, but he was well on his way to being blissfully oblivious now.

He lifted his drink and ran the cool damp bottom of the glass across his forehead, the glass wet his hair and a curl fell down, over his brow, curling up from the moisture. He didn't know where to go. He had his passport and about one hundred thousand dollars 'in cash', in the bag sitting at his feet. But, what he didn't have; was a real family or a home, or a friend.

He was glad that he'd set Mary Jane free, it had been the right thing to do. But now, there was nothing but emptiness. He wondered if she and 'her cop boyfriend' had been reunited yet; or if he'd managed to give Mario the money and somehow still remain alive? But mostly, he wondered what Mario felt about him now? Had he taken a contract out? Would he feel betrayed? Maybe miss him?

Jason shook his head hard, almost falling off his barstool. It was fairly apparent, even to him self; that he'd had quite enough to drink. He put the glass down, and looked around at the dismal, dark joint he'd wandered into. It was nearly empty, except one other man at the end of the bar and the bartender.

Jason didn't know anyone, anywhere, outside of the Cartel, and away from Mario. He had flown from Chicago to Boston on a whim, picking his flight strictly because, it left next; and he'd never heard of Corielli doing any business anywhere in New England, which had summed up his entire thought process before coming here.

Now here he was, and it looked just like any old bar in Chicago, and the guy nursing his drink across the room, looked like a cop to him. The type was easily recognizable; over forty, deeply disillusioned, wearing a cheap suit and a 'seen-it-all' attitude.

The man looked questioningly at Jason, he must have been staring.

"Do we know each other?" He queried.

Jason looked him steadily in the eye.

"No, I've never been here before, you just reminded me of someone else. Bartender, give him a drink for me."

The man told the bartender he'd take another of the same, and then carried it down the bar and sat down next to Jason.

"Thanks, what's your name son?"

"It's Jason, and you're very welcome." He was surprised that he'd given his real name.

"What brings you to Bean-town?"

"I'm just passing through, on my way somewhere else, my flight leaves in the morning. Are you on the Boston force?"

The man laughed, it was actually a very pleasant, very open laugh.

"Is it tattooed on me somewhere that I'm in law enforcement? Actually, I'm a federal agent, and in my experience only two kinds of people, make me that fast, another agent or a criminal. Which are you?"

Jason didn't even hesitate.

"The second…." He answered flatly.

"Want to talk about it son?"

Jason realized then, that he was looking into truly kind and concerned eyes. He was pretty intoxicated and the question seemed like it came from the heart and Jason simply wasn't feeling capable of being evasive.

"Yea, what's your name?"

He picked up his glass and the other man's and carried them to a table in the corner, almost as a knee jerk reaction; and for the second time that evening, the man moved and sat next to him.

The bartender showed no interest in either of them, except to note their drinks were still full.

"Well, my name is Gary Martell, Jason. It seems to me, you are a man who needs to talk, go ahead, I'm off duty, so whatever you say here is off the record."

He looked at Jason with kindly, almost fatherly eyes and Jason looked back steadily. There was a kind of unspoken communication of sorts, and somehow Jason knew he could trust him. Still, he didn't know quite what to say, or where to start, he just continued the steady gaze. Gary waited and looked steadily back. His eyes never wavered, but they were interested and very steady. Jason hadn't realized his drink was only a ginger-ale; Gary hadn't been in the bar to get drunk, only to think.

"I've never willingly had a conversation with a Fed, what area are you anyway?"

Gary answered simply.

"Racketeering. How about you?"

Now Jason had to laugh.

"Protection, for the most part."

"Well, then I guess we're in the same business, just on the opposite sides, huh?

"Seems like it; only I just retired."

Jason was beginning to enjoy the conversation. Gary was a good guy.

"Actually, I'm about to do the same thing, but I'm not very happy about it. But, that's another story. What's yours? As I said we are off the record."

The next thing Jason knew; he was pouring his heart out to this stranger, in a Boston bar. He explained how he'd met the man, he had worked for, and what he'd done for him in a broad sense. How more and more as the time had gone on, he'd faced tough inner battles over everything, he was expected to do. Jason never 'named names and particulars', rather the feelings encapsulated by being the perpetrator of certain tasks.

Finally, he recounted his most recent job and how he had been unable to follow through and had instead freed the woman, forcing himself into this self-imposed exile, and probably signed his own death warrant. Finally he summed up his total sense of loss, and inability to figure out, what should come next. As he finished his rambling account, he dejectedly put his head down on his hands and covered his eyes. His hopelessness and guilt was obvious and somewhat painful to observe.

Gary had listened without a single interruption. He'd heard the deep sadness, and watching him closely and with a trained eye, he also realized this was a kind, and even a good man, who had spent his entire life thus far, going in the wrong direction, just because of whomever had befriended him as a child.

Now, Gary couldn't help but admire the courage it had taken, to walk away from every thing familiar, and the only life and family he had ever known, in order to do the right thing.

He could see the loneliness that pervaded Jason's spirit, and he truly wanted to help him.

"What if, you could make some good, come out of all this? You know, like toppling a corrupt empire?"

Gary asked very softly, watching the other man carefully. He knew a question like this, could cause him to bolt.

Instead, Jason answered calmly.

"How? Maybe it is time for Mario Corielli to be stopped."

Now that the name was out there, Gary experienced a pang of elation, he'd had no idea, this man's confession, was going to be such a big deal. After the Pappas execution and the murders of several heads of the other Chicago families, there had been little doubt in anyone's mind that Corielli was the biggest and most vicious mobster left alive. His dramatic statements were legendary. Now as a total coincidence here he was talking to his closest friend, who had just crossed him.

Gary had thought he'd just bumped into a small time thugs 'second in command', now he knew, he needed to tread lightly. But if he could get this man, to turn his information over to the authorities, it might be entirely feasible to enter him into the witness protection program.

Then, at least Gary could do something big, even worthy, before his early retirement because of cancer. He'd be able to do a good thing for his country and this poor lonely man and retire with a flourish.

Very carefully and calmly, Gary explained to Jason, what he was thinking, and how it would allow him, to start over with a clean slate.

Jason listened and asked a few questions. Then he stood up abruptly.

"I'll think about it and I'll meet you here tomorrow night at ten; to tell you what I've decided."

With that, Jason was gone in a split second, before Gary could even react. He would just have to wait a day and talk to him tomorrow. But he felt pretty confident that Jason would be back. Despite his affiliations, he seemed a man of his word.

CHAPTER 49

After hanging the phone back on the receiver, Damon hurried over to the others who were waiting expectantly.

"So did you reach Mary Jane? Is she really okay?" Janice demanded.

Damon answered with great relief.

"Yes, she's fine."

"Then this nightmare is nearly over for you both. Now you can be together. But it would be best for you to both to go into hiding too, for a while."

Chaz spoke, after they all experienced the relief of the moment; as always the voice of practically and reason. He continued.

"But we've all been talking and we have a plan to share with you. Let me explain our solution." Chaz was talking very slowly, when James cut in.

"It won't relieve the problem right away. But we are convinced it will alleviate most of the heat; and bring a cease-fire to this on going vendetta."

Now Janice jumped in, they were all too excited to keep quiet.

"We give the money back anyway! Especially without our being under duress, they will have to appreciate the gesture, and it should take the wind right out of their sails."

Janice was so intense, wanting so much for Damon to see her logic. Before, he had always argued against returning the money to the mob in any scenario.

"Don't you see, we can't all live in hiding, and in fear forever? This would be our best chance to lead normal lives again."

Everyone had let Janice speak, until she had completed her proposal and the reasoning behind it. She had always been the one with the most to lose.

With great surprise, this time, no argument from Damon was forthcoming; he answered simply.

"Okay. I trust you have a plan?"

Now Chaz jumped in and quickly went over their plan. How it would be he and James, that would fly with Damon on to Grand Cayman and why. And that Janice would return to the ship and wait with Susan.

It was quickly decided, they would withhold $200,000 per couple as survival expenses while in hiding. Everyone felt a comfortable time frame to stay inconspicuous would be a year, past the five months left of the cruise.

The plans included Damon and Mary Jane. Then they could all stay in hiding comfortably, for as long as it took. The missing money would still be a mere drop in the bucket to the original billion dollars. Probably it wouldn't even be considered, when they returned the money voluntarily. A billion dollars was an amazing amount of money.

Mario Corielli wouldn't even believe it; that anyone would just return that much money, without dangerous consequences and coercion. So they assumed that eventually, he'd have to cool off, and eventually even forget about them. After all, he had an entire syndicate to run, and other types such as himself on the rise all the time. Surely he'd move on soon enough.

So having worked out all the details they caught a cab to the airport. They'd only need to exchange Janice's ticket for one in 'James' name then the men would be off, and Janice would head back to the ship. They were all confident that they had not been followed from the dock to the airport terminal.

There were no difficulties with the exchange at the airline counter which was rather a nice surprise. So spirits were all pretty high, as they approached the boarding gate. Damon and Chaz had worked it out, that after retrieving the money in Cayman, and when Damon had returned and found Mary Jane safe and sound. Then Damon would quite simply send all the money by special messenger directly to Mario Corielli; with a simple note, requesting a truce.

Damon wasn't even returning to the police force. They would all ere on the side of caution, and stay out of sight for a very long time, hoping that after more than a year, they'd be completely forgotten, a totally closed chapter.

There was even some discussion of Damon and Mary Jane signing on for the balance of the cruise. Janice really wanted to meet Mary Jane; and was good naturedly teasing Damon about it at the airport.

None of them, not even Chaz who was usually so observant, noticed the man watching them all so avidly from the next row of seats in the small terminal. As usual he was hidden in plain sight, and yet Vince had heard almost every word and realized that there would be absolutely no need to board the plane. It seemed his 'target' was only bidding all the men a fond farewell. They couldn't possibly have made his work any easier.

While Vince waited, his thoughts drifted. He was remembering another time in an airport. It had been two long years ago, an eternity really. He had watched as the only woman he'd ever cared about in his life, boarded a plane and flew out of his life forever. Tracy had normalized him. For four short months, he had been just like anyone else. Vince had once had a friend.

He'd met her at the library, where she'd smiled at him. No one ever did that to Vince. Either people didn't see him or they instinctively became nervous around him. She smiled several times and then asked him what he was researching so seriously. He showed her and instead of thinking the worst, she thought the best.

"Oh, you must be a psychology major. The abnormal stuff is fascinating." There was no condemnation in her voice. "I started out a Philosophy major, but there aren't many paying jobs for philosophers." She laughed.

Still Vince had not spoken. The truth was he'd never had a conversation in his life. People only told him things they needed to, or they completely ignored him. This was beyond him. Why was this young woman talking to him? Then he realized something. He was looking at her without any thought of making her an experiment. He found himself saying something he couldn't ever remember and the next thing he knew, they were at a coffee shop next door to the library, talking, or rather; he was listening.

They had talked like that on and off for the next four months and during that entire time he'd stopped his experiments, and didn't accept any new jobs. Vince had guessed that for a short period in his life, he'd been happy. She had spoken of Jesus and love and she had always been kind to him. Kind in a way he'd never known before. He'd spoken very little, but she never pushed him. Tracy Baxter was the only person he'd ever known, that he might have changed for. But at the end of the semester she flew home and away from him.

No one else ever spoke with him again, like she had; 'as if he were just a normal guy'. And after another month and a half went by, it was as if she had never been.

Vince's life returned to, what for him, was normal. But for a few short months in his life, he had not thought of killing anyone and he'd known a little kindness. It had changed him during that short time.

Now he watched as the men prepared to board, and leave Diane all alone. Vince thought, soon it would be just the two of them, and all his delicious plans. What a job this would be. Yet the random memories of Tracy, had somewhat dimmed the thrill he normally felt. Just remembering her for a moment had killed his edge.

So he pushed thoughts of Tracy and that time so long ago, forcefully out of his mind. He needed to focus on this job.

His eyes fixed on Diane Lindsey again, and this time, his eyes narrowed and his focus returned, along with his tight smile that meant death.

CHAPTER 50

True to his word; Jason was there at nine-fifty, to meet with Agent Gary Martell.

He had walked and walked that day through the Boston Commons. He'd spent the afternoon thinking about what kind of life he had now, versus an opportunity to do something good.

He had the power within him to take Mario off the streets. He could start all over as a whole new person; in the *Witness Protection Program*, sanctioned by the Feds.

They would help him with a job, a home, and a chance to go straight. The more he thought about it, the better it sounded. There was no downside.

Hiding from Corielli on his own, and his only real shot would be to leave the country and become a fugitive. If he assisted the Feds, he would have help and support. But most of all, he would be doing something good, ridding the world of Mario Corielli. Although once his boyhood friend and almost brother, Jason now recognized that there was no good left in him. He was strictly a power-mad mercenary. Jason would be doing the world a favor by putting him away for a very long time.

Gary stood to greet him, as he crossed to his table. He extended his hand and they shared a firm clasp. A certain understanding flowed between them.

They sat simultaneously and held each others gaze. Gary knew before Jason spoke that it was a go.

"Okay, how do I get started?" Jason asked without preamble.

"You'll come home with me. I'll make some calls. By morning, we'll be talking with the head, of the special task force for organized crime. He'll want to hear what you know. Then he'll arrange a safe place to keep you. Eventually the witness protection program will be brought in."

Gary recapped how it would all work.

"You know, he'll do his best to kill me, before anything can come to trial."

Jason spoke matter-of-factly.

"We'd be prepared for that, and we both know the odds."

Gary was honest and Jason felt better, not to be patronized.

"I guess my odds aren't any better on my own. At least this way maybe I can help stop him."

So the men were in agreement. Gary stood and without any more conversation they left together, a tentative, respectful friendship beginning to form.

The Fed and the Mafia enforcer, made a rather odd couple and yet they were actually two men with, a core-decency in common. That, was something, Jason had never experienced, in the company he'd kept all his life, prior to this.

He actually felt good about what he was doing. He'd been feeling better and better about everything, ever since freeing Mary Jane. Now he wished there were some way to tell her she'd really made a difference. He hadn't seen the Denver paper yet, so he didn't know what had happened to her. He hoped she was safe, and had been reunited with her detective and that they would escape retribution.

CHAPTER 51

Janice hated to see James leave, even for a couple of days, but she wasn't worried. It would be a huge relief; to get rid of most of the money. It had been such an obscene amount to be responsible for; and a constant reminder of what a farce her marriage had been.. She was very glad to see it returned to end this insanity.

As she kissed James good-bye, she heard a familiar voice approaching, and looked up to see Susan running over to say.

"I hated being left out. I took a cab and came to say farewell too."

She spoke while slipping an arm around Chaz's waist, but then she turned and directed her sincerity at Damon.

"Damon, I wanted to tell you how glad I am for you, that Mary Jane is all right. I know this must have been really awful. But now everything is going to be okay for all of us. And I'm here to safely escort my friend here, back to the ship, after we do a little sightseeing. So, no one has anything to worry about."

Which was true, they thought. So the men boarded the small jet believing, everything was going to be okay, and that the women were perfectly safe.

Janice and Susan chatted easily heading out of the airport. Neither paid any attention to the dark little man who fell in step so naturally, behind them.

Vince was walking on air.

"Twice the fun," he thought gleefully, as he followed the two women who were completely unaware of him.

"An extra added bonus."

His thoughts ran amuck; as he considered the joys to be found, with two beautiful women now at his disposal. This was going to be his best yet. He would have to be careful to journal every little detail. This would make a superb chapter for his book.

The only thing that worried him just a little; was the body he'd left behind in his motel room. He'd been so sure, he'd be off the island and far away when he'd left it to be discovered. But then, the room was paid up through tomorrow, so he was in no danger yet.

In fact, the more he thought about it, why not just go back there? It would be a perfect setting, to take the two new victims too.

It had been a total dive, comprised of all individual cabins; far enough apart to keep noise from being any problem. It was the kind of place, that wouldn't pay very much attention, to its guests; not as long as the bill was paid.

He felt assured the room would be just as he left it, the corpse neatly appearing to slumber peacefully. And 'that body' would serve as a terrific prop, in order to terrorize these new candidates. It would prepare them for their unique education that was still to come.

The hooker would be a horrific demonstration of what he was truly capable of. Probably enough of one, to drive Diane Lindsey and her friend crazy with fear, before he even did anything to them. The more he thought about his plan the more he liked it.

Vince felt completely in control, omnipotent, invisible, and invincible. He wasn't even concerned at the difficulty of getting two healthy, strong women to cooperate and go with him, without any trouble. He was plotting as he followed them and felt assured the moment would present itself, for him to nab them effortlessly. He was totally self-assured, as only the criminally insane can be.

He whistled under his breath as he followed closely enough behind them to listen to their animated conversation.

"Well it's just you and me kid, want to check out Devil's Island sights or just go have a nice lunch and poke around in town? We don't have to board the ship until eight o'clock tonight."

Susan was her usual energetic self always up for an adventure.

Janice responded carefully. For some reason her radar was working overtime, and the hair on the back of her neck seemed electrified.

"I don't know what I feel like doing, part of me would just as soon go lounge on the deck."

"Party-pooper, you can't cop out, just because our men deserted us in this port of call. Come on, don't be a spoil-sport, we'll have a good time, this is supposed to be a gorgeous place with an interesting, though grim history, don't you want to learn its secrets?"

Janice had to laugh at Susan's effervescence, she never ran out of energy, and nothing got her down. She just wished she could shake this feeling of impending disaster.

"Okay, you lead, I'll follow. We'll do whatever you like for the day."

"Good girl, you won't be sorry."

As Susan spoke, they reached the curb in front of the airport and she raised her hand and hailed a cab. One pulled up from the line of cabs waiting. She and Janice jumped in the back.

They paid no attention to the man hailing the next one; or the fact that his cab fell in right behind theirs.

Vince thought that they might be heading back to the ship. If so the pier would be a good place to pick them up. He never worried about how. A way always presented itself.

Susan and Janice bounced around ideas in the cab about what to do next. Their cab driver overheard and began to make suggestions.

"You beautiful ladies must see our beaches; they are the most glorious in all of the world."

His sing-song was lovely.

Susan was always interested in everyone.

"I love your accent. Were you born here?"

"Yes, um lady, I never wanted to go nowhere else. Everything I need is right here."

Janice sighed.

"Then you are indeed a very lucky man, it is so lovely. What's your name?"

It was not posted anywhere on the cab, as she had looked before asking.

"I am Kabe, pretty ladies."

"Well, Kabe; how far away is that beautiful beach and is it near a town, with a lunch spot?"

Susan inquired, grinning and feeling Janice lean more toward an adventure, instead of just returning to the ship. She could sense a 'holiday spirit' pervade the cab. They would have a great day. They could catch up on girl talk, walk some lovely stretch of beach, and have a terrific lunch, sitting outside, somewhere.

"Maybe twenty minutes Misses, then you see. It be very beautiful, just like you want."

They sat back and relaxed and enjoyed the lush vegetation they drove by. Not only palm trees grew here, rather there was a thick dense mass, of all sorts of different deciduous trees, vines, wild orchids and other exotic flowers. It didn't even look as if you could walk into it because of the density.

According to the brochures, without a machete and a very strong arm, it was impossible to infiltrate these forested areas at all. It had proven a virtual wall preventing any escape when the island had been used as a prison.

Janice and Susan chatted about unimportant things, while riding with Kabe, and he joined in, with an occasional piece of local lore, or to point out something of geographic interest.

His stories were delivered in his delightful sing-song, and the drive progressed pleasurably and quickly. There were many ghost stories and legends regarding the past prison population. In fact, almost all the stories, involved the prison in some way, shape or form.

Soon they entered a small coastal village. It was off the beaten track and had obviously, once been a fishing town. The buildings were mostly pretty run down; with peeling paint and old fishing nets draped everywhere. Buoys and anchors had been used as ornamentation, and it had a very authentic feel. Not like a tourist trap.

Kabe turned around in the seat of the cab and faced them.

"Dis be da real town, ladies. I want for you to see dat, and get a feelin for da island. Dis is how it be. Now I can take you to da new beautiful resort about a mile up a da beach, there ya got da restaurants and shops and stuff such as dat. We go now."

Janice spoke up.

"Wait Kabe, you say it is just a mile, is that right?"

"Yes mam, about dat."

Susan piped in.

"I can read your mind Janice, why don't we just walk up the beach from here?"

Kabe seemed uncertain.

"It be rugged, along da beach mams; with forest on one side and ocean on da otha, it is not a tourist area, ya understan?"

"A mile isn't far and I bet it's a gorgeous walk, let's go ahead and get out here. Okay with you?"

"Sure we can both use the exercise; we've been eating all too well, on the ship."

Kabe pointed them in the right direction; and they paid him and gave him a generous tip, thanking him for all of his help.

Neither of the women noticed the man exiting the cab parked about two buildings back, because he'd told his driver to pull between the buildings.

Vince told his cab diver to wait for him, he'd be back. And for waiting how ever long that took, he promised to pay him five-hundred-dollars! All he had to do was stay here.

Vince handed him a one-hundred-dollar bill in advance, and showed him the rest. It was fine with the cabby, 'just fine'.

The cabbie didn't make that much in a week. He'd definitely stay.

"No problem man! I'll be right here."

Janice and Susan poked through the tiny village. There really wasn't much to see, so shortly they ambled down to the beach.

It was a pink seashore, because of all the coral broken up by the waves and mixed with the pure white sand. The coastline's flatness, was relieved by large craggy boulders at the water's edge, many which sheltered tide pools, teaming with sea life.

Janice and Susan both enjoyed naming the creatures they recognized, in the pools. They were both scuba divers. Stories were recounted of trips they'd taken to Mexico, with Diane's parents, when the girls were teenagers.

They were having a ball and walking very slowly, chatting away, petting sea-cucumbers, randomly picking up shells, and picking up pretty smooth stones, and trying unsuccessfully to skim them into the incoming waves.

Nearly out of sight of the village now, they could just begin to make out the resort in the distance. It looked like a tiny, all pink sand-castle. Still it appeared quite far off in the distance. But, they were in no hurry. They had all day.

"This is really peaceful, isn't it? I think I'll take my shoes off and wade in. Want to stop here a while, before hitting the tourist area?"

Janice spoke animatedly, and was already taking off her shoes. She was still trying to shake off a disquieting and unexplained tingle of apprehension, by exhibiting a gallant effort at nonchalance. She new her nervousness could probably just be attributed, to the men leaving.

"You go ahead. I'll watch from here. I hate putting wet, sandy feet, back in to my good shoes."

"Oh come on, get your feet wet, the water is gorgeous."

"Okay, okay, what a nag, I'll be right there."

Susan responded to Janice's already retreating back. She commenced removing her shoes as Janice had. However, it was a little more time consuming since Susan struggled with ankle straps. She mumbled to herself as she struggled with one tiny buckle. She was sitting on the sand when a shadow fell across the beach in front of her.

Susan tried looking back and straight up at the owner of the shadow, but the sun was very strong. She couldn't make out any features looking into the glare, except that it was a man.

"Hello, beautiful day isn't it?" The man said pleasantly.

"Yes, It's quite a day." Susan answered squinting up.

"Have you been here before?"

"No, we're on a cruise and just got off to see the island for the day, do you live here?" Susan queried.

"No, I'm just visiting, the same as you and your friend, but I'm familiar with everything. Maybe I can show the two of you around, or be your guide. You know, two ladies shouldn't be running around all alone."

He spoke slowly and carefully and yet for some reason it felt stilted.

Susan felt a slight trepidation creep up on her. It was an indefinable something. She still couldn't see him clearly, yet it didn't feel like just idle chit-chat anymore. She suddenly wanted him to go away.

She glanced up and down the beach, there was not another soul in sight, except Janice, now at the water's edge, and she hadn't looked back or realized that Susan now had company.

Susan stood up, one shoe off and one still on. She gathered her composure that had seemingly deserted her. She simply didn't understand her own sudden, bizarre, irrational fear, but acknowledged it anyway. She was trying to put her finger on exactly what he'd said that spooked her, then realized it was the comment about being alone. How could he know that? They were only a short distance from a world-class resort. Why wouldn't he assume, they were staying there? That would have been an obvious assumption, not the one he'd made.

She looked back the way they had come, and there were three sets of footprints, in the sand. This man was dressed for business, a suit and leather shoes, not beach attire and she remembered seeing him at the airport.

Vince had been watching her face, and had read every expression. He was ready for the ensuing panic, and for her trying to cover it up.

It would be tricky, to get them both back to his little cabin, without a fuss. But he'd figured out exactly what he was going to do and say, while following them. He had a fool-proof plan.

Susan was looking practically level into his eyes, so he wasn't very tall, but there was something in those eyes that had frozen her, to the spot. He was terribly unattractive, but she didn't think she was letting that sway her. It was something else, something sinister. She couldn't put a finger on it; she just knew she wanted him to leave, he was giving her the creeps.

She saw Janice turn towards them, realizing that Susan had company, and then she hurriedly walked back toward them, looking more than a little concerned. Caution was very much a part of their lives recently.

After all, the last time they had been left unprotected, they had been shot at. And now, here was a stranger, alone with them on a deserted stretch of beach. A stranger that looked very much 'out of place', considering the way he was dressed, and worse yet; a stranger that had been at the airport as the men had left them.

Janice was even with them now. She knew this man was the reason for her uneasiness, earlier at the airport. She remembered seeing him too. But she tried to act nonchalant as she walked up.

"Hi, who's your friend?" She directed at Susan.

"We haven't gotten that far, I was about to tell him, we had to get back to the resort over there, we have friends that will be looking for us. It was nice to meet you though, we've got to go." Susan bluffed nervously.

Staying as casual as possible; Susan took Janice's hand firmly, pulling her away and in the direction of the resort. Unfortunately it was still pretty far away. She had an overwhelming desire, to get them in to the midst of other people, and off of this isolated stretch of beach, away from this still nameless man, that had followed them here.

She wasn't masking her fear well either. The tension was palpable.

Janice picked up on Susan's ruse; feeling all the same intense panic.

"You're right we'd better be going immediately, or they'll call out a search party. We are already late."

Janice spoke lightly, in direct opposition to the hair standing up on the back of her neck.

Vince smiled a slow, chilling smile, watching them prepare to run away from him, under a thin guise of lies. He could feel their fear. He knew they sensed his evil!

It was a remarkable, powerful rush; what he lived for, and he knew just how to play it.

"Let the games begin," he thought.

CHAPTER 52

Jason actually went home with Gary that night. It was late and Gary intended to make sure he was safe and sound. The men talked long into the night, and at some point they began talking of other things too. Then after a while, it became obvious to both of them, that they sincerely liked one another.

Gary confided, this would be his 'last hurrah', and told Jason about the cancer he was losing the battle to. Jason put a hand on his shoulder and they sat quietly for a while. There were no words. None were needed. Yet the empathy, each felt for the other, was tangible.

"No matter what the odds are; I guarantee your safety Jason. Putting Mario Corielli away, is the best thing you could possibly do. He's a cold-blooded mercenary and it's not just business with him. He's the worst of his lot, and you will really help clean up the streets by working with us. Evil prospers when good men do nothing."

"There are always new and worst guys in the wings to take over; you know someone else will just step in, when we put Mario away. I'm willing to do this, in order to clean my own slate and start over, and because Mario has gone too far. Yet a part of me knows that ultimately, it won't really make a difference. Not really." Jason said, sounding depressed.

"What if it saves Diane Lindsey? It will certainly make a difference to her, Jason. You said he wouldn't hesitate to kill her and the detective that saved her. He might even have killed your hostage, Mary Jane. So how can you say it won't make a difference? I would be willing to bet, that to those people, you've made all the difference. You have to personalize it. We can't know all the good you'll do in the long run. But, these are people, who will owe you their lives. Doesn't that make everything completely worthwhile? If not to you; certainly to all the people Corielli won't kill, because he gets stopped. Jason, I want you to do this, and I want to be a part of it too, because it's a good thing, a courageous thing, more importantly, a right thing to do. Crime can only be stopped, 'one bad guy' at a time. Corielli is the worst I've ever heard of, and stopping him wouldn't happen right yet, without you. But you have to be willing to see everything through. It won't be easy, to stay under constant guard, in safe rooms, moved frequently. But when it's all over, I promise you a new name and a chance for a new life. But best of all, you will have a clean conscience and you will have served your country. You are exactly the kind of man the *'witness protection program'* was designed for. Not the Anton Savions of the world. And I, for one, am proud to know you. Are you ready to commit and tackle this thing, believing 100% in what you are doing?"

Gary finished his litany and looked very tired all of a sudden. But somehow he also looked like a man ready to take on the lions. Cancer couldn't defeat character.

Jason couldn't help but admire his vehemence. He wanted to care that much. He wanted to stand for the right things. And suddenly he also knew he wanted to do this. He would make a difference. And he would redeem himself at the same time. His answer was simple and came from his heart.

"Lets' do it. Let's do this thing together. Here's my deal. I won't waiver, and you won't die!"

Gary laughed.

"Deal. Now let's get some sleep. We have a big meeting in the morning. The spare room is all made up. Make yourself at home. Goodnight."

CHAPTER 53

Damon had been filling Chaz and James in on all the events which had taken place; since they'd left Denver, and they were all animatedly coming up with ideas, for what he and Mary Jane should do next.

But, as Damon wisely pointed out, he had to work it all out with Mary Jane too. The important thing now was her safety, and then they had to ascertain where they stood with each other. Damon would go straight to her, as soon as he had the money, and then there would be time to figure everything out.

It was a fairly jovial group; considering the tension Damon had been living with, for the last several days. It was especially good, not to be so alone with such uncertainty.

The more they'd discussed it, the better the idea had sounded, for the two of them, Mary Jane and him, to also join the cruise for the remainder of the original six months voyage. He and Mary Jane could spend some down time, together and safe, among friends and in a totally relaxing atmosphere. After listening to Chaz and James go on and on about the ship, he was more than a little tempted. It sounded like a perfectly wonderful new start, for them to regain their footing as a couple, which is what he wanted, more than anything.

The flight to Grand Cayman was truly uneventful, and the banking matters, once more was unbelievably simple, considering the amount they were dealing with.

After their banking was completed Damon had in his possession more than $999,700,000 once again in bearer bonds.

The men had an early dinner together at the airport, before Damon was to board his plane back to Miami, and then on to Denver. There had been a flight with availability within a few hours of their arrival.

Flights back to South America were a little more sporadic, so James and Chaz couldn't catch a flight to Guayaquil, Equador until the next day. That would be the next port where they could catch up with Janice and Susan on the ship, the day after that.

Then they could all pick up right where they'd left off and go sightseeing on the Galapagos Islands together.

After Damon called Mary Jane advising her of his return plans and arrival time, he boarded his plane.

James and Chaz went to check-in at one of the hotels near the airport, for the evening.

Settled in to their room at the Airport Hilton by ten that evening, but restless and accustomed to being on the ship, it was a mutual decision; to place a 'ship to shore' call to Janice and Susan.

They could tell them all was well, and that Damon was now winging his way back to Mary Jane, taking the money with him.

James and Chaz weren't really very surprised, to not get an answer in either stateroom; until after the shows and a drink, they were seldom just sitting in their state rooms. There was just too much to do onboard ship. They left a message and contact number and waited for a return call, sure that they would get a call back before the evening ended.

James pulled out his laptop to get some writing done and Chaz turned the television on low and watched an HBO movie.

Mary Jane had hung up the phone, very much relieved after Damon called, with an arrival time.

She excitedly told Claire,

"By this time tomorrow, I'll be in Damon's arms. He's on his way back right now."

CHAPTER 54

Vince Pardrone looked at Diane Lindsey pointedly and as he did he pulled Joan over to him with a death grip on one of her forearm. He calmly placed the tip of a syringe against her throat, pointed straight at her jugular vein. It all happened so fast, that there was no time to react. Now both women stood frozen.

"I knew you were a couple of smart ladies. It would be a good idea to be docile, a very good idea. You see, in this hypodermic is a poison that can act so fast; that your friend here, could be dead in a matter of seconds, if I inject her. So you don't want to make me 'do that', now you both need to do, exactly what I say, and that's an order, not a request." He directed his chilling attention directly to Diane, while his eyes bored into her. Joan had not even breathed.

"Don't hurt her, please. We'll do whatever you say." Diane said very softly, trying to sound calm.

Joan looked straight at Diane, her back to the man.

"***GO!***" She mouthed silently.

"***RUN!***" She silently screamed, audible only in her own head.

Diane ignored her. There was no way she would leave her friend, not now or ever. Not even if it was smarter. Not even if it was their only hope.

Joan looked agonized, all her instincts told her they should fight back, yet she stood stock-still feeling the needle pressed tightly against her jugular, actually denting, even though not breaking the skin.

Vince just grinned. He could practically read their thought processes 'word for word'. He remained unconcerned. As always he was in control. Their terror would keep them in check, that and their loyalty to each other.

The one he held; had the right instincts. He had felt her silent scream. That was why she was the one he threatened, even though she wasn't his main target. Diane Lindsey would be more malleable if he endangered her friend. More so even than if, he held her directly. Plus, if he had to drop one of them fast, he'd dump the friend. After all he was supposed to take his time with Diane.

Those were his orders, and it would be his distinct pleasure.

Though minds were busy, it was painfully quiet. Except for Diane's small plea they were all still silent. Each was accessing the situation from every angle.

"There are two of us. He can't control both of us with one needle." That was the thought going around in Joan's head.

"If I can pull away without being injected, we can both run."

Yet despite her thoughts, she didn't move. He had too firm a grip, and the needle was nearly breaking the skin as it was. Still, doing 'something', seemed better than doing 'nothing'.

Diane couldn't process at all. Once again her friend's life was in danger because of her, and she felt completely helpless to do anything.

Vince was amazed at just how clearly he could read them both. He had felt this feeling before, this omnipotent state of transcending all barriers. He had won, they were his; no more powerful against him, than rag dolls. It was a state of heightened reality, more intoxicating than any drug. Finally he spoke, clearly and in command.

"Here's what we are going to do, and then neither of you will get hurt. Listen carefully. We are going back the way you came. I have a partner waiting, he's disguised as a cab driver. You will both come with us quietly. My boss only wants to ask you some questions. He already has your friends."

Vince spoke snidely. He was feeling very clever.

Diane's mind was considering what was said and she was calculating quickly. If they had the men, they would have the money shortly too. Then they would kill them.

Joan wasn't buying this. She'd seen the men board the plane and seen it take off; it had to still be in the air. There were no guns on planes. How could they have been taken? This had to be a ploy. She wished she could communicate with Diane, but it was a little difficult with a needle threatening her life.

"Now Ms. Lindsey, you walk just in front of us, and no tricks. I've got your friend, what's her name anyway?"

Joan answered fast, thinking dictated she not admit her alias; if Diane was Diane to him, then she'd be Joan. Her other name, could stay safe in case they got away. At least that was her immediate response.

"Joan, my name is Joan." she answered him herself. She wouldn't let him dehumanize her.

"Just don't hurt her." Diane's voice was barely audible.

Vince felt totally in control and replied convincingly.

"I told you, nobody is going to get hurt. Now just walk back to town, and do exactly what I say."

They did as they were told.

When they reached the edge of town he quickly changed his position. Now he had Joan tightly pulled against his side, as if they were sweethearts. The needle was pressed into her side, between their two bodies. It was a much less obvious looking position to walk into the little village.

However it didn't really matter. The streets were deserted. The cab driver was waiting, just where Vince had left him.

Everything was going so smoothly, he thought.

Yet he knew it could get tricky in the cab. Instantly he decided; the cab driver was a dead man, if there was any hassle at all. Human life meant nothing to him. He smiled, thinking that having them witness the murder, could be a kick anyway.

As it was, the three of them slid in the cab's back seat, with the cab driver paying very little attention. The ladies stayed perfectly quiet, drawing little attention to themselves. Vince snapped the command to take them back to his bungalow, giving the driver the name and location of the seedy rat-trap he was taking them to. The drive was uneventful. No one made a sound.

Reaching their destination was anticlimactic, too easy. Vince felt a little disappointment in the fact that there was no reason, to slit the cabby's throat. On the upside he didn't really need another body to worry about. Vince threw the rest of the promised money in the driver's lap.

Quickly he yanked the women out of the cab and forced them into his bungalow.

Much too late, Diane and Joan realized they had been had. That had been just a regular cab driver, not a partner, as he'd inferred. But it was useless to them now, that he might have helped them. The cab was already pulling away from the curb and they were being shoved through a door, motivated by the needle still lodged into Joan's ribs. So what could they do anyway? They were caught up in an ongoing nightmare, over which they had no control.

Looking around, before going in, they'd both noted that the grounds were deserted and the bungalow he'd taken them into was somewhat isolated, even from the other bungalows just like it.

The situation looked pretty grim.

Both Joan and Diane were separately hoping; that this would be just a talk like he'd said, with some mysterious boss.

They both just prayed hard, to get out of this alive; while their intuition belied their hope.

CHAPTER 55

Mary Jane and Damon couldn't let go of each other. As soon as he'd walked into Claire's front door, she had thrown herself into his arms. All their prior reserve was gone. Their fear for each others lives had shown them what was really important.

Claire considerately left them alone and shut the door behind her on the way out, giving them some privacy. She knew they had a lot to talk about, but that most likely would come later. For now, their hearts and eyes were doing all the talking.

"I love you." Mary Jane murmured between kisses.

"And I love you." Damon responded, looking deeply into her eyes.

They found their way to the sofa and sat, facing the fire blazing in the big stone fireplace.

"I'm so sorry, for what you went through my darling, please tell me they didn't hurt you."

Damon's voice cracked when he spoke.

Mary Jane laughed to soften the intensity.

"Actually as kidnappers go I was pretty lucky. Mine had a conscience."

She proceeded to tell him from start to finish exactly what had happened and all about Jason and his help.

Throughout the recitation they held hands and stroked each other, completely happy to be in touching distance.

Then Damon shared with her what it had been like on his end, and where he'd been, and about all the money he was going to send back the next day, and why. They talked uninterrupted, except for kisses, for hours.

Eventually Claire knocked, and reentered her family room.

"Are you two hungry? I was just getting ready to put dinner on the table. You're more than welcome, if you'd care to join us. Or I can put plates in the oven for you, for later, if you'd rather."

"That would be lovely, thank-you Claire, of course we'll join you. You've been terrific. By the way let me properly introduce you two."

And Mary Jane did just that.

Then they followed Claire into the dining room, and continued the introductions between Damon and Paul. Then the four of them shared a lovely dinner, friendly conversation, and a good bottle of wine, just like old friends.

Everyone kept the topics light, until the end of the meal. Then and only then, did anyone refer to what was going on and open up the subject; of the danger still in waiting in the wings.

Paul made it short and sweet, "We know your place isn't safe Damon, why don't you stay here, with us too, until you figure out the next move. You are both very welcome to stay here."

Damon and Mary Jane were both tremendously grateful and glad that the offer had come from Paul, so that they didn't feel as if he was only going along with his wife in helping her friend.

They answered simultaneously and simply in unison.

"Yes, thank you."

"But only for tonight." Damon added, not wanting to take advantage.

"For as long as you need to; do stay, it's no really problem. We have plenty of room, so don't worry about anything for a while. Just relax."

With that open hearted offer spoken out-loud, the conversation returned to simpler topics. The men discussed the ski season thus far while Claire and Mary Jane cleared the table, and made quick work of the dishes.

In the kitchen, Mary Jane gave Claire a huge bear hug, thanking her profusely for everything.

Paul stood as the women reentered the dining room, and gracefully excused him self and his wife.

Then they discreetly went upstairs, leaving the reunited couple alone again.

Damon and Mary Jane returned to the couch by the fireplace, and sank down entwined, to watch the dying embers glow behind the wrought iron grate.

"It is so good to hold you and to be able to touch you again. I'm even more in love with you now, than when we were younger."

Damon spoke, gently tracing the line of her throat and collarbone with his finger.

She answered softly.

"We've both grown and we know what's really important now. I never want to be apart again. I'm so sorry that I let my fear of losing you, make me run away. I was foolish and selfish. I'll stand beside you 'no matter what' for the rest of my life, if you'll let me. I can face anything together."

"I'm quitting the force. I don't want anything to ever come between us or worse yet, to put you in any danger. I'm so very sorry Mary Jane, so very, very sorry. It's time I used my law degree. Can you ever forgive me for being so stubborn before you left?"

"Done, now let me tell you why I was so afraid of your being a cop when we were young."

She reached over and pushed an errant lock of hair back on his forehead.

Then Mary Jane finally told Damon what had happened to her parents and unborn sibling, knowing she should have explained years ago.

When she finished telling him how they'd been murdered, and how that felt to her as a child, they were both crying.

"I wish I'd known. I'm so sorry baby."

Damon stood then and swept her up into his arms as if she weighed nothing. He cradled her against him tenderly.

"Which way is it to your room? You are exhausted."

Her room was on the main floor at the other end of the house. She directed him. He carried her all the way there. Damon laid her gently down on the bed. As he prepared to release her, she tightened her arms around his neck.

"You aren't going anywhere." She said pulling him down too.

Some how they managed to get undressed and under the coverlet or at least kick that off the bed. They reveled in rediscovering each other's bodies, completely at ease with their nudity. Damon kissed every inch of her while she looked at him lovingly and then ever so slowly returned his treatment, running her tongue tantalizing across his chest and over his straining abdominal muscles.

They kissed and murmured loving things to each other for hours, delaying their mutual satisfaction, until it was nearly unbearable.

Finally well into the middle of the night; they culminated their lovemaking with an incredible crescendo of passions having been spent, after such a long worthwhile wait.

They fell asleep still entangled, as if they had never been apart. They each had their first goodnight's rest in a very long time.

❧

It was midday before either of them stirred. The Colorado sun had been bright for a long while.

"Hey sleepyhead, you are the most beautiful thing I've ever seen." Damon said gently as her eyes opened.

He had been watching her breathe, for about twenty minutes. His arm was sound asleep, but he hadn't wanted to disturb her; he was caught up in the wonder of her being there, at long last.

She half sat up and then rested back on one elbow, looking down at him.

She arched one eyebrow.

"Boy, it's nice to wake up and find you here. I was afraid I'd been dreaming."

"No, I'm quite real and I want us to wake up every morning just like this for the rest of our lives."

"We still have some pretty serious things to face in 'the here and now' don't we?" Mary Jane asked earnestly.

He answered just as seriously.

"Nothing that will take us very long, I promise you. I'll resign, and then return this money to that 'murdering son of a bitch'. We'll disappear and live quietly for a while. I could go back with you to

Europe, or we could go on a cruise and just spend time together. Are you up to a honeymoon?"

"You make it sound too simple, my love. Are you really going to return the money to a mobster?"

"I do hate the idea. It goes against everything I believe in. However it's what the others want, and it is Diane's decision."

Mary Jane looked at him tenderly, seeing the way he was pulled in two different directions.

"You know, I don't really know this whole story, just bits and pieces. Why don't you start from the beginning and tell me everything. We'll look for the best solution together. I've paid my dues, and I am now involved in this case too. More than anything, I want to help and stand beside you. I love you with all my heart and I need to know, what we're still up against."

So Damon started at the beginning, he rolled out the entire sequence of events, beginning with the hit, two years ago on Anton Savion a man who'd become Rand Lindsey through the witness protection program, and told her what kind of man he'd been, that had cost Diane Lindsey her daughter. He explained her long healing process and how far she'd come.

He introduced Joan and Chase and Mark to the story in sequence and explained about hiding them all at her house. Next he detailed the attempted hit, at Joan's house, that had cost the patrolman his life, and had injured Damon in the explosion; and finally how Diane's phone call had brought her back to him.

When the account was finished, he asked her to tell him, every detail of her abduction.

He hated that she had been so scared and that he had been of no help. He was however, impressed by the total turn around, this Jason person had made on her behalf. What he'd done had taken a great deal of courage.

No doubt Mario Corielli would never forget having been crossed by his adopted brother. Jason was as good as dead. Of course, he was just another name on a very long list. Damon kept those last thoughts to himself. They would only upset Mary Jane. He just wished there was someone who could put Corielli away.

CHAPTER 56

At 8 a.m. the next morning, Gary Martel took Jason in to meet with the Organized Crime, Bureau Chief and testify as to his connection to the Corielli crime syndicate. Gary lead the interrogation and Jason answered his questions with enough detail to show what a powerful source he would be, and just how much insider knowledge he had been privy to. His answers held conclusive proof, of wrong doing in multiple cases, over a period of many years; and only someone very close to Mario Corielli or the man himself, could have known so many details.

It was a very long briefing, during which, barely a word, was interjected by the Chief.

Chris Baylor, although fairly newly appointed to his position, took it very seriously; he'd vowed, to 'take out' every head, of every major mob, during his administration. He was a man of high ideals, a good man, with morals and values.

He'd listened intently to the testimony, his upbringing hadn't been so very different, from the one Jason described. He too had been orphaned in his early childhood; only he had very fortunately, been adopted by a wonderful family.

He listened with empathy and tried to understand the choices that had been made for this man, because of his circumstances. Chris believed in free will. However, he also knew that, being in the right or wrong place, at the right or wrong time, played a huge role in people's lives too.

Jason had finished his account, of his connection to Corielli, recapping which acts, he could knowledgeably report upon from the inside, and his own involvement in full detail in each case.

Chris believed it was enough solid ammunition to get Mario Corielli put away for good. He also discerned that this was valuable enough information; to warrant a new start for Jason. In fact he had never met anyone who deserved the witness protection program more. It was a program that had been so often abused by authorities in the past. Whereas this was exactly what the program had originally been intended for; hiding good people, who'd been in bad positions, that were capable in assisting the authorities in 'bringing down the bad guys'.

After thinking for sometime, he realized that the other two men were waiting quietly and with a great deal of tension for his response. He kept it simple.

"We have a deal."

He stood up and extended his hand to each man and shook them firmly.

"I'm not going to waste any time at all. We will pick-up Corielli immediately. I'll request that he be held 'with out bail', as a dangerous criminal with the ability to flee our jurisdiction. Jason, you are to go into protective custody immediately. However at both your requests I will assign Gary here to be your direct liaison. Does that suit you both?"

They both nodded. It did.

Within the hour Baylor was victorious and Mario Corielli and two of his key players were in custody. It was the lead story on every major news station and would be the headline for every major paper at the next printing. The source of course, was left unnamed.

But Corielli knew instinctively who'd betrayed him. He'd been combing the planet for Jason, ever since he'd disappeared with the detective's girlfriend. He knew Jason was the one person who could help the Feds 'nail him to the wall'. Jason had been on the inside, of everything Mario had ever been involved in, for the last ten years. No one, aside from himself, knew more about both his own and his fathers before his business. Jason had to die; and it had better be fast!

Jason Sedori and Gary Martell were being comfortably housed in a safe place, just outside of Chicago, in a yuppie neighborhood called Schaumberg in a very ordinary split level house. They would only be there about a week, and then they'd be moved out of the state. Mario's contacts were too good in the state of Illinois. A Federal attorney was taking his statement on the record. And after he detailed everything Jason could recount for the next week; then Jason would be hidden somewhere much safer, until the trial.

Baylor intended to keep this man alive. He believed Jason was a truly good man, willing to risk his life to bring down a bad man, who was practically his brother. That took real courage. He knew it must have been a very difficult decision. Now he intended to make it all happen, and keep he and Martell, a very good agent, both alive. Baylor was also aware that this would be Gary's last case and why. He'd read his dossier too. He would help him retire and die a hero.

Damon and Mary Jane heard the news that evening, a Special Report on the television in

Claire's family room. They were dumbstruck. Mary Jane knew immediately that this was Jason's doing even though the news release hadn't named an informant.

They could certainly rest easier now. Maybe, they could even go home.

It was the next day before Chaz and James read about it in the paper at the airport. But they had much bigger worries. They had never gotten a return call from the ship. Their subsequent calls even in the middle of the night had gone unanswered.

Now they were frantically boarding a plane to leave Grand Cayman. Originally unsure of whether to go back to the ship now in Equador, or back to Devil's Island to pick up the search.

Since it appeared the girls weren't on the ship they decided on Devil's Island.

CHAPTER 57

As Vince shoved the two women into the bungalow, it took a moment for their eyes to adjust. All of the shades were drawn and there was very little light in the room. The needle was poised at Joan's throat again.

Diane's eyes scanned the room and settled on the bed, since it was the largest thing in the room, and as such, dead center. It appeared that someone was sleeping and very soundly. Face down and with the covers pulled up, the only thing really visible was long hair. The sleeper was obviously a woman, and out cold. So where was this boss? What was next?

Similar questions rebounded in Joan's mind. It was strange, but a person can grow accustomed to anything; the needle at her throat was becoming almost natural. Now bigger fears were rearing their heads.

Joan's eyes had fixed on the woman on the bed. She was unnaturally quiet. It was a very small bungalow and some sleep sounds were to be expected. Yet, there were none. She didn't appear to be breathing either, and there was a distinct odor of decay in the air. Her eyes met Diane's and spoke volumes. Once again she mouthed the word.

"GO!"

But Diane's eyes responded sadly, as she gave an imperceptible shake of her head. Wise or not, she would not leave her friend.

Once again Vince was enjoying the fact that he could hear every thought. He realized that only fear, had entrapped them thus far, and he had worked it all totally to his own advantage. Two very healthy, strong women, with a witness in the cab, or in town could have bested him. He reveled at having played a great mind game and won. It was heady stuff, yet he knew it was time, to play it even smarter now.

In another couple of minutes, he would have them bound and gagged, and be fully in control, and they would have lost their last chance for freedom.

Finally, he spoke, directing his comments to Diane once more.

"On the dresser is a roll of electrician's tape, bring it over here and wrap your pretty little friend's wrists."

When Diane failed to move quickly, he snapped.

"NOW! Don't mess with me!" Diane picked up the tape, and came toward he and Joan haltingly. Her eyes crestfallen, she looked into Joan's and saw defiance.

Joan thought about it; once he got them tied up, this was game over. She couldn't let that happen. It was time to act.

As Diane crossed the room, closing the space between them Joan reacted on automatic pilot and a burst of adrenaline. In the blink of an eye, she rolled her body violently away, from the needle, twisting and falling purposely at their captors feet. Joan jammed her fist straight up in his groin with all of her strength and simultaneously pushed her body weight violently against his knee, relieved to hear it pop, as she reversed its natural angle. She had broken his leg.

She rolled away from him, and mercifully, out of his reach. Diane gave her a hand and they were both running for the door, as his hand closed around Diane's ankle. Diane turned and kicked him viciously in the head, trying to get free. He finally released her, as Joan hit him over the head with the dresser lamp. Vince fell nearly unconscious to the floor, but not before stabbing the injection, firmly into Diane Lindsey's calf muscle!

CHAPTER 58

The commercial plane carrying Chaz and James landed on the tarmac at Devil's Island. They were planning to begin the search for the women exactly where they had left them, the day before; at the airport.

That morning, they'd reached the ship's purser and verified that their cabins were indeed empty. No one from their party, had checked back in, before the ship sailed from Devil's Island the night before. The ship personnel had not found that at all unusual, since the jet setters that frequented the cruise, came and went at will.

However, Chaz and James were now frantic. They knew absolutely that Susan and Janice should have been on board.

They must have missed something. There must have been a tail on Damon after all. Sick at heart, they each blamed themselves, while trying to figure out where to begin searching?

With Mario Corielli in custody, were the women to be used as hostages? Or could they have been murdered, just for revenge?

Chaz as Chase, was an excellent investigator, and James as Mark, was a reporter skilled when it came to digging up information, but this was personal, intensely personal. This concerned the safety of the women they loved and it was hard to think clearly in a foreign atmosphere and while in a panic. Plus the trail was a day old and they hadn't caught something they should have the day before, so they were both mentally kicking themselves.

Now frustrated, they didn't know what to do next. They both stood at the gate, where they'd left the woman just yesterday morning and were transfixed, staring at all the people milling around, all of the people who were not; Diane or Joan, women who'd each already suffered at the hands of the mob.

"Let's call Damon, maybe he's been contacted. I kept the number he called for Mary Jane. It's a place to start anyway."

They nodded at each other and both turned to walk to the terminal and find a phone. Perhaps Damon could at least get the local authorities to cooperate. They weren't even sure how to approach them or what names to use. It was a tangled web they had all woven, in trying to keep safe. One, that had failed them all anyway. The women had still wound up in harms way, alias's or not.

As Chase picked up the phone, Mark uttered only one heart-felt comment.

"Please God, just let them be alive." He could so easily picture a smiling Diane, kissing him good-bye here, only twenty-four hours ago.

Their alias's fell away as real life encompassed them once again. Their idyllic cruise had come to an end abruptly; their fake identities hadn't been enough to protect Diane and Joan after all. They'd all been living in a fool's paradise; believing they were safe. The tentacles of the Corielli family had reached them even here.

Claire answered her phone on the second ring, listened a moment and answered simply.

"Just hold, I'll catch him; he was just going out the door."

She ran and caught Damon and Mary Jane in the driveway.

"Damon, Chase is on the phone. He says it is an emergency."

Damon bolted back into the house, with Mary Jane right on his heels. He'd noted the absence of his cover name, they must have heard about Mario Corielli's arrest.

"I'm here, Chase. You know they've arrested Corielli right? Is that why you called?"

He was pacing with the kitchen cordless as he spoke. Intuition warned him, it was more than that. He listened, grabbing a pad off the kitchen desk.

"Give me the number there and let me call you right back." Damon wrote; than read back the number, verifying its correctness, and hung up; dialing again immediately.

He had already called his department once that morning and they had pointedly told him, to rest; he was still officially on medical leave. Now, he simply called the dispatcher and made her aware that a foreign department would be calling to verify his position and to please do that, without hesitation.

Then he contacted the Devil's Island main Police Department. Quickly, he identified himself and asked to please be connected with their Chief of Police. They put him on hold only a moment, and then connected him to a Captain Poitier.

In less than a minute, Damon had given his credentials for the Denver force and held while they were verified.

Before he could even completely describe Janice and Susan, the Captain interrupted him, and took over the conversation.

"Listen Detective Matthews, we have two dead bodies here and some real confusion about their names. If you have someone in the area that can shed some light, send them down."

The Captain's English, was heavily accented and difficult for Damon to understand.

Damon could barely respond intelligibly.

"How and when?"

"That's what we need to know. We are having a hard time making sense out of any of this. We have very conflicting stories. You said your friend's husband is a private investigator, well send him down and tell him to ask for me, I'd like some answers."

Then the phone went dead in Damon's hand. He couldn't believe it, the Captain hadn't even told him how Diane and Joan had died, and now they were disconnected.

A shaken and deeply saddened Damon, dialed the number that Chase had given him, dreading what he had to tell them, angry that it wasn't more detailed, and feeling both helpless and responsible. In fact, he had tears in his own eyes. Nothing else really mattered if they were dead.

The phone rang only once. Chase answered.

"Damon?"

"Yea, it's me. I have very bad news. You need to get straight down to the police department on Prince Road. The street number is 147. Ask for Captain Poitier. Oh God, Chase I'm so sorry, they're both dead. He is expecting you. I'll stay right by the phone here. Call as soon as you know something. Chase, I'm so sorry. Let me know ...."

The phone was dead in his hand. Damon understood. He knew that Chase and Mark would be headed straight down to the precinct. They would be frantic. Now all he could do was wait for a return call.

He turned and explained to Mary Jane what he knew at this point, which wasn't nearly enough. She began to cry.

Chase placed the phone back in the receiver, and turned to face a terrified looking Mark. He'd been observing Chase's face and had heard half of the terrible conversation.

"What?" Mark for once was at a loss for more words.

"We have to get straight to the police station. They're dead. Mark, they're gone."

No longer a tough guy, Chase's voice caught in his throat.

Both men looked sick. How could Diane and Joan be dead? They'd just left them yesterday. Yesterday they had been laughing and very much alive, and they just couldn't be dead. They couldn't be.

Meanwhile even more was going on in Chicago. Mario Corielli had been imprisoned awaiting trial. Meanwhile some of the other Mafia families saw their chance and put a 'hit' out on him. That was easier to do then people realized within the penal system.

Corielli hadn't exactly endeared himself to his contemporaries. He was found within a matter of hours; 'an apparent suicide', alone, and hanging by shoelaces he shouldn't have even had, in his private cell.

There was a guard on shift that night, which had never been seen before and never would be seen again. That man was now $250,000 richer.

The outcome was that Corielli was gone, and everyone was thinking good riddance; thus ended his reign of terror.

The general consensus on every front was; 'what goes around, comes around.' Corielli had indeed; 'reaped what he sowed.'

This was one case in which the Feds and the other cartel bosses agreed; they were all glad he was dead.

A trial would have hurt business for the cartel and would have been expensive for the government, without a guaranteed outcome. There would be very little investigation regarding the 'suicide'. That was the way his death would be recorded.

Only Jason would feel a moments sorrow; for the shadowy memory of the boy who had taken him home and been like his brother.

No one else would mourn him, or the legacy he'd left behind.

CHAPTER 59

Joan had broken a heavy lamp and then an absinth decanter over Vince Pardrone's head; after he'd stabbed the deadly syringe into Diane. She'd not taken any chances, when she'd hit him the second time.

They had both been terrified, standing over the unconscious body of their captor, as Joan reached down and carefully pulled the needle out of Diane's calf muscle.

The glass syringe was still full of fluid; it appeared as if the monster on the floor, had not managed to depress the plunger.

Diane was shaken and had hit her head hard, on the corner of the dresser, as she went down to the floor. But she had managed to get up, and she was cringing against the wall, turned away from the bodies, as Joan felt for, but did not find a pulse, for the woman on the bed.

Hurriedly vacating the awful scene in the room; together they crossed the large expanse of scraggly lawn to the motel office. The manager called the police based on their near hysteria.

Since arriving at the police station, Diane and Joan had been relentlessly grilled; with so many questions, for which they had no answers.

They'd further confused the issue by giving their real names, while carrying other identifications.

They were holding them as murder suspects, since there were two dead bodies at the seedy motel bungalow; one of which Joan had admitted to battering.

They couldn't tell them exactly who the man was that they'd killed, or anything about the dead woman either. Just that he'd been trying to kill them.

In fact they were having a hard time, just explaining, who they really were, and what the circumstances where; that had them traveling with false passports. That was a serious crime too.

There were the language barriers, along with the fact that Diane was confused from her fall; and Joan was frightened Diane might have had a small amount of the poison injected, or might have a head injury.

Joan was still trying to get them to call in a doctor to check Diane, but they were being held in cuffs in an interrogation room.

At the mention or the name Mario Corielli; as the reason that they'd been in hiding, they were informed and stunned, by the fact that he'd been arrested yesterday and committed suicide that morning. The story had just made the international news.

To further complicate things, someone at the motel, had stolen Vince's wallet and the woman on the beds purse, after Diane and Joan had fled the room to run to the office, leaving the door open.

It was a lousy part of town, so close to the airport, and no one would know until they were discovered, in a dumpster out back, stripped of cash several days later.

For now, things were definitely more complicated by both corpses being unidentifiable.

Meanwhile, the inability to name the two dead bodies, complicated by the crazy allegations coming from these two women, were keeping the local police chief confused and more than a little frustrated. Add the general confusion, of the accents and language barrier, false or no identifications, and the possibility of an unknown poison in the syringe at the crime scene and the whole ordeal was a circus.

Diane was the first one to see Mark and Chase enter the front door, from her vantage-point, seated at the back of the station; she could see out through the glass of the interrogation room.

Then they disappeared from sight, as they were directed in to another office out of her field of vision.

It seemed an eternity passed, after Diane told Joan that she'd seen them come in. They were forced to wait and wonder, but at least they had hope now. The man questioning them continued until the phone at his elbow rang.

Of course Chase and Mark were being examined with very little information revealed to them as yet.

They too, faced the complications of proving their actual identities; while handing over passports that made them appear to be liars. Plus there was the added complication of their misinformation; which had caused them to conclude that Diane and Joan had been murdered.

They were fighting with their own fears as they tried to solicit information about the two bodies they'd been told about.

Eventually at Chase's suggestion, the Police chief called Damon Matthews back and sorted through his calm version of the facts, police officer to police officer. After an in depth discussion it was finally revealed to Detective Matthews; the fact that the women were alive, and being held at the station for the murder of a man and a woman. They were not the victims.

Chase and Mark finally understood from the one sided conversation at their end that Diane and Joan were alive.

The Chief continued to listen for a time while Damon vouched for them and explained what must have happened; that the women in the interrogation room were the ones being stalked by a killer, and that he could only assume that the other woman had been his victim too.

Since that concurred with the account given to him during his interview with Diane Lindsey and Joan Phillips and explained their phony identification, the chief picked up the phone and ordered them to be released.

It was with tremendous relief, the cuffs were finally removed and Diane and Joan were escorted out of the claustrophobic little room.

Crossing the room at a near run were Chase and Mark; and in seconds they were in each others arms.

There was would still be paperwork and a statement to record. But the police chief had believed the Colorado detective and released the two women as long as they promised to return the next morning and not leave the island.

He'd never really been able to imagine them as killers. He might not know who the victims were yet, but his gut told him the man on the motel room floor, had deserved to be hit over the head, and based on condition the female body found in the bed, those women had done the world a favor by killing him in self-defense.

Naturally the four of them went to the hospital straight from the police station. Diane was checked for a concussion or any poisoning. She was looked over but released as stable. Both she and Joan seemed subdued and probably were in shock, but otherwise they were fine.

In a few days the ordeal was over, and they were all free to leave the island. The four of them returned to the tranquility of the sea and rejoined the cruise.

Within a week Damon and Mary Jane caught up with them and came aboard too. Chase and Damon had arranged it as a surprise for Diane and Joan, they needed a distraction from horrific memories.

There would be nightmares to deal with for a while, but time would heal and love really had conquered all. Plus with Corielli dead, Damon still held the money he'd never had time to return and he wanted to return it to Diane.

The refraction that had begun when Diane Lindsey went through the glass of the windshield two years ago, had ended a life of lies and deception; and released her into a place of healing and love.

It hadn't been an easy path, but it had been a worthwhile one and she and her friends had all been blessed by the journey.

CHAPTER 60
IN CONCLUSION

For four and a half more months; the three couples enjoyed the life onboard 'My Fair Lady' and at wonderful ports of call.

They'd unanimously agreed it was best to let any contracts floating around out there, placed by Corielli, have time to die out. And Diane and Joan and Mary Jane had all been through ordeals; that they needed time to recover from.

Within a short time though, with lots of love and sea breezes, all the nightmares stopped completely. The human spirit was very resilient and the atmosphere was very therapeutic as were the bonds of friendship and love. Diane and Susan had liked Mary Jane immediately. They all had.

Now all the couples were very close, as only so many brushes with disaster could possibly have brought them. It had made them all appreciate life so much more and revel in the fact that they were together and in love.

Along with all the fun, there were many serious plans and discussions too. There was still a huge sum of money to consider. And over the months a solid plan was decided on. One on which they could all agree.

On the day before they were leaving the ship; three couples stood up together; and the ship's Captain preformed a beautiful wedding ceremony; which not only created three marriages, but also entwined the six friends forever.

When they returned to Denver a foundation was formed with the money. It was christened 'Lexie's Gift'. The goal and purpose of the foundation was to help 'inner city youth' get off the streets and form productive lives. It was a multi pronged program and fortunately its funding was unlimited.

Each of them had a contribution unique to their own talents.

Damon and Chase taught drug awareness, martial arts and held self-esteem workshops for former gang members. Eventually they involved many other police officers who volunteered their time. Within a year they had thirty-seven different instructors and had helped more than five hundred gang members to leave their gangs, find jobs, and help mentor younger kids.

Mary Jane started art programs in every medium, and she sponsored several art scholarships with the help of other artists and galleries who would exhibit student works. Her students began to clean up the city's graffiti, painting beautiful wall murals throughout the projects, with the help of recruited local teens.

Diane completed her degree in Social Work and with Joan's help started all kinds of clinics, with satellite offshoots. Their remarkable concept for unwed mothers were all inclusive, with birthing and motherhood classes, and a day care center, so the new or pregnant mothers could attend high school classes or take college credits. They had clinics that specialized in depression, abandonment and child abuse issues. They had teachers and dieticians and therapists in every area, with so many volunteers wanting to be a part of such a wonderful center, they were overwhelmed by all of their generosity.

Mark wrote. He wrote for grants, for media attention and of course his books too. He started writer's workshops for the kids at the center. He helped them express themselves and journal as a means to vent creatively. With them he published 'Hear our Voices, Teenagers in America Speak out', a book written from the hearts of all the kids.

All the programs constructed together to create 'Lexie's Gift' became a model project; one that many other cities wound up copying and thus seeded, many other similar projects. The foundation was founded on mob money, but it became a blessing to everyone who was touched by it.

At the grand opening of the birthing center, one year after they'd all first begun the foundation, Diane found out she was pregnant. The announcement was shared by she and her husband and six other very happy dear friends and partners.

Jason was given his new beginning as the Feds had promised, and he and Gary would remain friends. They liked and respected one another. The only new start he really needed was a new identity and a job referral and reference.

In a matter of months in a small New England town on the coast of New Hampshire, Gary would serve as the 'best man' at Jason's wedding to a lovely woman he'd met at the restaurant he worked in. He'd found his calling in his cooking.

As William Oberman, Jason was eternally safe from the mob. He was a chef, at a little Italian restaurant in town and very, very happy, content with his life for the first time since his birth.

Everything in his life had changed for the better. He had a family now too; his wife Jodi was expecting their first child. They had friends, and she had a huge family that he'd become a welcome part of.

He stayed with Gary, as a friend until the end. He was an usher at Gary's funeral in Boston. When William and Jodi's son was born, a month after the funeral, he was christened Gary Jason Oberman in memory of the bond the two men had formed.